Shepherd's Gaze

Shepherd's Gaze

Marsha Newman

Shepherd's Gaze

© Marsha Newman 2018

This book is a work of fiction. Named locations are used fictitiously, and characters and incidents are the product of the author's imagination. Any resemblance to actual events or places or persons, living or dead, is entirely coincidental.

Published by
Lighthouse Christian Publishing
SAN 257-4330
5531 Dufferin Drive
Savage, Minnesota, 55378
United States of America

www.lighthousechristianpublishing.com

Chapter 1: The Bella Ava

The brand new charter cruise ship, Bella Ava, slipped smoothly and speedily through the clear crystalline blue Australian waters. Her return from a maiden trip up the coastline from Sydney to Cairns in the Great Barrier Reef had been a tremendous success to the owner, a prominent business man and socialite of Sydney.

But none of those important details mattered at all to the spell-bound girl hanging over the deck of the ship hoping upon hope to see one last glorious mystery hiding in the waters below. So captivated was she, no notice was given to the stern looking man who approached her quickly from offside and swiftly grabbed the twelve year old by the back of her jacket.

"Srenna Adelaide James! I swear you shall bloody well render me heart failure one of these days!" the man scolded, as he pulled the startled girl off the ledge and away from the railing.

"Daddy! You nearly frightened me to death!" Srenna exclaimed, twisting to see the expression on her father's anxious face. Harrison James tried desperately to hold his rambunctious child's gaze with as much parental firmness he could muster. But once again, it was no use. Even as he looked down at Srenna's serious dark eyes, he shook his head and began to chuckle at her while gripping her in a big bear hug.

"What am I to do with you child? Tell me what?" he scolded, still laughing, still hugging.

"Oh Daddy, it's almost over. The greatest adventure of my life is ending and I haven't seen everything!" the young girl lamented dramatically.

It was indeed nearly over. The ship was even then beginning to turn towards its home harbor in the early evening sunset and the sight of land would be sooner then Srenna could bear.

"What more could you experience, child, what greater mysteries unravel?" her father asked of her in his best dramatic tone. As he spoke, he guided her carefully back to the railing and with one protective arm around her waist and the other on a post, he allowed Srenna to continue her observations of the waters below.

"One more dolphin, maybe a whale or a great creature like the ones in the Bible, you know, Levia…Levi…" she stammered.

"Leviathan," her father finished and then added, "That is the greatest of all whales; the largest creature still on Earth."

Harrison James loved telling his inquisitive daughter all about the creatures of the world. He was after all a prominent veterinarian in Sydney's upper class community. He had done quite well for himself, his wife Sara of twenty years and their three children, Srenna, and the boys, Douglas and David, five year old twins. It was this life they had come to know that had afforded them this surprise holiday aboard the Bella Ava for a five day trip up the coast. Many of her father's acquaintances were aboard as well with their families. But Srenna had not engaged much with the other children, even at the insistence of her mother, who adored the social life, or the gentle coaxing of her father, who in comparison, tolerated it.

Srenna found most of the girls her age boring and silly, already too interested in boys, and flirting, giggling too much and too loud.

This annoyed her. She was more interested in where and how the ship was going and what was beneath her in the fathoms of water below. She and her father had explored wondrous findings the one day they anchored and went to shore for swimming and sunbathing. They had searched as many crevices and pools as they could, collecting breathtaking samples of shells, conches and other great treasures. Harrison had taught her how to swim at an early age and her natural abilities allowed him to venture into deeper waters to see the breathtaking spectacles of the under water world of the reef.

"I have spoiled you for land for ever, eh?" he laughed again, realizing his energetic offspring, much like himself even now, would jump the forty feet into the water, if the ship were at a standstill.

"Come on with you," he started, "you were supposed to be helping your mum watch the boys while she finished packing."

With one hand on Srenna's arm to assure she was obeying him, Harrison James turned to head towards the door leading to the cabins below. She was just about to beg for one more minute, when a noise so deafening, a noise as though metal were ripping metal, steel ripping steel, came roaring up from the other side of the ship. Srenna's father barely had time to react instinctively upon hearing it. He pulled Srenna towards him when the Bella Ava violently lurched, gave up a deep shudder across her body and came to a grinding halt.

Before either one knew fully what was happening, Srenna and her father found themselves hurled to the deck floor and separated by several feet. But Harrison was up within seconds. He knew the moment he stood that the beautiful cruise liner was already beginning to list to her starboard side. He checked his footing as he scrambled to Srenna.

She was trying hard not to cry, looking at her father with wide eyed fear. Already screams and shouts could be heard from all over the ship as the obvious dilemma became known. The Bella Ava had either struck something or had been struck. None the less, Harrison James quickly assessed the situation as he lifted Srenna up from the floor.

"Daddy, what's happening," she cried staring at her father who was sure the maiden ship was probably sinking. The modest charter, though luxurious, was indeed much smaller then most cruise liners these days. It was meant for exclusive trips. To her own fault, Harrison James could tell she was taking on water, and she was taking it fast.

He never answered Srenna. He only pulled her along to the wall, trying to get his footing. Passengers had started flooding out of the doorways in sheer terror and panic, headed for the few life boats tethered to the ship's side. He watched in horror as one, then another loaded quickly, not even remotely full and attempted to lower to the churning waters below.

Harrison knew for a certainty they would hit the side of the ship, rolling people into the unforgiving sea. He ignored Srenna's sobs racking her as he began pulling her along the wall towards the bow of the ship He knew there was only one chance for his beloved daughter to make it away from the sinking ship. He intended to look for his wife and sons, but he knew Srenna would slow him down. He knew he had to move quickly. He reached for a cushion off of a toppled lounge chair and carried it with them.

Barely had he reached the bow, when another sound, an explosion, gave way to the rancid smell of fuel. Another swift shudder nearly sent them both over the edge.

"Hold on to the rail Srenna!" he yelled, as he pulled her up and against the side. He looked around one more time at the terror aboard the holiday ship and then looked at the terror in his daughter's eyes. He put the cushion in Srenna's arms and kissed his daughter's tear stained face. Then to her horror, he lifted her in his arms and placed her on the railing.

"Daddy, what are you doing!? No Daddy!...Please...don't,...I can't do this,...please," she begged fearfully, clinging to her father.

"Srenna stop!" he commanded in a voice she had never heard before. "I have to look for your mother and your brothers. I can't leave without trying!"

"I want to come with you, please, don't make me jump, Daddy, please!" she sobbed uncontrollably. Her father knew he was spending precious minutes.

"Hug this Srenna. Don't let go. When you hit the water, kick! Kick as hard as you can away from the ship. Head towards the sun. Don't look back, don't stop. Just swim! Do you understand?" he instructed her as he held her face in his hands. He could feel his child digging her fingers into his arms, unwilling to let go. He pried them away from his body and continued to stare earnestly at her.

The fear was suffocating Srenna, but so intense was her father's voice, she nodded her head without anymore argument. With one last kiss to her forehead and "I love you Srenna", she felt herself being hurled out from the railing. Try as she might to hold onto the cushion, she hit the water with such force she felt it yank from her arms on impact.

But the resilient twelve year old only remembered one thing as she came up from the angry waters and still hearing the terror in her father's voice from the deck above, she turned quickly away from the dying ship as soon as she retrieved the cushion ...and kicked. She kept moving in spite of the many horrific sounds and smells around her.

After only a few moments Srenna had ceased hearing her father's shouts but another voice was ringing in her ears. It was a quieter voice, sure and steady; one she had learned to hear already many times in her twelve short years. It was no longer her earthly father who commanded her attention, but her Heavenly one who continued to encourage the child to swim. She was unaware of how close the Bella Ava had been to safe harbor when a scientific sub fatefully struck the ships starboard side. Additional explosions rang out behind her only adding to the adrenaline that was pumping the girl's legs involuntarily. At one point an unforgiving wave slapped her so hard she slipped from the cushion and felt herself sliding into the relentless sea trying to claim her as a casualty. But she fought back only as Srenna James knew how. A driving force made the tired child fight once again to gain the surface of the water and keep going, this time without the cushion. She felt like she had been in the angry waves for ever, but realistically only twenty minutes had passed when the first of Sydney's Coast Guard found the exhausted child swimming in the direction of the harbor. When the rescuer in the water attempted to pull her into the rescue boat, Srenna fought him, still kicking, panic overtaking every muscle in her body. He pulled her into his arms, holding her as tightly as he could against his strong chest. For a few fleeting moments Srenna, even in a state of terror, was able to look back at the scene being played out where the Bella Ava once floated, beautiful and proud. Thick black smoke was coursing out of her body and only a slight amount of her prestigious form could still be seen over the waters surface. Everywhere Srenna looked she could see people in the waves, whether alive or dead she did not know.

When she was finally aboard the rescue ship and carried to a stretcher it took the medic only moments to realize the deep shock the girl was going into. He hesitated only briefly before sedating her. Srenna felt as though she were sliding back into the waters she had just come from, only this time they were placid and quiet. Again she heard a reassuring and peaceful voice whispering in her ear, "The Lord is my shepherd, I shall not want. He maketh me to lie down in green pastures, He leads me beside still waters…"

That scripture continued on, but it was the voice she had heard in the waves that spoke firmly and lovingly to her, "Stop kicking Srenna …and rest". The medic watched the devastated little girl as she succumbed to the sedative he had administered. It wasn't until then that her arms and legs ceased moving. But he wasn't completely convinced that it was that which sent the child into a deep comatose sleep or even the Chaplin who had been quoting Psalm 23 in her ear. He wondered if the undeniable presence of a peaceful Being in the room hadn't just taken over. He was just simply grateful that the exhausted youth had stopped kicking and sobbing …and crying out… for her "Daddy."

Chapter 2: Srenna's Angel

The streets of Sydney's section were particularly busy this late spring afternoon, but not too busy for the experienced school girl weaving in and out of moving vehicles and pedestrians on her bicycle. She had grown quite agile running errands for the head mistress at Devon's School for Girls. Srenna James had begged Mistress Harvey for the privilege of picking up and delivering items after school for the soul purpose of breaking out of the boring routine of school.
The sixteen year old had spent the last three and a half years earning the trust
and respect of the school's dowdy overseer by studying hard and getting good grades and doing more then her share of chores at the moderately prestigious school. It had not been an uncomfortable place to be. The teachers for the most part had taken sympathy on the young girl placed there by the children's services after the tragic loss of her parents.

Fervent tries to reach any relatives in Melbourne had been unsuccessful, whether due to negligence, health or other matters. Even the family's parish leader, Reverend Carmel had tried extensively to find a family for the twelve year old orphan when she finally came out of the hospital. But in the end the girl became a ward and placed at Devon with what was left of her father's estate monies. Reverend Carmel had been able to obtain permission for Srenna to retrieve her personal belongings and some family mementos, but everything else had been sold in an estate sale to cover expenses at the hospital and immediate costs at the school. Her family had been well off, but not rich by many of Sydney's "elite" standards. Still enough had been available to cover the girls' room and board, schooling and meager personal needs since arriving.

The Reverend and his wife, Ruth, had known Srenna and her family for many years, meeting them when Harrison and Sara James had moved to Sydney from Melbourne. Like many young families the young couple ventured to the shores of the bustling city with the promise of a better life. As a veterinarian, Harrison James was able to establish a great reputation with the horse owners of Australia's upper class.

But the James family remained true to their strong beliefs in God and Harrison faithfully attended the Anglican Church with his wife and later with his children as well. Daniel Carmel had become quite fond of the oldest child and her vivacious and always inquisitive personality. In a silent prayer one night at her bedside, he made a promise that he would stay in touch with the dear child. And so far he had been able to keep that promise, visiting her at the school every week and now as she had grown older, he looked forward to her consistent visits and her faithful attendance on Sunday morning, come rain or Australian sunshine. He kept abreast of her welfare, her grades, her health and especially her challenging spiritual needs. He was constantly reminded of his own biblical shortcomings when he saw the depths in which the girl attempted to understand the promises in the scriptures and how much unswerving faith she had in spite of the horrific tragedy she had suffered. He was however very concerned that the girl's reliance to survive nearly drove her sometimes to keep going; even to a fault. His greatest of all concerns was that she had somehow buried any trauma suffered by the horrendous sinking of the Bella Ava and the subsequent loss of her family. Try as he had he could never seem to break into Srenna's memories of that life changing event long enough to see if she had processed her grief adequately.

The James family, along with 128 other passengers had never been recovered. Reverend Carmel had held a memorial service for the family and several others lost, but Srenna remained hospitalized for two months following the tragedy due to the pneumonia she succumbed to after being in the salt water.

There were no bodies, so there were no burials, no graves, no closure for the girl, yet in all of that, once the powers to be had decided her immediate future, Srenna jumped headlong into her new life, school, classes and other challenges.

It was a new challenge approaching that sent Srenna bicycling the five miles to the Carmel's parsonage this sunny afternoon. Reverend Carmel had left a message by telephone that he wished to see her after school. He had been ill earlier in the week so he offered Srenna the chance to get away from her usual routine. She quickly pedaled the final mile up to the large church and the adjacent home where the Reverend and his wife lived.

Srenna couldn't imagine what he wanted to see her for. Her grades at school had been excellent. She had not had any problems lately with discipline or anything of a negative nature other then the usual feeling of not fitting in with the other girls her age. She still disliked the silliness of the other girls concerning boys and parties and fashion and all the giddiness that went with those things. She still much preferred to figure out why things were what they were, where they came from and seemed to have a million questions more then all the girls put together.

One thing she did not seem to question at all was her appearance. Much to the other girls disdain, Srenna James was beautiful. And worst of all, she cared little about it. She had grown from the skinny little girl with dark auburn pigtails and dark eyes to an attractive young woman nearly sixteen years old. Her figure had definitely filled out but only in a graceful and modest way. Her fellow students could not help but notice the way boys looked at Srenna when they had outings or gatherings with other schools. But Srenna wasn't concerned about those things at all. To her, the boys were even sillier then the girls.

As she rode up to the gate at the parsonage she could feel her pulse quicken, not from the ride there but from the anticipation of the unknown. She pushed the bicycle through the iron gate and laid it on it's side before running up the few steps to the front door. Once she rang the bell, she began her usual fidgeting, shifting from one foot to another, for Srenna had a difficult time standing still at any time. She had boundless energy and found it hard to be motionless for any amount of time.

She didn't have to wait too long before the Reverend's dear wife Ruth opened the door quickly. She seemed very happy to see the young girl as always.

"Gidday Srenna! How you going?!" the cheerful woman greeted her. Her arm went around Srenna immediately and she crushed the girl with one of her infamous motherly hugs. "Why, you must be tuckered out child, riding all this way after a hard day at school."

Srenna laughed at the robust woman she had known all her life. "I'm good as gold Mrs. Carmel, as always," she answered, knowing full well the Reverend's wife would huff and puff just walking across the courtyard to church let alone trying a trip on a bicycle. Srenna loved her though and the Reverend. Their faithfulness to the dear orphan had had much to do with Srenna's continued trust in God in spite of everything.

"Well good then, good. Now, he's waitin' for you and his tea as well in the office," she chuckled, leading Srenna down the hallway to the familiar room she had been in many times in her life.

Ruth Carmel knocked on the door and then picked up the tray she had left on the table beside it. She barely waited for the "Come in" when she motioned with her head to Srenna to open it and step inside.

Srenna entered the parsonage office Reverend Carmel had established as his study and his hideaway from the frequent "drop bys" he received during his busy week. Widowed Mrs. Campbell would "drop by" the church and end up staying to chat for an hour. Frank Barnett, retired mechanic, would "drop by" to see if anything needed "fixing". Any other countless visits finally caused the gentle but frustrated parish leader to designate Tuesdays and Thursday as his "drop by" days. The rest of the time he took sanctuary in his study, well protected by his gracious, but firm wife. Today, however, he had waited rather impatiently for one of his favorite visitors to arrive, but only because he needed to speak to Srenna about some issues that were about to affect her life in a dramatic way again. He was a bit on edge as the lovely young girl walked in and crossed the room to give him her usual greeting.

Without any hesitation Srenna walked right up to the elderly man and threw her arms around his waist. He in turn hugged the adored child as if one of his own offspring had entered the room, though they had been gone from him and his wife for several years now.

"Srenna. I believe you've broken your record, you! School's only been dismissed for twenty minutes. Did you fly here child!?" he laughed holding her back and trying to sound surprised.

"Yeahr. I'm right shagged too. Got bored with the cycle," she quipped back with her usual bantering with the beloved man.

"Now girl, what'd I tell you about fibbers?" he laughed again, knowing the child could no more lie then God himself could. They had been testing one another's light jocularity for much of Srenna's young life and Daniel Carmel found her joy and humor to be greatly refreshing and a true gift as well. He hoped it would serve her now as he remembered why he had summoned her here.

"I'll leave you two to your tea," announced Mrs. Carmel as she set the tray down on the desk and headed for the door. With no other word, she smiled at Srenna and nodded at her husband reassuringly, then closed the door behind her.

Before another word was spoken, out of a delightful habit, Srenna poured a cup of tea for Reverend Carmel and handed it to him. She took joy in serving him his tea and spending time with him in his office. Knowing full well he would insist on her pouring herself a cup, she did so and then took a seat in her favorite chair in front of his desk. He had taken several sips as he walked around behind the desk and lowered himself into his comfy chair. Srenna sensed he was savoring the moment of relaxation and calm. She was beginning to wonder even more so why she had been summoned to visit with him. She needn't have wondered very long.

"Srenna, I trust everything is well with you at school, what with the end of the session and finals over. Most of the girls will be leaving for holiday break, eh?" he asked the young girl.

Srenna set her tea cup on the end table next to her and answered quickly, "Yes. I'm certain I passed most of my tests. It'll be very quiet at the school this time next week." She looked at the dear old man and saw concern on his face and continued, asking, "Why? Has Mrs. Harvey said otherwise?"

Reverend Carmel heard the change in Srenna's voice go from the jovial to concern almost immediately and knew he must simply get to his point of calling her today. Srenna James didn't miss anything. So he leaned into the desk and caught the girl's serious eyes.

"Srenna, I've absolutely no doubt you have given everything to doing the best possible job to finish your school year. Mrs. Harvey tells me you continue to be a tremendous asset with the younger girls and your willingness to help with chores and all. She has even told me you are very close to simply completing your classes and graduating. That's not at all why I needed to speak to you today." At this point the dear man stood and walked over to his window overlooking the courtyard between the house and the church. He was finding it suddenly very difficult to look into Srenna's dark brown eyes, knowing full well he was about to shake her world again.

"Then if everything is sweet, why are you upset?" the insightful child asked.

"I'm…just…well, I'm afraid I have some difficult news to break to you," Reverend Carmel began. "I'm not sure…"

"You could just tell me, eh? She'll be right. Always is," the girl smiled slightly, trying to assure him, and assure herself also.

"Well, you and me, we're going to believe that, now, eh?" he responded, pulling himself away from the window and coming back to the desk. This time he leaned on the front of the desk directly in front of Srenna. He looked down at her, into her eyes and began to explain the situation concerning her.

"Srenna, I'm afraid finances to continue your schooling at Devon have quite run out. You'll be able to stay for a few more weeks till new arrangements have been made. According to Mistress Harvey, you could even receive your certificate of completion, you've done so well." He hesitated for a moment, trying to read the girl's face and any reaction to his announcement. But Srenna sat frozen and fixed on what her parish leader was telling her. "You'll probably be transferred to Chapman's Children's Home in Newcastle until your seventeen. They will help you become emancipated, find a job. I'm not sure what all. There's another proceeding scheduled to finalize the rest of your wardship." At this point, Daniel Carmel leaned forward and took the bewildered teenager's hand and gently squeezed it. She only sat and kept those haunting dark eyes fixed on the agonized man.

"I have to leave?" she finally questioned softly. There were tears behind those eyes that had learned to laugh again. Now there was confusion in them, even a bit of fear. It pained him to have to be the one to put it there. It had been he who had finally closed the door of hope on the devastated little girl when neither her mother or father were found and no one came to "get her". It was he and Ruth who had begged the Anglican District leaders to allow them to take the child in; but their answer was no. All along, for over three years he had taken her part, stood for her on behalf of Harrison James. Now he could do nothing; only break the disturbing news to her and try to prepare her for yet another emotional upheaval in her life.

But he suddenly saw what he'd seen many times with this phenomenal girl. She sat up straight, took a deep breath and looking at the wall behind him, stated in a voice, trembling only slightly, "Well, I guess that's it then, eh? If I must leave, I must. After all, it's like you've said before. It's not like God didn't see it coming, whatever He does with it, right?" She looked at the Reverend, wanting agreement, his reassurance that the faith she had learned over the nearly sixteen years of her life, the promises she knew coming from the word of God he had delivered every week, were truer now then ever.

"Yes my dear child, He knows. We'll pray, you and I, and ask Him to show us both, to help you as you go through this," the kindly old man responded. He said it with all the conviction he had known in his forty years of shepherding, as much, if not more to convince himself as well as her.

"Mistress Harvey wanted me to talk to you first. I'll be with you during the proceeding and when the caseworker takes you to Chapman's. After that we'll see if we can't arrange for visits and even see you at holidays," he offered.

But Srenna stopped hearing the plans the compassionate friend had been making. Her mind was struggling with the news she's received. She could feel herself beginning to lose composure, in spite of what she knew in her heart. The thought of leaving familiar surroundings and loved ones she had left in her life, was threatening to flood in uncontrollably. She did what she knew to do to maintain control.

"Reverend Carmel, I just remembered, I have to run a quick errand for the cook before I go back. I promised I would do it," she sputtered hurriedly and stood up. She pulled her hand away so abruptly and moved towards the door that he wasn't sure how to react. But he had seen this behavior before. She threw herself into her problems with almost a vengeance, just as she had school, her challenges, her changes. He simply did not know if she was just that trusting….or just that able to suppress.

Srenna made her way back through the quieter streets towards the boarding school, only this time in much less of a hurry.

Her mind was spinning almost as fast as the wheels on her bicycle, with all the news she had just received. Mrs. Carmel had tried to convince her to stay for supper: they would drive her back to school later, hoping she would let them help her sort out the changes that would be happening in the weeks to come. But true to her nature, Srenna was off in a flurry of energy.

"She'll land on her feet, that one will, eh?" Daniel Carmel said to his wife, trying to convince himself as they watched the determined girl speed away.

"Right after she tries to climb this mountain at a full run all by herself," Ruth Carmel chuckled softly, "poor little lamb."

But this time Srenna was losing speed. It seemed the more she pedaled, the more her mind was racing. The more her mind raced, the more she wanted to cry. She was lost in the dilemma, when the sound of an automobile horn snapped her back to where she was and what she was doing. She had crossed in front of a driver and was only missed by the man's quick reflexes as he came to a screeching halt. He yelled angrily at the girl who first just stared at him as though she were dumbstruck by what almost happened.

Then it came. The flood of tears she had been holding back, the disconcerting news she'd gotten, the uncertainty of what was going to happen; it all came crashing over her like the angry waves when she had been in the water fighting for her life.

When she realized people were watching her and even coming towards her, she used what was left of her energy to push her bicycle off the street and literally run from the scene. From behind her she could hear people calling to her as to see if she was hurt or needed help. But she turned a corner into an alley and didn't stop until she reached the other end.

Srenna stayed just inside the alley, leaned against the brick of a building and sobbed. She gripped the bicycle against her as if it and the wall were the only things holding her up. She couldn't even form the words of a prayer on her lips, her emotions were so deeply drowning out her young faith and any reason at the moment.

"My dear child! Has someone hurt you? Are you injured or lost?" a gentle but concerned voice spoke over Srenna. She had buried her face in one hand and the sound of a woman addressing her startled Srenna enough to make her stop crying and look up. Before she'd had a chance to answer, Srenna saw a lovely young lady, probably several years older then herself come towards her and without thought or hesitation the woman placed a calming arm around the devastated girl.

"Whatever it is, she'll be right." The beautifully dressed woman hugged Srenna and spoke to her as if she'd known her all her life and strangely enough, what she'd been through.

For some odd reason, Srenna, who hated people to see her cry, began weeping and telling the stranger all that had just happened, her disturbing news and how she felt. As she sobbed and spoke, the woman quietly listened, stroking her hair with one hand and supplying her with a beautiful lace hankie in the other. She said nothing until the heartbroken girl had spent herself in sobs and words and then for several minutes simply held Srenna against her shoulder.

A few more minutes passed as Srenna began to calm down a bit. The woman reminded her of both her mother's arms when she'd fallen down and gotten hurt and her father's, when she'd been disciplined, forgiven and then reassured how much he loved her. These thoughts threatened to send her back into a tearful encore, when the young stranger began to speak to Srenna.

"You know, several years ago, I needed employment. A friend of mine sent me to see a woman who trains and hires out governesses. Her name is Marilyn Crawford. She's always looking for bright, energetic young girls," With that the woman pulled a card from her handbag and gave it to Srenna.

Srenna took the card in her hand and stared down at it blurry eyed and exhausted. "But I'm only sixteen," she stated despairingly, "No one is going to hire someone as young as me."

"Srenna," the woman smiled, speaking firmly to her. "We can never doubt that God knows exactly what we need and when we need it. And remember," the woman spoke as she hugged Srenna and then suddenly moved towards the street. "He will keep you in perfect peace if you keep your mind on Him." She smiled again as she took the last few steps and turned the corner. Srenna stared at her as she disappeared around the building onto the street. Then she looked down at the card again.

Suddenly, she realized as she saw Marilyn Crawford's name and address on the card that she simply did not have a clue as to who the woman was that she had just poured her heart out to, but as quickly as she grasped that she realized that the woman had also just called her by name.

Srenna pushed the bicycle as quickly as she could to the street, looking down the sidewalk, hoping to see the lady walking away and ready to ask her for her name. But the mysterious Samaritan who had just held her as lovingly as any mother could was no where to be seen. Srenna pushed the bicycle along the store fronts wondering if her comforter had stepped inside one of them. But all were closed for the day and it baffled the girl as to what had just happened.

She was still walking slowly down the street when she came to the last doorway before turning the corner. There on a sign above the door were the words, "Marilyn Crawford Agency". Dumbfounded, Srenna felt her heart pounding and a strange sense of strength and peace coming from out of nowhere, a sense of Him, a feeling she had known before, a feeling that slammed into her one moment and slid in quietly at another. She looked up and down the street again, then at the card in her hand again. Then she realized she still held the hankie. Two initials were embroidered on the lacy cloth; the initials S. J. Srenna stared in awe at the evidence she had of the woman who had ministered to her in the alley only moments ago. Her thoughts tumbled over the idea that the initials were her own. She looked up with tears in her dark eyes at the information on the window of the agency. She knew whatever had transpired just now had been no accident and that somehow tomorrow she must come back. She was still uncertain what it would hold, but she was sure of one thing.

God had just sent her an angel!

Chapter 3: God and Mrs. Crawford

The last day's events of school were painfully slow and mundane to Srenna especially after what had surely been an angelic visitation the day before. She felt compelled to tell no one at the school about her experience and no one asked why the orphaned girl had arrived late for the evening meal. Head Mistress Harvey assumed that Srenna might be upset upon receiving the news from the Reverend about leaving Sydney. She already felt somewhat badly for the poor child, but now she really pitied the homeless girl and her uncertain future. Everyone was talking excitedly about their holiday plans for summer break so when Srenna excused herself early feigning a headache, she was allowed to retire to her room without question.

But today she had a plan! School would be over at midday. When Srenna asked early that morning if she might return to the parsonage to talk to Reverend Carmel some more about her imminent future, Mistress Harvey said yes almost immediately, assuming the disturbing news was upsetting her and Reverend Carmel would know best how to console her. But it wasn't the parsonage she headed for the moment school was dismissed. Many of the girls would be leaving by that evening, all fairly gone by tomorrows end. Srenna hugged a few of the younger girls whose trust she had carried the last 3 years. But she could barely keep her mind on what they were telling her about their summer plans. So she quickly disengaged herself from their circle of conversation and headed out to the bicycle rack. That morning she had pulled and pinned her long dark auburn hair the way the older girls and teachers wore theirs, she stayed in her uniform skirt and blouse and donned a short jacket as well trying desperately to appear older in any way she could.

As she carefully pedaled her way back to the street she had left last night her mind went over her plan until she knew what she was going to do and say. Only a few minutes had passed when Srenna came up to the building and doorway she had stood in front of in a flurry of emotions. There again she saw the name Marilyn Crawford Agency on the door sign. In her hand was the business card given to her by the lovely mysterious woman in the alley.

Srenna stared at the card for a long time, her heart pounding in her chest and then reaching in her pocket of her jacket she pulled out the hankie with the initials S.J. on it. Again she felt a deep sense of peace all around her as she reached for the door knob.

But upon entering the lobby of the agency office, Srenna nearly turned and ran out. It was obvious by the furnishings of the room that this was no trite business. Rich leather chairs and beautiful oak tables spanned the room's cozy dimensions. A handsome brick fireplace graced the back wall and everywhere fine paintings and vases were placed in grand opulence. An immaculately dressed woman sat at a desk far richer then Reverend Carmel's had ever been. The woman looked at Srenna in what must have seemed to her extremely drab and plain street clothes, making the girl feel suddenly very awkward and hugely inadequate. But the receptionist broke the uncomfortable silence asking quickly and professionally "May I help you, young lady?"

Srenna sucked in as much air as could possibly be gotten by one very nervous girl and plowed forward with her plan. "Yes... yes mum, I'm... My name is Srenna James. I ran into an acquaintance of Mrs. Crawford's yesterday while looking for a governess position. She gave me Mrs. Crawford's' business card and suggested I come see her." Srenna walked to the desk and held out the card trying desperately not to lose it out of her trembling hand.

"Well, yes, this is Mrs. Crawford's' card. But who did you say gave it to you?" The woman questioned skeptically.

"I'm sorry" Srenna began "We only met a short ways from here, while shopping. We got to talking and I told her I was looking for a position, as I've finished with school and I'd like to train for a career as a governess. I've quite forgotten her full name but I believe she said her first name was Susan or something of that nature. Her last name started with a J." Srenna stopped to catch her breath fairly certain that at any moment either the receptionist would show her to the door or worse, the ground underneath her would swallow her up into hell for lying. She remembered the hankie as well and pulled it out to show the receptionist. "She gave me this to use. Said Mrs. Crawford would recognize it."

But much to her surprise neither one occurred. Instead the woman gave Srenna a confused look and exclaimed quickly, "Susanna Jarvis, Yes. Fine young woman. One of Mrs. Crawford's finest protégés. Governess to the Mayfields. Why…you wait right there and I'll see if Mrs. Crawford can see you," the woman responded. To Srenna's complete shock she walked through the door behind her and into the next room before Srenna could begin to thank her.

Srenna stood frozen to the floor, afraid that if she walked about at all she might bolt and run back out the door. But again the news of yesterday, the impact of having to leave Sydney and go to Newcastle, flooded over her both to despair and to desperation. And well that it did for suddenly a fierce determination came over her as well and she resolved to carry out her plan.

It was a determined Srenna who was just about to move from her spot on the floor to examine the room when the receptionist came out in a flurry through the office door. But it was again a desperate Srenna that was ready to hear any good news possible. Judging by the warm smile on the woman's face, Srenna felt a glimmer of hope.

"Oh… Mrs. Crawford will see you Miss. Says she wants to meet you," she gushed to Srenna, coming over to the surprised girl and putting an arm around her. "Come on in and you'll have your interview."

Srenna was speechless and felt as though she were some actress preparing to go on stage to deliver her performance. The problem was she'd completely forgotten what she had planned on saying. The usually quick witted youth felt suddenly very addle brained as she walked through the door into an equally rich and eloquent office. Coming towards her was another older woman dressed in a finely tailored dress and jacket. The woman could have been old enough to be Srenna's grandmother and austere enough to scare her to death, except her eyes held a twinkle in them and her smile to Srenna was patient and genuine.

"Gidday, Miss James. I'm Margaret Crawford," she addressed the nervous schoolgirl as she extended her hand.

Srenna gave her own hand in response, though it was trembling fiercely. She was acutely aware how sweaty her palm must have felt to this impeccably refined business woman. Somehow she found enough volume in her voice to acknowledge the greeting and replied, "Mrs. Crawford. I'm so very pleased to meet you."

"Come, sit and let's have a talk you and I, shall we?" Mrs. Crawford motioned to Srenna, showing her to a comfortable overstuffed chair in front of her desk. "May I have Alice bring you some tea, dear?" she offered as she moved to her own chair behind the desk.

"Oh no, Mum, I'm fine, really, but thank you so much," Srenna replied quickly. She knew full well at that moment that given a cup of tea, not a single drop would make it to her lips should she even attempt to drink it.

"Very good then. I understand you were referred to me by Susanna Jarvis. Is that correct?" Mrs. Crawford began, holding the business card in her hand.

"Yes… yes Mum. We met only yesterday, while shopping a short ways from here. She started sharing her love for children, caring for them and all. I told her I was interested in becoming a governess myself," Srenna spilled out, trying to remember little details she recalled about the kind lady in the alley. Before she could deliver her next rehearsed line, Margaret Crawford simply and pointedly asked the girl the one question she had hoped would not come up at all.

"Exactly how old are you, my dear?" the woman asked gently.

Srenna thought for sure the next large breath she inhaled would deplete the room of all oxygen and yet only one word found the ability to escape her lips.
"Seventeen," she responded, hoping her face had not drained all color from it or that she would simply not be struck dead at that precise moment.

"And your school? I assume you've completed your education this session, have you not?" Mrs. Crawford went on looking down and writing on a clipboard in front of her.

"Oh yes, …yes, I have. All passing grades. High test scores. I've done very well," Srenna added quickly, realizing some of her responses were indeed true. But only for a fleeting moment.

"And what boarding school did you attend, dear? I'm afraid I didn't catch it," Mrs. Crawford pressed her.

Srenna felt herself hesitate this time as she determined whether to stumble on deeper into her fabrication or turn and run.

She chose the former.

"No boarding school, Mrs. Crawford. I was taught privately. My father was a veterinarian, for race horses. We traveled a lot. He allowed me to travel with he and my mother." Srenna was dumbfounded by how this lengthy statement tumbled out of her mouth. She waited with her heart pounding to see what the intrigued woman would say.

"Well, I'll need to see your certificate of completion and of course a letter from your parents agreeing to your employment with us, as well as references from at least one person. Your private teacher or parish leader would do. From there we can determine where and when you can be trained and a possible position within a year. Since Susanna Jarvis seemed to think you held some possibility and she was one of my prized governesses, I think we should have no problem…"

But Srenna heard nothing past "a letter from your parents". Before Mrs. Crawford finished her last statement, much to her surprise the seemingly poised young lady suddenly stood from her chair, wringing her hands and fighting back a wall of tears ready for the second day in a row to spill relentlessly down her cheeks.

"I'm sorry Mum…I…I can't do this. I'm really sorry…I need to go…please…" a distraught Srenna stammered, as she quickly moved towards the door. She was nearly ready to escape as she reached a trembling hand for the doorknob, when a firm but quiet voice commanded her.

"Srenna. Come back and sit down."

Srenna blinked, sending a flow of tears from behind her eyelids and quickly down her face. She heard the authority in Mrs. Crawford's voice, but another sound also flooded her ears. It was the calm knowing quality of her father's voice when she'd done something wrong as a small child and gotten caught. But it held that tender reluctant tone, the one that hadn't the heart to scold her, or even remotely get angry with her.

It was that tone of voice and Srenna's despair that made her turn and sit back down in the chair. She choked back every sob that was attempting to rack her entire being as she looked at her lap, ashamed and horrified that she had gone as far as she had with the deception. She couldn't bear to look at the woman sitting across from her and was really wishing this time that the floor would open up and swallow her whole. All the while Srenna gripped the lacy hankie in her hands, twisting it fiercely.

Mrs. Crawford stood from her seat and moved calmly to the door. Upon opening it, she addressed the receptionist in the waiting room quietly and evenly.

"Alice, we will need our tea now, if you please." She closed the door behind her and returned to the desk, but this time much in the same manner as Reverend Carmel, she positioned herself directly in front of Srenna.

"Now, let's start this over and why don't you tell me what I really need to hear and what you really need to say," the gentle woman suggested. As she did she reached for some tissue on her desk and offered it to Srenna. She then reached for the handkerchief in Srenna's hand and unfolded it looking at the familiar initials embroidered in yellow. It still held a faint scent of lavender. She looked intently at Srenna.

Never raising her gaze past Margaret Crawford's skirt, Srenna once again poured out her heartbreaking story. From start to finish, every detail came tumbling out until she sat back in the large chair, exhausted and nearly ill. All the while Mrs. Crawford sat patiently against the desk and listened to the distraught teenager sob out her tale. When a knock indicated that Alice had afternoon tea, she stepped to the door, received it and came back. She poured a cup for Srenna and handed it to her. Nothing had been said; no response to all Srenna had spilled out up to that point.

Finally the kind woman ordered in a calming voice, "Sip it carefully child. And while you're sipping, allow me to share my own tragedy with you."

For the first time since Srenna had sat back down in the chair and lamented her trials to this stranger, she dared to look up at her, a bit surprised by what she had just said. But Srenna listened, unable to take her eyes off this matronly woman as she unfolded the tragic loss of her husband in World War One. Her life was brought full about when she determined to throw herself headlong into helping other families and their children, instead of immersing herself into grief and despair.

The result over the last couple of decades had been first her own position as a successful governess and then the founding of the agency and training of those young women desiring to follow that path as well. When she finished, Mrs. Crawford once again ordered Srenna to "sip her tea" as the awestruck girl stared at this amazing woman. Srenna was so busy listening to every detail of the heart wrenching story, the cup remained on her lap. Still an occasional solitary tear found its way down her wet cheeks.

"Srenna, how old are you?" Mrs. Crawford asked again, holding the young girl's eyes.

Without turning away and feeling somewhat relieved that she felt she could answer honestly, Srenna replied quietly, "Sixteen, just." She held her breath as before, sure now that she had spent Mrs. Crawford's complete patience, as the kindhearted woman stood and walked behind her desk. As she sat back down, she once again reassured the girl in front of her.

"You remind me... of me, Srenna, when I was younger, even a few years ago. Determined, driven to survive. But...you're not a liar," she stated, as though she had known Srenna her whole life. At that, Srenna's eyes dropped again. But then to her surprise, Margaret Crawford briskly and forcefully commanded her in a quiet tone, "Lift up your head Srenna! Look me in the eyes."

Srenna pushed her gaze up and fixed her eyes on the woman's wise blue eyes.

"You couldn't go through with it. It took more honesty and courage to admit you'd done something wrong, something you wouldn't have if you didn't think you had too, eh?" Mrs. Crawford questioned.

"I didn't want too, but I don't want to leave Sydney either," Srenna replied firmly.

"Maybe you won't have to," the elderly lady stated, winking suddenly at Srenna, a slight grin forming on her lips. She moved a ledger in front of her as she spoke and began turning the pages of it. Then in a more serious tone, she began explaining something to Srenna.

"Srenna, many of Australia's finest men are preparing to join the war both in the Pacific and in parts of Europe. In the last few weeks I've had numerous requests for governesses, mother's helpers and the likes, as many of these men's wives will need assistance while they're gone." As she explained this all to the girl she wrote down some information on a card.

"Now, here is what we might be able to do and I stress might, as it will have to be approved no doubt by the court overseeing your custody."

As she spoke, Srenna felt another flicker of hope, this time real hope. Mrs. Crawford handed her the card and looked encouragingly at her.

"Take this information to your headmistress. I will call her myself after you leave and see what has to be done to place you with one of these families. If she believes it is a possibility, I will set up a time for you to visit the people on that card. The Havilland's are a very prominent family in Sydney. Mr.Havilland will be leaving in one month as an officer in the Anzacs. Grace Havilland is due to have her third child anytime. She has a live in nurse, but wants a mother's helper for her other two boys, ages four and six years.

"Boys?" Srenna questioned, feeling a twinge of memory come over her. She quickly realized though that as determined as she was right now, she would take care of some ones dogs if it meant staying.

"Yes. Boys. You'll be keeping them occupied, going out with them, helping the oldest with school and other chores around the house," Margaret Crawford explained. "Does it sound like something you could do, would want to do?" The woman tried to read the reaction on Srenna's face as she gave her the information. Srenna looked away for the first time since Mrs. Crawford had held her attention with this possibility. For only a fleeting moment she thought of her young twin brothers who she would never see again, never watch them grow, play with them, fight with them. Mixed emotions threatened to confuse her, but for the still firm voice of Margaret Crawford.

"Srenna, could you do this?" she asked the girl softly.

Srenna let out a huge sigh and answered quietly, "Yes...yes... I think I could." She forced a faint smile at her extremely benevolent host.

"All right then. I'll call Mrs. Havilland. You speak to Head Mistress Harvey. I'll call you in the morning with an appointment and we'll go from there, eh?" the woman said with finality and confidence, as she stood and came around the desk. She motioned to

Srenna to stand, took the teacup from the girl's hand and began walking Srenna back to the door with a matronly arm around her. Just short of the door, she stopped and turned the sixteen-year-old around and looked her full in the face.

"I've no doubt Susanna Jarvis had great words of encouragement to share with you and thought you would be a wonderful asset to someone for all you've been through." With that Margaret Crawford handed the girl the hankie and added, "You'll want to keep this, I'm sure."

Srenna fought hard to hold back the fresh new tears brimming in her dark eyes as the woman spoke her final words to her.

"I believe she was right. Now it's up to you to believe it too, yes?"

"Yes mum…yes," Srenna answered, feeling suddenly empowered, now that a new and truthful plan was in motion.

"Go on with you then," Margaret Crawford smiled, "and I'll talk to you tomorrow." She finished walking Srenna back through the waiting room and to the front door, gave the girl a hug and gently pushed her through it.

Srenna grabbed her bicycle away from the side of the building, but not wanting to ride just yet, she walked back the way she had come. When she reached the alley where she had met the mysterious woman the day before she suddenly remembered the words the woman had shared with her.

"Remember, Srenna…He will keep you in perfect peace if you keep your mind on him."

Srenna uttered first a prayer of repentance and then a prayer of thankfulness to the One who had truly just helped her. She didn't know yet just how this would all turn out. But she had new confidence that it would.

She also didn't know that her mysterious Samaritan who had found her in the alley, sent her to Mrs. Crawford's doorstep and had given her new hope,….had been dead for over two years, killed in an automobile accident.

Srenna was also oblivious that as she climbed on her bicycle to race back to the boarding school, a dumbfounded business woman, dedicated to helping others, had locked herself in her office, fallen on her knees in her own prayer of gratefulness and thanked her God for supplying all her needs "according to His riches in glory."

She could only wonder what great and wonderful measures He would go to to supply the needs of the child that had just left her office.

26

Chapter 4: I Will Lift Up Mine Eyes

The large black horse carrying the thirty eight year old sheepherder up the steep incline moved with a poetic deftness and agility. John Patton could have taken the long road up leading to his higher grazing fields where woolly fat sheep and their lambs were feasting on rich grass. Today, though, he was in a hurry to find his fifteen year old son, Matthew, who had taken the thousand head of Romney sheep up for him while he made a trip down to Masterton. The New Zealand countryside was livid with color even for a cool autumn afternoon. And only a slight hint of rain could be seen in the distance and smelled in the air. All of this seemed to go unnoticed by the rugged country man, still young by many standards and yet seasoned after nearly fifteen years of establishing and running the 1500 acres of hilly lush grazing land. He had worked tremendously hard to build a good steady life for he and his beautiful wife, Miriam and what now numbered five children. It was the oldest, Matthew, he was searching for now, so he could relay extremely important news to him. He had even chosen to speak to his teenage son before his beloved Miriam, in the hopes that the breaking news would be easier to bear with Matthew's support.

The news had been anticipated for a couple of years now and was really no surprise to John when he went into Masterton to speak to the Anzacs recruiting officers. Anzacs was the combined military alliance formed by the Australian and the New Zealand governments in support of the ever increasing threat by the Japanese in the neighboring South Pacific Islands. The war that had only touched the European and African continents, now threatened the whole of the South Pacific region. John Patton had hoped beyond hope it would never mean defending his homeland of sheep country, but since the taking of China and the bombing of the South Pacific islands, the threat was very real. He had put off the tug on his conscience to enlist mostly due to the birth of his last child, Emma and his wife's increasing work load with five energetic children. He dreaded leaving her behind with the incredible responsibilities of mother and caretaker of their large sheep station.

He had great confidence in his strong and dedicated oldest boy. Matthew had been helping his father since he was old enough to ride. The young boy, the image of John when a youth, followed his father's daily routine with great joy when he was allowed. When at school, he thought only of getting home and to the fields. He woke every morning at six a.m. so he could help drive the sheep to graze and then rode on to school. The minute school was over he made his way to the hills and took over so his father could spend time at the pens or time with his mother. John recognized early on a deep natural passion Matthew had for the land and the sheep he had been born into. He hoped now as he spotted his tall blond, blue eyed offspring that that passion would serve his son well.

John was not surprised either as he rode up to the small grove of trees that Matthew was engulfed in his other passion. The boy's head barely bobbed up to acknowledge his father's approach, but only because he was fervently trying to complete whatever train of thought he had been writing down when he heard the big black horse coming up the path.

"Eh, Dad. How ya going?" the boy yelled, as he closed his journal and stood to meet his father. John dismounted Samson and gave the faithful steed a loving pat on his rump sending him off into the field to graze along side Bear, Matthew's four year old colt. From the nearest group of sheep came the bouncing ever energetic Duke, the best Border collie in all the North Island as far as John and Matthew were concerned. He beat Matthew to his master before the boy could reach his father to hug him.

John Patton had always been quick to show his children undeniable and noticeable affection and had equally displayed affection towards his greatest love in life, their mother. Now his children gave it back without thought or embarrassment, even in public. He and Miriam's warmth and unfailing love for one another had truly bonded all of them together like a three stranded cord. Again he hoped their strength as a family would encompass them as life was about to change for all of them.

John tusseled Duke's black and white head and then ordered the dog to go back to the sheep. He then reached for his son's already broadening shoulders for a routine hug and answered him with a forced smile. "I'm doing okay, son. I'm doing okay. It's your mum I'll be worrying about now, and you."

Matthew lost the grin he had shown his dad when he first approached. He had learned his dad's tones of voice well and he knew his father was trying hard to be encouraging and positive, but was really struggling with the news he had come to give his son.

"You'll be going then, eh?" Matthew asked quietly, sure he already knew the answer.

"Come sit with me, Mattie," John Patton ordered gently, his arm still around the boy who wasn't yet as tall as he was. They sat sown on the log that Matthew had been leaning against and John looked out in front of him at the hills around them and the mountains just beyond that. Looking at them reminded him as always that what would help them now, who would help them now, was the Creator of those majestic mountains. No doubt his God fearing, God loving son had been looking to them as well while he waited for his father's return with the inevitable news neither one wanted to hear.

"Yeahr son. I will," John answered quietly, with finality. He tried to see the reaction on his son's face but Matthew had turned it away, looking off into the trees so his father couldn't see him fighting back the tears.

"Listen, Matt. I have to ask you, son, to help me encourage your mum that everything's going to be right. Your brother and sisters are going to need ya to be strong," he stated firmly. He hesitated for only a moment, giving Matthew time to gain control of his feelings before stumbling on.

"Now… I've already stopped at the Rainga's. They know. Jimmies gonna help ya all he can, and Irmani too, and you know Tom's right there with ya," John Patton explained, referring to their family's closest and nearest neighbors. Jimmie Rainga, a native Maori man and his wife Irmani had taken John and Miriam under their seasoned wings when the young couple first arrived in New

Zealand from England. Their son Tommie, the same age as Matthew had been his best friend since the two were barely walking.

"Won't Jimmie be going?" Matthew finally asked, trying desperately to control his shaky voice.

Nawr. Jimmie? His no young man anymore, Matt. They wouldn't take him if he wanted to go. But he feels strong about staying here and watching out for all of you. Said so, he did," John answered, with as much humor as he could muster for his son.

"How soon?" Matthew dared to ask.

"Two weeks," his father answered quietly.

"Two weeks?!" Matthew responded as a tear found it's way down his cheek

"Son, the sooner we can get this war over, the sooner we can stop living in fear that some Japanese dictator is going to try taking all of this away from us, eh?" John explained adamantly.

"Yeahr, sure. I guess," Matthew answered, looking down forlornly at the rich green grass under his feet.

"Matthew, your mum and I, you, all of you, have worked hard to make this our home. I can't just sit by and wait until their dropping bombs on any piece of our island. Do you understand that?" John inquired of his son. He waited patiently for his dear child to take everything in.

Matthew rubbed the back of his hand across his eyes and pulled his head up. His gaze caught the mountains in front of him. Then to his father's encouragement, Matthew began to recite a verse from the Bible that had been dear to him since he was old enough to read. "I will lift up mine eyes unto the hills from whence cometh my help."

John Patton joined him in the 121st Psalm. "My help cometh from the Lord which made Heaven and Earth," they quoted together. They looked at each other as they finished the passage and then John grabbed his boy's shoulders, pulling him into his arms. He let Matthew cry. And when the fifteen year old was through, he stood, keeping his arm around his son and whistled for the horses to come.

"Let's go tell your mum, eh?" he said softly. He never hesitated a moment to kiss the top of his son's head, the son he would be leaving behind to fill his shoes while he was gone. He wondered as they made the trip down the road toward the house how his boy had grown up so fast. A thousand things came to his mind that he wanted and needed to tell him before leaving for Australia and then Hawaii.

He silently uttered up a grateful prayer that Jimmie and Irmani would be there for Matthew, for his three daughters and nine year old son. He was all too aware of what he was asking of Matthew. He would probably have to leave school and do his lessons at home. John wasn't sure if that would be welcomed news or distressful news as his oldest child wasn't a great fancier of his classes anyway. The boy enjoyed reading and he was always writing something. But his other classes bored him. John could only hope his son would strive to finish his courses during his absence.

There was one thing John Patton knew about his young shepherd son. He had the heart of King David and that heart was after God. It had been from an early age. Then at the pivotal age of thirteen after Matthew and Tommie had gotten into trouble, Matthew had made a straight line for the alter when Reverend Davidson gave the invitation to give his heart to God at the Anglican Church in Castlepoint. Matthew had wept like a baby in front of the whole church and proclaimed he was "a sinner, going to hell" and he wanted Jesus in his heart. John and Miriam were not really shocked or surprised as their oldest child had been passionate from the day he was born. He had never done anything halfway and John was even convinced the boy had encountered the presence of the Almighty numerous times while sequestered away in the fields much like the boy of Bible times.

John put much hope in those comforting memories as the sprawling homestead came into view and they approached the archway leading down into the valley where the comfortable two story home stood. He admitted to himself silently that if it were not for Matthew's strength of character, his beloved Miriam's strength of heart and joy, and his dear friends and neighbor's undying support, he could not do what he was about to do.

He turned his gaze one more time at his son and caught Matthew's glance as they reached the house. He faltered for a second when he thought he saw a slight hint of fear behind the boy's eyes. But Matthew grinned at his father, that infamous boyish grin that made his father's heart soar many times already in his young life. John Patton took courage.

"She'll be right, eh?" his boy declared more then he asked.

"Yeahr, Right," John smiled back.

They both turned their heads towards the front door as they heard it open and Miriam Patton, baby Emma on her hip, came out on the porch and to the top of the steps.

"Good as gold, son. Good as gold," he finished, as he lowered himself out of his saddle and headed up the walk to meet his cherished wife.

Chapter 5: Srenna's Birthday Surprise

"It was my turn next, you. I'll box your ears for sure," exclaimed a very irate eight year old Thomas. His cries of injustice were ear splitting enough to wake the dead, but when his taunting eleven year old brother William grabbed the ball and moved away, again, Thomas had had more then anyone could expect. Even Srenna, and her endless patience, usually beyond expectation, was growing extremely thin.

"Alright you two, I've heard all the fighting I'm going to tolerate today," she announced, as she swiped the ball out of William's hand long before he could react. She motioned to all three of her charges to head for the sidewalk and the path back to their comfortable Sydney townhouse. As far as she was concerned, the outing in the park several blocks from the boy's house was over. Only five year old Henry, the youngest child of Frank and Grace Havilland, was equally ready to call it a day due to the spitting and spatting of his two older brothers most of the morning. For some reason the boys had been irritable most the week and Srenna knew that Grace would probably send both of them off to take a much hated and much needed nap after lunch, in spite of their ages. She noticed poor Henry was a bit disappointed that they had their outdoor adventure cut off early, and she resolved to report to his mother that the boy had really been very good in spite of the older ones displaying such ugly behavior.

Srenna normally had only minimal trouble from any of them, but there were times when they just got too competitive with one another and had it out. The last five years of employment with Frank and Grace Havilland had been both a blessing and many great lessons for her as well. Her placement in the home after being hired through Mrs. Crawford's agency for governesses, had proven to be a real challenge, but it was one Srenna embraced with a vengeance. She had been so determined to do whatever she must to stay in the Sydney area, that every instruction, every guidance given by Margaret Crawford had been received with much passion and resolve. It didn't take the well known business woman any time at all to realize she had found a girl filled with the ability to give and care for people.

Placing Srenna James with the Havilland family was like a perfect fit and at just the right time in both their lives. Frank Havilland left to go to war in less then a month, leaving his dear wife at home with a brand new baby and two energetic boys. He knew his wife would need all the help she could get. He was more then willing to spend his well earned and abundant money on hiring the young girl sent over to them by the agency.

The blessing then for Srenna was a job, a home and in short order a friendship in Grace who was less then ten years older then Srenna. The two hit it off so much that in no time Srenna felt comfortably at home and thrilled that she was able to remain in the area she had grown up in. She was reminded even today, that so much had happened in just five years. She could hardly believe the young girl of sixteen who completed her certificate of schooling, started out as a novice governess, was now twenty one and felt so much more mature. Only two weeks ago when they had celebrated her birthday she could scarcely believe how God had taken care of her every need. The joy she received from helping Grace with the boys, even on their worse days, solidified her sense of calling as a governess. She loved the boys dearly and knew they felt the same way about her.

But right then she was reminded that at times they could undo the most peaceful thoughts with out a moments notice, as one bumped into the other on the sidewalk. Before either one could retaliate she stepped between Thomas and William and smiled reassuringly at them both that they were headed for bed and maybe more the minute they entered the door.

Somehow as usual, Grace Havilland had a sense about these things and was waiting at the door for them. She had only to look at each face to know that the morning outing had been taxing on Srenna and Henry, and was going to be even more taxing on Thomas and William when she got done with them.

"Judging by the look on Srenna's face, I'm going to guess the two of you have been fighting again, eh?" their lovely young mother stated. She turned to Srenna, smiling softly, "Another lovely morning in the park? How do you do it, Miss James, without leaving them hanging from a tree by their feet. I believe I have some rope somewhere in the house. Perhaps they should be tied together and hung upside down in their room for the afternoon!" she continued, looking sternly at the boys, trying hard not to laugh at the whole notion of stringing them up.

Srenna covered her mouth with her hand, because she knew she would laugh. She also knew Grace Havilland had learned a long time ago to be tough on the boys at the absence of their father and at the same time tolerable, as they were after all, boys.

Srenna had learned so much from this young woman, married to one of Sydney's most prominent business men. She was a real woman of stature, even for her age, and well liked among the elite crowd in the social circles. Her husband had returned, gratefully unharmed and ready to pick up the pieces in his shipping business after the war. Though they and thousands of others had their lives disrupted by the world's dismantling battles, the Havilland's were fortunate to have pieces left to pick up. Less then a year after the end of the war, many families were still devastated by the grueling number of soldiers that fought with the ANZACS and returned home to hospitals due to severe injury or worse yet, to graves. Srenna was thankful that every one of her and Grace's prayers had seemingly been answered and Frank was home, safe and well.

She regained her composure long enough to report to Grace the details of the infamous squabble in the park and as was predicted, they boys were ordered up the stairs to take lunch in their rooms, Henry excluded, and spend some quiet time "reflecting" upon their behavior towards one another. Srenna was ready to follow them upstairs to see to it they obeyed their patient mother, when Grace motioned to her to let the boys go up alone and pulled the young governess aside. She held Henry's hand as she squeezed Srenna's shoulder.

"I'll take care of organizing the boys and having Mrs. Dually get their lunch upstairs," she announced to Srenna, smiling at the girl.

"You have a visitor in the parlor, a Mr. Harold Garner. He's been waiting to speak to you for about fifteen minutes."

"Mr. Garner?" Srenna asked, with a puzzled look on her face. "I don't think I know anyone by that name," she added, looking toward the parlor door. "Did he say what he wanted?"

"He indicated that he had some news for you. I'm going to make sure the boys are locked away. Get Henry to Mrs. Dually and then I'll join you," Grace offered reassuringly. She could see the concern on Srenna's face and wasn't about to let her protégé deal with a complete stranger on her own. She smiled one more time, as she headed up the stairs to corral the boys and Srenna turned with Henry to take him to the kitchen. After depositing the hungry five year old to the Havilland's cook and housekeeper, Srenna headed back into the hallway leading to the parlor door. She was tempted to make the gentlemen on the other side of that door wait until Grace returned.

But Srenna James never let much hold her back when it meant finding out what was going on. So with her heart pounding just slightly more then a few minutes earlier, she turned the doorknob and entered the room.

Sitting in one of the comfortable overstuffed chairs by the fireplace sat a very distinguished gentleman, maybe in his forties. He was enjoying a cup of morning tea and seemed relaxed, for having just waited a good twenty minutes or so. At first sight of Srenna, though, the man jumped from his chair and nearly sent his teacup flying.

"Miss James, I'm assuming," the gentleman addressed Srenna politely. "Allow me to introduce myself. My name is Harold Garner." He extended his free hand towards Srenna and smiled a graciously warm smile towards the girl.

"Mr. Garner. It's my pleasure. Mrs. Havilland told me you've been waiting for awhile. I do apologize, "the young woman responded, as she offered her hand to be shaken.

"No. No. It's quite alright dear. You've had a busy morning from what I understand. I couldn't help but over hear the ruckus the boys were giving you as they came in," he chuckled. "I would have rung up first, but quite frankly I didn't have a telephone number, only an address. I do hope you will forgive the impertinence of me just showing up like this."

As the man apologized again, Grace entered the room and stood beside Srenna. Almost immediately, Srenna could tell the poise with which her employer seemed to take command of the conversation, not in a controlling way, but in a protective one. She slipped her arm around Srenna's shoulder even as a mother would her own child and before Srenna could say anything more to the gentleman, Grace Havilland motioned to the man to sit.

"Now Mr. Garner, let's all have a seat and find out if we can what this visit is all about," Grace stated firmly, with still a polite but deliberate start. She motioned to Srenna to sit on the sofa with her and then continued to wait for Mr. Garner to respond.

"Well, yes, then. I suppose I should just get right to it, for your sake Miss James," he began, still somewhat composed, but realizing he had a captive and commanding audience where Grace Havilland was concerned.

"You informed me, when we spoke that you were with a law firm, in Melbourne?" she asked inquisitively. Srenna looked first at her and then at him when the words law firm were spoken.

"Is there something wrong, Grace? Have I done something wrong?" the girl asked with a tinge of fear in her voice.

"Oh, no dear, no," Mr. Garner responded quickly and gently, realizing he had concerned the young woman with this announcement. He then reached down beside the chair and pulled up a briefcase that had been propped against it. As he began opening it and shuffling papers about, he continued to smile at Srenna and went on with his explanation. "I'm with the law firm of Barnes, Barnes and Garner, myself, of course being the Garner referred to. Our law offices in Melbourne were acquisitioned by your maternal grandmother, Mrs. Paul Hughes. It's been a little while now, maybe two years ago, after your grandfather passed away." With this the man looked kindly at Srenna for any reaction from the girl concerning the news about her grandparent. The girl however only stared back in puzzlement at what he was even explaining.

"Go on Mr.Garner. Please get to your point, if you can, for Srenna's sake," Grace Havilland suggested firmly as she took a hold of Srenna's hand on her lap.

Mr. Garner cleared his throat before going on. "Well yes, I'll try to be precise about all this legal rhetoric, if I can." He took a deep breath and began again. "As I said, I represent your grandmother, but I am terribly sorry to be the one to indicate to you that she also passed, about eight months after your grandfather. We were pleased to help Mrs. Hughes arrange her affairs after the death of Mr. Hughes, his estate and all, and as you might have known, it was quite an estate. However, there was some concern as to who would stand to become the beneficiary."

Srenna looked hard at Mr. Garner, and then turned to look at Grace with more question in her eyes then her employer had ever seen in the usually confident girl. There was so much confusion on the poor girl's face that Grace Havilland was becoming just a little annoyed with Mr. Hughes for taking so long in his explanation. But the man knew, and painfully kept going.

"Miss James, you had no contact with your grandparents to my understanding. Is that correct?" Mr. Hughes asked gently.

"Well, no, at least none that I remember. My mother was estranged from them after she married my father and my parents moved to Sydney. My grandparents did not approve of my father." Srenna hesitated for a moment, reliving the memory of her devastating knowledge that no one came for her after her parents died; not either one of her grandparents. Both Grace and Mr. Garner could tell the young woman was beginning to slip into a very painful place and the mere look on Grace Havilland's face suggested the struggling man had better speak quickly.

"Miss James, here is the long and the short of it," he started with a slight grin on his face. As he pulled a legal document open, Mr. Garner continued with an even broader grin on his face. "For what ever reason your grandfather felt he must separate himself from your mother, know this. Your grandmother did not feel the same way. She simply could not go against Paul Hughes. The man was set in his ways, though he adored his wife. He left her everything, with no conditions whatsoever and your grandmother decided to reconcile what she could in spite of her being extremely ill. I have papers here that would resolve this issue, Miss James, in the form of a living trust, set up for you by Mrs. Hughes. It was to be kept until the date of your twenty first birthday, which I do believe you just recently celebrated?" he inquired of both ladies.

"Mr. Garner. What are you saying?" Grace asked in utter amazement, as she could see by Srenna's expression the girl was dumbstruck and unable to ask anything on her own behalf.

"Mrs. Havilland, Miss James, I am most pleased to inform you," he hesitated only long enough to read from the document, "that

Srenna Adelaide James is sole beneficiary to the Hughes estate." He stopped and waited for both woman to discontinue staring wide eyed and unbelieving at him and then watched them both, with a bit of amusement, as they stared dumbfounded at each other.

Srenna felt as though the room was spinning, as she tried desperately to process the news Mr. Garner had just delivered. She didn't know what to say. She even felt a bit faint. She had started squeezing Grace's hand harder and harder and harder as the man from Barnes, Barnes and Garner announced her inheritance, and the inevitable realization began to sink in.

Finally, Grace Havilland found her tongue again. She tried to loosen the grip that Srenna had taken on her hand and gently patted the girl, and then put a supportive arm around her shoulder. In less then ten minutes, Mr. Garner had told the child she had lost her grandparents she didn't even remember and then told her she was apparently an heiress. "Mr. Garner, do you mind me asking you for Srenna, as she seems to be in a bit of shock, just how much the "estate" is worth?" Grace Havilland never minced many words, and at this moment she felt it necessary to finish this information so Srenna could begin to realize what she had truly just been told.

"I have here, legal documents spelling out in detail what is left after legal fees, taxes, any probate costs, etc, etc, but all told, not including the estate home, which is also left to Miss James, the amount is roughly eight hundred and sixty thousand dollars. The properties, including the house and grounds in Melbourne are roughly worth another two hundred thousand easily. All together Miss James, YOU are worth approximately one million dollars." With this the satisfied man sat back in his chair and retrieved his cup of cold tea from the table beside him and smiling one more time at both women, resumed sipping the cup. He watched the expression on both of the ladies faces with a great measure of amusement that his news had indeed come as a complete and unexpected shock.

"Srenna, are you alright?" Grace Havilland asked her young helper softly, wondering if the girl would just simply pass out at any moment. She waited patiently for an answer; her arm still around the girl's shoulder, much tighter then it had been only minutes before.

"I...I...think so, I...don't know quite what to say. I mean...what does one say?" Srenna answered her in a shaky voice, looking around the room in utter disbelief.

Mr. Garner set his cup down again and turned to Srenna, somewhat in sympathy for the confusion the young governess must be feeling. He felt as though he must follow through with his information and begin to shed some practical light on this new found wealth.

"Miss James, I want you to know that our law firm is here to assist you in any way possible to set up your new finances, your properties, any changes that might transpire from all of this, whatever you need. Your grandmother wanted you to have every comfort you should have had after your parents died. She however, knew through an investigation that you were well taken care of here in Sydney, under the employment of Margaret Crawford and this fine family. She did not want you to be disturbed with her illness, her care, and what she knew to be her time close at hand. Whether right or wrong, doesn't matter now. What matters now is that you have a large enough sum of money that you are well taken care of for the remainder of your life. Invested wisely, used intelligently, there is no need for you to ever want for anything again. It was her way of making restitution."

Srenna finally found her voice, and burning tears as well, as she tried to sort out the emotions crashing over her at the moment. She had just received news that would have sent anyone into a frenzy of joy, but at the same time she was feeling some disturbing regret. Regret that she had not been given the opportunity to even know her grandmother before she died; regret that all these years, especially the initial ones after the Bella Ava claimed her family's lives, she had no family to call her own. Her mixed emotions were beginning to consume her,....and Grace Havilland could tell.

"Mr. Garner, would it be possible to resume this conversation a little later, perhaps tomorrow sometime?" the sensitive woman requested. She could see the tears in Srenna's eyes waiting to spill over, but she knew Srenna all too well. She hated to weep in front of strangers, and had only cried a few times since Grace had known her. At this particular moment, Srenna was holding back with all her might, and Grace knew it.

"Why, I don't mind that at all," Mr. Garner affirmed, gently, looking at Srenna with great concern. He took the cue to stand and prepare to leave, returning the legal documents into the briefcase, leaving a copy of what he had just read on the table. "Perhaps, Mr. Havilland, being a seasoned business owner, will be able to enlighten

Miss James as to the measure of this news. I can return at your leisure to secure any transferring of funds, financial arrangements, any questions. As I assured you at the first, I assure you now, Miss James, I am here to make this transition as easy for you as is possible."

With that the kindly man began walking himself to the door. Grace Havilland let go of Srenna and stood up to follow their visitor out, but turned to Srenna first and bent to look the young girl in the eyes. "Will you be alright for a moment, while I see Mr. Garner to the door?" she asked Srenna lovingly, as though the dear child was her own. Srenna could only nod, and continued to sit quite still. Even after Grace had exited the room with Mr. Garner, she sat frozen to the sofa, her hands folded in her lap and stared at the wall directly in front of her. Her mind was running in a blur of speed as she attempted to think of all she had just been told. She was still in a semi state of shock and disbelief when Grace reentered the room and quietly sat down beside the shocked girl.

"Srenna," she started softly, smoothing the dark curls back away from her face. The gentle touch of Grace's hand across her skin sent a flood of tears down Srenna's face and her head into the woman's arms. "Oh my dear, my dear child," she cooed tenderly and compassionately. "I can't even begin to wonder what you're feeling right now. Such mixed emotions. But we'll get it right. It's really quite astounding." As she spoke she rocked Srenna in her arms and tried calming the girl. "Tell me dear what you're thinking, what's going on in your head," she gently coaxed Srenna to respond.

"I don't know….I can't even think straight. I never knew either one, my grandfather or my grandmother. Mother tried numerous times to reconcile with them both," the stunned girl explained. She stopped crying and sat up, pulling herself away from Grace's arms, "I'm not sure if I should be sad or ecstatically happy."

"I know you must feel some sadness for not having had them in your life, not getting to know them. I know you must have felt so alone when you survived the accident. But Srenna, God does have higher ways then ours. Even if your grandmother couldn't or wouldn't contact you, it's obvious she wanted things to be taken care of for you in the end. The old lady must have felt terrible about not being able to see you or help you while her husband was alive."

"But why not after he died?" Srenna asked through a veil of tears.

"I don't know luv. I can't answer that for you. And you may never know. What you do know is this. As of this hour I do believe you are quite worth more then any governess I know," Grace commented with a grin on her face, trying very hard to lift the bewildered girl's spirits.

"I'll tell you what, let's see if Henry has turned the kitchen upside down, get you and I some lunch and then we can talk some more about all of this, eh?" the dear woman suggested. "Might I suggest as well that I call Frank and see if he would come home a little earlier and help you look these papers over?" she went on. She guided Srenna towards the door in the hopes that maybe just getting the girl to move would begin to shake loose the sadness about her news and help her to begin to process the enormity of the good news.

"Yes,…yes I suppose that would be wise. I don't even know what to ask Mr. Garner or what to expect from here." Srenna leaned her head against Grace's shoulder as they made their way towards the kitchen. She was thinking way too far ahead, wondering what all of this news truly meant as far as her future. It did seem to dawn on her suddenly that she had gone from a well off little girl in the midst of Sydney's elite community, to a penniless orphan, and now once again found herself surprisingly and incredibly endowed.

"I do know one thing, Grace," a much more subdued Srenna began.

"What is that, my dear?" Grace inquired holding the girls shoulders tightly as they walked.

"I've never a dull moment in my life, have I?" she jested lightly.

"No my dear, you do not," Grace Havilland smiled, glad to finally hear the Srenna James she had come to know and love as her children's tenacious governess.

Chapter 6: Miriam's Prayer

Twelve hundred miles away the unpredictable New Zealand weather was presenting itself as a very unwanted visitor. The day was already as bleak as any could be in the tiny town of Castle Point on the east coast of the north island. Ordinarily most in the area would welcome the sometimes daily rainfall that kept the sub tropical beauty of New Zealand lush and unending. Today, however, it only lent to more spirits being crushed under the weight of it's soaking; spirits and hearts that were already crushed and saddened by the funeral procession to the little cemetery located on the bluff above the sea. The service for the still somewhat young mother who had finally succumbed to an imminent death after months of illness was heartbreaking for the friends and church members who had come to show her surviving children their unfailing love and support. Reverend Davidson, the Anglican parish leader of the church by the coast, was heavier hearted then most of the onlookers as he himself had led this mother and her husband to the Lord and then led them into a quick and faithful service to the church and community

John and Miriam Patton had been two of his fondest friends from almost the moment they landed in New Zealand to start their new lives as sheep ranchers. They were young and energetic and grew in their trust from the very beginning, sometimes encouraging the Reverend more then he ever did them. They brought a boy into the world and into their church family only a few months after arriving; a boy that would grow into one of Hamilton Davidson's favorite students of the Bible, always asking questions, always challenging him, always challenging God to show him more, speak to him more.

Today that boy, now nineteen years old, was certainly challenging his God as he stood over the grave of his dear mother. In his arms was his youngest sister, Emma, known fondly to him as "Little Bug", completely unsure what was happening and clinging to her oldest brother with all her might. Next to Matthew Patton stood his oldest sister Mary, only three years younger then him, with her arms around yet another sister, Lilly. Standing beside them, cowering under his raincoat stood an angry but painfully quiet boy, their thirteen year old brother Stephan. Directly behind all of them was the closest semblance of relatives to the young brood, Jimmie and Irmani Rainga. Their son, Tommie, had not moved his hand off of his lifetime friend's shoulder since they stopped in front of the freshly dug grave. They all listened now to the words about the sweet woman who had brought each one of them into the world with great aspirations and hope.

It was the child missing from the grave site service that would never really know how much his dying mother had given up for him. Baby Benjamin had no clue how much of a struggle his mother had just bringing him into their lives and then how much she withered away in just seven months. Try as everyone might to encourage the woman to recover from the difficult birth, it was really Miriam's heart that just gave up even though she made some attempts to tell herself she must recuperate for the sake of her children. Daily she made the effort to nurse and respond to the baby's base needs, yet at the end of that day she lay drained and exhausted, too tired to carry out the demanding requirements of a house, a ranch and six children. As the days waned into months, it was obvious that Miriam's own grief for the loss of her precious John in the war would take its ultimate toll.

And that day had finally come, only two days earlier, in the wee hours of the morning. In a room at the hospital in Masterton, Matthew, Mary, Stephan and Lilly said their final goodbyes to their struggling mother with the help of the same close friends with them now. Hovered around the heartbroken children, Jimmie and Irmani had also said their goodbyes for the woman who had been as close as a sister to both of them.

Jimmie knew his strong and usually opinionated wife. She was falling apart inside, but for the moment all she could do was hold the babies she had helped to bring into the world as the area midwife. Every Patton child had seen and felt this robust island native woman even before their mother had. Having only been a little over eight miles from their home every day of their lives, Irmani had been one of the strongest influences in the lives of all of them. But now she stood with them, totally helpless and herself grief stricken at the loss of her closest neighbor and best friend. Even with Jimmie's strong arm around her broad shoulders she was struggling to maintain the composure the children desperately needed her to have at the moment.

Hamilton Davidson spoke as gently and encouraging as he could muster. He was also crying out for his faith in God right now that all of this would somehow make sense in the days and months to come. His words about Miriam's strength and courage seemed almost hollow to him as he looked at the slight coffin in front of him and then at each of the children's faces.

His eyes couldn't help but light on Matthew as he watched the boy's expressions, trying to read his thoughts. But as was usually the case in a crisis, Matthew was standing tall, his gaze out over the ocean in front of the little cemetery. The Reverend had to wonder if the oldest of the Patton children wasn't even really hearing him, but was instead already in a silent conversation with the God he had trusted all of his life. That was the way with Matthew. Although he had broken down in the hallway of the hospital, only moments earlier he had assured his mother they would all be alright, promising her he would take care of everyone. He even promised her he would keep them all together.

It was Miriam's last request. She implored Matthew, with Irmani and Jimmie looking on, that the children not be split up, not sent anywhere but their home, the home she and John had worked so hard to provide for them. She didn't know how that would happen, but true to her nature, even in the midst of leaving the bonds of Earth and her tired and stricken body, she prayed over her children one more time as they gathered around her bed.

The prayer was a simple one. Send Matthew an angel. It could barely be heard over the weeping in the room by those who had also gathered to support the children through this most difficult transition. But Matthew heard it and so did Mary. Irmani heard the soft whisper that escaped her beloved friend's lips. So did Reverend Davidson and his wife Patricia as they stood over and around the children gathered at their mother's side.

When it was over, when Miriam breathed her last struggling breath, the children held onto her for a few moments, weeping. But it was Matthew who raised up his head from his mother's silent heart, looked at the doctor who had been painfully standing off in the corner and ordered the tubes and all to be removed from his mother's body. Irmani nodded at the doctor, assuring him he'd better comply and the nurse stepped in immediately to extract the breathing tube and IV from Miriam's lifeless body. It wasn't until that task was finished and each of Matthew's siblings were safely in the arms of the Reverend, his wife or Irmani, that the brokenhearted boy walked from the room, with Jimmie and Tommie close behind him and crumbled to the hallway floor. He wept harder even then he had the day his father had been laid to rest. He was tired and his feelings were so raw at that moment, he didn't even care that his best friend and his father held him in their arms and let him sob like a baby.

Now, two days later, everything seemed a blur; a numb blur. Everyone had been in a mode of just getting through the next few days. Irmani or Jimmie had been at the house everyday, along with others in the church, bringing food, cleaning, helping each one of the children to prepare for the funeral and any measure of closure accomplished in it. There was a small measure of relief after so many months of their mother's illness that it was over, but none of them had really had time to think about the days to come and the repercussions of her death. Right now friends and neighbors were abundantly present.

Jimmie and Tommie tried to take over the responsibilities of herding the sheep to the fields, but the moment Matthew knew the children were looked after by one or another caregiver, he insisted on being out in the fields with his sheep. Tommie, who had known him since they were old enough to crawl, followed close behind his best friend, keeping some distance if Matthew needed it and making sure he was available at a moments notice should Matthew cave in again. But Tommie, as well as Jimmie, both knew that Matthew had become a man long before any boy should have had to. He would keep his moments of weakness very private, sequestered somewhere up in the hills, where only his flock and God could hear him. He had been for years; especially after the death of his father.

No one was remotely prepared for that news. It seemed as though it should have never happened, but as it were, only months away from the end of a bitter war in the Pacific, John Patton became one of thousands of New Zealand men to give their lives for their homes and their fellow countrymen. So much hope was dashed that day when the officer from Auckland came to deliver the sad news to Miriam and the children. Only six months earlier, John had managed to obtain a long weekend pass for R and R, and by no small miracle he hopped a freighter plane coming to Auckland and then the train to Masterton. Everyone was so surprised to see him after being away nearly three years, they all hardly knew where to start catching up. He tried desperately to spend time with each of his precious children and then later that night, pulled Miriam aside and fled to their little cabin on the hill where they had first lived.

The next day, John painstakingly took his oldest son into the fields alone, the same young son he had left every responsibility to. He knew he must make sure Matthew was alright and that he could hold out a little bit longer. He assured Matthew that all the talk of the war coming to an end was true and that it was only a matter of time and he would be home.

But today Matthew saw what being home really meant for both his father and his mother. He kept telling himself as he glanced at the grassy grave where his father lay and the freshly dug grave where his mother would lie next to him that somehow they would all get through this nightmare. But his mind couldn't help but wander away to the weeks and months ahead of him, ahead for his orphaned family.

He didn't have to look at his sister, Mary, to know she was trying as hard as he to stay composed and strong for the younger children. She was like that. She too had become extremely grown up and responsible over the last four years. She had only been twelve when John Patton left. She was only just becoming a young lady when Matthew had taken over much of the ranch's business. Their mother had helped Matthew as much as she could, so Mary had many more chores then usual. She learned early how to cook and take care of the house. Her younger siblings were her responsibility most days before and after school. It was fortunate for her that she had been a strong student and was able to maintain her scores in spite of her increased burdens.

At the moment Matthew was grateful she stood beside him and could be expected to do whatever it would take to keep this parentless family together. He knew he could count on her to keep at the house and the chores until he could work out something else. He didn't know what, just something.

For a moment his eyes wandered the crowd a bit. Sympathetic and supportive onlookers were listening to Reverend Davidson as he continued to speak more words of encouragement to his audience. He knew many of them would help for a while, for as long as they could, but reality was most of those here today also ran sheep stations, many larger even then theirs. In time, most would have the burden of the tremendous work it took to maintain their livelihoods each day. This was a rural community. Hard work was a way of life everyday and some days even harder. Matthew thought ahead briefly to the month they would sheer the sheep, not very far off. And the cutting of the spring's choice lambs for market would only be three months off. So much, so many things flooded his mind right now he felt himself becoming overwhelmed.

But as though someone snapped their finger in his face, Matthew suddenly heard the end of Reverend Davidson's eulogy and he found himself very alert to the task at hand. Hamilton prayed one last prayer, and then motioned to Matthew to lay the first handful of dirt onto the coffin containing his mother's body. As he walked up to the grave, he placed little Emma on the ground in front of him and stooped down beside the tiny girl. With one arm around his baby sister, he showed her with loving tenderness how to scoop up a handful of dirt and sprinkle it atop the beautifully carved box. The child followed her favorite brother's motions and from all over the crowd, woman could be heard crying softly as they watched Miriam's little girl and then another and still another, give their final tribute to their mother.

Only Stephan held back, frozen and still sullen and Irmani shook her head at Matthew when she thought he might force the thirteen year old to follow suit. Matthew knew not to argue with the woman and let his brother go. When it was finished nearly everyone there came up to the children, hugging them, promising and assuring them they would help in any way they could. He knew they meant it too.

Almost an hour had gone by and most had filtered away from the cemetery. Patricia Davidson and Irmani Rainga, women worlds apart and yet both equally concerned about the immediate welfare of the Patton children, jointly decided that Matthew and his family had had enough. They both began routing the children to awaiting cars with the help of their husbands and in no time at all everyone was headed for the Patton home. It had been decided early on that no dinner and no reception would be held at the church or anywhere else for that matter. Irmani knew they needed to go home and rest.

But Hamilton and Patricia followed, along with the Rainga's and their offspring. A quiet meal had been prepared earlier that day for the group to partake together. When they arrived, both women moved around the kitchen as though they had been in it many times over the years. And they had. Both had loved Miriam as a dear sister and friend. Somehow even though Irmani and Patricia were as different as night and day, they worked together, caring for the children in any manner needed. Little Emma succumbed to a much needed nap almost the moment she hit the door and even nine year old Lilly was exhausted from the day's events. Stephan disappeared nearly as soon as he had filled his belly and no one seemed terribly concerned with the young boy going bush to whatever hiding place he chose. Matthew, as well as Mary tried desperately to be some kind of host and hostess to all their faithful lifetime friends and neighbors but even they were beginning to feel the incredible weight of a grueling day; and a grueling week for that matter.

The Rainga's oldest daughter, Nula, had stayed behind at the house to take care of her baby brother, Irmani's last child of only eleven months and the Patton infant. Benji Patton was frightfully fussy and uncertain as he had been most of the week as to why his mother was simply not beckoning to his cries of hunger. The tiny seven month old had not weaned and Irmani, herself strapped with her own nursing baby was attempting to wet nurse the little boy until he could be weaned.

But Benji was not doing so well. His base memory of his mother's warm bosom and tender, though weakening arms was still fresh in his baby mind. He fussed for Irmani, nursing only just enough to barely sustain his appetite and then was fussy again a short time later. Even for the seasoned mother with eight children of her own, the task at hand was beginning to take its toll on her. But she wouldn't give up. Not for Miriam's sake. In the last few weeks had it not been for Irmani's undying devotion to her dearest friend, the dear child might have starved to death as well. Irmani disappeared into the master bedroom to the infant's adjoining nursery to once again try to nourish the little boy.

When the kitchen had been cleaned adequately by Patricia Davidson's standards, she and the Reverend began saying their goodbyes. Before they finished they had instructed Matthew as to what they would be doing to help them out in the weeks to come, assuring the boy that much help could be expected as they made the transitions needed. It was highly suggested by both that the children not be expected to return to school for the remainder of the session. Only a few weeks were left before their summer break. The Reverend's wife offered to speak to the school director and the children's teachers to get their work for them to do at home.

Many other things were said as well as first Hamilton and Patricia departed, and then Jimmie and Irmani began to roust their brood towards the door. Irmani wanted to stay. Usually she got her way, but tonight Jimmie took charge, knowing full well they were all exhausted. He insisted Irmani come home and maybe bring Benji along so he could be nursed during the night if need be. In the end that plan was greatly welcomed, even by Irmani's demanding standards. Neither Matthew or Mary had any fight in them to do otherwise and the minute the Rainga family drove away in their multiple vehicles, they were glad for the quiet calm that seemed to settle over the otherwise grieving house.

Matthew felt like his head would explode if he had to think of anything concerning the next day or the ones after that. He offered to make sure Stephan was in and settled upstairs and knew that Mary would do the same where the girls were concerned. Someone would be by tomorrow to check up on them and help where help was needed. He thought for sure they had at least come to the close of the longest day of their lives as Mary headed for the stairs leading to the children's bedrooms. He had heard Stephan come in a short time ago through the back kitchen door and turned to join his younger brother there when he heard the sound of an automobile outside in front of the house.

Matthew wondered immediately if Irmani had reversed the decision to stay as she so commonly was able to do when she wanted her way or truly thought someone was in need of her. He thought nothing of opening the front door, actually prepared to banter with the robust island woman as he had done so often in his young life and even began to address the woman in a joking manner.

"Managed to get your way after all, eh?" he quipped and then caught himself before going on. He found himself instead face to face with another rather stout middle aged woman. The woman was startled by Matthew's abrupt opening of the door and even gasped a bit when the young man snapped the door open as quickly as he had. Before Matthew even had a chance to apologize to the stranger on his front porch she began her introductions with a question

"Excuse me, young man, but this is the Patton farm, is it not?" she asked in a clipped British tongue.

Matthew stared hard at the woman who had neither a New Zealand dialect about her or even that of the British one of those living on the island. For a moment he only stared, wondering why this complete stranger was there, on of all days, this one, and then why the automobile she had come in was driving away. It was only then that he realized that the obviously proper English woman was holding two bags in her hands. It seemed like many minutes went by before he found his tongue and his manners to answer her as she began to get frustrated with him.

"I'm terribly sorry, Mum, I'm not usually so slow in my manners. Please, tell me how I can help you," Matthew began, trying to gain some semblance of politeness in spite of how tired he was.

"Well young man, you can help me by taking my bags and showing me to my room!" she addressed him curtly.

"I beg your pardon, Mum," Matthew responded , now with a tinge of agitation in his voice and a ton of confusion on his face. "Maybe you have the wrong "farm". We weren't expecting anyone to visit right now. We've only buried our mother this day and we are all very tired. But I'll be very glad to take you back to town or wherever it is you need to be."

"I need to be right here, son. I'm Mrs. Wrightman, your new governess!"

Chapter 7: More News For Srenna

As it turned out, Srenna's grand news was not the only profound announcement waiting in the wings. Frank Havilland did indeed come home early that day and after examining the will left behind by Mr. Garner he sat Srenna down and meticulously went over the details with his children's young governess. It was determined that an appointment would be made with the lawyer from Melbourne in the next few days to find out what procedures needed to take place to transfer funds into an account for Srenna and then any other legal work that needed to follow.

Srenna's mind was still swimming from the things her employer had explained to her. Grace had the presence of mind to suggest the girl call Reverend Carmel and let he and his wife know what had happened. They were astounded and ecstatically happy for her. Neither were surprised that Martha Hughes had come forward in any way after the death of her husband. Daniel Carmel had always been suspicious that given the chance she would have reconciled with Srenna's mother long ago but the longer time went by the more likely it was it would not happen. The determined parish leader had tried several times to contact Srenna's grandparents, but there was never any reply. After awhile, he simply gave up because it discouraged him so much where Srenna was concerned.

But today the news seemed to bare mixed emotions for Srenna. Even after the reality began to sink in she felt a strange sense of her whole world being catapulted into a new realm again, both good and for some reason,… bad. She couldn't explain to anyone how she felt. The money was more then she even remembered her parents having had though she seemed to know her mother's family had been very well off and high on the social ladder. They had so completely rejected her father that Paul Hughes had threatened his daughter to never be with Harrison James or he would cut her off. Srenna remembered hearing her mother cry and her father encouraging her many times when any attempt to mend ways with her parents failed. "Some day," Harrison kept telling his beloved wife.

Though it was too late for either of them, today that reconciliation on her grandmother's part was about to change the course of Srenna's life again. It was the uncertainty of how that seemed to shake the girl at the moment.

Grace continually reassured her dear helper that she and Frank would help in any way possible as the brevity of her new found wealth unfolded. She finally convinced the tired young girl to take the remainder of the day off, rest, go to the Reverend's or what ever she needed to do to process her news. In the end Srenna simply retired upstairs and lie for a very long time on her bed trying to sort out her feelings. It wasn't until she finally began praying that any measure of peace started to take over.

Money had never been important to Srenna even when her father had made it in his field as a veterinarian and was in high demand by Sydney's high society race horse owners. It wasn't important to Harrison James either but he strived to make his beautiful wife as comfortable as she had been accustomed to growing up. Over the last few years Srenna had made more then enough at the Havilland's home to sustain herself and her employers had amply taken care of her immediate needs in their home with great benevolence. Their lifestyle was elite by every measure of Sydney's social circles and Srenna had evolved from the poor little orphaned girl into the mainstream of high society once again.

This time though, she came in under the guise of a wealthy family's governess, a position well sought after by many young women in Australia. She found herself there largely due to Margaret Crawford's influence in that circle. Now she wondered how this might effect her position with the Havilland's for the exact opposite reasons. She was now herself quite wealthy.

"Too much to think about," Srenna whispered to herself, as she stared at the ceiling and tried to continue praying. But her emotions had drained her, her thoughts were exhausting her and in the end her tired mind and body got the best of her as she drifted into a strangely deep sleep; so deep in fact she never heard Grace Havilland knock and then enter the room quietly when Srenna did not answer.

Grace was concerned about Srenna. She had grown quite fond of the girl over the last five years. She had struck a bond with her almost immediately and she knew quickly that Srenna would be exactly what her boys would need while their father was gone and Grace was left with the sole responsibility of raising them. She truly felt that God had sent her precisely what she needed. And in a short time became fully aware that they were what Srenna needed as well.

As she crept to the bed quietly so as not to disturb the sleeping girl, Grace couldn't help but wonder how all this information today would alter Srenna's life; especially in lieu of her husband's own breaking news. She knew tomorrow there would need to be more discussion of events unfolding. But for now she was just grateful that the silent girl on the bed seemed to be in a peaceful slumber so much so she never even flinched when Grace covered her with the comforter at the end of her bed. As Grace silently tiptoed from the room and gently closed the door she was equally grateful that all the news today had really been good news albeit, life altering.

But that was after all, life.

The next day found everyone in the Havilland home fluttering about Srenna's news. The two oldest boys had heard enough that Frank and Grace felt they should explain what was going on. They were all of a sudden much more congenial with Srenna then they had been the previous day. It was exciting to them to think that she had a lot of money, though it had never even been an issue with them concerning the state of affairs with there governess. They really did adore her and found her quite a challenge most of the time in a pleasant and playful way. It never dawned on them that she was not in the same financial class as they were. It just hadn't mattered.

Srenna still felt the next day as though she simply did not know where to even start where her knew found wealth was concerned. She also wondered why Frank Havilland lingered at the house this morning… but she was soon to find out his reason. Shortly after breakfast and when the boys had been sent to play in the garden with the housekeeper she finally decided that maybe she should indeed talk to Reverend Carmel and get some input from him as well.

But before the Havilland's gladly gave her the keys to one of the automobiles so she could drive to the parsonage they asked Srenna to sit down with them in the parlor. Once again that strange feeling of apprehension came over her as Frank and Grace sat down across from her on the same sofa she had been sitting on when receiving her news the day before. She could tell by the look on Grace's face that they too had some kind of life changing announcement to make.

Frank Havilland smiled first at his wife in a reassuring way and then smiled graciously at Srenna. "We've all been very surprised by all your good fortune my dear girl. It has been quite a lot to process the last twenty four hours, I must say," he started slowly. Srenna listened intently to him but couldn't help but notice how fidgety Grace was as he spoke. The boys' mother was indeed preoccupied even though she was attempting to follow what her husband was saying. "We have a bit of our own news to share with you Srenna; news that we've been contemplating for awhile now but wanted to be certain of before we brought you into it," Frank began hesitantly.

Srenna was aware now as well that even Frank seemed a little nervous where the news was concerned but before she had a chance to question anything he plowed on.

"Srenna, for some time now I have been pursuing a business venture with one of the officers I served with in Hawaii. He too has an import/export business but is located out of San Francisco in the United States. We talked quite a bit while together about possibly merging our businesses when the war was over. The market in the States is booming, especially west coast, and well to put it as gently as I know how, I've decided....we've decided," he started, looking hopefully at his lovely young wife for moral support, "to do exactly that."

As he finished the sentence, Srenna gazed at Grace to see what her reaction to the announcement might be. She could read her face fairly well and knew that Grace Havilland was also having mixed emotions about her news much the same as Srenna had had with hers. The woman was holding her dear beloved husband's hand or more likely gripping it, and at the same time trying desperately to give the man the backing he needed from her at the moment.

"It sounds wonderful for you both," Srenna responded politely, still sensing there was more to this venture then Frank had completely divulged.

"Well, it truly means a bigger market to be sure, better opportunities and my future partner is hoping as well to gain some benefit from my ties with the Pacific buyers I've worked with over the years," he continued to explain. "It does however mean that there will be some changes in the near future, changes for all of us." With that statement he looked once again at his unusually quiet wife to be sure he still had her moral support. Grace was indeed watching her husband, although with some uncertainty, with a great amount of pride and trust in him as he unfolded their family's future.

Grace finally found her tongue as Frank hesitated for a moment to size up Srenna's reaction to more life altering news. "Srenna, what Frank is trying to get at is we are probably going to be relocating to the San Francisco area," Grace spoke gently. As soon as the words were out of her mouth, she saw the astounded look upon Srenna's face, first staring at one and then the other.

"How soon!?" was all Srenna could answer.

"Inside of a few months, Srenna, as soon as I can establish a sound staff to take care of things here while I'm State side. I want Grace and the children to go with me for now, until both ends are up and running smoothly," Frank plowed on. Before either Srenna could ask or Grace could answer the question in the young girl's eyes, he added, "Of course we would want you to come. We could truly use you while the boys are going through this transition and well,"

Before he could go on, though, Grace Havilland seemed to find the directness she always seemed to have when most needed and she lovingly cut her husband off. "Of course, Srenna, we also know you have a lot to think about yourself," she started, gazing at her husband with a definite   "wait a moment please before you say another word" look upon her face.

Frank Havilland waited.

No one said anything for a moment or two. All seemed to be literally reeling with all the information that had been processed over the last twenty four hours; all good news in many ways; all life altering news in every way. Grace was trying to be her husband's greatest support at the moment, but knew full well what she was up against in the months and possibly years to come as her husband made this business transition. Frank was only hoping this indeed would be the best thing he could ever do for the future of his young family.

And Srenna's mind immediately contemplated the thought of "how" they would make the transition, not so much when. A very familiar knot began to fill her stomach; one she had encountered numerous times over the last nine years; one that never allowed her the freedom of enjoying the one thing most of Sydney's elite families found a routine holiday as well as travel.

A journey on a ship.

Her mind was screaming at her at this very moment, telling her absolutely not. Her body was tightening even as Frank explained more details. Her heart rate was faster and she new she was breathing harder. Grace knew it too.

"Alright Frank. I think we've just about exploded Srenna with news today as well as yesterday, eh?" the kindly woman suggested, standing from the sofa and joining Srenna at the chair she sat in. "We all have a lot to process and some time yet to do it. For goodness sake, this child never has to work again in her life if she so chooses, remember?" Grace added, kneeling at Srenna's side and patting the girls hand encouragingly while she caught her husband's gaze.

Frank Havilland took the cue his bright and sensitive wife was accustomed to giving him at times. "Yes, Grace, you are right. I'm so sorry Srenna. I didn't mean to overwhelm you with this announcement.'

"No…no it's quite all right really," Srenna offered, realizing they had seen her struggle with the news and probably felt badly. "Really, I'm just…you know…there's just so much to think about."

"Of course there is, dear, for all of us. But we'll talk about it later after you've had some time to speak to Reverend Carmel and his wife about everything. I know they will be able to help you sort things out," Grace assured her. "Let's let this child get on with her morning and go on over to the parsonage, eh?" she finished as she stood and held her hand out to Srenna and then the other hand to Frank. That was the way Grace was. She always seemed to know when enough was enough.

And this was certainly enough for the moment.

Within only a few moments Srenna was on her way to the parsonage across town in one of the cars. Even as she drove the streets and turned the corners she knew all too well, she couldn't help but wonder what corners she would be turning this time in her young life. Her mind raced ahead at the mere thought of having to take a ship to embark upon the shores of America. She loved the children and was as equally fond of Grace and Frank. They had become family to her just as Daniel and Ruth Carmel had been.

But her intrepid fear of the sea and her deep seeded memory of the tragedy her own family had lost their lives to was not about to allow the girl the freedom to travel on the ocean. She would not and had not even visited the shoreline any closer then was necessary in the seaport city of Sydney. Now more then ever she was certain her answer to the Havilland's would simply be no.

Once arriving at the Anglican Church she had grown up in, Srenna made her way up the parsonage steps and knocked on the front door. Within only seconds Ruth Carmel was at the door and gushing happily at Srenna, hugging the girl as though she hadn't seen her in weeks when in fact it had only been days.

"Srenna girl, I do believe no one has more excitement in their lives then you, eh?" the Reverend's stout little wife chuckled. She reached for the girl and hugged her with one of her enormous and robust hugs she had been freely giving to Srenna for most of her life. As she hugged, she led. She walked Srenna through the front parlor and into the hallway leading to her husband's study chattering al the way about how incredible the news was about Srenna's inheritance and the estate being left for her.

Ruth Carmel would never even think of gossiping this news to another soul, but Srenna knew the elderly lady would indeed talk her leg off finding out all the details. As fortune had it though the walk back to the study door was only a few minutes at best and Daniel Carmel was waiting for Srenna with great anticipation. They had only walked up to the door and it swung open wide. Reverend Carmel grabbed her in another big fatherly bear hug.

"My dear child come in, come in. I want to hear all your news, every bit of it," he chattered excitedly to her. Srenna couldn't remember when the kindly parish leader had been so intrigued with anything other then his sermons, or how he was going to solve a dilemma in one of his church member's lives. She couldn't help but smile at him and Ruth as they escorted their favorite visitor to one of the overstuffed chairs in front of the desk as though she were some kind of royalty.

"It's really astounding, actually, quite unbelievable really," she began, looking at both of them with her eyes wide with amazement. "I don't even know where to start, and as it were I have even more news to give you."

As she unfolded the account of Mr. Garner's visit, both her dear friends listened, spellbound with every word proceeding from her lips. Daniel Carmel was not the slightest bit surprised though that Martha Hughes had come through in the end whether Srenna thought too late or not. From the tone of her voice he could tell there was some regret in her heart that she had not had the least bit of opportunity to meet her grandmother. He knew this dear girl sitting in front of him would question the deeper things concerning these matters. The money at the moment was not even an issue.

Both Daniel and Ruth let Srenna spend herself explaining everything, including the news of the Havilland's eminent move to the States. Just as many other times, they knew Srenna welcomed their input and advice with open arms and when she finished every last thing she could think of she hesitated to let either of them respond. For one of the first times Srenna could remember Ruth Carmel was speechless. She stared incredulously at the girl and then looked to her husband hoping he would have something profound to say.

Daniel Carmel simply stood from the front of his desk where he had been leaning while Srenna recounted her last two days of events and walked to his favorite window in his study. It overlooked the garden between the parsonage and the church. It was peaceful there for the most part. But today it reminded him of another garden; a garden where his Savior had to make a tremendous decision to stay or to go. To stay was for him. To go was for all. He turned his warm brown eyes towards his wife of nearly forty years and then looked at the endearing inquisitive child he had known all her life waiting for him to deliver some formable speech that would give her direction and clarity right now.

"Srenna, I must say, you have a knack for keeping us all on our spiritual toes, or more likely on our knees, to be sure," he smiled lovingly at her. "I wish dear girl I knew what to say to you. I'm overwhelmingly happy for you that this good fortune from your grandmother has landed in your lap and equally disconcerted about the thought of you leaving Sydney and going to America. I know your fears about going. You've shoved this away for a very long time, eh?" he added gently.

Srenna diverted her eyes away from her parish leader. For what seemed to be a lifetime Daniel Carmel had cautiously and tenderly encouraged Srenna to come to terms with the day of the tragedy that had ripped her family away from her in a single hour. But the grieving youngster had first simply been too saddened by the event and then had begun to survive. She simply would not address it after that. But now here it was; right back in front of her. To go meant she faced her fear. To stay meant she lost a dear family she had actually belonged to and loved dearly for the last five years.

"My dear beloved child, in all the years I have prepared God's messages for his flocks I have stumbled few times to not have anything to say. But I must tell you today," he began hesitantly and even a bit painfully, "I know not what to tell you, except this. You will have to wait on Him to show you, to tell you, to give you direction. This is one of those times when all you've learned from those around you, everything you've staked your beliefs on are going to have to lead you now." The gentle man stared hard at her but with as deep a love for any of his flock as he had ever had. "I wish I had more for you," he finished with an encouraging smile and a hope that she wouldn't begin crying.

But Srenna James was not discouraged. His words cut deep but were more truthful then any other person had ever been with her. Even her own father had often times softened the truth to protect Srenna and her mother never really wanted to hear all the truth. But today Srenna knew she had some tough decisions to make and they would be altering her life, maybe for the rest of her life.

"Do you want me to stay?" she hesitantly asked Ruth. Srenna knew full well the motherly woman was more likely to molly coddle her as any mother would do her own children sometimes, but even Ruth Carmel, looking first at her husband for moral support and then at Srenna seemed to understand the brevity of the decisions to be made.

"Srenna, luv, of course we both want you to stay," she began, but then caught her husband's expression and quickly added, "but darling, we both agree that you are at a crossroad and you have to make a hard decision as to what is right...for you." Ruth looked back at her husband to see if her statement met his approval and Daniel was indeed nodding his head in agreement.

Srenna lowered her eyes into her lap for a moment and the Reverend quickly prayed for something, anything to encourage the struggling girl and all the news she was trying to process.

"All we are saying Srenna dear, is listen, pray and listen. You know we'll be praying for you and with you," he suggested off the top of his head. But then just as he had quickly stated those words, a thought came to Daniel Carmel's mind.

"Srenna, do you remember what you told me you heard, when they pulled you out of the water, when the young Chaplin was praying over you? You told me he was praying the 23rd Psalm." The Reverend was about to begin the popular chapter when Srenna interrupted him almost out of habit.

"The Lord is my Shepherd, I shall not want. He..." she began haltingly, tears beginning to brim her eyes.

But Daniel picked it up with her as she stumbled a bit, "He maketh me to lie down in green pastures." As they both recited it, Ruth joined in and added, "He leads me beside still waters."

When they had finished the whole chapter, they were all sniffling a little but certainly all felt much comfort in hearing the promises written by a little shepherd boy who trusted his God everyday of his young life, especially as life changed dramatically around him.

"Srenna,... listen for His voice, your Shepherd's voice and I believe you will know when you've made the right decision, eh?" Reverend Carmel grinned.

Srenna smiled, finally with a bit more hope and encouragement then when she had come. Oddly enough she had no new direction really, only the reminder of what she already knew, promises that had been greatly overshadowed the last couple of days with the chain of enormous events.

When the Carmel's said their goodbyes to her at the door, Srenna hugged them both. She had been so reliant on them as she continued to cope with the loss of her family, the mere thought of leaving them to go anywhere was painfully hard. But it seemed a certainty that she was once again at a crossroad of some sort and decisions were at hand any way she looked at things.

"But what road, Lord?" she prayed quietly as she pulled the car into the traffic and headed back to the Havilland's home. The weight of her thoughts were solidly heavy. Memories she wasn't quite sure she wanted to deal with were threatening to overwhelm her. But Srenna had gotten very good at shoving away that which she did not or could not deal with at the moment. And right now she couldn't think and drive and contemplate taking care of the boys later this afternoon while Grace went out. What was immediate would gain her full attention as usual.

"He said to listen for your voice. I'm trying to do that but there's so much noise from all this news I can't really hear anything," she continued whispering up her prayer. "Could you help me to hear what I'm suppose to hear, even if it means drowning out everything else," she finished.

"Oh, …and Father,.. I suppose I should thank you for all this money you've given me, though for the life of me I have no idea what to do with all of it." Srenna laughed at that notion, knowing full well there were many people in the world that would gladly take that problem off her hands.

One thing was for sure. Whatever road she chose, it appeared it would at least be lined somewhat with gold.

Or at least that's what she thought.

Chapter 8: The Lie

"I have to bloody well come up with something here soon or I'm going to go off my rocker!" lamented Matthew, as he rubbed his tired eyes and looked just about as miserable as any nineteen year old person could. "Mary has had enough too. Stephan is being a jack ass as much as he can, the girls are into everything and Benji…well he won't stop crying, he won't eat right. Even Irmani is at her wits end. I can't do this anymore!"

Hamilton Davidson sat quietly and calmly in the chair across from the boy he'd always known as strong and resilient. But he knew by the tone of Matthew's voice he had indeed reached the breaking point after four weeks of coping with his young family and the loss of their mother.
Even with all the help given by the church family and friends, and daily help from Irmani and Jimmie Rainga, his resilience was nearly used up by the fifteen hundred acre sheep station, twelve hundred head of sheep and five children to look after.

"Matthew," he started slowly, "I think we may have to be a bit creative in finding another governess this time."

"Creative?" Matthew snapped. He was weary beyond belief, discouraged beyond encouragement, and at this moment in his life even teetering on the edge of having his faith seemly crushed. The third of three governesses had up and left the little orphaned family to itself after only two weeks in the home. The first sent by Miriam Patton's mother left after only four days. The second made it one day. They were now alone, again. "What could we possibly do differently to get someone here and keep them here?"

"Well... we may have to entice someone here and then just never let them leave, you know, hold them against their will," grinned the Reverend. The look on Matthew's face indicated that he wasn't going to be humored out of his dismal outlook on the matter.

"That's not even funny," Matthew mumbled as he rubbed his head and his eyes once again.

"Matthew, we will find someone, but maybe the problem isn't your family. Why goodness, you're a normal bunch really, just....energetic is all," he offered still grinning and trying desperately to gain any ground in lifting the boy's spirit. The last four weeks had indeed been the roughest that Hamilton Davidson had ever remembered anyone in his parish going through, even during the war. He knew all too well that Matthew had done everything possible to keep his family going, keep the ranch functioning, and try to keep his sanity. But he was, after all, only nineteen. The children had not gone back to school, the sheep shearing was only weeks away and lamb cutting was looming close behind. It was an enormous task for any set of parents, let alone a young man not even out of his teens.

Hamilton and his wife Patricia had hoped that Miriam's mother, Madelaine Brewster who lived in England would have showed up after a wire was sent that her daughter was nearing her death. But instead a governess arrived the day of the funeral along with a letter of regrets. The regrets were brisk to be sure. The children's maternal grandmother had not seen any of them in nearly seven years. She was a prominent owner of a British boarding school in London and as headmistress herself she rarely left England to attend to anything, including the death of her own daughter.

That was alright with Matthew. He had never liked her, ever since she had come to New Zealand in an attempt by his parents to reconcile with her. But instead she tried to convince his parents to send Mary to her school. They of course had flatly refused and Grandmother Brewster left in a huff. She never showed up when John died and due to what she called "uncontrollable circumstances" also neglected to attend her own daughter's funeral. But she did send the governess. Matthew disliked that woman almost as much as his grandmother and as it were with his grandmother, the governess seemed to completely despise Matthew as well. He found maintaining any control over his own home a constant battle. The woman usurped any authority Matthew should have had as his brothers and sister's caretaker.

The woman had little or no patience with either Lilly or Emma, and Benji sent her into a frustrated whirlwind every time he fussed, which was most of the time. Her frustration seemed to perpetuate his frustration which led to more frustration and then confusion. Chaos followed close behind. Most nights when Matthew finally came in from the grazing fields with Stephan he was met by total pandemonium in the house. He could hear Benji's woeful cries and knew the day had not gone well. He just wasn't sure what to do. He was use to laying down the rules with the girls, attempted to keep Stephan in line, but where the baby was concerned he found himself despairing for his infant brother. Irmani Rainga had helped as much as anyone could but she too was at odds with the strict British governess. Having had her eighth child only a short time ago Irmani threw up her hands and told her husband she would "see that woman to the train station on the end of my barefoot."

But that woman left quickly in the afternoon, shortly after Irmani's last visit and when there had been an altercation between her and Mary. Matthew could never stand for anyone yelling at any of the children but least of all Mary. She had been trying to fill her mother's shoes with as much grace and poise as was possible for a sixteen year old girl. She missed school and all her friends, but Mary would not complain. She dutifully helped take care of whatever task was at hand with the girls, the house and little Benji. But nothing she did seemed to be good enough for the woman. Matthew and Mary agreed on one thing. They were both glad she left.

The second lady, even older then the first, simply could not handle rural life. She was nervous around the children, the house, the sheep and especially Irmani. The native island woman who had known all these children their entire lives sent her packing after only one day; not directly, but one look at the robust Maori woman living up the road from the children made the poor woman change her mind and leave the next day. The third as afore mentioned, lasted two weeks. She left after Lilly tattled on the woman and told Mary she had been drinking something "odd smelling" on the back porch, "and not tea!" had been Lilly's recount.

"Whatever do you think we could possibly do or say to anyone that would make them stay, let alone come," Matthew moaned disconcertedly as he slumped farther into the chair.

"Well… to begin with, maybe an older woman is not going to work for your family. Did you ever consider that," suggested the Reverend.

"And I suppose some younger woman is going to want to give up what ever life she has left in her to come to this back hills community, and tend children, while I tend sheep," he jested cynically.

"Well…you really don't need a much older woman feeling strangely about taking orders from a young man such as yourself. I think it makes them feel odd for some reason. But a younger woman, with more energy, more adventuresome, more…." He stopped when he could see that Matthew was not convinced that this would ever happen.

"Matthew, maybe the problem is overwhelming for most. No father and no mother, that is a lot for any governess to consider. But to be honest with you, if she were the right kind of governess, one that truly loved children, truly felt a calling on her life, she'd stick it out. She'd know that it would take some time for the children to adjust after all they've suffered, eh?" the concerned parish leader asked with tender compassion. He was through jesting with Matthew and knew things were at a crucial point where these children were concerned.

"Anyone learning we have neither one is simply not going to come, and that is as they say, that," Matthew stated despairingly. He gazed off over the room and found a spot on the wall to stare at.

"What if we could find someone but didn't tell her right away that both of your parents are indeed gone," Hamilton Davidson suggested slowly.

"What!? Lie to her?" Matthew exclaimed in unbelief. Never in all of his nineteen years under this man's tutelage had he ever heard him remotely suggest anything of the nature he heard now. Matthew had sat up in his chair and stared at the man across from him, his eyes wide in amazement.

"Well, I'm thinking of it this way," began the Reverend. "What if you write a letter on behalf of your father? You could write it as though he were requesting the help the children need. You know what he would say Matthew if he could ask for help for all of you," Hamilton suggested cautiously. "You would simply just not mention that John is deceased as well."

"Oh…I see. It would be alright because I really wouldn't be lying, I'd just simply be forgetting to tell her only the most important part of the truth!" Matthew snapped. He was getting angry now and really could not believe they were even having this conversation.

"Matthew…look. Desperate times sometimes call for desperate measures," the Reverend stated firmly. "You are nearly out of choices. We can't keep the social services away forever and sooner or later your grandmother is going to find out her little gift of a governess is no longer here.

Now, all I'm proposing is that in order to find someone that fits a younger description we may need to first entice her here. Then after she's met the children and you, if she really cares about children, she's likely to be sympathetic to your needs. Are you at least understanding this part of it?"

Matthew had at least not come back with a snide response and was looking down at the floor. He was out of snide, out of patience and definitely out of ideas. "And where do you propose we find such a saintly person, Reverend Davidson?" he asked tiredly, his voice quivering just a bit.

"Well… as Providence would have it, I just happened to wire a close friend of mine in Sydney, Reverend Carmel, parish leader of St. Andrew's Anglican Church. I felt compelled to ask him if he might know of anyone in Australia who is a governess or an agency for governesses. As it were he just happened to know of one who has just determined not to follow the family she has served for the last five years to the States next month when they relocate. She has been a member of his congregation since she was very little. When I shared a bit of the circumstances here he wired back and told me he thought she might fit the criteria."

Hamilton Davidson paused to see if Matthew was showing any interest in anything he was saying. The boy was at least looking at him now and no longer staring a hole in the floor. But his expression still indicated he was very unsure of this plan.

"Look mate,…from what I'm gathering from Daniel Carmel, this young woman is vivacious and a real fighter. She too is an orphan. I don't know how, he didn't go into that detail, but think about it Matthew. She would certainly understand all you and your family have been through," he argued enthusiastically. At this information he was pleased to see finally a touch of interest on Matthew's face. He plowed on hurriedly to make his point stronger.

"She has experience. She's been taking care of three boys for a very wealthy family in Sydney."

Matthew's expression took on a discouraged tinge again at that detail. "And you think she's going to give up the city life of an elite family and come to sheep country?" he asked despairingly.

"Yes," was all Hamilton Davidson would say.

"And once again, enlighten me on how I am to entice this vivacious young city bred elite governess to our rural little island," he quipped sarcastically.

"Matthew…you've been writing up there on your mountain for as long as I've known you to be able to hold a pencil. You have a way with words. A God given way, I might add. Can you still remember how your father might feel if he were here right now instead of you, seeking desperately the help you children need?" the patient man suggested. That question threatened to bring tears to the boy's eyes and Hamilton quickly changed his tone to the gentle shepherd he truly was.
"Son…I have a feeling about this. I think it's time to try something like this with the full intent of coming clean after she gets here and has seen the children, seen what you need."

"How young is she?" Matthew thought to ask suddenly.

"Twenty one from what Reverend Carmel tells me."

Matthew lowered his head into his hands for a moment and then looked back up at the Reverend. "How do we ask her to come without giving everything away."

"Write a letter as if you were your dad. Write it from John's heart if you could speak for him. Tell her what the children need, who they are," Hamilton instructed. "Assure her that you'll make arrangements to get her here and even send her back if she so desires after meeting your family."

"And what about me?" Matthew asked quietly, "What if anything do I say about me?"

"I would say nothing about you, only the children. You're not a child Matthew. You need her to take of the children, eh?" the parish leader finished. He waited carefully, watching Matthew's face and knew he had possibly convinced the young man to at least try this for the sake of his fragmented home. "All I'm suggesting is this. Go home, try to pray about this and then write the letter to her asking her for her services. I will forward the letter to Daniel Carmel and then we'll see. That's all we can do."

"Does Reverend Carmel know my father and my mother are dead?" the boy had the presence to ask.

"He knows you're mother has passed recently. I did not want to put him in a position of leading this girl on, so I spoke to him as though it were indeed your father asking for help," Hamilton explained cautiously.

"So…the lie has already begun," Matthew stated blankly.

"Could we just try this and then I will repent, I promise," the Reverend smiled at Matthew, hoping he hadn't just sent the entire conversation back to the beginning turmoil they had both felt.

But Matthew had no more fight in him. He pulled himself out of the chair and walked to the office door and as he put his hand on the doorknob he turned to the man he had trusted as much as he had his own father all his life. He looked at Hamilton Davidson with complete frustration on his face. It seemed as though Matthew would simply just walk out the door without another word. As fate would have it though the young man found some humor left in him before leaving.

"Just make sure when this is all over that you leave plenty of room for me at the alter beside you when we both repent, eh?" he jested, only a slight grin on his face and a shake of his head. With that he exited the room and left. Hamilton Davidson watched as the young sheepherder who had in fact been taking care of his family now for almost four years climbed into his truck with the weight of the world on his shoulders and headed back to his home. The Reverend sighed heavily as he truly thought about what they were about to do.

"You can intervene anytime Lord, anytime now," he prayed, as he watched the truck disappear up the road. "We could all use that angel Miriam prayed for right about now."

Chapter 9: The Letter

"Five children! And two of them teenagers?" Srenna exclaimed amazed at the details Reverend Carmel had just given her about the governess post in New Zealand. "What do I know about taking care of teenagers?"

"It's not all that long ago, my dear that you were one," Daniel Carmel chuckled, looking fondly at the young girl sitting once again across from him in his study. She had been frequenting his office and home more this last month as she attempted to make several huge decisions about the next phase of her life. She had firmly decided not to accompany Frank and Grace Havilland with their children to the States next week even though she already felt the enormous weight of missing them all. "Would you just read the letter that came for you. Mr. Patton has most assuredly taken great pains to write a request for your services. The poor man must still be grieving after the loss of his wife," he finished, holding out the letter for her to take. He then added quickly, "I took the liberty of giving Reverend Davidson your name when suggesting you for the post."

"How thoughtful of you," Srenna smiled forcefully.

She stared at the elderly gentleman sitting at his desk. She had trusted him most of her young life with enormous and miniscule decisions, and everything in between. Now, though, he was actually encouraging the Australian born and bred girl to leave Sydney and embark upon a new country. And a very rural one from what he had just told her.

"Sheep? Twelve hundred of them! And five children," she repeated.

"Well, yes, my dear girl, you already acknowledged that detail," Reverend Carmel jested with her in his usual jocular manner.

"But…" Srenna responded, wrinkling her nose at him, "not the twelve hundred sheep, eh?!"

"Srenna, it sounds to me as though Mr. Patton has established a comfortable life for his family, albeit in a back hills setting, but that is the nature of New Zealand's sheep country. I understand from Reverend Davidson that the community of Castle Point is a tight knit bunch, a strong mix of native Maori islanders and good British families. They all get along quite nicely from what he has told me in the past," he explained. He wanted to go on with his pitch but a little voice inside of him told him it was time for Srenna to simply read the letter and then let God do the rest.
He waited for a moment to see what, if any, response came from his favorite visitor all these years.

Srenna was staring at the closed envelope now. Her mind was running at top speed once again as she tried to sort out the facts that the Reverend had just presented, but somehow she was getting nowhere. Her reasoning was muted, as though not even there, as she thought about this family on the little north island twelve hundred miles south east of Australia. Thoughts of a new baby crying for his lost mother were beginning to play on her imagination.

Daniel Carmel knew what was going on in this young woman's heart right about now. So still he waited. It wasn't until he heard the familiar sigh come from deep inside of her that he knew he could get up. "I'm going to leave you alone for a bit, while you read the letter. I'll be in the church working on that blasted door that doesn't want to shut properly. Come and find me when you're ready," he suggested gently as he rested his hand on the girl's shoulder, squeezing it encouragingly before leaving the room.

Srenna sat frozen in her chair for what seemed like a long time. Really only moments passed before the curious and always inquisitive young Aussie opened the envelope and pulled the letter out into her hands. Even before she unfolded several sheets of stationary, she could feel her heart pounding harder and that familiar anticipation of an unknown adventure seemed to wash over her as it had many, many times in her life. She even found her hands trembling a little as she adjusted the first page in the afternoon light. Then, taking a deep breath, Srenna James began reading the written plea from the children's father.

Dear Miss James,

It is with the greatest of hope that I write this letter of request. After much   discussion with Reverend Davidson and his mediation between myself, your Reverend Carmel and of course yourself, I would like to offer you a governess post at our sheep station on the North Island of New Zealand.

Castlepoint is located just east of Tinui and Masterton, about two hours northeast   from Wellington. We are by measures a relatively average sheep ranch and most days it requires a full twelve hour day of work to maintain. Due to the recent passing of my beloved wife Miriam I am in great need of a dedicated woman such as you to oversee the care of my children. They have suffered a great loss in our home with her absence. I have been assured by Reverend Carmel through Reverend Davidson that your experience with children is wonderful and your devotion to them special. I am in great need of both.

My oldest daughter Mary is sixteen and she is desperately trying to maintain some semblance of her mother's influence. Most days she is fully overwhelmed with the care of her younger brothers and sisters and I can see how quickly she is losing any memory of what it was like to just be a young girl in school. She is extremely bright, and I know she misses her classes and friends incredibly.

Stephan is thirteen. He is all boy, energetic in every way and struggling probably the most excepting his mother's death. He is angry about it and we are all trying to figure out how to help him go through the transitions. He is not a bad child, just a sad one.

Lilly is nine and is definitely the most vocal of all of the children. She has a way of saying things right out, many times for the good and some, just not. But she is truthful to a fault. And she is, as it seems, her little sister's best friend and guardian.

And that would be five-year-old Emma, still the baby by her own rights and struggling a bit with the arrival of another baby in the family. She is pretty much inseparable from Lilly. She understands very little about why her mother is gone.

And of course there is the baby. Benji is just shy of being eight months old. He understands nothing about what has happened and is in deep need of a consistent and loving caretaker. The previous governesses seemed unaware of what he truly needed. Mary can only do so much for him and our dear neighbor and friend who had been assisting us has had to shorten her stays due to the needs of her own baby.

As you can see, I am more then likely asking the impossible. But I am not above telling you I am desperately asking. I am aware of the reputation and standing you have in the Sydney area and am as equally aware that you could probably find a much better post and stay in your familiar surroundings. But after being informed about you by Reverend Davidson and spending much time in prayer about the children's needs, I am more willing to take the risk of asking, then to take the risk of not and missing the right person for this job. I need someone with a calling for children, a heart for my children, and a true desire to meet their needs.

I can offer you room and board and can assure you of a monthly salary for your personal needs. As well, I have sent in advance a ticket aboard the shuttle ship between Sydney and Auckland for next Monday. I will arrange train fare as well to Masterton if you decide you can indeed accept this request. I will also assure you of return arrangements in   the untimely event you change your mind once here.

Once again it is with much hope that we can look forward to a reply for this post. I will look forward to your decision as soon as you have had time to prayerfully consider all I have shared. Please feel free to wire me with any and all questions prior to that decision.

With deepest sincerity,
John Patton

For the longest time Srenna sat and simply stared at the letter. Then for some odd reason she read it again. As each name of the children leapt out at her, she could feel her heart being tenderized by an unknown image of each one.

But it was baby Benji that broke her. A single tear found its way down her cheek as the thought of the infant crying for his departed mother threatened to overwhelm her. Her own memories of her lost family and how it felt when they never came for her, flooded over her senses.

Then as if someone were in the room with her, she heard that unmistakable voice in her head. It reminded her that someone did come and she was now sitting in the study of that dear man and his wife who had relentlessly come everyday to be with her and take care of her.

Srenna stood from her chair and moved to the window overlooking the garden between the parsonage and the church. If not for one struggling thought she would have run from the room and found Daniel Carmel and told him yes, yes she would go. But that thought was sending chills up and down her spine even as she contemplated it. Nevertheless, being who she was, she grabbed up her handbag, letter still clutched in her fist and headed for the back door leading into the garden. It took the girl only a minute to reach the side door of the Anglican Church and only another one to find the parish leader on the other side.

"It's out of the question, really, isn't it?" she began speaking out of breath.

"Is it really? And why would that be my dear child?" Reverend Carmel asked with a knowing look on his face, but one that never left the door he was working on.

"Well you know why," Srenna returned, exasperated with the man who was fishing for a debate. She knew he was. It was his way of not telling her she was wrong or what she should decide. He had been doing this with her all her life. Still she could not hesitate, even as much as she did not want to admit what was troubling her. She looked away as she spoke what she thought was the obvious. "I could never go on that ship. Never!" she snapped adamantly.

"Who ever said you had too?" the gentle man answered, grinning at her as though he had a secret.

"What do mean? He's already sent me a ticket! He's expecting me to answer and then board that dreadful ferry and cross that horrible water!" Srenna was beginning to lose any composure or control now and Daniel Carmel could feel the struggle, the fear that had plagued this beautiful child for nearly nine years. He quickly got up and moved to her side, placing his fatherly arm around her, hugging her.

"Srenna, calm down and answer one thing for me please. If you could get there without a ship…would you?" he asked in a much more serious tone and yet still with a twinkle in his wise eyes.

"Well…I….well…yes. I do believe I could go. But that's not going to happen any way you look at it," she lamented.

"Well I suppose not, if you're looking at it from the viewpoint of the deck of a ship. But what if you were looking at it from the viewpoint from the air?" the man asked grinning an enormous grin.

"Fly!?"

"Do you have something against planes?" the dear Reverend asked softly, not jokingly, for he knew Srenna's fear of any ship was a serious and even reasonable one.

"Well…I don't know. I've never been on one before, eh? Besides, there are no commercial flights from Sydney to Auckland, is there?" she retorted back, becoming even a bit more frustrated with the process of deciding her fate.

"Well, I'm not the one to talk too, eh? But I'm betting Frank Havilland can help you there," suggested Daniel Carmel. "The important thing here, Srenna is… do you want to go?" He looked straight into the girl's large dark eyes still threatening to spill tears down her cheeks. She turned her gaze away from him and blinked and they came anyway.

"I can't bear the thought of those poor motherless children struggling without someone taking care of them, but…"she began.

"But what, luv?" he asked gently

"It means everything changes again. It means going away from here, away from you and Ruth and…" her words trailed off as she succumbed to both of Daniel's arms as he pulled her into a full hug.

"Of course it does. But think of it Srenna. You use to be the little girl who couldn't wait to get outside in the wide open spaces and all the mysteries God has in His great big creation. Look what He's offering you. Why… I'm told that New Zealand is the most breathtakingly beautiful country in the South Pacific. You'll be doing what you do best and enjoying God's glory while you are," he argued. He waited for a moment to give Srenna time to consider what he'd just shared with her. Then he pushed her back and looked into her face again.

"Do you remember what I told you a few weeks ago when your world "changed" again, when you got the news of your inheritance and then the Havilland's move?" the Reverend challenged her. Then he added quickly, before she had a chance to answer. "What do you hear, Srenna, in your heart. Or better yet, who do you hear?"

Srenna went back to the day she had finally come to the Carmel's and sought out their advice as to what to do about all the news she had received. She wanted Daniel to tell her then what to do and he wouldn't. Neither would Ruth.

"You told me to listen for my Shepherd's voice," she answered quietly.

"Who do you hear, what do you hear?"

"I hear Him telling me how much those children need me," she stated, her own voice quivering, "But…"

"Go home and talk with Grace and Frank. See if he can help you. See if that doesn't put the peace on your decision," the wise and loving man offered. He would have allowed the girl much more time to argue her points but he knew this was a step of faith God was asking of her. No amount of arguing was going to change that.

"I took the liberty, again, and you can be angry with me if you want, and talked to Frank myself. He can indeed set you up on a freight flight leaving on Monday bound for Wellington. Go home, Srenna. You have a lot of packing to do," the man chuckled. At first he was sure Srenna would scold him as she had so lovingly done over the years when he wasn't taking care of his health or doing something a man his age shouldn't, but she was at a loss for words, strangely enough.

She turned toward the side door of the church where she entered only moments ago, and suddenly realized her whole life would change the minute she walked out of it and went back to the Havilland's house. She turned back to Daniel and smiled at him. How could she be angry with him? He never missed a single opportunity to challenge her to wait on the Lord, or in this case, to leap.

"Should I write him a letter, telling him I'm coming, or a wire?" she asked quietly.

"I believe a wire would make it there before you, where a letter will arrive after you've pretty much showed up," the joyful man laughed. "I've no doubt, Srenna, you will know if you are doing the right thing. I truly believe you will hear Him, just as you have many times in your life.

"Five children," she repeated, shaking her head, and then adding, just to get a grin out of Daniel, "and twelve hundred sheep."

"Listen for your Shepherd's voice, Srenna. You might be surprised where it will come from," the Reverend answered, patting the girl on the shoulder and gently pushing her through the door. Daniel watched the little girl he remembered all these years walk away towards the drive and the automobile she'd come in. He was conflicted in his feelings, as though he had indeed just pushed one of his own children out of the nest. He and Ruth would have gladly raised her without a moment's hesitation. And in many ways they both had. Now he knew that in one short week, she would be gone. But his heart told him that was good…good for her. And exactly what these children needed. Another comforting thought came to his mind, recognizing where this one came from and who it came from. Unmistakable peace blanketed him as her car disappeared.

"We'll be seeing you again, Srenna James, eh?" the elderly parish leader whispered, a single tear sliding down his wrinkled cheek.

Chapter 10: The Reply

Dear Mr. Patton...stop...It is with greatest joy that I am answering your request for the governess post with a sound yes...stop...however, will be returning your ship fare and will be taking a freight flight to Wellington on Monday...stop... Current employer has also made arrangements for me to stay at a hotel in Wellington Monday night and train tickets for the ride to Masterton...stop...will be arriving sometime before 12:00 P.M on Tuesday....stop...If not much trouble, will be bringing two trunks with personal belongings...stop...will be looking forward to meeting you and the children...stop....sincerely, Srenna James.

Matthew stared in disbelief at the wire that Sam Mathers had brought to the house. The postman, who also delivered the mail in the rural ranch areas, took care of wired messages coming through the little post building in Tinui. When he saw the wire had come straight out of Sydney, Australia he dropped everything to bring it out to Matthew. Mary had sent Stephan after Matthew in great haste when Sam told her where it had come from. Now they all stood frozen on the front porch as Matthew read the wire once and then to everyone's urging, read it again. Then they just stared at each other as though none of them could believe this prestigious city bred woman would come to their corner of sheep country.

It was Mary who finally broke the silence, when it dawned on her how behind she was on everything and how messy the entire house was. As if someone had catapulted her out of a cannon, she handed Benji to Lilly and stepped into the house. She feverishly began scooping up everything she could get in her arms, at the same time barking out orders to Lilly and Emma to do this and do that.

Matthew excused himself politely to Sam and following Mary into the house he gently but firmly grabbed Mary's arm and turned her around to face him.

"What are you doing Mary?" he asked his oldest sister, who generally was in more control of her emotions then he was. But he could see by the expression on her face that the news had mixed blessings for her.

"Don't you see? This house is a mess Matthew! One look at all of this and she'll turn and run just like the others," she cried. She was not even trying to hold back the tears as they spilled down her face and she pulled her arm away from her brother. "We have to clean. It has to be perfect if we want her to stay." As she lamented that last statement she proceeded to pick up clothes and toys and move towards the kitchen.

But Matthew caught her again and this time he pulled the items from her arms and placed them on the chair beside the hallway door. Then he pushed Mary into what was left of the chair and squatted down in front of her.

"Mary…why do you think we need her to come? Do you honestly think someone who has taken care of three boys for the last five years doesn't know what a mess looks like?" her brother asked, grinning at her lovingly and patiently. He wiped away some of the tears from Mary's tired face and dropping to his knees, put his arms around her.

A quiet sniffle behind him indicated to him that everyone had followed them into the house, including Sam Mathers. Except for Stephan who as usual stood off to the side with a disgruntled look on his face, everyone had tears in their eyes, including Sam.

"Now listen all of you. Mary's sort of right, eh? We do need to clean up this place a bit and Mary's tuckered. No time to muck about, right?" he ordered gently extending his arm out for his sisters to join him in hugging Mary. The little girls came gladly into their brother's arms with baby in tow and he hugged them all and Mary as well. He looked over at Stephan wishing he knew what to say to the boy to make him feel better, but all he could muster was, "She'll be right, Stephan. You'll see."

At that encouragement, Sam stepped over to the thirteen year old and tried to put his arm around the boys shoulder to affirm what Matthew had just said, but Stephan would have none of it and slipped out of the door and disappeared. Matthew sighed heavily and peeling his sisters from his embrace, stood up and turned to Sam. "Ignore him, mate. He's not sure who he's angry with, but it's not you, eh?" Matthew apologized.

"No worries Matthew. I know he must be missing your mum and dad something awful," the kindly man offered as he walked towards the door. "Will you be sending a response to this Miss James? Sounds to me like she could be a keeper, this one. For your sake I hope she is."

"I suppose I should let her know I'll pick her up at the station on Tuesday," Matthew admitted, following him to the porch.

Sam took out a tablet and pencil he always carried with him for messages. "Fire when ready, mate," he told Matthew, standing poised and waiting.

"Dear Miss James…stop…gratefully responding to your decision to except post…stop…will be meeting you at the train station with the truck…stop…have a safe trip …stop…sincerely,…

At that Matthew hesitated, looking at Sam and realizing that he had no idea what Matthew and Hamilton Davidson were up to. He almost gave him his own name. He finished the wire with, "sincerely, Mr. Patton." He watched Sam Mathers' face for any reaction to such a formal sign off, but Sam seemed oblivious to Matthew's closing. He dutifully wrote everything down, handed the tablet to Matthew to sign and then stuck it back in his pocket.

"I'll take care of this as soon as I get back to the postal," he promised. "I hope this works for you, mate." With that Sam trotted to his truck and left to continue other deliveries. Matthew walked back into the living room and realized everyone had dispersed into another part of the house. Along with them went the pile of things he had dropped on the chair. From somewhere upstairs he could hear Lilly and Emma talking and even laughing. But Mary's voice was not heard, so he headed for the kitchen. She wasn't there either.

He finally found her in their mother's bedroom sitting in the rocking chair with Benji. She was trying desperately to get the infant to take the bottle Irmani had made for him earlier that morning during her short daily visit. But he would not have it. He wiggled and squirmed, pulling franticly at Mary wondering why no one would nurse him. Once again Mary seemed close to tears, frustrated and discouraged with her baby brother and wondering why she couldn't help him.

"Let me try, Mary," Matthew suggested gently, putting out his hands to take the fussing child.

"You!? As if you can do anything at all to help him Matthew Patton," she snapped. Right away she felt awful for having been cross with her oldest brother. She didn't mean to be angry with him, but she in fact knew what it was he and Reverend Davidson had planned. "Do you really think this woman is going to stay after she finds out what we've done?"

"What I've done Mary, not you. I should have never told you. Then you could be faultless when she's gets angry. I'm sorry I dragged you into this," Matthew apologized as he took Benji carefully from her arms and began to walk the floor with the boy, gently rocking him in his brotherly arms. When the infant had settled a little Matthew attempted to give him the bottle as he walked back and forth across the floor. Mary had leaned her head back for a moment but when she saw that Benji just might eat and nap for a small while she slipped from the room and headed for the kitchen.

Matthew watched his sister walk out of the bedroom and felt as though he were looking at a much older woman, the responsibility of all she'd been doing weighing heavy upon her. The baby in his arms brought him back to full attention as Benji's little doubled up fist hit Matthew in the chin. He had only swallowed a few drops of the goat's milk Irmani had left behind and Matthew knew his littlest brother could not go on at this rate for much longer.

The stark reality to Matthew was when he had seen lambs die when they would not suck from another mother or take the bottle he attempted to give them after their own mother refused them or had themselves died. Now he held his own kind, desperate to feed him and sustain him. He knew every day was crucial as the infant struggled to nurse, still remembering the closeness of his mother's breast. Benji was sleeping more only because he was becoming weaker, worn out by all his fussing and crying.

Matthew was worn out as well. He sat down in the chair with Benji and looked down on the curly blond head in his arms. He knew Benji was the very image of himself when Matthew was born. His mum had said it over and over as she grew sicker and weaker. Every day she made her oldest son hold the infant, building what she knew would need to be a strong bond, brother to brother. And her plan had worked. Matthew knew he had to do what ever it took to keep Benji well and taken care of; And Mary and Lilly and Emma and Stephan. He had promised her.

All these thoughts were whirling through Matthew's head as they suddenly shifted to the young woman who would be descending upon them in less then a week. He didn't even have a clue as to what she looked like and he realized he would be going to the train station blind.

"Oh well," he whispered softly to Benji as the child finally nodded off. "It's not like I could give her any description of me either, eh? I guess I'll know when this sophisticated butterfly floats off the train." His attempt to be amusing was missed on the sleeping baby in his arms, and it really missed him too. "What am I doing?" he asked himself, quietly laying his head back against the back of the rocking chair. He was not prepared to hear that still small voice in his head answer him back even more quietly as if not really in his head but his heart and his spirit.

"You're doing the best you can, son, the best any shepherd can do for his flock. Don't despair. Just trust me. I know what you're doing. More importantly, I know what I AM doing."

Matthew heaved a deep sigh before uttering up a prayer for his family and for the governess preparing to leave Australia. He stood carefully and placed Benji in his crib in the little nursery off the end of the bedroom. He watched for only a moment as the child slumbered, twitching every now and then still a bit fitfully. Then he crept from the room and closed the door. He would have gone and found Mary and the girls if only he had the strength to deal with them at the moment. But he did not. Instead he stole quietly out the front door and headed down the path to his father's horse, Samson, who had been grazing at the front gate.

Matthew needed to get alone for awhile. He was fully aware that Stephan had probably gone bush after hearing about the new governess. But he couldn't deal with him right now either. Mary would be doing what she always did and would have started supper, so Matthew mounted Samson and headed back to the fields where he had left the sheep. As he rode the large black stallion up the road to the lane leading to the pastures he thought again how he was going to break the news to this woman that his father was indeed dead. As quickly as the words of encouragement had enveloped him, a cloud of doubt began to overtake him. But he knew from experience what he had to do to find any peace.

Matthew stopped Samson in his tracks as they came up on the first gate to the fields. He dismounted and led the horse through the gate and then gave the animal his freedom and let him begin to graze again. Matthew walked a bit away from the horse that had carried his father for several years before going to war. Now the boy who had become the man of this house rode him. But right now Matthew did not feel much like a man, especially not one of honor. He was struggling greatly with the plan he and Hamilton had devised. But looking back down the road and seeing the house down in the valley below the fields he felt his heart crying out.

As if at a crossroad of decisions himself, Matthew first looked at the house, then the fields where he could see the sheep dotting the hillsides. He was torn, confused and even scared. What if it didn't work and she did leave, he wondered. He was entertaining this horrid thought when his eyes caught the movement of something in the trees, something larger then the sheep and not as large as the horse.

It was a red deer. It walked out of the trees and headed straight at Matthew and Samson as if there were no fear in the animal at all. Stopping just short of possibly twenty feet away from the boy, the deer stared hard as if suddenly it realized there was something or someone there. It seemed unafraid by Matthew's presence and actually appeared to size up the nineteen-year-old. Matthew could not take his eyes off the deer, a doe with large dark eyes. She seemed to stare right through to his soul and then as quickly as she had appeared she turned and headed up into the trees and higher ground. A number of times she stopped and looked back as if making sure he was watching her.

Matthew was frozen stiff for several moments as he pondered the appearance of the animal at such close range. Then, as he had many times while in these hills, he remembered a verse from his Bible his father had made him memorize years ago.

"The Sovereign Lord is my strength; He makes my feet like that of a deer. He enables me to go on the heights." One more look up the hill in the direction the deer had walked and Matthew knew that God had just spoken loudly and clearly to him just as He had many times during the countless hours spent alone in the fields.

"Alright, I'm going. I'll stop worrying and start planning for her arrival, eh?" he jested with his Heavenly Father. "But just one small request if I might. I don't care what this woman looks like, but could she at least be too small to clobber me too hard when she finds out what I've done."

He waited for a moment hoping he would hear yet another encouraging answer, but only silence followed.

"That's what I thought," he chuckled, shaking his head as he walked the rest of the way up the hill where the sheep waited patiently for their shepherd.

Chapter 11: The Arrival

Srenna looked around one more time in the train seat to make sure she had recovered anything she had been occupying herself with on the trip from Wellington. The morning trip had flown by quickly since the train pulled out of the station in Wellington taking her farther away from the life she had known in Australia and closer to her new destiny. Her departure the day before from the airport had been one of the most difficult things she had ever done. Leaving everything behind, the Havillands, Daniel and Ruth, Mrs. Crawford and just the familiarities of her life and her relationships with those people, was by and large a momentous time for her. But as difficult as it was, even in the midst of goodbye tears, deep down in her heart she was sure she was hearing from God to go.

That week, from the time she acknowledged Mr. Patton's request and wired him that she was coming, was so full of preparations, it flew by with the force of a whirlwind. Final arrangements for her inheritance, the care of the estate by Mr.Garner and other last minute plans were prepared in a flurry. Gifts for each of the boys, Grace and Frank, Daniel and Ruth, and Mrs. Crawford were purchased on a shopping spree unlike any Srenna could remember. She also purchased gifts for her new children she would be meeting, as well as new clothes for a governess who would be frequenting a country ranch instead of an elite city townhouse.

Frank Havilland worked feverishly to help her obtain her papers to travel to New Zealand, making arrangements to fly her over on one of his freight flights to Wellington. This promised to take off the edge a little for Srenna even though she had never flown before. It was a far cry better then trying to board a ship and sail across the Tasman Sea to her destination.

She found it incredibly hard to pack with Grace's help. The two of them would be folding Srenna's belongings and suddenly simply start crying. They would hug each other and then one or the other would say something encouraging, which would console them for awhile. Then sooner or later something would set one or the other off again, they would cry again, hug again and console again. Several times the boys entered Srenna's room when they heard them crying, but they finally backed out and stayed away.

It seemed as though Srenna and Grace would actually finish packing the day before with no other crying incidents, until Grace came into Srenna's room with a going away package to add to one of her trunks. It was wrapped in a special box and laid in among the layers of Srenna's clothes. But Grace made Srenna promise not to open the package until after she arrived and unpacked in New Zealand; Not a moment before she knew she was suppose to open it. Again both young women clung to each other and wept. All and all Srenna was sure she had well spent her tears just in the packing process.

But she was wrong. When she said her tearful goodbye at the house on Monday morning to the boys first and then one more time to Grace, Srenna was sure she would simply just cry all the way to New Zealand. It seemed that was highly possible when Frank Havilland drove her to the airport. When they pulled in at the hangar where the freight plane was preparing for it's weekly flight she saw the two people she knew she would be missing the most.

Daniel and Ruth Carmel had promised to see her off and as true as any loved ones could have been in her life there they were standing on the tarmac waiting to give her their last hugs and kisses for what might be a very long time. Her emotions were so heightened and so mixed she was sure she might just change her mind and stay. But in the end, with last minute words of encouragement, in a blur Frank whisked her aboard the plane, made sure she was fastened into one of the few seats behind the pilot's cockpit and then hugged the girl who had lovingly cared for his children the last five years.

Though he tried not to show it, tears were also brimming in the stoic business man's eyes. When he had departed from the plane it was no time at all before the crew began the taxi out onto the airstrip to take off.

Srenna waved furiously at those waving her goodbye and then closed her eyes as the plane prepared to take off. She wasn't sure if closing her eyes was due to the fear of leaving the ground, or more likely, leaving everything behind. She did however know she did not wish to look out over the ocean they would be crossing to reach their destination of the north island twelve hundred miles to the south east. Once well into the air she forced herself to look out the window next to her but their altitude was high enough at that point that clouds and distance made the water below them seem miniscule in size. The pilot himself, at his employer's orders came back to Srenna to make sure she was alright. She began to actually relax in a short time and even realized what an incredible sensation it was to be so high in the air and above the clouds.

Srenna took the travel time to pray for what lay ahead of her, the children, her life with them and helping John Patten care for them. At each step of the trip she found herself becoming more and more excited to reach her destination. As they landed in New Zealand's bustling city on the south end of the island, Srenna saw only the beginning of the tremendous mountainscape running through the heart of the country. Never before had she seen such incredible and picturesque beauty. As they circled Wellington, the height of the mountain range made her feel quite small and insignificant. That night in Wellington at the hotel, she could barely sleep for all the anticipation of the next day's train ride to Masterton.

Srenna couldn't take in all the sights fast enough the next day as the train pulled out of the station and began heading up the tracks where Mr. Patton would be meeting her and to the beginning of her new post. Like a small child she kept her nose pressed to the window for nearly the whole trip, feeling a growing intensity of excitement. She tried to relax as the tracks wound in and out of the foothills and along the awe inspiring mountain range along the way, but she was beginning to feel more and more nervous as the tracks brought the train closer and closer to the Masterton station. She had pushed her feelings as far away as she could since leaving Sydney the day before, but now the desire to finally reach her destination and this new family was more then she could shove away. She had been watching as the breathtaking landscape of New Zealand's north island unfolded before her, barely able to drink in all of its glorious God given beauty.

She had never seen such towering majestic mountains as those from her window. Everywhere there were mountains, she saw vast sky so blue it almost hurt her eyes to stare at it. The rolling hills leading up to the foot of those mountains were as equally beautiful and along the way Srenna saw the hillside dotted with woolly white sheep and cattle herds on ranch after ranch. Comfortable homes, nestled amongst small groves of trees, gave a warm welcoming feeling.

She wondered if the sheep ranch she was heading for, or station, as the New Zealanders called them was as inviting and alluring. Right now, though, her thoughts were quickly becoming anxious ones as she smoothed out her dark blue skirt and crisp white blouse she had put on early this morning. She brushed back her long dark curls and made sure the clip holding it up and back away from her face was securely fastened in the back. She wanted to appear as mature as possible when Mr. Patton first met her.

She was suddenly and painfully aware of how young she might seem to him; a man with children in their teens. Srenna knew very likely he was nearly twice her age and was beginning to thoroughly unsettle herself with negative thoughts of inadequacy and inexperience. She could entertain those thoughts for only a moment, as she was jolted out of her self assesment by the train coming to a stop in front of the station platform.

It was a quaint and quiet little station nestled amongst some other small buildings on the outskirts of Masterton. As Srenna waited for the attendant to announce they could exit from the train, she gathered up her purse and bags, took one more look around her and then stood to stretch her legs. The attendant was coming down the aisle towards her and stopped to see if she needed any help. The kindly man took her bags and she followed him to the exit. As he turned to offer his hand to Srenna, she stopped for only a moment, took a deep breath and descended onto the platform.

Very few people were leaving the train to stay in Masterton; most going on to Auckland. She thanked the attendant for his hospitality, and taking her bags, she walked towards the opened door of a small lobby. Before she stepped through it, she looked up and down the platform to see if anyone was coming towards her, but the platform had emptied quickly. She did see several trunks at the far end and assumed they were hers. Upon entering the lobby she set her bags down and quickly scanned it remembering that she didn't even have a real description of John Patton. It really didn't matter though as the few occupants in the lobby seemed to have already found those they were expecting, and Srenna found herself standing quite alone.

As the train pulled out, she stepped away a little from her bags and turned towards the entrance she had just come through. Beyond the line of trees across the tracks was yet another view of the snow capped mountain range to the west and it made Srenna take another deep breath to try to calm her jitters. Just as she exhaled she heard someone approaching from behind, but before she even had time to turn around she heard a soft, low voice speak hesitantly and yet with a tinge of hope.

"Miss James? Srenna James?"

Srenna felt the need for yet another deep breath as she turned slowly to face the person who had just spoken her name. Expecting to see the face of a middle aged man, Srenna found herself strangely surprised at the one that stared back at her with eyes as blue as the sky she had just been admiring. No middle aged face looked back at her as though seeing something he himself had not expected. This young man was, had to be, near her own age. He stood nearly a head taller than she, with sun streaked hair the color of wheat. His face had the distinct glow of one use to being out in the field all day, but not yet weathered by years of ranch work. She wasn't sure if the sound of taking a deep breath was her own or his, as he too seemed to be sizing up this young governess from Australia. She wondered if this stranger had expected a more matronly school marm just by the way he stared at her. He seemed unsure what to say or do next and Srenna realized suddenly she needed to answer him.

"Yes... Yes, I'm Srenna James," she smiled and offered her hand in a formal attempt to shake his. He looked at her small hand extended towards him and nervously took it in his. He knew the moment he took it how refined and proper she must be. It was as soft as the lamb fleece he had been use to all his life. He let go of it quickly, conscience all of a sudden at how rough his own hand must feel in comparison. But she didn't seem to mind. The young man did see the puzzled look that replaced her smile.

"Mr. Patton? Are you John Patton?" she asked with a tone of confusion.

"Well... No Miss.... I'm not John Patton. I'm Matthew. Matthew Patton, his oldest son. I'm.... my father ...couldn't make it... so he sent me." Matthew turned his eyes away at that statement and quickly busied himself by stepping back to pick up the two bags Srenna had left a few feet away. "I assume these are yours and maybe the trunks on the platform. I pulled the truck in at the end, knowing you would have something to load. I hope you don't mind the truck. It's a might bit weathered and all but she's sweet. It gets us where we need to go."

"No, I don't mind at all," Srenna smiled politely. She did however add quickly, "Your father failed to mention you in his letter. He..."

"He probably didn't think he needed to, me being nineteen and all," the boy explained quickly. "I pretty much take care of myself. Gone most of the day." He seemed to Srenna to be even more on edge then she as he rambled on while stepping back through the entrance and out onto the platform. She followed behind him trying to match his strides and walk beside him.

They reached the end of the train platform and both stopped only long enough for Srenna to nod her head in acknowledgement that the trunks were indeed hers and then Matthew resumed his quick movement down the steps to an old truck with wooden running boards and wooden slats along the bed. He placed Srenna's bags over the side by the front of the truck bed and then opened the passenger door for her to climb up. Climbing in was not such a graceful thing to do in her modest straight line skirt but she pulled it up and quickly lifted herself up to the seat while Matthew held her arm to steady her. He closed the door and bound back up the steps to Srenna's trunks and she watched as this New Zealand boy lifted them one at a time as though they were empty boxes and carried them to the truck. Once he had loaded them he climbed in on the driver's side and started the engine. He glanced quickly at Srenna as she straightened her skirt and again couldn't help but notice how proper and mature she seemed. He was also intrigued by the warm color of her skin and wondered if she had had much occasion to frequent the beaches in Australia. She would fare well in the New Zealand sunshine if so. She looked to be one who had definitely enjoyed a high society styled life. As he pulled the truck around and into the road leading away from the station he was very aware of every rut and bump he was hitting and apologized several times.

"How far is it to the ranch or… I'm sorry…station?" Srenna inquired, looking again at Matthew and smiling at her slip. She had tried to read up a little about the many sheep stations in the North Island.

"It'll take about thirty minutes to get out there. We're north of Tinui and Castle Point, closest to Castle Point" he answered her, glancing quickly her way and then turning his eyes back to the road. "I hope your trip was pleasant enough, the flight and all. You must be pretty brave to get into a plane and pretty tuckered."

"I'm alright. The trip was a short run. I barely looked out the window at all. But when we came in for the landing I did peek at the moutains. They're astounding! I can't wait to see them closer," she smiled and laughed a nervous little laugh. Matthew smiled back at her, both feelling a bit awkward and unsure what to say next.

They were silent for awhile, Srenna taking in everything they passed by and Matthew trying hard to figure out what he was going to say to her before they reached the house. The closer they got the more anxious he felt and he fidgeted with the steering wheel until Srenna thought it might come off in his hands. She decided to ask him about the children, hoping if she could get his mind on something else besides making small talk he might relax.

"Tell me about your brothers and sisters. I can't wait to meet all of them. I've read your father's letter over and over trying to get an idea of each one," she stated. Matthew glanced at Srenna's face and her great big round dark eyes and for a moment all he could see was the genuine desire of this young, very pretty woman to leave everything she knew in her city life and come to this sprawling island countryside to help the children.

"Well," he started slowly, "there's Mary after me. She's sixteen and wants to be thirty. She's been trying to hold down the fort. She spends most her day just keeping up with the little ones and the housework. Then there's Stephan, who is thirteen and gives her as many fits as he can. He works hard enough, but he's all boy. I'm afraid he has more energy then I ever had at that age."

They both laughed a little at that idea and Srenna could feel Matthew begin to relax.

"And then there must be Lilly, eh?" Srenna asked.

"Yeahr, Lilly, percocious little Lilly. She'll ask a million and one questions, some that will embarass us all, but she expects an answer to be sure and a truthful one. She'll be ten in about three months." Matthew took a deep breath and looked to see if Srenna was still listening to what seemed to him like boring facts about his siblings, but Srenna was watching him intently as he gave his description of each child. He was acutely aware of her eyes being fixed on him as he spoke and again felt awkwardly young and simple compared to her sophistication.

"Go on please. There are two more, aren't there?" she coaxed him.

"Yes mum, Emma, she's next. Was the baby for a long time and having a bit of a struggle with not being one now. She hangs on Lilly a lot... and me. She's five and will start school when it's in session again... end of January," Matthew finished his sentence.

Suddenly he realized how much time had passed and how close they had gotten as he turned onto the road that would lead them through the ranch gate and down into the valley where the house and sheep station was.

"And the baby, little Benji. How is he? The poor little thing must be confused about all that's happened," Srenna interjected, not quite prepared for Matthew's sudden change of emotions. Almost as quickly as she had sensed him beginning to ease up, Srenna felt his mood change and she turned to see what it was he was peering at through the windshield as he brought the truck to a stop. They had come to the top of a lane with two gate posts and a sign over the posts with the name 'Shepherd's Gaze' carved on a wooden sign. Below at the end of the lane sat a home much like those Srenna had seen all along the way, two story sprawling house, weathered by the sun, wind and rain, yet in an inviting way a most welcomed sight. Behind it were the gentle rolling foothills and beyond those the gradual incline of the New Zealand mountains. The fields a short distance beyond some larger stock barns were covered with flocks of sheep everywhere Srenna looked. A myriad of pens laced the fields just beyond the barns. A quiet river could be seen just a short distance beyond the house, meandering through the hills and small groves of trees.

She was trying to drink it all in. The beauty of the valley seemed to be clothed in a blanket of warm peace to her and for the first time since leaving Srenna felt something sure and definite about the place she was about to embark upon.

"Oh Matthew...it's absolutely beautiful." She turned to smile at him, but was caught off guard by the incredably strained and miserable look upon Matthew's face. She stared at him with great concern, for he was gripping the steering wheel so hard his knuckles were white. Srenna asked him with intense worry in her voice. "Matthew, what's wrong? Are you alright?"

He let go of the steering wheel suddenly and quickly got out of the truck. Srenna watched as he walked towards the back of the truck and began pacing back and forth across the lane. She hesitated for a moment, confused as to what to do. She climbed out of the truck and walked to the end and stood wondering what she had said or what had happened that had upset him so.

"Matthew...I'm sorry if I asked you too much. If I said something about the baby or anything to upset you, I'm..."

But before she could say anything more, Matthew looked up from the ground he had been pacing and staring at and shook his head at her. "No...no you're not to blame and certainly not the one to be apologizing. It's me to blame. Me to be apologizing. I can't believe I tried this or agreed to it. I can't do this to you. I'm not a liar...I..."

At that, he turned his face away from Srenna and turned his back. She knew she had seen tears welling up in his eyes just as he turned and could only imagine how he must feel embarrassed by her seeing him cry. She took a step towards him and was going to put her hand on his arm to try to console him, but he quickly moved around to the passenger side of the truck.

"Whatever it is, I know you must be feeling so much grief right now," she began softly and gently, following him, "But it's alright. I'm here now to help your father...and in time I'm sure..."

Before she could finish her sentence, he cut her off sharply, " You're not here to help my father!" he shouted, "Your here to help me!" The young man looked hard at her, his face stricken with despair. " I'm the one who wrote the letter!"

Srenna stared at the boy's distraught face and the tears now running down his cheeks undammed. She wasn't quite sure what he was telling her, but a large knot had formed in her stomach as he spoke those words.

"What do you mean, you wrote the letter?" she asked, not sure at all she wanted to hear the answer. "Does your father even know I'm coming?" she asked, beginning to feel a twinge of fear.

Suddenly Matthew could no longer look at her, look at her face and those eyes. He closed his and turned his face towards the house as he let out his complete confession.

"He does'nt know...because he's dead. He's been dead...for over a year. He was killed in the war. He was suppose to come home." Matthew was crying now, his voice breaking as he tried to fight back his feelings. "She never got over it you know...losing him. She had such a hard birth with Benji and then we all thought she'd recover after awhile, but she just got weaker and weaker and depressed........sad."

Srenna stood frozen in her spot, taking in all Matthew was saying. She heard everything, yet her mind kept running back to the fact that this boy had just told her both his parents were gone. She could feel herself trying to stay calm but her mind was racing. The sudden realization that there was no parent, no father as well as no mother in that house below sent waves of mixed emotions through her. Then suddenly, anger began to rise up in her and she found her tongue.

"You lied to me," she stated in a dead quiet voice.

"I know I shouldn't have," he stated in a voice not unlike a small child. "I didn't know what else to do. I need help! The governess my gran got us after mum died, left four days after the funeral. I've tried to keep things going but I just can't do it! Mary can't do it!"

"Reverand Davidson helped you lie," she said clipping her words with distinct feelings. She remembered the words of encouragement by Daniel about "Mr. Patton and his need for a governess."

"I didn't want to. I wanted to just ask someone out right, but every one that came was just all wrong. They all left. I can't do this alone!" Matthew looked forlornly at the young woman, feeling horribly ashamed and desperately tired.

Srenna began to feel something break in her heart as she stared into Matthew's tearful blue eyes. She began to feel that strange compassionate calm that always came out of nowhere at the most intense times. Just at that moment a heart wrenching sound rang up from the home below. The woeful cry of a baby made both of them whip their heads towards the front porch and they could see all of the children standing, waiting for Srenna's arrival. A young girl about her age was rocking a wailing baby in her arms.

Srenna's heart broke like glass on a rock as she heard the mournful cries. "What's wrong with the baby?" Srenna demanded, looking hard at Matthew.

"He hasn't been taking a bottle. He fusses through the whole thing and then he just spits it all up. He's barely eating enough to stay alive," he replied, his voice still breaking with anguish.

"Was he weaned before your mother passed away?" Srenna asked bluntly with great concern as she moved to the truck door. When no answer came she raised her voice, "Was he weaned?"

Matthew shook his sad face and answered in one misearble word "No."

"You'd better get me down there. Now!" she ordered, as she climbed back into the truck.

Matthew stood for only a few seconds, wiping his face with the back of his hands and climbed in without question. He said nothing, his only concern, her only concern was the wailing child on the porch. It only took Matthew a few moments to fly down the road leading to the house. He was no longer concerned about the ruts and bumps. Srenna braced herself as much as she could to take each shock against her body.

Matthew brought the old truck to a jolting stop and jumped out and hurrying around to help the young governess out of the front seat. But before he had even rounded the truck, Srenna had climbed out and was headed through the little white gate leading to the front porch where the children stood waiting and the baby still wailed. Halfway up the walk she stopped suddenly and turned to speak to Matthew in a tone of command. Her action nearly caused him to slam into her as he hurried up the path close behind her.

"I need my bags!" she spoke sharply and then resumed her quick walk up to the porch.

"Right ... got them mum," he responded, turning back quickly and grabbing them from the truck. He felt frantically and painfully aware that she was angry and mostly irritated with him right now. But he watched in amazement as her entire mood went from that to a steady, controlled approach of the children and the screaming infant. Srenna walked straight up to the girl holding young Benji and stopped only long enough to address the bewildered youth.

"You must be Mary," she spoke, smiling reassuringly at her. "May I?" Srenna asked, holding out her arms to Mary, who nodded and gladly handed over the distraught boy. Srenna smiled again at the girl but immediatly gave an order to her directly. "Come with me. I'll need your help." She could see the tears brimming in Mary's eyes, but she neither waited for them to spill over or to even address the other children who had parted quickly to allow this young woman access to their baby brother. She did turn her head as Mary opened the door into the house and commanded Matthew's attention. "Bring the bags! Please!" Her tone with him was stern, but to Mary she asked gently, "Where can we go… to be quiet?"

Srenna had no time to take in her new surroundings as Mary hurried across a large room and opened a door off the left side. Srenna followed her into a bedroom where a crib stood at one end beyond some louvered doors. A rocking chair at the end of the bed was exactly what Srenna wanted and she lowered herself into it trying to console the now flailing baby. She suddenly realized Matthew had followed them into the room and he stood holding her bags with a beaten, miserable look about him.

Srenna literally barked at him this time. "Leave the bags there and get out!" She looked down at the crying baby, not wanting to look at the young man's tortured expression, but she heard the door shut obediantly and then heaved a deep sigh. Srenna looked up at Mary who stood waiting anxiously at the door. "Lock it, Mary, and then bring the larger bag here," she spoke in a quieted tone, calmly, again smiling at the girl who was barely holding back her own flood of tears. "Take a few good deep breaths, dear. We'll get this righted, but we've got to keep our heads about us, eh?"   As   Srenna spoke she held the boy in one arm firmly, even though his little arms and legs were kicking and fighting this woman he didn't recognize at all. "Now, in the bag there's a container," she instructed, to which Mary quickly opened and began searching. She noticed as she searched that Srenna was unbuttoning her blouse and she was distracted for a moment by what the young childless woman was going to do. "Hurry, Mary. He's only going to be fooled for a few minutes," Srenna told the infant's sister. Srenna slipped the blouse off her shoulder and then the strap of her braziere. The baby seemed to know instinctively that he could begin to rut and before Srenna could expose her breast to the distressed and hungry child he was trying to latch onto her with all his might.

And latch he did! Srenna winced at the desperate baby's need for just a moment. He fervantly began to nurse, finding some temporary comfort in what he was used too; a warm bosom and quiet arms. Srenna spoke calmly to Mary as the girl pulled out a container from the opened lugguge.

"There's a special nursing bag in there. Put his milk in it and make sure the nipple is fastened on tight with the band," the young governess instructed. Mary took the bottle of milk she had been hopelessly holding all this time and hurridly emptied its contents into the soft bag. She fastened the odd looking end back on and rushed to Srenna. As was predicted, Benji had figured out that his new governess had no nourishment to offer him and was fitfully rutting again. Before he could screw up his helpless little baby face into another round of deafening wails, Srenna slipped the bag against her breast and guided the special end up to the frantic child's little mouth.

To Mary's surprise and relief, her baby brother latched onto the nipple and immediately began to suck as though his life depended on it. Srenna watched him for a few minutes and then looked up at the amazed girl and grinned. So satisfied was he that the tired infant's eyes began to flutter and then droop, but not before he fixed his gaze on the face of his new caregiver. Srenna could feel him relaxing more and more in her arms and try as he might to keep his gaze on her, he finally fell into a sleepy trance. His little head gratefully nuzzled against Srenna even after he stopped sucking the nearly empty bag of milk.

Srenna watched him for a few more minutes before she realized his sister was still in the room sitting on the edge of the bed. She had a look of both amazement and deep relief on her face. She was unsure what to do, what to say, but a grateful "Thank You" formed on her lips to Srenna. She then stood up and quietly slipped from the room, closing the door behind her.

From somewhere off in another part of the house Srenna heard muffled voices, a few noises of footsteps moving about and then the closing of a door. Then a deep silence fell over the house and only the occasional distant bark of a dog could be heard. Srenna sat rocking the sleeping baby, feeling suddenly overwhelmed by the events of the day. She put her head back against the rocking chair and thought to herself,"What am I doing here?" She realized though, that as quick as she had formed the thought from her struggling heart another heart was hearing her question. She looked down at the beautiful child in her arms, this curly blond headed motherless orphan and clearly heard that still small voice she'd heard so many times in her young life.

"Be patient, child, and I will show you how to do this."

Srenna put her head back again, but this time it was her eyes that fluttered and drooped shut. Even as that incredible, peaceful thought consoled her temperarily asleep, she held onto the contented boy snuggled to her heart.

Chapter 12: The Memory

"Swim Srenna! Swim towards the sun. Don't stop, and don't look back. Keep going. Keep kicking! Keep going, …keep kicking... keep going... keep kicking..." The fervent commands were becoming harder and harder for Srenna to hear, lost in the distance somewhere far behind her as she kicked and paddled and kicked some more; away from the sinking ship, away from her past and those familiar to her. She wanted to stop but she couldn't. Her legs and arms wouldn't let her. Her eyes were fixed on something ahead of her. She thought it was still the sun setting over what must be land. The she realized it wasn't something, as she frantically swam on. It was someone. She saw them, standing just above the waterline as if on land. A tall lad, his blond hair gleaming in the sun, was waving to her as if to assure her she had almost made it to shore. Around him, others, smaller ones cheering her on, when suddenly… she felt a small fist hit her in the chest.

Srenna's eyes opened quickly and she saw immediately that she was nowhere near the frothy waves of her deepest and most fearful memory. Instead she saw all around her a quiet, lovely room painted in subdued hues of blues and yellows. She realized instantly that the baby boy she held was the one she had just fed and rocked to sleep. His tired little eyes were still closed and his breathing was still even and quiet. He was still nuzzled contentedly against Srenna's breast. She wondered if she had made his tiny fist strike out because she was dreaming. None the less he slept on and Srenna stood slowly and carefully so as not to wake him. Laying the empty nursing bag on the chair, she then laid Benji in his crib with great care and waited for a moment to see if he would stir. When she was sure he was still in a deep slumber, Srenna walked silently from the little boy's nursery and gently pulled the louvered doors closed. She listened for only a few seconds, breathed a deep sigh of relief and turned to assess her surroundings.

As she pulled her clothes back together she scanned the bedroom she was standing in. It was somewhat roomy in size, having a large double bed, a tall dresser and a small vanity and chair. There was also an old wardrobe. Beside the bed was a nightstand and Srenna saw right away that the lamp beside the bed was an old oil lamp, beautiful in style but definitely not electric. She wondered about that for only a moment when she saw a lovely green vase with white lace-like etchings on it filled to overflowing with flowers of all colors and kinds. A card leaned against the vase and Srenna crossed the room to pick it up. Crayon colors nearly matching the flowers themselves were drawn and written on most of the surface of the inside of the handmade card. One single word was written in the center, WELCOME. Srenna could tell that childish hands had scribbled and doodled their very best while another pair of hands showed some practiced artistic abilities and yet another more mature pair had added the final touches to the card.

Srenna put the card in her skirt pocket and took another look around the room. White lacey curtains covered one window beside the dresser. She went to it and looked out the window to see if anyone was outside. It was still very quiet all around her. Even the barking of dogs could not be heard as she had earlier. Srenna's curiosity was beginning to peak as she wondered where a house full of children could have disappeared to. She realized she must have dozed for about an hour by the sun's position now as to when she'd arrived at midday, so listening one more time for the sleeping baby and then content that he might sleep on for a while longer Srenna stepped through the bedroom door and into the rest of her new surroundings.

The bedroom and nursery she stood outside was off the left side of a large cozy room, having a huge fireplace at the opposite side. Three older looking over stuffed chairs were positioned all over the room as well as a worn but comfortable looking sofa facing the fireplace. Another rocker sat off in the far corner next to a closed door and the front corner where she stood had a beautiful spinet piano. Numerous oil lamps were positioned on end tables, the mantle and another desk on the outside wall close to the front door. The floor was dark wood but beautiful woven rugs were strategically placed around the room giving the living space a warm, cozy air. Two large opened windows again framed with lace curtains flanked either side of the door she had first entered. They were fluttering in the warm New Zealand spring air. All the wood was an unusual and rich looking wood Srenna had never seen before.

Srenna crossed the room looking curiously at each object, each piece of family heirloom scattered across the mantle, the tables, and the desk. Everywhere were toys, shoes, books and other items that six people could easily have strewn across the room. Beloved family portraits hanging on the walls and reminders of the family that still remained here, tugged at Srenna's memories of her own family. It seemed like a lifetime ago to her. She quickly pulled herself back into the room, pushing thoughts of that life, for the time, far away. She finally heard hushed voices coming from somewhere to her left towards the back of the house. Moving to an open archway and hall along the back wall Srenna saw a door to the left, a stairwell and an open door to her right. At the far right end an open room appeared to be a dining area.

She turned down the hall to the left towards the first door and much to her relief it was the bathroom. Stepping inside the room she gratefully used, to her delight, a working commode with a water closet above it. There were also two lamps on the wall in this room, both oil and Srenna realized she was not seeing any electrical fixtures anywhere. The room did have a beautiful deep claw-toothed bathtub, a welcome sight for a much needed bath later. Both that and the free-standing basin had what appeared to be water pipes running down from the wall to them from outside. After turning the pearl-white handle she was as equally delighted to get warm water from the faucet. She washed her face and hands and checked her appearance in the oval mirror above the basin and moved back to the door. She assessed the room before walking out and couldn't help but notice that even though someone had obviously attempted to clean the room, everywhere was evidence of many bodies using the room. Baskets of clothes in the corner were full to overflowing and towels were hung on hooks across the walls, some on the floor, where they had been left in a hurry.

Five children, she suddenly thought to herself, not able to push that thought away; five children and one boy trying to be the man of the house. She was beginning to feel overwhelmed by this thought as she stepped back into the hallway, but it was quickly blotted out when she saw the round cherub-like face of a little girl, staring at her wide-eyed from the door beyond the stairway. The little cherub gasped when she saw Srenna and then disappeared in a hurry into what had to be the kitchen. Srenna smiled and slowly followed the youngest of the Patton girls through the door and found her self staring at a large, warm and lovely kitchen, again containing the rich dark wood seen in the front room. Not even the piles of dirty dishes and clutter around the room seemed to dampen her impression of the spacious love worn room. Mary turned from the sink where she was attempting to wash dishes, to see the young governess appraising the conditions.

"It's a bit of a mess, I know, Mum. I've been trying to get caught up since yesterday, but I....." the teenager explained hurriedly and painfully.

"Oh no, Mary. It's quite alright," Srenna answered her, quickly crossing the room. She immediately put her arm around the girl and gave her an encouraging squeeze and then assured Mary in a light tone, "She's sweet. We'll get it done together. You'll see." She smiled at Mary and then turned to the two younger girls at the table watching Srenna's every move, sizing up the Aussie woman who had come to take care of them. "And what's this?" she inquired of the littlest child, still staring at Srenna. The girls had a large basket filled with peapods and each was shelling as much as they could at the big wooden table in the center of the room.

"These are peas and we are having them for supper," instructed five-year-old Emma, as she popped a pea into her little round mouth.

"These are peas and you are having them now," retorted nine-year-old Lilly, with an air of frustration in her voice.

"Ahh..." Srenna responded, kneeling down between the two girls, trying very hard not to grin or laugh at the seriousness of the older girl. "Maybe I could help you first and then your sister with the dishes." She stood and pulling out a chair, sitting next to Emma, she began shelling peas and filling the empty bowl on the table. Lilly seemed a bit more content that maybe they would now complete their chore sometime that day and smiled gratefully at Srenna.

Mary continued to wash away at the dishes piled on the counter as she watched Srenna engage her sisters in small talk about the garden, what was growing there and what they liked to eat. She was relieved to see how at ease both the girls seemed to be around this strange newcomer, but not really surprised because of how she had felt herself in the bedroom when trying to calm and comfort Benji. She had not made Mary feel at all at fault or inadequate for not being able to quiet the hungry baby. Instead Mary was amazed how quickly a cloud of peace seemed to fill the room. It seemed to fill the kitchen now. She kept glancing over at the three of them while laboring at the piles of dirty dishes, when Srenna calmly stood up suddenly and encouraging the younger girls to keep shelling she came to Mary's side and gently moved the girl over.

"You rinse and I'll wash for awhile," she smiled warmly.

Mary gratefully began rinsing and stacking the dishes on the drain board. As the two worked side by side Srenna questioned her helper about food for the supper meal. It was already 3:00 in the afternoon by the clock on the wall.

"Stephan got a couple of chooks from the coop this morning and they are in the icebox," she informed Srenna.

"And we'll have peas of course," added Srenna, looking at the girls, encouraged by the growing uneaten amount in each bowl. "Do you have potatoes?" asked Srenna, looking around the kitchen for a vegetable bin or pantry.

Mary stopped rinsing and walked to a door at the end of the counter. It was indeed a large walk in pantry. Srenna followed her, towel in hand and was relieved to see a well stocked array of canned and dried vegetables and other supplies. A large wooden bin with a lid sat in one corner still stocked at least half full of potatoes. Another smaller bin on the shelf labeled 'onions' was also still full.

"Mary, you're mother was a hard worker to be sure. This is all so lovely and organized," she marveled.

But Mary was choking back the tears again as she answered Srenna. "Mum was too sick to do the canning this last time," she explained, "This mostly came from Irmani and her daughter, Nula and some from the church ladies. They've been helping as much as they can."

"Then I'll have to meet these wonderful ladies who have helped you so much," Srenna smiled. She quickly assessed the abundantly stocked shelves and then began pulling potatoes out of the bin. As she handed them to Mary she grinned at the girl and laughed, "Say when, eh?" not knowing at all how much everyone would eat. Ten in all were counted out into Mary's apron and then both went back to the long kitchen counter.

"Let's get things started and we can wash dishes as we go," suggested Srenna. She went to the icebox beside the back door and pulling it open found the chickens or chooks Mary had referred to earlier in a large pan. She was very relieved to find them plucked and ready for cooking. She was also relieved to find the icebox was electric, a wonderful gift to John Patton's wife just before he left.

Srenna decided to let Mary lead her as much as was possible in order to win the girl's confidence and help.

"Baked or fried, Mary?" she asked.

"We like it fried," the girl offered.

"Good enough then, much quicker too," agreed Srenna, with and adamant nod of approval. "Let's bake the potatoes though. There's still time, I think. When do you usually eat your evening meal?"

"The boys will be back from the fields around 5:30. We eat round about 6:00," Mary explained. "Stephan goes out to the fields at the noon meal to help Matthew. He takes lunch out to him."

"And what time does your brother leave in the morning?" Srenna asked, trying to absorb all the information concerning her new surroundings and daily schedule.

"Very early, 6:00 A.M. usually," the girl announced.

"6:00 A.M!" Srenna exclaimed with a great deal of surprise, and without hesitating she added quickly as if asking, "So... he's gone nearly all day?" As soon as she had said it she realized her tone might have sounded critical of this young man. The look on Mary's face and that of her sisters told her how they felt about this.

"He has a lot of work to do and only Stephan to help," Mary answered, just slightly sounding defensive of her older brother.

Srenna felt badly immediately for having made Mary feel as though she must defend Matthew's daily routine and she quickly apologized to the girl and smiled encouragingly. "Of course he does, dear, poor thing trying to keep up with the whole station."

Mary seemed to except this amendment and for several minutes nothing more was asked and nothing else was offered as they cleaned and prepared potatoes for baking and readied the chickens for frying. Lilly and Emma finally finished the peas as well. The stove was also electric, to which Srenna breathed another sigh of relief, but she did finally figure out that no electric was wired for lights or a water pump. The water coming in to the kitchen sink however was piped in from an enormous water tower located outside and off the end of the house.

Srenna was impressed with the ingenuity of the rural ranchers to use the more then abundant rainfall she had heard about, sometimes on a daily basis, to supply water to their families and stock. Though the water was somewhat warmed by the sun itself, water however still had to be boiled for baths and dishes. There was a hot water boiler outside according to Mary. She set her mind to learn as quickly as possible how the children's mother had provided such loving care for such a large family. In the meantime she was happy to rely on Mary's tutelage to complete the chores.

As they completed each task Srenna kept her ears and eyes opened and tuned. Everywhere she looked, even pass the clutter and struggle of this family for the last seven weeks, a mother's touch could be seen, could still be felt. Once again Srenna found she was uttering up a silent prayer for her loving Father to help her find her footing in this beloved home and provide what these children needed.

She was shaken suddenly out of her prayer when she heard the sound of a crying baby coming from the bedroom. Srenna marveled at how the dear child had napped when she looked at the clock and saw that it was already 4:30. She started for the door but Mary offered to go retrieve her baby brother from his crib. Srenna nodded and after Mary left the kitchen she looked in the icebox to find more milk. Beside the regular bottles of milk she saw another container that appeared to also have milk in it.

"What is this Lilly?" she asked the nine-year-old who was still shelling peas.

"Goats milk, mum. 'Mani brought it. Said it's better for his, "poor li'l tum," Lilly quipped, trying to mimic what Srenna could only imagine was the twice referred to person who had been helping this struggling brood.

"And who is 'Mani? I simply must meet this person," she asked curiously, starting the milk on a burner in a pan. Just then Mary walked into the kitchen with Benji in her arms. She carried the nursing bag with her as well. Srenna knew she would have to wait for an answer, for the moment the infant caught sight of her his gentle fussing in Mary's arms became the frantic cries of a hungry baby. He fidgeted until Srenna reached for him and Mary gladly handed him over.

"Can you wash this quickly? The goat's milk should be warm enough?" she instructed the boy's sister. Mary obediently moved to prepare her baby brother's bag of milk. Even though only a few hours had passed she knew the poor child had not sustained much in the last few weeks. As she feverishly got it ready she saw Srenna offer the child the security of her warm breast again and her safe arms. Lilly and Emma watched in silence at the young governess as she slipped the special bag up to the unsuspecting boy who went from breast to bag even quicker then before.

"We will be alone for a little while yet, right Mary?" Srenna asked looking at the clock as it hit 5:00.

"Yeahr. They won't come in till around six," Mary answered quickly.

"All right then. This will be our little secret. And this dear little gentleman," Srenna giggled into the boys soft curls. This brought a round of giggles from them all and Srenna was glad the girls felt a bit of merriment already the first few hours since she'd arrived.

As she fed the hungry baby, she encouraged Mary to begin frying up the chickens in a large skillet. The girls gave Mary the peas to be boiled and then set on the back of the stove to keep warm.

"I'll get the bread," offered Lilly, to which Emma added loudly, "I get the butter!"

Srenna finished feeding the quieted and satisfied baby and was going to hand him off to Lilly, but already the boy had decided Srenna was to be held onto for dear life, so she held him in one arm and scurried to help carry clean dishes to the dining room table. She was really delighted at how at ease Mary completed the task of supper while she wasn't trying to appease Benji.
"This is good," she thought to herself, glad and relieved to see how easily the girls pitched in and helped. They would be a good team. There was so much to do. Three fleeting hours had passed in a flash just washing a few dishes and preparing a meal. It would take all the willing hands she could enlist as the days unfolded.

The table set and supper nearly ready, Srenna actually began to feel a pinch of anxiousness at the thought of Matthew returning for supper. She painfully recalled that her last words to him were agitated and even sharp and she wondered how the meal would be if he and she were still on uncomfortable terms. She wondered how she might even take him aside before they sat down and apologize to him for being so short with him. But she got her answer quickly when promptly at 6:00 P.M. Stephan bounded up the front steps, announced he was home and "Let's eat," came impatiently out of his mouth. Then as though an after thought as he barreled through the kitchen to wash his hands, he looked straight at Mary and informed her in a somewhat sarcastic voice, "Don't bother to wait for Matt. He's got work to do in the barn. Said he'd eat later." With that, the boy flew into the dining room and plopped himself into a chair. As if in taunting defiance he began to help himself immediately to the food on the table. Srenna hesitated for a moment while trying to size up Mary's reaction and she could see how quickly the thirteen-year-old was aggravating his older sister.

"Stephan! Wait!" she snapped angrily and grabbed the platter away from him. As fast as order had seemed within grasp, Srenna saw one child undo it. She had been use to three small boys challenging her on occasional bad days, but nothing prepared her for this young teenage boy's open attempt to unsettle the mood they had all just been in. He kept looking directly at Srenna to see what effect he had on her with his rude behavior.

Srenna knew though that his actions were a deliberate attempt to unnerve her and she wasn't so sure it was his way of saying he would be the boss. She too began to get agitated with him and as she put Benji in his high chair, she was nearly ready to snap at Stephan as well. But instead, something rose up in her not in anger at all. She pulled herself up to her full five foot five, looked the boy straight in the eyes and calmly responded, "My rule for eager hands wanting to eat before everyone else is this. You'll be done first, so you'll be able to do more cleaning after." She fixed her gaze on the boy's startled face with a steady stare.

The girls were watching him with horrified looks waiting to see if he would defy Srenna, but before he could even think of a rebuttal to sputter back at his new governess, Srenna made herself sit down at the end of the table next to Benji's chair. She motioned to the rest to sit and they quickly and obediently did.

"Who would say grace tonight?" she asked scanning the table with a warm smile. Mary was trying hard not to smirk at Stephan with a vindictive, "You've been told" look on her face. Emma sat with her hands under the table so as not to suffer any remarks from anyone, but Lilly piped up eagerly, wanting very much to gain some, any, approval she could from Srenna.

"All right Lilly, go on," Srenna encouraged.

"God, thank you for this food," she began. "Thank you that we could fix it very good today. And thank you that Mary has help so she won't burn supper anymore, and Benji will stop crying all the time and Stephan will..."

"Amen!" Mary finished soundly and firmly. She gave her sister a threatening look, to which Lilly stuck out her tongue, and Emma chirped, "Amen." Srenna looked up and brought it all to a halt, including Stephan's preparation for some form of retort, with her own quick "Amen" and then "Let's eat, eh?"

She began passing the bowls and platter around the table but waited till they came back around to take any. As the food reached Mary, Srenna encouraged the girl to put some food on a plate for Matthew to eat later. The table was already painfully devoid of the loving parents that had probably surrounded the children each night with attention and conversation. But Matthew's absence set even a greater cloudy mood over the room and Srenna wanted very much to lighten it as the meal continued.

As she attempted to feed the baby some mashed up potatoes and peas. Srenna looked around the table at the solemn faces. Then suddenly she remembered the fight that the three Havilland boys had gotten into one night while their parents went out for the evening.

And Srenna began to giggle!

The children stared at her as though she were crazy. They looked at each other wondering what any of them had done that was so funny. Srenna stopped suddenly realizing they were staring wide eyed with great curiosity on their faces.

"I'm so sorry," she sputtered, trying to contain her self. "I wasn't laughing at you. I just remembered something very funny that happened at my other home, something very naughty the boys did."

Immediately Lilly questioned, "They did something naughty and it was funny?" She, along with everyone else, looked puzzled.

"Well it was naughty, but it ended up being hilarious," Srenna explained, beginning to chuckle again.

"What did they do?" asked little Emma, leaning close to the table to hopefully hear a story.

"Well...Henry, the youngest, threw a pea at Thomas, the middle one. Then Thomas got mad and threw bread and butter at him, only it hit William, the oldest. Then they all started throwing everything, except the cake in front of me." Srenna realized all eyes were on her now and she knew she would have to finish the story or suffer the consequences.

"What happened then?" asked Lilly with great excitement.

"Why I threw cake at them!" Srenna stated as a matter of fact, with a mischievous twinkle in her eyes. There was a collective gasp around the table and a look of disbelief on Stephan's face.

"You didn't!" Mary laughed.

"I did!" Srenna admitted levelly. "They were all so stunned they quite stopped and then began to cry."

"Were they sad?" Emma questioned.

"Oh very, I think, for you see, they got no cake for desert. I made them clean every last morsel of food off the floor and furniture and then…" she trailed off.

"And then what?" Lilly quizzed.

"And then they got a bath, all three of the little buggers and they went to bed," she started laughing again. To her delight the girls joined in. "I found peas in my hair for two days!" she added.

"Like you'll find in his?!" scoffed Stephan sarcastically, pointing a finger towards his baby brother.

Much to Srenna's dismay Benji had indeed smashed numerous peas into his blond baby hair and suddenly everyone started laughing at him and with him for the child knew he had done something funny. The young governess looked around the table and was grateful they had laughed at the story. Stephan had even laughed a little, though he tried hard not to let it be known. But even as Srenna excused herself from the table to clean Benji's hair she was still acutely aware of Matthew's absence and she was even more determined to speak to him before she retired for the night in this new home. She wasn't sure how or even what to say to him to reverse their shaky beginnings, but she had to try. As she bathed her brand new infant charge she thought of all the children and wondered how they had managed these last seven weeks without their mother or for that matter all the time their father had been gone.

Especially Matthew. Srenna had seen the broken heart of a young man barely out of childhood himself beg her at the top of the hill. Then she suddenly and vividly remembered the name on the sign over the gate posts, Shepherd's Gaze".

"Shepherd's Gaze," she whispered softly over the baby's clean hair. "You saw everything, didn't you Father?" she smiled. "Their shepherd, my shepherd. You've never taken your eyes off any of us, eh?" And then in a form of a plea Srenna lifted up her voice out loud, "Help me to show them you're still here." Her last words spoken made little Benji turn his face up to the stranger, this young woman who had drawn him in almost immediately just because of his base needs. He reached his chubby baby hands out to Srenna and she picked him up from the bathroom sink where she had just bathed him. She wrapped a clean towel around him and buried her face in his wet curls. He clung to her as though he had been all his eight months of life.

"You've already twisted me around those chubby little fingers haven't you, little beggar?" She playfully kissed his fingers and cuddled him as she walked to the bedroom and nursery.

Srenna dressed him quickly wanting to get back to help the children finish the supper mess, but before she had a chance to make it back into the kitchen the table had been cleared, the dishes started and Mary was looking quite pleased with the progress made already that day.

Srenna asked Lilly if she and Emma would play with Benji for just a while till he grew tired and both willingly accepted the challenge just to get out of clean up.

"And where is Stephan?" she asked, concerned with the absence of the boy who had tested her at supper. Srenna saw that it was already 8:00 and becoming dark outside.

Mary frowned and admittedly told Srenna, "He wouldn't help and I'm tired of fighting him. He went out, probably to the barn." The cloud of frustration came flying over the girl's countenance as quick as a summer storm, but Srenna wasn't about to lose any of the ground gained today. She squeezed the girl's shoulders once again and then picked up a dish to rinse and dry.

"She'll be right, Mary, one battle at a time is what my father always told me. And right now these dishes are our battleground," Srenna laughed remembering how her father would encourage her to not get overwhelmed when faced with a challenge or many of them at once. She looked around the kitchen at the children. Right now from where she was standing, four out of six Pattons safely in the house, fed, and happy was a battle won. She would deal with the other two Patton boys when the time was right.

Chapter 13: The End of a Day

The day had come to such a quick end as Srenna rocked the infant boy in her arms that she had barely enough time to even feel homesick or bewildered by all that had transpired upon her arrival at the Patton home. By 9:00 P.M. it was Lilly and Emma's bedtime and the baby was already showing signs of the need for sleep again. He had fussed on and off most of the evening everytime Srenna even hinted at putting him down or turning him over to Mary or the younger girls. She could only imagine what trauma the little boy had suffered unknowingly at the loss of his dear mother. There was no way to console the small child except to give in to his base needs and at that moment Srenna realized she would likely have to give in to him the most or the chaos she entered into would resume. She only hoped the other younger ones would be a little understanding and not all expect individual attention immediately. She who prided herself on facing any crisis was pushing away overwhelming feelings of the enormous task set in her lap earlier in the day.

Srenna's thoughts suddenly wrapped themselves around the image of the young man who had picked her up at the train station this morning, the young man who had fallen apart on the hill leading to the house after his painful confession, the young man whom she had angrily spoken too, and the young man who had refused to join them for her first supper with the children. As she held little Benji close to her and hummed a sweet lullaby to him she watched his eyes once again give way to exhaustion. But her mind wouldn't stay off of

Matthew and what he must be feeling wherever it was he had gone. She was sure he was avoiding her out of embarrassment, even hurt, his own hurt and grieving. Srenna wondered how this young nineteen-year-old had coped with the enormity of all the events that had occurred in this home over the last year or for that matter ever since his father had gone off to war. She had watched Grace Havilland deal with the departure of her husband to fight the war in the Pacific and many times had seen the toll their separation from each other was taking on Grace and the boys. But to be only a young teen and be faced with the strapping responsibilities of this family and a huge sheep station, Srenna couldn't even fathom. Again she felt her heart give way to her struggling mind wondering where he was and how she was going to minister to him let alone all the brothers and sisters he had. She uttered up another desperate prayer to God that she would be able to find a way to make amends with Matthew and start fresh and new with him tomorrow if she didn't see him tonight.

Finally satisfied that Benji could be laid down Srenna carefully stood and deposited the weary child into his crib. She gently brushed the top of his curly head and sighed deeply as she stood for a moment and watched him sleep. She hoped and prayed he would sleep well tonight as she began to feel her own fatigue creeping over her body and her own deep need to rest. However, she knew except by the grace of God she would probably not get much rest tonight as she realized she still needed to see what the other children were doing and how much more work she had to finish.

Srenna found her gifts for the children in her larger luggage and then crept silently from the room after pulling the doors closed to Benji's nursery. She found her way into the quiet kitchen where there were dishes everywhere on the counter and the drain board was full from earlier washing and from supper. To her relief they all appeared to be clean. She made a quick decision to leave everything right where it was and tackle putting them away tomorrow. She took one more look around the room to make sure she could leave it and realized that the plate made for Matthew was gone off of the stove and a bit of peace came over her that he had at least received his meal, however he may have gotten it. She suspected that Stephan or Mary had been involved in making sure their brother had eaten. Once she scanned the large room one more time Srenna headed back into the hallway and made her way to the stairwell leading upstairs. As of yet she had not even been upstairs to the bedrooms, but as she climbed the stairs she could hear the voices of the children coming from one room at the end of the hall. The door was partially closed so Srenna knocked quietly and waited for an answer.

"Come in, Miss James," she heard Mary's voice. Srenna pushed the door open and walked into what was obviously the younger girl's room. Mary and Lilly were sitting on Emma's bed, with the younger girl already tucked under the bedcovers. Lilly was leaning against Emma's pillow with her and Mary held a book in her hand attempting to hopefully persuade the youngster into slumber. But the minute Emma saw Srenna her head popped up and the five-year-old exclaimed to her sister in no uncertain terms, "I want the lady to read to us!"

"Oh dear, I'm afraid I've disturbed your wonderfully quiet and calm bedtime routine," Srenna apologized. "Maybe tomorrow night I can read to you."

But that idea was met with boisterous opposition from both girls especially when they saw Srenna bearing packages in her hands. Before Mary could chide either one of them Srenna quickly cut her off and responded, "I don't mind Mary, if you need a break." She handed the girl a small package and explained to her that she had brought her a little something from Sydney.

As Mary stood up and handed the young governess the book she took the gift in her hands and smiled knowingly at her. Still grinning, she answered Srenna, "I could use one, but..." she whispered to Srenna as she passed her, "I'm guessing you do too. And thank you so very much." She stood at the doorway for just a moment watching Srenna make her self comfortable on the bed next to the girls, giving them each a gift. She turned quickly to retreat from the room. Tears started to well up in her eyes as the image of her mother reading to the girls not so very long ago came slamming into her memories. She stood outside the room and listened to the expressive tones of Srenna's voice as she narrated the children's book to them much the same way her mum would have done. The tired, but relieved girl made her way into her bedroom and began preparing herself for a much needed night of rest. A vague hope came over her as she realized that they had fairly made it through the first day of the new governess, even if Matthew was somewhere sulking and feeling sorry about what he did.

Mary had known he was going to go through with it and that he didn't want to, but she also knew that none of them could go on much longer without badly needed help. She was glad now that he had. But she also knew that Srenna James could as easily leave them after she understood what she had gotten into. Mary heard the tone of voice the governess had used on her brother and for a fleeting moment she feared the worst. Then as suddenly as that thought crossed her mind another thought pushed it away.

Mum had prayed for an angel, right before she died; an angel for Matthew, an angel for all of them, someone to help him, to help Mary. From her room next door she could hear the sound of her little sisters laughing at the story Srenna was reading to them. If she wasn't the angel prayed for, Mary thought, she was the closest Mary had ever been to seeing one.

Srenna had only finished the book and closed its cover when Mary walked back through the door. The girls showed her the beautiful drawing paper and crayons Srenna had given them and begged to use them immediately. Both Emma and Lilly protested loudly when their sister and governess agreed on a resounding no, and Mary stopped them immediately knowing full well that everyone needed to call it a day. The girls whinged and complained, but as Lilly grudgingly climbed into her own bed, Srenna remembered the homemade card she had stuffed into her skirt pocket hours ago when she first arrived. "Why look at what I've found, "Srenna smiled as though she had found a treasure. "Now I wonder where this came from. I found it in my room," she added with an air of mystery in her voice.

"We made it!" exclaimed little Emma, nearly coming up off the bed again. But Srenna quickly leaned over the rambunctious child and hugged her dearly, kissing the top of her head as though she had been doing so forever.

"I thought maybe you did," Srenna laughed at her and looked over at Lilly just in time to see the older of the two get a, "Don't leave me out" look on her face.

"So did I!" came Lilly's retort.

Srenna moved over to the other bed and gave the nine-year-old an equally loving hug and kissed the top of her head as well. "I know!" she smiled at the frustrated sibling. "You both did an excellent job and the flowers are the most beautiful ones anyone has ever picked for me.

"We didn't pick them for you. Matthew did!" Emma proclaimed with a very proud look on her face that she had given away her big brother's gesture of kindness.

"He did, did he?" Srenna answered, surprised at this announcement. She gazed over at Mary who was leaning on the door post watching the scene.

"Most of the flowers in the vase are from the hillsides. Matthew used to pick them for Mum every day when he was little," Mary explained, once again trying not to let the tears take over.

"I'm glad you told me. I'll remember to thank him tomorrow. You've all made me feel very special today," Srenna offered, hoping to bring the close of the day to a much better end then when it had started. With that she told both girls good night and that she would be there in the morning when they woke up. She walked past Mary to the door and smiled at the young girl encouragingly as if to say, "I will be here in the morning." She then went down the stairs and let Mary say her good nights to the girls. In only a few minutes Mary came to the bottom of the stairs to say good night to her new caretaker and found Srenna trying to pick up a few of the articles strewn across the living room.

"Those can wait until tomorrow, unless you want me to help you now?" Mary offered. But the look on the girl's face gave her away and Srenna put the stuff on one of the chairs and turned to agree with the tired girl.

"You're right Mary, it can wait. But I do need to know if your younger brother is okay and in the house yet," she wondered out loud, remembering that the boy had gone out to the barn after supper. She had not seen him since.

"Yes, he's in his room. Has been for about an hour. Matthew brought him in," Mary reported.

"They're both in?" Srenna asked, wondering if they had slipped in while she put Benji to sleep. Her eyes went to the stairwell she had just come down and a strong urge filled her to go back up and try to reconcile with Matthew before turning in. "Maybe I should talk to your brother before going to bed. I really hate leaving things the way they were earlier when I got here." She looked at Mary for any sign of approval as she moved back towards the hallway.

But Mary dashed that idea when she answered Srenna in a soft, low voice, "He's not up there. His room is right there," she informed the young woman, as she nodded her head towards the shut door at the opposite end of the living room. Srenna stared at the door she had seen earlier this afternoon, wondering then what it led too. She still had her eyes on the door when Mary suggested quietly with a knowing tone of voice, "He's best left alone for awhile, when he gets like this," she whispered gently. "He's feeling pretty stupid right now and incredibly ashamed. It's not like him to lie or to hurt anyone deliberately. That's not Matthew's way," Mary said again in defense of her older brother. "He'll be sweet. Just give him some time."

Srenna turned her gaze back to Mary's face and saw such maturity on it, she knew at that moment she was not alone in this new endeavor, nor was Mary alone anymore in her day to day struggle to be mother to this orphaned little family. "I'll let it go tonight, Mary, even though I hate going to sleep with things unresolved. But I am glad you told me this about Matthew. I guess I can't blame him for being desperate enough to take care of all of you any way he had too." She smiled at the girl and gave her a hug and urged her to head upstairs to bed herself, to which the exhausted teenager gladly complied. As Mary walked back to the stairs, Srenna remembered the other gift she had brought for Stephan and asked Mary if she would leave it for him or give it to him before she went to sleep.

"I'm not at all sure about him either Mary," she admitted to the young girl. "He seems very angry." Srenna watched Mary's face for any sign of agreement. Her face immediately went from the happier expression of only a moment ago to the frustrated one earlier at the table. Srenna knew then that Stephan had probably been testing his sister's authority and position in the home since their mother's passing. Before the girl could answer Srenna offered a suggestion for both of them.

"Why don't we just kill them both...." she started with a mischievous look on her face. She added quickly, "with loving kindness!" She saw the look on the poor girl's face change from bewilderment to amusement when she realized that the new governess had a sense of humor. Mary liked that. Srenna was going to need it. She smiled and once again said good night.

But as soon as the girl had disappeared up the stairs Srenna found herself wondering, now that she knew where Matthew was, if the young man was asleep or sitting in his room thinking about all the events of the wearisome day. Part of her was still a bit upset at his tactics to get her here, but an even bigger part of her was painfully remembering her own deceptive attempt to arrange the course of her own tragic life.

Srenna uttered up a prayer of thanks that God had shown her more patience then she had shown Matthew today and resolved to find a way to make peace with him tomorrow. She suddenly felt so tired she could barely walk into what was now her bedroom, move her bags off to the floor and climb into the bed fully clothed. She had no idea how long Benji would sleep through the night, but she never finished that thought as her tired body succumbed to the comfort of the bed and it's covers and the incredible stillness that now hung over the house. Her mind was too tired to think any more about Matthew sleeping just across the living room from her or how he was feeling. The last thing she recalled was the mumbled prayer that escaped from her lips. Then the New Zealand quiet overcame her and she fell into a deep, dream-laced sleep.

Chapter 14: Srenna's Second Day

There was no seeing Matthew the next day either. Srenna got her prayer answered when the baby who had fussed so loudly for her the day before slept far longer then she could have ever hoped for. And so she slept. And so did the others, at least past the time their older brother left the house and stole away to the fields for the day. Srenna only woke when she heard Benji stirring in the little room attached to hers. At first he seemed as though he might simply wake up quietly, but when his first attempts to be known went unattended he let out his best and loudest eight month old cry of despair. It sent Srenna straight up out of the bed she had fallen into fully clothed the night before. She quickly stumbled to the child's crib and scooped him up, hoping that alone would calm him, but he seemed as disoriented as she was from the rude awakening. She knew if anyone had still been sleeping anywhere in the house they would surely be awake now, and probably hungry.

Her senses were being flooded with many thoughts as she laid the little boy on the layette table and began changing him. While he whimpered and cried Srenna tried consoling him and reassuring him he would have what he wanted as quickly as she could retrieve it from the kitchen. It crossed her mind briefly that she was still in the same outfit she had started out in early yesterday morning when leaving her hotel room in Wellington. "What a life time ago that was," she thought to herself as she completed the task of a wet diaper to a dry one while Benji kicked and fussed. She was feeling a bit fussy herself when a knock was heard on the bedroom door. She grabbed the boy up in her arms and without even thinking who it might be Srenna swung the door open quickly. Much to her relief, it was Mary, and she was holding the coveted and badly needed nursing bag in her hand.

"I heard him start fussing. I figured you were going to need this and soon," Mary smiled, still wearing her robe and noticing Srenna's disheveled clothes still on her body.

"Oh, Mary. You are an angel, dear! Thank you, thank you," Srenna gushed warmly, grabbing the nursing bag from the girl's hands and heading for the rocker. "Let's see if he will just take the milk...without any of me!" she chuckled, hoping she could bypass the procedure used the day before to feed the distraught infant. But it was not to be. The baby boy had found solace in Srenna's warm bosom and he was not to be interrupted anymore by anything in the world directly around him. Try as she might to slip the special nursing end to his hungry mouth he still required the assurance of her safe breasts. Srenna finally gave in to him to calm and quiet him and when he was ready she traded herself for the bottle. Once again he was perfectly happy to receive the sustenance she could not really give him. All the while Mary sat on the edge of the bed and watched the young woman she had known less then twenty four hours and marveled over the lengths to which Srenna would go to comfort her baby brother.

"I thought we'd never hear him stop crying. Thank you, Miss James!" Mary exclaimed with deep gratitude.

"Well, we did it together, Mary, but please, just one more thing," Srenna said with a grin on her face. "Please call me Srenna. Miss James makes me sound so...old and spinstery, eh?"

Both the girls giggled at this description of Srenna, but then Mary asked her in all seriousness."Do you mind me asking?" she started hesitantly, "Just how old are you?"

Srenna grinned again and shook her head at the oldest Patton sister as she looked down at the satisfied baby in her arms. "I don't mind and I'm just twenty-one."

Mary smiled back at Srenna and answered her with a bit of disgust in her voice, "I'm only sixteen, and I wish I was twenty-one." The pretty young girl looked frustrated about her age but Srenna wondered if it was really all the responsibility she had been given since the death of her mother. Srenna had to think the girl felt somewhat inadequate at times. She quickly assured the girl how hard it was for her most of the time and that Mrs. Havilland had been her greatest mentor and teacher for the last five years. "Do you like taking care of other people's children?" Mary asked hesitantly, not wanting to pry too much but at the same time wanting any sign whatsoever that this lovely young governess would not get disgruntled right away like the other governesses and leave. This question went unanswered as the sound of footsteps coming down the stairs from the hallway interrupted their conversation. Before either of the younger girls could burst through the bedroom door, Mary had reached it and stopped them with her finger to her lips.

"Shush, you, or you'll set Benji to wailing again!" Mary commanded in a loud whisper. She turned to Srenna and quietly suggested to her that she would start some breakfast and that they would all see her after she had a chance to use the bathroom and get dressed. Mary's tone of voice once again held a tinge of maturity that Srenna found reassuring in a way and very welcomed as the oldest sister took her younger sisters and herded them towards the kitchen.

Srenna leaned her head back for a moment looking around the room that had become hers overnight. The vase of flowers still graced her bedside stand and she remembered the girls telling her that Matthew had picked them from the fields she had seen as they drove in. They brought a smile to her face briefly. It was peaceful in this little alcove nursery and bedroom. There was no opulence here to be sure as there had been in the Havilland's distinguished townhouse in Sydney's elite neighborhood. But Srenna could feel the love that had been put into this room and the house itself as she moved around it yesterday. For the first time since she had arrived she had time to think about the mother and father who had shared this room together for many years and wondered how hard it was for the children to have a total stranger occupying it now. She knew Benji didn't mind, having only his immediate needs to be met, and Stephan....Stephan just seemed too defiant right now to care. Mary was obviously relieved to finally have help, and Matthew... she wasn't sure about. She wondered most about the little girls who were with Mary in the kitchen waiting for breakfast for yet another day without their mother. She knew that in many ways their needs were also base, but mixed with an ever present memory of their mum and all the things she did for them. Srenna had not needed to show so much affection to the Havilland boys as she had needed to just keep up with them day to day. But she resolved to show Emma and Lilly as much affection as either one of the little girls would allow, just as she had done with the much younger girls at the school. Everything else would have to fall into place, she thought as she peered into the blue eyes of her youngest charge. He was happy for the moment. He had fixed his gaze on Srenna again and looked at her as though memorizing the woman who had found a simple way to comfort him.

"What a beautiful little man you are," she cooed into his ear. "You and I are going to be fast friends then, eh?" As if understanding what the lady was whispering to him his little baby hand came up reaching for her face and Srenna kissed his fingers and pretended to bite them. Much to her delight the child actually giggled and it made Srenna's heart sing that he'd responded to her with some measure of joy in this house that had known so much suffering. As he finished the remnants of the goat's milk from the nursing bag, she began thinking about what the rest of the day would hold, remembering the piles of dishes in the kitchen, the piles of just plain stuff in the living room, and the endless piles of laundry found in the bathroom yesterday afternoon.

And she was dead sure she needed a bath. But when that would happen she did not know. However as soon as the bag was drained and Benji was burped, Srenna laid the youngster on her bed and pulled some fresh clothes from her biggest bag. "I might smell, but at least my clothes won't," she giggled, speaking to the small child who had already figured out how to roll and scoot across the bed towards the floor. She hurried as quickly as she could, grabbing him several times as he reached the edge and then plucking him up in her arms she sat down on the chair in front of the dressing table. One look in the mirror sent a groan from her lips and a disgruntled look on her face as she realized just how badly she was in need of a complete makeover. But she took a deep breath as she put Benji down on the rug at her feet and gave him something to play with for a moment. She pulled her hair out of the twist it had been in and rewound it behind her head in a rushed effort to simply get it out of the way. A few pins and one clip later and she felt much more ready to take on what ever met her outside the bedroom door; at least for now.

Srenna scooped Benji back up and headed for the kitchen. Mary had the girls setting at the table both engrossed in what appeared to be a bowl of hot cereal and toast. Mary was attempting to put some of the dishes away already when Srenna walked in, but as soon as she saw the new governess she reached her arms out to take Benji from her. "I can take him while you freshen up if you'd like," the boy's sister suggested, hoping the child would indeed come to her so Srenna could have at least enough time to wash and use the facilities. "Even if he cries a little," she added with some determination for Srenna's sake.

He did protest a bit, but Srenna desperately needed to let Mary hold him for just a little while. "All right; but I won't be long, no bath or anything like that. I'll just wash my face and try to get on with the rest of the day," she gladly agreed. As she spoke she moved slowly towards the door hoping Benji would not begin howling again as he had done several times last evening. But Mary distracted him with a piece of soft toast and the boy was engrossed with the morsel he'd been given long enough for Srenna to slip from the room. She made a dash for the bathroom and the solace of some fresh water. The large bathtub looked very enticing to her but instead she settled for slipping her clothes off and giving herself a hurried sink bath. Just splashing her face made her feel renewed and better. She tried not to be overwhelmed by the laundry in the room that she knew would eventually have to meet with a better washing then she had just gotten, but first things first, she told herself.

Srenna dressed back quickly into the slacks and blouse she had put on earlier and made one more check of her hair before returning to the kitchen. Mary had put Benji in his chair and he was busy playing with a wooden spoon she had given him, but the minute he saw Srenna his baby face began to screw up in a probable attempt to fuss again. "Oh no you don't little beggar," she laughed kissing the child's head and pulling his chair closer to the one she sat down in. Mary had set a plate of toast in front of Srenna with jam and offered to pour her governess a cup of tea. "Thank you Mary. I'll have tea this morning. Although…I thought I smelled coffee. I usually drink coffee first thing," Srenna explained.

"Alright then, coffee it is," said Mary turning back to the stove and reaching for another pot. Much to Srenna's surprise there was indeed coffee in the pot, hot and strong.

"Did you make this early this morning?" she asked remembering the lovely aroma being the first thing she smelled as she woke out of her sleep.

"Matthew did," Mary offered in a matter of fact tone. "Be careful. It will definitely get you going," she chuckled, watching the young woman's face as she sipped the dark drink.

"Indeed it might, Mary. Remind me to thank him for this too," Srenna smiled, thinking about the young man who had followed his routine this morning faithfully and had already gone out to work in the fields. As she ate a piece of toast and chatted with the girls about the days events, Srenna couldn't help but wonder what it was going to take to see Matthew and get things right with him. She really didn't want any more time to elapse before she spoke to him and apologized for being so hard on him the day before. "Did he eat before he left and by the way... where is Stephan?" asked Srenna suddenly, remembering the other boy she had tangled with yesterday.

Mary smiled at Srenna when the young woman changed gears so quickly and admitted without saying so that she had quite forgotten Stephan. "He's been gone for awhile too. Out in the barn doing his chores or at least he'd better be. He has to take care of all the other livestock, you know," she explained. "Matthew gets him up before he leaves to take the flocks out. Stephan does his chores in the morning around the barn and then goes out to help Matthew in the afternoon. He takes Matthew his lunch when he goes." Mary stopped to catch her breath as she tried to give Srenna as much information as she could.

"Really Mary. You all seem to have a very good schedule. I'm very glad to see how organized you really are," Srenna said, genuinely impressed.

"Mum and Dad always had us follow schedules when needed; especially during the school session. It's...just ...well…" the girl began, her voice breaking a little as it had several times yesterday. She turned towards the kitchen sink, averting Srenna's eyes and tried to compose herself.

Srenna got up quickly from her chair and went to the young girl and immediately put her arms around her, bringing the tears brimming in Mary's eyes to overflowing and spilling down the poor girl's face. For a moment Srenna forgot that there was anyone else in the room but Mary, but that notion was gone in a flash when she heard sniffling and quiet crying from behind her. Emma and Lilly had both begun to cry when they saw their big sister lose control and start weeping. Mary heard them too and immediately pulled herself together and broke free of Srenna's embrace. She and Srenna both took the girls into their arms and onto their laps, one each and tried to console and quiet their tears. Srenna had Emma on her lap but reached a hand out to Lilly's arm, comforting the older of the two.

"I'm sorry," Mary said remorsefully, still trying to keep her own tears in check.

"Don't be Mary. It's alright to cry. It's alright to feel sad sometimes; really," Srenna encouraged the girls. Little Benji sat seemingly dumbfounded that everyone but he was crying. The poor little boy looked at his sisters as if to ask what was wrong with everyone, but he sat perfectly still until tears were spent, at least this go-around. Srenna and Mary hugged the girls again. "Let's agree to cry when it's needed and then when we are done we'll do something great and wonderful to remember something happy about your Mum and Dad, eh?" she suggested. The girls surprisingly liked this idea and it seemed to bring a sudden shift in the mood everyone had been in only moments ago. Too help the matter, Benji gave a very loud smack on his tray with his spoon as if to say, "Okay!" This action literally brought a round of badly needed giggles from the girls and turned the conversation to what they would do special this morning. It was finally decided to make Mum's very best cookies, or at least try. "And," thought Mary to herself, it didn't hurt that they were Matthew's favorites as well. She decided at the moment to keep that bit of information to herself. But she knew it might go a long way in making him feel better. She too was beginning to worry about the way her brother was feeling and she hoped Srenna would indeed have a chance to speak to him before the day was over.

"You'll have to show me around, girls, how you do things, where you do your laundry and all, where everything belongs, especially..." she began with a whimsical look on her face, "all the things in the living room. When we're done mixing up the cookies we'll have a contest to see who has the most stuff and how fast the winner can put it away." Mary turned her head so the little girls couldn't se her grinning at the creative way this young but obviously seasoned young governess convinced them to engage in "picking up". Neither one even had time to realize that she had gotten them to agree to do so and they both began to discuss what they had left in the messy room and who was going to win. Srenna was pleased too, knowing full well the time would come soon enough when they would figure out her scheme. But for now they were both just happy to please her and win her attention any way they could.

Srenna found the rest of the morning to be quite a whirlwind as cookies were mixed and baked, items were retrieved from the next room and deposited in their perspective places, (winner being both girls), and lunch was made. She found some time to bathe Benji again, began sorting the endless piles of laundry and took a tour of the outside of the house. To her delight there was an outside shower on the back of the porch next to an old wringer washer. It was supplied with fresh rain water from the water tower behind the house, as she found out rain was in the forecast nearly every other day. Off the back of the house a short distance away was an out-house or "long-drop" as the New Zealanders called it. The decision had been made to leave it as more children came along over the years. However, plumbing ran into the shower, the bathroom inside, the kitchen sink and the washer all by a series of pipes that John Patton had designed himself from the water tower. She was highly impressed with the way the sheepherder had used God given commodities to make this rural home work a little more efficiently. But she also finally realized that limited electric had been wired to the house into the kitchen for the refrigerator, the stove, and a hot water boiler on the back porch, but not for lights or heat. There was no dryer save for the several rows of clothes line off the back of the house. There was clothes line along the end of the porch as well for rainy day hanging. This really didn't disappoint her though as she realized how much work she could do while being outside in the fresh air. And for Srenna that alone was a welcomed thought as she assessed the enormous amount of work she would have to do every day. The girls also proudly showed her the magnificent garden that they had all worked on earlier in the spring and was already yielding a harvest of vegetables and herbs for eating. She was informed once again that "Mani helped" and Srenna found herself still wondering who this incredible woman was that everyone kept referring to. She made a mental note to herself to ask Mary the details of this mystery person.

Stephan came in on cue ready for his lunch at noon and ready to go to the fields. His manner was still impatient and pressing, even though his first encounter with Srenna the day before had been challenged and did not go the way he had hoped. This time he wanted his lunch and he wanted to go. He badgered Mary with a great degree of pressure and Srenna could see immediately how the boy triggered his older sister to frustration. She had anticipated his behavior as the time approached his arrival from the barn and his chores and Srenna was willing to just get the boy his and Matthew's lunch bucket and let him go. She just wasn't ready yet to deal deeply with him. She had not ever had experience with a teenage boy and their quirks. David Havilland was only ten-years-old when she departed from Australia. So as of now she only wished to tolerate Stephan as much as she could until she felt more confident. He also appeared to only wish to tolerate her where his sustenance was concerned. He took the food and left without a thank you or any other acknowledgement. Srenna had thought she might ask him to tell his brother she wanted to see him later before supper but she completely forgot as the boy hurriedly ran out of the front door and made his escape on his horse. She pushed the idea of speaking to Matthew tonight into the back of her mind as she prepared to feed Benji, and the girls and then take on the second part of her day.

Srenna's afternoon went by nearly as fast as the morning with the exception of toting Benji around. The tired child went down for his routine nap after lunch and Srenna found herself desperately praying that he would sleep as long as he had the day before. She had the girls play with him as much as he would allow to wear him out and he was unable to resist drowsiness when Srenna fed him and laid him down. She stood over his crib for only a few moments before the little boy succumbed to weariness. Again she found herself being quickly attached to this beautiful little baby and she would have simply stood and watched him sleep if time and work would have allowed. But it did not and she felt the tug of chores overtake her as she remembered the enormous mountain of laundry waiting on the porch where she and Mary and the girls had deposited it.

Srenna slipped quietly from the bedroom and headed for the back side of the house. It was already 1:30 in the afternoon and she wanted to get some laundry done and hung in the bright afternoon sun. She had contemplated all morning how she would accomplish a hopeless looking task without becoming overwhelmed and in the end decided with Mary's help they would only do what they absolutely needed. Srenna had the girls sort their clothes and then pull out what they truly needed washed immediately, as well as the boys things and diapers and Benji's things. They were in bad need of clean linens, but Srenna chose enough to give them all a fresh set of towels and wash cloths. She would tackle bed clothes the next day if possible. All in all, this plan still afforded her and Mary three piles of clothes to be washed and hung during the afternoon.

She kept in the back of her mind to also decide on supper ... and soon. Earlier that morning while helping Mary put the rest of the dishes away Srenna had mentally assessed the provisions again both in the pantry and the icebox. A trip to the market was needed in the near future but she did find a good stock of basic staples needed for meals. She wanted to involve the older Patton girl in every way she could to meet the needs of her brothers and sisters and she was already realizing that their lifestyle and customs were a bit different from the ones she knew in Australia. Mary suggested something easy like a stew or soup over what she called a "hangi" or the outside fireplace. It was a wonderful stone fireplace only a dozen or so feet away from the back of the house, down wind from the clothes lines and near enough for them to watch as their pot of soup cooked. Underneath the stone ledge where a pot could be hung over hot coals was the actual "hangi", a pit under the coals where food was placed in a cast iron container, buried and steamed for several hours. Srenna immediately found great enjoyment in this brand new method of cooking that had really only been used back home in Sydney for holidays and picnics. She found out from Mary though that this mode of cooking outdoors was very common and practical for the warmer months in New Zealand. She looked forward to becoming more adept to using it.

The chores were moving along fairly well while Srenna washed clothes and Mary hung them. She had Lilly and Emma pull carrots right after lunch and washed more potatoes in a bucket of water. The girls seemed to enjoy helping but Srenna wanted to see them play as well, so when they were finished with there contribution to supper she sent them off to play for awhile. She looked at Mary for some idea as to where the girls were allowed to wonder. "They can be around the house and no farther then the line of trees behind it," she explained to Srenna pointing to a grove of trees a hundred feet or so behind the house. "The river is just beyond those trees and they're not allowed to go there by themselves. They're not allowed to go to the barn alone either, except Lilly can go get the boys if they are there. We walk sometimes to the low fields to take Matthew his lunch or for picnics. But even then they have to stay with one of us. Lilly can go to the chookpen with Emma but it's just off the drive between the house and the barn. Did you see it yesterday when you came in?" Mary asked her.

"Yes I did. I'm glad Lilly and Emma can be such helpers. I don't think I'll be very good with the chooks, getting eggs and all," she chuckled, shivering a bit at the thought of tackling the fowls for their bounty. She remembered too, yesterday, that Stephan had been the one referred to concerning the gratefully prepared frying chickens in the icebox. She felt another chill come over her at the horrid thought of having to kill or even clean a chook or chicken before preparing it for their meal.

Mary watched her new governess squirm a little thinking about some of the challenges that were upon her in this unfamiliar land. She wanted to reassure her quickly before she had time to think of a million reasons to take flight and leave. She hurriedly added to the overview she had been giving Srenna. "Stephan is responsible for the chooks. He'll take care of getting them for you. He and Matthew also hunt and fish every week, especially Matthew when he's in the fields. We eat fish and lamb, of course and beef we get from the Rainga's station. They have both sheep and some cattle. Irmani and Jimmie make sure we have what we need."

"There's that name again, Mary. I've heard Irmani spoken of several times now. Who is this incredible person? And what an unusual name," Srenna finally asked, wondering since she arrived yesterday who this mysterious person was.

"Jimmie and Irmani Rainga. They have the station next to ours. They were Mum and Dad's best friends ever. We've known them all our lives, ever since our parents moved here from England," the young girl explained. She hesitated as she took another load of clothes from Srenna and headed to the clothes line. Srenna followed her, wanting very much to know more about the person that must be the nearest woman around the area, and the woman who had apparently been attempting to care for this brood of orphans since their mother had become ill and passed away. Her curiosity was getting the best of her as she drilled Mary for more details.

"Rainga. What kind of name is that Mary?" she asked with genuine innocence.

It's Maori. They are native islanders. I think you'll like Irmani, even though she is a bit raw, as Mum would put it," Mary explained. She watched Srenna's face to see how the refined city girl would react to learning that a big part of this family's life was the couple on the next fields over. And that they were not "Pakeha" which meant they were not "white".

Srenna was even more excited though to meet this family who were the closest neighbors and badly needed allies in helping Matthew and his desperately young and parentless family. "Do you think I'll be able to meet her soon?" she asked with real interest. Mary was relieved to hear the excitement in Srenna's voice and she smiled at her caretaker knowing now that city girl was obviously not prejudice or judgmental about people being different.

"I can call Irmani and tell her to come over this week if you'd like. She's dying to meet you too. She wanted to give you a few days to get your bearings and all. She can seem a little, um …aggresive at first. She means well and all. She's got eight children of her own, and she knows a lot about being a mother," Mary described.

"Eight children! How does she do it?" Srenna exclaimed. She was beginning to get an impression of some tremendous woman of great wisdom and experience. She wondered now if she would welcome the woman in the house or run and hide the first time she met her. Srenna was painfully aware of her great shortcomings in age and maturity where this outstanding Maori woman was concerned.

"Don't worry. The Maoris stopped eating the white folks a long time ago," the girl laughed, but she saw immediately that the joke fell on unknowing ears and the look on Srenna's face made Mary laugh even harder. "I'm sorry, Srenna, I'm just pulling your leg, eh?" Mary giggled. Srenna tried to laugh at Mary's attempt to lighten the moment. "Actually, Irmani is a midwife. She pretty much brought all of us into the world, starting with Matthew. She's also a nurse."

Srenna found that thought to be a reassuring one about the native woman and once again she felt a desire to meet the one that had so influenced the lives of the dear children she was trying to learn more about. She knew now that the Maori woman would probably be one of her greatest allies in taking care of the children the best way possible. "Will you call her tomorrow and ask her to come for tea as soon as possible? I really do want to meet her," Srenna admitted feeling a bit of relief concerning this neighbor.

All laundry finally hanging in the warm spring sun gave Srenna and Mary a much needed break from the long morning and equally long afternoon. They sat down for a short while to discuss plans for the next day and watched Lilly and Emma playing in the grass under a small tree with their dolls. But Srenna's break was short indeed when she heard the distant sound of an awakening baby and knew that once more he was in great stress not knowing where everyone was and why they weren't coming to his aid immediately. She told Mary to stay put and watch the girls and the soup on the hangi fire. She rushed to get the milk warmed and bag filled as quickly as she could. When she walked into the room Benji was peering through the slats of his bed whimpering as though his little heart was about to break.

"Oh, you poor dear. So neglected and lonely," she cooed at the boy. She scooped him up into her arms and hugged the boy kissing the side of his cheeks and consoling him, "You're alright, eh? Not too hungry I'll bet," Srenna chuckled as she changed him quickly and more efficiently as he seemed more content that she had even come to his rescue. He actually stopped his fussing for a few moments while Srenna pulled his outfit back on and headed out the door with him. But when she did not immediately offer him the milk as she had done several times he began screwing up his little face in an awful promise to howl to the whole world. "Just another minute or two, you. We'll go outside and do this," she explained to the distraught child. She hurried to the chair next to Mary and sat down, holding the bottle up to Benji's lips in a grand attempt again to get him to suck the bottle only. But again the hungry infant remembered all too well the bond of nursing and proceeded to fuss and fumble. Srenna was only a little frustrated but twice as understanding that the child couldn't be weaned all at once from something he had known for nearly eight months. She willingly gave in to him once more but within only moments he had latched onto the nursing bag instead of Srenna, giving her some hope that at least the process was going as was planned and really better then expected. He was calm and happy. That's what mattered.

"I'll get the girls to help me finish up supper," Mary offered, "They can get the table ready. It's nearly five. The boys will be back soon." With that the young girl walked to the tree where her sisters were still playing and asked them to come with her. They were reluctant to quit, but they both looked at Srenna to see what her reaction would be if they did not obey their sister. Srenna saw their look and smiled at both of them. She called to them to come over to her chair.

"I have a very special assignment for you both," she whispered to them as though she were about to give them a great secret mission. The girls leaned into her chair to hear what it was they were about to be asked to do as if it was indeed a wonderful request. Srenna continued to whisper in a low soft voice. "I want you to help Mary find the prettiest plate or bowl to put our lovely cookies on for Matthew and Stephan when they come for supper. Then take a sheet of your drawing paper I brought you from Sydney and color it any way you want and we'll give each of them a beautiful place mat you both made."

"Why do they get a place mat?" asked Emma, with a puzzled look on her face.

"Why.... because they've been gone all day and we missed them, eh?" Srenna offered, hoping this was all the reason she needed to engage the five year old again in some work and make it seem like play. It seemed to do the trick and in no time at all the girls had gotten the drawing paper Srenna gave them yesterday and busied them selves with coloring for awhile. Mary pulled the hot soup off of the hook over the pit and carried it into the kitchen to keep it warm. She got out several of her mother's favorite plates for the cookies and let the little girls pick the one they wanted to use. She placed the cookies on the table in front of them, with the plate and told the girls they could arrange them onto the plate any way they wanted. It made her happy to see the girls enjoy helping as they had their mother many, many times. Srenna had come in with Benji and sat down at the table, watching Mary interact with her sisters much like any mother would her children and again she was pleased that Mary seemed so mature and capable. But she also made a mental note to find out what kinds of things were important to the just sixteen-year-old girl. Srenna wanted her to be less and less pressured to do so much around the house especially since the teenager would need to go back to school along with Stephan, Lilly and Emma in February when it started again.

The supper hour came quickly and Srenna found herself feeling a bit of angst about Matthew coming home. She had mulled over in her mind what she wanted to say to him and how she would get him alone for a few minutes to do it. But all that was for naught, since he once more decided to evade her presence by staying out to do more work. Stephan almost seemed to take delight in telling the young governess that his brother would not be in for the evening meal that night as well.

Srenna almost was unwilling to except this answer when she saw the devastated look on Lilly and Emma's face that he was not eating with them again. But she knew too that even as her anger with Matthew seemed fueled by his distancing of himself that it would not be good for her to engage him for awhile. She desperately tried to salvage the evening meal by having the girls make a beautiful plate for him with an extra bunch of cookies on the side. She assured them that their brother would be very proud of their accomplishments today and they could tell him tomorrow.

She didn't tell them, any of them, that she fully intended to find him tomorrow and confront him, even if it meant climbing the mountainside to the fields he would be in. She was beginning to find his behavior to be slightly childish. And she could see how his absence was truly affecting the girls who needed him to be there. She resolved herself to find some way to bring this to a head and one way or another get it reconciled.

Supper over and clean-up almost finished, Srenna sent Mary out to take down the dry clothes. Lilly went with her and Emma stayed in to play with Benji. Srenna could tell that the youngest Patton sister was very attached to her older sibling when she began asking Srenna why she couldn't go outside with Lilly and Mary. The truth was Srenna wanted to see just how independent little Emma could be on her own and without clinging constantly to Lilly. She remembered that Matthew had told her yesterday on the way to Castlepoint from the train station that Emma was struggling with not being the baby anymore. She watched the child watch the door for the return of her big sister of nine-years-old and knew full well it was Lilly who was keeping Emma in check since the tragedy of their mother's death. Srenna realized as well that this child of only five years had probably not ever had a chance to really know her father before he went off to war. She would have been barely one when he left.

This revelation, as she looked at the beautiful curly headed child made her aware even more of the role that Matthew Patton had been playing in this family for the last four years of his life. Srenna found herself feeling almost guilty for being angry with him again when she thought of all the responsibilities he had had to face as only a teenager. The idea of his desperation to find help made her remember her own desperation to do what ever it took to stay in Sydney.

"Oh bloody rubbish," she mumbled under her breath, frustrated and confused as to what to do. Her thoughts were quickly snapped back into the large kitchen at the tug on her apron and the sound of a small voice.

"Are you angry at us?" came the little whisper at her side.

Srenna looked down into the big round blue eyes of the child who had cried in her arms earlier that morning. She immediately felt remorse for having been angry with Matthew at all. "They are all suffering," she heard that still small voice, even smaller then the baby voice beside her. She knew now she had to rely totally on God to tell her how to make things right with the young man and not just go off to confront him.

She suddenly felt the tug again of the little girl's hand in hers and scooping her up in her arms, Srenna smothered the child with kisses laughing at her till she giggled. "Of course I'm not angry with you. She's sweet. I'm....I just missed your big brother at the table tonight, eh?" Srenna answered her honestly. Emma put her head down on Srenna's shoulder and put her arms around her new governess' neck. She clung to Srenna so tightly that for a few moments neither wanted to let go of the hug, until the whimpers of a jealous baby were heard at Srenna's feet.

Srenna looked down at the sound coming from directly below her and felt Benji pulling at her slacks. He was on his knees and bouncing up and down as if to say, "Me too, me too!" Both Srenna and Emma began laughing again. "Whatever am I to do with you two? I need four arms to hug you both at the same time!" she exclaimed while sitting the five-year-old on her feet and squatting to pick up the infant who was beginning to show much more disapproval of Srenna's attention for his sister. Srenna dropped to her knees and holding Benji in one arm she drew Emma back into the other one. She breathed into the little girl's ear, "Can you give your baby brother a hug? He really needs to know you love him and you will take care of him. After all, you're such a big girl now and such a good helper," Srenna encouraged the small child.

This seemed to placate Emma to the greatest degree, for she squeezed Benji and Srenna with all her might and answered soundly, "Yes, I am a good helper. Even if Lilly says I'm not!"

"What did Lilly say, you?" came a resounding question to that, as Lilly came through the kitchen door with Mary and the laundry. Her face was screwed up ready for a thorough sticking out of her tongue at her younger sibling, but Srenna gave her a look to discourage her, and since Lilly wanted to please the young woman nearly as much as her sometimes annoying baby sister did she reluctantly complied. She did however have a look of being left out that made Srenna laugh and open up her arm around Emma to welcome the other Patton youngster into her embrace.

"I'm going to have to ask God to grow more arms out of my body if I'm going to hug all of you at the same time," she giggled just before they all went tumbling. She glanced desperately at Mary for help as she struggled to get up and the teenager reached first for Benji and then ordered her sisters to get up and off of Srenna, trying not to start laughing herself at the pile of arms and legs on the kitchen floor. Benji decided he did not like all this sharing of his caregiver and continued to fuss until Srenna realized how late it was getting for the infant. "Mary, I'd better get him settled down for the night." She promised the younger ones she'd be up to hear their prayers and tuck them in as soon as she had Benji down and went straight way to the bedroom with the infant, his evening bottle in hand.

As Srenna prepared the boy for the evening she went back over the events of the day, assessing what had been accomplished on only her second day in this busy home. She made a mental note of what went well and also what would need more attention, especially in lieu of the girls earlier display of grief. It was bound to come out, she told herself. They would get more comfortable with her as the days went by and there were going to be rough days. All in all she was not too disappointed with what had taken place already, in spite of her dilemma with Matthew and her sureness that Stephan thoroughly hated her being there. But just as yesterday when she resolved herself to be content with some progress, Srenna resigned the day to be a good one after all, even though it was not quite over.

Benji fell asleep at Srenna's bosom again, only half finishing the bag of goat's milk this time and relaxing quickly after a hard evening of playing with his sisters. She was very glad he went to sleep so fast. She was really beginning to feel the weight of the last two days on her body, and it seemed a life time ago that she had bathed or spent any personal time of any quality. She knew sometime tomorrow no matter what she would desperately need to take a bath and wash her long hair. If not she was certain they all might want to send her back. But that thought suddenly made her realize that even as she had not taken one, neither apparently had the rest of them for the two days she'd been there. Something made her wonder how often the beautiful claw tooth tub in the bathroom really got used, especially when Srenna remembered the shower on the back porch. She registered this in her mental notes as well to ask Mary what their bathing routine was after all, especially a family of their size.

Benji down and sleeping well, Srenna slipped from the bedroom quietly, barely breathing so as not to disturb him at all and headed to the second floor and the girl's room. Mary was with them attempting to read to them but once again at the sight of Srenna both girls squirmed and begged the young governess to take over. Srenna watched Mary to see if the older girl was offended by her sister's request but she saw a look of relief on the teens face, and Srenna knew that many a night it had been her responsibility to put the young ones to bed. "Go on Mary, do whatever you want or need to do for yourself. I can get them settled," Srenna offered her young helper. Mary hesitated for a moment until Srenna looked at her with a look of insistence and then thanked Srenna silently. She left quickly and headed for her own room to prepare for bed.

One story, two prayers and two hugs and kisses later, Srenna insisted the girls quiet down and go to sleep. She knew if she didn't keep somewhat of a schedule for them as Miriam Patton must have with this large brood, that she would lose control of everything in a heartbeat. But the girls were tired and really didn't give her too much fuss when she turned down the lamp and closed the door halfway. She stepped into the hallway just in time to see Stephan walking into his room, and for a moment she thought she might go to his door and see if there was anything the thirteen-year-old needed. Her hesitation gave him time to close his door though and she found herself even a bit intimidated in knocking at it to speak to him. None the less she took a deep breath and walked up to it knowing that sooner or later she would have to deal with him just as much as dealing with his older brother. She knocked lightly on the door, waiting with held breath for the teenage boy to respond. She heard only a "What?" gruffly flung at the door from across the room.

"It's only me, Stephan. Srenna. I was only wondering if you needed anything before you went to bed?" she asked gently against the closed door.

"NO! Nothing!" he announced with a resounding response.

Srenna bit her tongue as she felt the frustration with this Patton boy bubbling up in her. She composed her voice before answering the belligerent youth. "All right then. I'll see you in the morning for breakfast. Good night," she finished as sweetly as she could muster herself to do. She walked away from his door and glanced at Mary's but saw neither lamp burning or door closed and thought perhaps the girl had indeed snuck downstairs to use the bathroom before bed. Srenna wondered too if Matthew had come in from the pens and barn and whatever he had busied himself with again tonight, but she was far too tired once again to confront him or deal with him before going to bed. She knew Stephan had snuck his plate out to him at Mary's prompting and had let it go one more time.

She had just hit the bottom step when Mary appeared in front of her with a hand full of towels and wash cloths. She was coming from the direction of the kitchen where they had left the laundry, and Srenna was puzzled at the girls next statement. "Here, you'll need these," Mary smiled, looking towards the bathroom door. From inside Srenna could hear running water and she suddenly felt her heart lighten as she realized exactly what Mary had been doing while Srenna was retiring the girls to bed.

"Oh, Mary, what did you do?" she gushed as she made her way to the door. There in the tub was lovely hot water and more running into it as they spoke.

"You'd better hurry before it runs over. I'll see you in the morning." And with that and a quick hug the girl walked out. Srenna stood there for a moment and watched the tub filling up with wonderful hot water, much to the thanks of John Patton's ingenuity and the magnificent boiler outside. She turned the faucet off and quickly made her way back to her room to retrieve her robe and toiletries. As soon as she returned, locking the door behind her, she peeled off her clothes and sank into the delightful water slowly and gratefully. For as long as she could she sat under the warmth of the water and allowed it to soak away every frustration, every challenge she had met in the last few days and every one she knew she would have in the next few weeks. Nothing else mattered right now except the healing warmth of the bath and its soothing calmness. She found herself uttering up thankful prayers that this country home she had found herself in was not all that back country or rustic. She also found herself lifting up prayers for each one of the children as she relaxed and enjoyed her short luxury. But most of all she found herself still wanting very much to know how and when she could reach Matthew, start fresh with him and how she was ever going to meet his needs as the head of this household. All these thoughts started to overwhelm her again, until she heard HIS voice, again. The same thing she had been hearing for five years now. The same lesson she was learning over and over and over. "I will keep him in perfect peace, whose mind is stayed upon Me because he trusts in Me."

It was the last thing she remembered even as she dozed off later in bed, clean, happy and ready to take on whatever the next day offered.

She could only imagine what that would be.

Chapter 15: More Honey

Any hopes of any more laundry being done the next morning were dashed when Srenna rolled over and heard the clamoring sound of rain drops beating against the window at the end of her bed. She rolled back to the wall and wondered if she might actually be able to sleep a bit longer as no sound was coming from the baby's crib. Neither were there any sounds any where in the house that she could tell. It was hard to judge the time of hour due to the overcast conditions outside but suddenly she did hear the distinct bark of dogs and that sound made her jump up quickly and leave her room to look out the window in the front room. There, just leaving the barn fully enveloped in a rain slicker was Matthew's undeniable six foot frame. The happy border collies were delighted by the rainfall and Matthew followed behind them leading his horse, Samson, as though the weather neither discouraged him or stopped him from his daily routine. Srenna watched him as he disappeared into the sheep pens.

She was, however, discouraged, realizing she would not have the opportunity to speak to the young man, again, possibly until later in the evening. She turned from the window with a disgruntled look on her face and nearly ran into Mary, whom she had not heard coming into the room. "Mary! You startled me. I didn't think anyone was awake yet," she gasped at the girl. Mary smiled at her as though she knew what had been going through Srenna's mind as she watched Matthew leave.

"He'll be taking the sheep up into the foothills. There are more trees up there. Some protection from the rain then down here in the valley," Mary explained. She saw a look of genuine concern on the young woman's face concerning her brother, as Srenna looked back at the window and then listened to the rain pelting the house. "Don't worry about Matthew. He's use to the rain. He's got all kinds of little lean-to's on the mountainside to keep him dry. Besides, "she began to add, "This never lasts very long around here. We've actually been very lucky it hasn't rained before this. It will probably stop before lunch time."

The girl smiled reassuringly at Srenna and then looked at her standing there in her nightdress. She quickly added, "Stephan, however, has not left yet and may be down any second."

Srenna looked down at her nightgown and suddenly blushed just a little standing there without a robe. At the same time both girls heard the unmistakable whimper of a waking baby and Srenna moved towards the bedroom door immediately. "I'll just grab my robe and go get his milk, then," she suggested.

But Mary waved her on telling her she would get it and bring the bottle in to Srenna. Once again Srenna smiled at Benji's sister and how willingly she assisted with everything concerning her baby brother.

Srenna stepped into the room and met the gaze of a fully wakened infant letting the world know he had joined it from his peaceful slumber. But his peace was short lived when Srenna stopped to pull her night dress off over head and slip a pair of slacks on and a blouse as quickly as she could grab them from the wardrobe. He wanted her attention immediately, but she knew she could not appease him in her night clothes. He finally sat back on his little baby bottom and began to cry as though he had been abandoned, and Srenna rushed to his crib to pluck him up and console him.

"We are going to have to do something about weaning you and very soon," she fussed over the child as she changed his wet diaper and then settled into the rocker with him. As soon as he knew he could nurse he quieted. But already Srenna could tell he had figured out the routine and in only a moment he was fussing again for milk, something she could not give him. She wondered what was taking Mary so long and tried to get the frustrated infant to suck for just a few more minutes. But it was no use. Fortunately Mary came rushing in with the nursing bag and glorious goat's milk and as soon as it was slipped between Srenna's breasts the boy rooted and latched onto it. He fussed for a little bit, letting both girls know he was not to be reckoned with or fooled. "He's on to me Mary. The little beggar is too smart. I think it might be time to simply expect him to take this and not me anymore. I think he already knows I'm going to be here when he needs me."

"Are you …going to be here?" the boy's sister asked, looking at the governess holding her brother dearly. The expression on Mary's face, the tears brimming her blue eyes again, made Srenna want to put Benji down and take his sister in her arms instead. Srenna felt the tears well up in her own eyes as she reached her hand out to the young girl and motioned to her to come to the rocking chair.

"Mary…Dear Mary. Of course I'm going to be here. Do you really think I could leave now?" she exclaimed. "Why, you've all quite snagged me, eh?" she laughed as she grabbed the girl's hand and pulled her onto the floor in front of the rocker. "That is …at least you girls and this little one. I ….. I just am so frustrated with your brothers, especially Matthew," she added.

"Maybe you could go talk to him. When it stops raining," Mary suggested, looking hopefully at the governess she was already beginning to love and admire. "I know if you'd just talk to him you'd find out how Matthew really is. It's just….he's had so much, so many things, and the sheep shearing is soon and then the lamb cutting,….."

"I don't know what all that means, Mary," Srenna cut her off. "But I believe you about your brother. I believe he has the weight of the world on his shoulders and has had for a very long time."

Srenna sighed deeply and looked towards the window in the direction she had seen Matthew go this morning. Then she looked back at Mary. "Do you think Stephan would take me to him when it stops raining later, on his horse?" Srenna asked hesitantly.

"Do you know how to ride?" Mary returned, sure this city bred woman would say no.

"Actually, I use to ride all the time when I was a little girl, but it has been a long time since then," Srenna chuckled. "It's going to take awhile for me to remember those days. Better I ride with Stephan if he promises not to buck me off."

"I'll ask him for you, tell him he has too, eh?" said the teenager. A look of determination came over her face where her thirteen-year-old brother was concerned. She would take delight in telling him what to do and then making him do it; especially if it meant bringing Matthew back into the house in the evening.

"All right then, but be gracious to Stephan, you know, not too bossy. I want to be in one piece when I get up there," Srenna joked, even though deep down inside she was a bit nervous about the thought of submitting herself to a ride up the hillside on the back of Stephan's horse and then confronting Matthew as well. But it had to be, she told herself. It was day three and far too much time had transpired since she'd got there. She wanted things settled one way or another.

Then, suddenly, Srenna had a thought. She had brought gifts for each of the Patton children from Australia, something to show a gesture of caring for them. At least the ones she knew about. She realized that because she had not known about Matthew she had not brought anything for him. She looked up from the contented baby in her arms who was just happy to have safe arms and warm milk to nourish him. The girls were easily pleased, and even Stephan had had his base needs met in the last two days even if he was testing everyone. But Matthew, she wondered, what did Matthew need. She looked at Mary who was still sitting on her knees at Srenna's feet. "Mary, what does your brother like to do? I don't mean what does he have to do, but what does he love doing when and if he has time?" she inquired of his sister.

"Well..." Mary thought for only a second, "that's not hard at all. Matthew spends so much time out there by himself and only the dogs and sheep around him...he's always got a book with him. He loves to read. And he probably will kill me for telling you this, but....." the girl hesitated.

"What Mary? I need something to make amends with your brother. You know the old saying, "You can catch more flies with honey?" Srenna begged.

"Yes. Well... Matthew loves to write. He's been writing since he was old enough to hold a pencil," she confessed. "He' got all kinds of journals and poems and...don't tell him I told you about the poetry, all right," his sister grinned.

"It will be our secret. But I think you just might have given me the ammunition I need to butter up your brother," Srenna grinned back. They both seemed very pleased that maybe by the end of the day Matthew would be back at the supper table and over his misery where Srenna was concerned.

Just about then any peace in the house was broken when yelling and fighting could be heard from somewhere upstairs. Both Srenna and Mary recognized the anguished crying of Emma and Mary stood quickly and moved to the bedroom door. Benji was nearly finished with his milk and Srenna stood to follow Mary, but before she could reach the door the distraught and brokenhearted five year old came through the door and running into Srenna. From beyond the door she could hear Mary raising her voice distinctively at her younger brother who had apparently already started his provocations on his sisters that morning. Srenna glanced over at the clock on the dresser and was aghast that it was only seven o'clock.

It was going to be another long day!

Mary had no luck in solving the sibling disturbance and Srenna seemed to have little or not much more affect on the boy who had been teasing his baby sister relentlessly about being a baby sucking her thumb. He had actually pulled it out of her mouth, to which Lilly threatened to slug him soundly, which in turn brought more threats from him and led Emma in her descent down the stairs wailing. Mary tried to stop her and when unsuccessful, continued up the stairs and threw herself into the infraction. In the end, before Srenna could peel Emma off of her, place Benji on the floor and order Emma to watch him and then begin the climb up the stairs, Stephan had already decided he was finished with his morning disruption and nearly knocked her over on his way down the stairs. He stopped at the front door only long enough to screw up his face at Emma, stick out his tongue at her and snap, "Baby!" one more time before disappearing through the door and out into the rain. It all happened so fast that Srenna nearly ran after him just out of anger, but Emma began crying again, and Benji joined suit simply because someone else was crying.

Srenna scooped up Emma in her arms and looked down at the baby trying desperately to pull himself up her leg. Mary came into the room looking discouraged and near tears herself, but she immediately took Emma from Srenna's arms and forced a smile. "I'll take her and you get him," she suggested, trying to salvage some measure of peace and plans they had both just shared.

"Where is Lilly?" Srenna asked the discouraged girl.

"She's sweet. Just angry, that's all. She can't stand it when Stephan picks on Emma. She's the only one can do that," Mary answered trying to lighten the distressful moment.

"All right, then. Let's keep our focus on what we planned, in spite of this…this, whatever this was," Srenna said with great determination. "We need your brother back in this house, and I need Stephan to help me."

"He'll be hungry soon enough, especially since he didn't get breakfast. Why don't we make an extra special lunch for both of them. You know…..more honey, eh?" the bright girl suggested, winking at Srenna and grinning mischievously.

"Now you're getting it, Mary," Srenna smiled, grinning at Emma and kissing the youngster on her tearful cheek. "Let's get this day started the right way. We have some work to do."

As it turned out Mary was exactly right about the rain and Srenna learned her first lesson concerning the fickle New Zealand weather. Before the morning was even half over the rain had ceased, the sun came out and a light breeze was blowing the grass and trees dry. By mid morning Srenna, who had heeded the girls prodding, had finished two more loads of clothes and had them ready for the lines. She was delighted when the rain stopped and the sun lent its bright warmth to dry the clothes. Mary kept the girls up on the porch playing while she hung line after line of clean garments, diapers, and anything else that had been dirty. Srenna busied herself in the kitchen preparing some beef to slice for the boys' "special" lunch. It was decided that a true picnic lunch would be prepared with all the trimmings, including more of the cookies baked the day before. Srenna even set a kettle of spiced ice tea with lemons to brew to take for their drink when she found out how much Matthew loved tea.

She let Benji crawl around the floor with some toys to play with while she worked. Already the eight month old infant was moving about with great ease and speed and several times she plucked him up and away from this and that as the inquisitive child explored the confines of the kitchen. He could hear the girls outside on the back porch and was determined to see what they were doing. After only a short hour of wrestling with his adventurous baby's curiosity she tried putting him in the high chair and giving him some pieces of bananas. This satisfied him for roughly ten minutes. She laughed at the blond headed boy when he displayed such stubbornness to still figure out what his sisters were doing without him. Finally, Srenna opened the back door and dragged the child, chair and all out onto the porch.

"He misses his sisters!" she laughed, exasperated with the child and at the same time happy to see how much he wanted to interact with Emma and Lilly. They were gladly willing to entertain him, at least for awhile, much to both Srenna and Mary's delight. She left the door open to keep a watchful eye on everyone and proceeded with her work. She had also hoped this morning to take a real assessment of the food and staples in the pantry and Frigidaire. There was some concern as to when a trip would have to be made to the market, where it was and how she would get there. She had driven a little while living and working for the Havilland's. But the thought of driving the truck that Matthew had picked her up in was a little intimidating. None the less it would either have to be her or Matthew, she thought to herself, since she was sure Mary was not driving yet.

Things were not so bad though as she took stock of the food and items in the fridge. A few more days would be alright. She wanted to keep her mind focused on her unannounced meeting with Matthew. All morning she had been praying and asking God to help her know what to say to the young man to appease his feelings and reconcile with him. Srenna thought back to the first moment she had heard his voice on the train platform, how quiet and peaceful it had been. But nothing was as startling as those blue eyes that stared at her when she turned around. She had been quite unprepared for his introduction and she was suddenly very aware of the fact that since her arrival and their harsh words on the hill, Srenna had not spoken to him or looked at him except to be angry. Now she was going to face him, her true employer, she told herself, not a mature middle-aged father, but a young nineteen-year-old boy trying desperately to be the father.

True to his nature, Stephan came bursting through the front door around twelve o'clock, hungry, impatient and attempting to unsettle the house again. But this time Mary and Srenna were ready for him.

Srenna had his lunch bucket on the counter behind her along with Matthew's but she wasn't about to give it to the famished boy until she got what she wanted.

Mary came in and stood at the door ready to back Srenna up. But it was she who started the conversation with her brother. "Srenna needs you to take her up to Matthew. It's very important that she talks to him today." She waited to see what his reaction was going to be, but when he turned to look at Srenna and saw his lunch being well protected he knew he was outnumbered. To make matters even worse for the belligerent teen, his younger sisters appeared in the doorway united as well. Between the looks on their face letting him know they were tired of being pushed around and the two older girls staring him down, he begrudgingly gave in.

"I'll be ready in two minutes," Srenna responded quickly looking at Mary for any help she could get to leave.

"Go, I'll take care of things here, including supper. Just go," Mary laughed hoping their plan was indeed going to work. "I'll guard the lunches too," she added looking at her brother with a warning in her eyes to not even think about grabbing them and bolting.

Srenna rushed to the bedroom and grabbed up the package she had wrapped only an hour ago. She had brought out the three writing tablets Grace Havilland had given her as a gift before Srenna left Sydney. The dark green cover on the one made Srenna think of Matthew being in the fields all day in the lush grass and beautiful trees. It looked like it could have been chosen just to suit him so she had the girls color yet another picture for their beleaguered brother and wrapped the journal as a much needed peace offering.

As quickly as she could Srenna took a look at her appearance in the mirror and smoothed back her curls from her face. She had changed into a clean spring blouse and freshened up a while ago, wanting to, at the very least, be somewhat together when she talked to Matthew. She nearly ran to the kitchen hoping Stephan had not figured out a way to side step his sisters and flee. But he was sitting at the table mumbling something about being blackmailed and groaning all the while about having everyone "gang up" on him. Once Srenna appeared he was up and ready to go, impatient and well…just Stephan.

She didn't disappoint him though when she grabbed the lunch pails and walked out of the kitchen heading for the door. She was in a bigger hurry then he and she only stopped to ask him to grab the container of iced tea. He grumbled again, grabbed the tea and followed her out the door. His horse Bear was tethered to the front gate waiting more patiently then either of them, nibbling at the grass at the fence. As Srenna got closer to the animal she felt a definite knot in her stomach as she realized it had been well over nine years since last riding. She hesitated for a minute until she saw the look of distinct pleasure on Stephan's face that he might have some leverage over this Aussie governess. But she defiantly stared him back. He was not going to have the better of her, she decided.

"My father was a veterinarian," she announced with deliberate confession, "for horses! I've been around them since I was born." With that she motioned to the boy to mount, which he did reluctantly and then she handed up the buckets. She held out her hand for help and kept her stare fixed on Stephan's face. Again, not because he wanted to but because he was beginning to see her tenacity, he slipped his foot from the stirrup, reached his hand down and helped her up onto the back of Bear. She tucked the pails between her and Stephan and adjusted herself only in enough time before he nudged the horse to leave. She grabbed the boy's middle to keep from pitching off. He thought he was going to make Bear trot unforgivingly, but Srenna knew what he was thinking and she stuck her mouth right up against the ornery boy's ear and whispered, "Don't forget, I have your lunch. It would be a pity if it went all over the ground."

To his despair, the rest of the trip was a calm and gentle ride.

Chapter 16: The Compassionate Confession

As magnificent as they were, the New Zealand Mountains seemed obscure to Matthew Patton this rainy morning. The drenching weather seemed fitting for the mood he was in again for the third day in a row. He sat now under the little hut his father and he had built six years ago to protect them from the rain that occurred with faithful frequency on the east coast of the island. The lean-to's and shelters were located all over the Patton land, to keep them somewhat dry and warm while the coveted rain kept the lush grass growing and green. It was this endless sub-tropical climate that gave the sheep owners the edge they needed to raise such splendid and productive herds. Matthew was use to being out in it sometimes all day. Most of the time the rain was a temporary visitor and the warm south sea winds always dried things up quickly. But today he didn't care if it rained for the rest of the week.

He'd tried praying. But he felt like his prayers were hitting the ceiling of the hut and bouncing right back into his lap. He was certain that God was angrier with him then He'd ever been, even angrier then when he and Tommy Rainga had stolen his dad's truck and snuck out to the beach when they were twelve. Matthew remembered the look on his father's face when the constable in Castlepoint brought them home. Matthew felt like he'd broken his father's heart and he felt horrible for weeks until his father sequestered him away for a few days. When they came back Matthew had sat in church feeling miserable because everyone knew. Before

Reverend Davidson even gave his closing invitation Matthew was headed for the alter to repent and beg for forgiveness. Even when they could begin to laugh at the incident, long after Matthew had been punished, he felt a twinge of guilt and remorse that he had disappointed his father.   But John Patton knew his son's heart, and that he was still all boy. He knew Matthew needed a right of passage from being a little boy to being a responsible young man. It wasn't until John took his son and left with him for two days and went bush with him that Matthew found some peace and forgiveness for himself. Matthew desperately wished just now that he and his dad had had more times like that together…before…

The nineteen-year-old pushed that thought quickly out of his mind as he felt more miserable missing his father. As he had done many times in the last year, in many of these shelters, during many rainstorms, he put his head in his lap and cried. He would never think to let anyone see him cry back at the house, especially the girls, but he remembered once again in agony that he'd actually allowed this new governess he didn't know at all, to see him do just that. But for some reason he couldn't control his feelings with her up at the top of the hill. All he could painfully recall were her searing words to him, "You lied to me!" He also recalled her tone of voice with him at the house and in the bedroom. The memory of it cut him like a knife and it made his tears flow with even more pain. Each day that had gone by he wondered if she would simply request to be taken back to the train station and leave. Truth was he'd barely been able to eat for the last two days his guilt was so heavy on him.

"I don't know what to do Father!" he cried out, his hot tears nearly as drenching as the pelting rain outside. "I can't do this. I can't, I don't…." his words gave way to deep sobs and for what seemed like an endless amount of time Matthew simply wept.

Then that unexplainable thing happened. The same one that had come over him at the hospital the night his mother died and he sat huddled on the hallway floor in Jimmie and Tommy's arms; the same one that came over him in the barn the day the military officer arrived with the news of his father's death in battle in the war. It was that warm, quiet peace, like a heavy blanket, as though someone or something had just entered the hut and laid it over his back and all around him. Matthew knew the presence of the One he had just been crying out to was with him in the hut, right now as real as life. As simultaneously as could be possible, the clouds parted and the rain stopped outside. He listened for a moment at the absolute stillness all around him and was afraid to even breathe or move for fear it would end.

But it did not end.

Matthew finally looked up from his position in front of the hut door. The sheep were moving out away from the trees happy to eat the grass in the field, and Samson was also walking out to graze. Matthew looked at the sunshine that had come out and was dancing on the raindrops as though they were little crystals all over the mountainside. He pulled himself up and out of the hut, stretching his long legs and taking in the sight in front of him. The air was fresh and clean, the grass and trees so emerald green it nearly hurt his eyes to look at. But most of all Matthew saw the mountain range in front of him. Because he'd come up to the foothills just below the incredible line of snowy peaks he was reminded how very small he was and how very huge they were comparison. It was the same God he had just cried out to that had slipped into the hut that formed the majestic landscape above him. The peace he'd just been given was also the reassurance that that God would have an answer.

And Matthew didn't have to wait too long for it. In just a little over an hour he saw Bear approaching with Stephan in the saddle. But to his great surprise he saw another passenger perched on Bears backside clinging to Stephan with all her might. He recognized immediately that it was not Mary. Then almost with a bit of dismay, he saw that it was the governess. For a moment he felt an absolute feeling of panic rise up in his throat as they approached. But it was too late for him to hide and too silly and immature for him to run. So he uttered up a mumbled prayer to the affect of, "This is my answer?" He felt badly in an instance for having doubt, but the painful memory of his encounter with her was flooding over him again.

Stephan pulled Bear up and gave his brother a distorted pleased look when he saw the tortured expression on his older brother's face. He gave Srenna a hand down from the horse after taking the lunch pails and tea from her and then leaned down to offer Matthew his. He smirked at his brother as Srenna straightened her clothes and smoothed her hair back and whispered to him, "Enjoy your last meal!" With that he turned Bear around and headed off into the fields.

Matthew stood there with the lunch pail and tea container looking like the little whipped puppy he had felt like the first day

Srenna came. He was frozen to the ground wondering what in the world this woman could possibly say to him that wouldn't make him feel even worse then he did. Srenna stood equally frozen, waiting, hoping she would remember what she had planned on saying to this young New Zealand sheepherder. She had a million and one things she needed to say but right now all she could do was stare at him. As they both stood wondering what would happen next one of the border collies came bounding up to introduce himself to Srenna. It was dear old Duke, the Patton's oldest and most trustworthy of sheep dogs. Much to Matthew's surprise Srenna seemed neither put off by the wet dog or his rambunctious greeting for her. She bent to hug the hyper collie.

"And what is your name you fine old man?" Srenna cooed over the dog, to which he wiggled and wagged for even more attention.

"This would be Duke," Matthew answered quietly watching the young woman fawn over the aged canine.

But then suddenly Srenna looked past the dog at the scene behind and above him. Matthew watched the expression on her face as she drank in the sight of the mountains this close and he moved back when she stood up and walked towards him and then past him as though she were being drawn to them like a magnet. He held his breath for fear at any moment she would remember why she had come all this way to find him. He was sure it was not good.

Srenna finally turned and caught Matthew's eyes. The moment she did he shifted nervously away from her gaze and not able to stand it any longer he quietly asked her, "Why did you come up here?"
He waited for a second and then fearfully glanced at her once more. He was sure she would have a look of disdain or disappointment on her face. He was nearly shocked when what he saw was a slight smile and a look of some kind of compassion gracing the lovely face he had stared at on the train platform. Her dark eyes bore through him as though for the first time instead of getting angry she was sincerely trying to figure him out.

"You must be hungry, Matthew. You need to eat," she started, moving towards him and taking the pail out of his hand. "Where do you usually sit when you eat?" she asked as she walked past him.

Matthew took a deep breath and followed her a few steps and then answered in still a quiet tone, "Over here will do, on the log." He sent Duke back to the field and proceeded to lead the way to a log that had seen many years of father and son lunches and motioned to Srenna to sit. But before she could lower herself onto it Matthew realized how wet it was and quickly told her, "Wait! It's very wet. Let me get something for you to sit on," he offered. He went back into the hut and grabbed up his rain slicker, and as he walked back to Srenna he opened it up and laid it out on the log for her to use. He motioned once more for her to sit and then stood waiting, wondering what he should do next. Srenna answered that for him when she patted the spot next to her and indicated she wanted Matthew to sit next to her. He reluctantly lowered himself onto the rest of the slicker and sat painfully next to her.

"I just can't get over how magnificent the mountains are here," she commented trying desperately to lighten the awkwardness of the moment. But when she saw just how miserably difficult this all was for Matthew, she simply ordered him, in a gentle tone of voice, "Eat, Matthew. If you're not going to, I am. I'm famished. It's been another busy, busy morning. I barely ate breakfast and I had to smell this all morning while I was fixing it. It's roast beef. I hope you like it. Mary said you did. The girls sent you more cookies too. And some fruit salad. And Mary showed me how to make the spiced tea with lemons that you like....." Srenna rambled on trying to figure out what she could say to make this young man feel more at ease. Then she realized she could talk all afternoon, but what she really needed to do was what she came to do and not wait another second.

"Look, Matthew, you and I....we... well we got off on a pretty rocky start. I'm really sorry I got so angry with you, eh?" she began haltingly. She glanced over at him, staring at the lunch pail as though he was about to start crying again. Srenna looked back out over the landscape in front of her and saw all the sheep gathered in groups all over the hillside. As far as the eye could see it seemed there was no end to fluffy white animals she knew nothing about. And then a thought came to her mind; a memory, a time when someone told her something about themselves to help her understand why they were doing what they were. That someone had been Mrs. Crawford, the woman she had lied too when seeking a job as a governess.

Srenna pulled her slight frame up and drew a long breath. Matthew still had not said a word and was staring a hole into the tea container. "Matthew…would you allow me to tell you a little story about something that happened to me several years ago, something I did, when I felt alone, at the school?" Srenna waited only for a second and then plunged on. "It was about four years after my parents died and I was living at the girl's school in Sydney." This statement brought Matthew's eyes off of the container and for the first time in many minutes he actually looked at Srenna with a curiosity he couldn't hide. So she began her story.

"When I was twelve years old, I lost my family very suddenly in an accident. I was sent to a girl's school in Sydney after my recovery and …well…I was there for almost four years. Then one day just before the end of my school term, I found out from Reverend Carmel that my father's trust fund he'd set up for me when I was little had run out and I was going to be sent to an orphanage in Melbourne, far away from everything and anyone I knew. I was devastated when I found out and I fell apart in an alley on the way back to school. This lady found me there and after I told her what was wrong she referred me to an agency that hired young women as governesses. I went to see the owner the next day but I knew she would only hire and train girls who were at least seventeen and finished with their education," Srenna hesitated for a moment to see if Matthew was following her and to her surprise he was watching her intently as she spoke. "Well the long and the short of it was…I was terribly desperate. I didn't want to leave Sydney, the Carmels, my friends and teachers I'd come to know, just ….everything. So when Marilyn Crawford asked me how old I was…well…I lied," Srenna admitted, looking down at her feet and then back up at Matthew.

She had his full attention now.

"I told her I was seventeen and done with school and that my parents wanted me to work as a governess. I was almost in the clear, I thought….until Mrs. Crawford announced that she would need permission from my mum and dad, and a transcript of my finishing grades at my school. I thought I was going to throw up. But somehow even in that I managed to get up, graciously thank her for her time and then….." Here Srenna waited for a moment, looking back out at the grandeur of the mountain peaks in front of them.

"And then what?" came the burning question on Matthew's mind as he waited for Srenna to finish.

"And then I lost it at the door. I started crying and apologizing to the poor woman and admitting my horrendous sin and well…. I fully expected her to just boot me out on the street. But you know what she did?" Srenna asked him, grinning at her captive audience. Matthew could only nod his head no and wait again for her answer. "She made me come back in, ordered me a cup of hot tea and then told me how she had lost her husband in World War One. She never remarried and decided to dedicate herself to helping families with children. She was so understanding and patient with me and she ended up taking me anyway. Said she admired the fact that I couldn't go through with the lie" Srenna looked sideways at Matthew again and saw that the boy had lowered his eyes to the ground. She could feel the remorse in him so strongly it felt like hers all over again. She hurt for him. "Do you know what she told me?" Srenna asked in a soft low voice.

"No," was all Matthew could say.

"She told me it took more courage to admit I was lying and come clean. She said she saw strength of character in me because I couldn't go through with it. She said a lot of people would have simply walked out the door and never come back. She said a lot of things that day that I will never forget. And because she gave me a chance and she believed in me….well…I'm here today, talking to you." With that Srenna put her hand on the young man's arm beside her and smiled knowingly at Matthew. He dared to smile back slightly and hopefully for the first time in a long time. He looked deeply at Srenna for a moment and then suddenly sighed heavily.

"I didn't want it to be this way, believe me….I…." he started.

But Srenna cut him off with her hand up and smiled even harder at him. "I know that!" she laughed, "I know that." She repeated with a more serious tone in her voice. "And that's why I'm here, so you and I can start over….We can start over…..can't we?" she asked sweetly.

"Does this mean you intend to stay?" Matthew asked hesitantly.

"Um…let's see…I think the answer is… yes. That is if …" she waited for a split second, "if you think we can start over," she stated firmly. She looked at Matthew hard and fixed her eyes on his. He knew she was not going to budge and truth was he didn't want her to. He wanted her to stay. He needed her to stay. But he needed to be at peace with her. He wanted to be at peace with her.

"I think that would be possible, that is if you do," he smiled back.

"I do... and to show you my gratitude for tolerating my temper and forgiving me, I have something for you. I didn't know you existed when I got gifts for everyone else so I hope you like this. A little bird told me you like to write," she offered as she pulled the journal from her slacks pocket. She handed it to Matthew and watched his face to read his reaction to the gift.

"You really didn't have to..." he started.

But once again she waved him silent and smiled. Before he could argue with her she motioned to him to open the package and then she pointed out the lovely carvings on the dark green cover. She told him to open it and showed him the inside cover. She had written in it to him, "To Matthew Patton, a true shepherd....from Srenna Adelaide James."

Matthew held the book open for several minutes and then remembered his tongue and that this young governess was telling him she would stay. Only a short time ago he had felt such despair and now...he felt a glow of hope burning inside of him; real hope. "Thank you," he answered simply and quietly.

"You're welcome," she responded with notable reassurance that tonight Matthew would actually be joining them for supper. She stood up all of a sudden and looked towards the path that Stephan had brought her up. "And now...I think I probably should be going back, before Mary runs away, Benji starts wailing again and Lord knows what Emma and Lilly cook up," she chuckled. She actually heard a bit of a laugh from Matthew as he too stood, but just as quickly he allowed a shadow to cross his face.

"I've really dumped a lot on you, eh?" he painfully asked.

Srenna only smiled another sweet smile back at him and sighed deeply. "You have. But not nearly as much as has been "dumped" on you," she stated bluntly. She watched the young man shuffle his feet and look a little beaten again, but she was not about to let the progress they had made slip away. "Matthew," she started, coming closer to him, "Neither one of us can do any of this alone. Mary can't do it alone. But you know what they say about a three stranded cord, eh?" she grinned reassuringly. As quickly as the weight of everything had tried to overtake him, he felt it melt away.

"It can't easily be broken?" he finished the Bible verse.

"Yes…exactly." She answered softly. "Now, can I get back the same way I came if I walk?" she asked him beginning to head for the path.

"You can, but we'll miss you at the supper table tonight if you get lost," he jokingly answered and then in a much more serious tone simply instructed her, "I'll ride you back, at least till you can see the house."

Srenna did not intend to argue with him there. She had been so busy trying to stay on Bear that she missed much of the route they had taken to get up here. She waited patiently for Matthew to whistle to the big black stallion to come from where he was grazing. In no time at all she found herself positioned behind Matthew on Samson's back and on her way back to the house. It wasn't until they were nearly to the low fields that Srenna realized that neither one of them had taken a bite of there lunch. As Matthew helped her down from the big horse's back she looked up at him with her dark eyes and smiled. "Will you be in for supper tonight?" she asked hopefully.

"I'll be there, I promise," he answered as he pulled Samson about and waited for Srenna to head in the direction of the house below.

"Oh…and Matthew," she began, with a serious look on her face.

"Yes?" he asked with a puzzled look on his.

"Eat your lunch, eh?" she ordered softly, yet firmly.

"Yes mum," he responded with a grin on his face. He headed Samson back up the path only stopping briefly after a few seconds to make sure Srenna was indeed on her way towards the house. He watched the young Australian woman walk slowly down in the direction of his home. He couldn't help but notice how she took the time to look all around her at the new sights, her new surroundings. Again he felt hopeful, that just maybe this was the person God intended to send them after all. And something else was stirring in him. For the first time in well over a year, he had laughed, he had even joked with her. He had felt…happy. He watched for a few more moments as she disappeared over the last hillside before hitting the road to the house.

As he rode back to the fields he found himself uttering up a different prayer then the despairing one a few hours before, a prayer of thanks, a prayer for his brothers and sisters, and most of all a prayer…for the brave young woman who had just chanced everything to come make things right with him. He prayed God would give both of them wisdom to know how to help this family stay together like his mother wanted. He didn't know how it was all going to happen, but he did know …it could happen, with the help of a very determined and tenacious young governess. The journal he had slipped into his back pocket bore witness to that. It told him she saw his heart. "To Matthew Patton, a true shepherd" he read again and again. Aside from his mother and Irmani and sometimes Mary, Matthew had never had a girl "see him", or "hear him". He found himself remembering everything she shared that afternoon, everything she admitted, everything she said. He actually found himself looking forward to going home tonight, and sitting around the table with his family. And …Srenna Adelaide James.

Chapter 17: The Family That Prays

There was little time to celebrate the victory up on the hillside when Srenna made it back to the house. She filled Mary in on the results and to the girl's delight she heard that her older brother would be home and in for supper. As she and Srenna worked side by side to prepare something delicious for the boys when they came home, Srenna told her some more and Mary felt her heart lighter then it had been in a long time. Truth was she felt horrible for Matthew and all he had been expected to do the last four years. He had barely had time to be a teenager and certainly had not had a moment of peace since their mum died. Mary wanted to help him but she didn't know how, other then to feed him and keep the children taken care of. They had both felt like instant parents for the last eight months or more.

Srenna was so overjoyed that she and Matthew had come to terms over their beginning that she found herself babbling on and on about Matthew's reaction to her story and her desire to start over. She described every look on his face and every word he had spoken to her. Mary grinned while listening to this lady go on about her brother that way. She couldn't help but catch the tone of Srenna's voice when telling the pivotal moment Matthew agreed to begin their acquaintance over. She was delighted that Matthew had bent, given in to the charms she had already recognized in this beautiful young woman. Maybe now they could relax a bit; begin to move on. The younger children needed that very badly. They needed Matthew here and at the table.

Suddenly Srenna changed the course of the conversation as they peeled potatoes and remembered something spoken of the day before. "Mary, did you call Irmani Rainga and invite her over for tea," Srenna asked abruptly.

"Why, yes as a matter of fact I did," the sixteen-year-old responded lightly.

"Oh my, is she coming?" Srenna asked half afraid of the answer, half hopeful it was soon.

"Tomorrow, mid morning, for coffee, not tea. She said to make sure the pot was hot and strong." the girl laughed, "She says tea is for "Pakehas", white folk, and not stout, robust Maori woman."

Srenna heard the mimic in Mary's voice as she imitated what could only have been the strange native islander's take on things. She wondered again if she would be completely intimidated by her guest or immediately love the woman to death.

There was no more time to worry about any of the next day's agenda when Benji woke from his nap around four o'clock. Srenna fed him quickly, not even fighting with the infant as to whether to allow him to suckle for awhile. She wanted him to be happy and contented when his big brother came in for supper. That done she hurried the girls to get cleaned up and then help Mary set the table. All was going rather well, since Mary had started vegetables baking earlier with the broth form the large roast Srenna had baked this morning. The potatoes were nearly soft enough to mash and Lilly was carefully cutting a loaf of bread for the meal.

Srenna watched the girls get excited about Matthew coming in as though a special guest of honor was coming. She hadn't realized just how much the little girls had truly missed their oldest brother. It did bother her though suddenly at the thought of Stephan and how he would feel with all the attention aimed at his brother and not at him. For some odd reason she felt even a little sympathy for this boy who seemed to be stuck somewhere between a little boy and a young teenager, and no parent to guide him. Now that she had made amends with Matthew and they were on better terms, she resolved herself silently to find some way to reach Stephan as well. He was, after all she had experienced in the last few days, the most explosive Patton child. It would indeed be a new challenge for her to find some common ground with him and help him process all that had happened in this home.

The girls were all in the kitchen when Matthew and Stephan came in from the barn. Matthew excused himself for just a little bit and disappeared out on the back porch. In only about ten minutes he returned inside with wet hair and clean clothes and Srenna knew the young man had showered before sitting down at the supper table. She was anxious to get everyone to the table and get the meal started while everyone was in a good mood.

In no time at all a very noisy bunch of Patton children had filled the table. Lilly and Emma were trying to win Matthew's attention feverishly, each coming up with a greater tale to tell him about the last few days. Stephan was the only silent one, sulking in his chair, unable to get a word in edgewise. Srenna watched him with some concern but she also kept a close eye on Matthew as he attempted to catch up with his sister's events. Finally, Srenna cleared her throat and gently suggested they pray so they could all start eating.

"I believe you have the best idea of the day, Miss James," he answered with the tilt of his head and a grin on his face. He looked straight at Srenna as he held his hands out for Mary and Lilly to take as they had always done around the table. Srenna grabbed Emma's hand and held her other one out for Stephan to take, but when the boy hedged, she waited patiently until Matthew jumped in and quietly responded to his brother, "We're waiting on you Stephan. We can eat when we're done praying." That said Stephan reluctantly let Srenna hold his hand and grumbled as he lowered his head.

"Now, whose turn is it to pray, I wonder?" Matthew asked looking around the very full table.

"Yours!" Emma answered loudly and firmly.

"Really?" Matthew asked his baby sister teasingly. "Are you sure, Little Bug?" he challenged her. To her delight he used his endearing nickname for his baby sister.

"Absolutey," she quipped back, grinning so hard that none of them could stifle their laughs.

So Matthew prayed. He was very thankful to be back at the table with his siblings, with new hope and a new smile at the end of the table where once there was an empty chair. He glanced up while thanking God for the food and for the ones who had prepared the meal, and for all of them being safe and together, and saw Srenna looking up at him, smiling. He couldn't tear his eyes away from her gaze as he finished the prayer and everyone said a resounding amen.

She had tears in them. She was fighting them back. But he was sure they were there. He remembered the painful confession she had made to him that afternoon as they started the food around the table. She knew what they were going through. She knew how much they had lost. Reverend Davidson and Reverend Carmel had hand picked her to come here and help Matthew, knowing full well this young twenty-one-year-old girl had had enough of her own tragedy to understand all of theirs.

As they ate and talked, he heard new sounds around his dining room table, something he had not heard in a long time. It was joy! Happiness! Even plans being made for the next day and the next and the one after that. Several times he had to choke back his own tears, but not tears of grief… tears of hope, maybe even healing tears. Even looking at his brother's disgruntled expression didn't discourage him tonight. If God could help Matthew come to terms with his guilt, he knew God could help Stephan come to terms with his anger and grief. He smiled at his brother fidgeting with his fork hoping he would look at him long enough for Matthew to reassure Stephan, encourage him. But Stephan kept his eyes diverted from everyone.

"She'll be right," Matthew encouraged himself one more time, looking at his brother and whispering a quick prayer up for Stephan. But tonight he wanted to concentrate on the little ones. He looked back around the table at each one and then found himself landing his eyes on Srenna once more. She was smiling at him again, a very pleased look on her face. She nodded ever so slightly, just enough for Matthew to notice and he in turn nodded ever so slightly back.

But Matthew and Srenna were not the only ones that noticed their unspoken acknowledgement.

Mary felt her heart bursting inside her chest as she watched her brother's face. She was happy for him that he was finally feeling some relief, some peace, some joy himself. It was about time. And she couldn't help but be a bit glad that some of his smile was due to the lovely young governess occupying her mother's empty chair. She tucked that thought away in her mind and continued to drink in the events taking place all around their happy table this spring October night.

Chapter 18: Irmani Rainga Visits

Srenna wondered if her plan would work this morning. Just as she had hoped she smelled the strong aroma of brewing coffee coming from the kitchen. The night before after everyone had retired to bed, after she was sure all lights were out and even Matthew was tucked safely away in his room, Srenna opened up her door just enough to hear any noise coming from the living room and definitely smell Matthew's wonderful pot of coffee. And she did. First his quiet steps across the living room and then a little noise from the kitchen awakened her. Srenna waited for a little bit until she thought he was nearly ready to leave. She knew he was true to routine most mornings, according to Mary, and would grab some fruit and cheese, along with some bread for his breakfast and eat it on his way to the fields.

Srenna finally rolled out of the bed silently, as not to wake the still slumbering infant in the crib in the little alcove nursery. Pulling her robe on around her gown, she slipped from the room and headed for the kitchen. She was determined to make up for the two days she had lost being on good terms with her new employer. She wanted very much, also, to find out what ways she could help Matthew specifically. Now that they were talking she intended to ask him on a regular basis.

When she walked through the door of the kitchen she gave little thought as to how she looked after only just getting up. Srenna was never one to care much about what others thought or saw in her physically. But for some reason upon entering the room and Matthew turning from the sink to see her standing there made Srenna blush unlike never before. For a moment she found herself tongue tied and a bit uncomfortable, but when Matthew smiled and said, "G'day. What are you doing awake so early this morning?" she found herself glad she had made herself get up.

"I was hoping to see you before you left for the day to see if there was anything you needed," she started, smiling back at him. "Or anything you wanted me to do today."

"I need you to have a cup of coffee while it's still quiet and get your senses about ya before Irmani Rainga descends upon this nest," he chuckled. Srenna was amazed at the jocularity of the young man in comparison to his mood earlier yesterday and the two days before. She liked him much better this way.
The grin on his face seemed to brighten the whole room and it made her feel as though he would have a much better day then he'd been having.

"Should I be worried; you know … about her visit," Srenna asked painfully, with a bit of a concern in her voice.

"Nope. She's a little rough around the edges, that one, but she's got the biggest heart on the whole of the north island. Regular mother hen, Irmani. Everyone around here under the age of twenty-five has felt the slap of that woman first thing in their life," he continued to joke about the Maori mid-wife.

"Well, actually, I am looking forward to meeting her, especially if she can give me any advice," Srenna admitted.

"Oh, you'll get plenty of that, to be sure!" Matthew laughed as he picked up his saddlebag and canteen. He finished swallowing his cup of coffee and set it in the sink. He saw the look on Srenna's face and grinned at her again as he moved toward the door. "She'll be right, you'll see. If you survived the last three days with this brood, Irmani Rainga will be a piece of cake." With that Matthew walked to the front door and after turning to Srenna and grinning one more time he started to leave.

But before he could walk out Srenna felt a strong urge to say something to Matthew before he left and was gone all day. "Matthew,… it is alright to call you that isn't it?" she fumbled awkwardly, "I mean, if you want me to call you Mr. Patton,… I mean… that is your proper name and I am your employee and all…."

"Matthew will be fine," he stopped her, still grinning at her. He couldn't help but notice the long dark hair running down her back and the stray curls falling in her face and for a moment she looked more like a little girl standing there instead of the refined city bred governess he had escorted off the train platform. "And would it be Miss James I should call you," he bantered with her.

It was her turn to grin, along with another slight blush, but her answer was, "Srenna will do."

"I'll be in then, around six, ...Srenna,.... with Stephan, who will hopefully be in a better mood," he finished and started out the door.

"Matthew," Srenna thought of one more thing.

"Yeahr," he turned toward her and waited.

"Have a great day and I'll see you tonight," she smiled softly.

Matthew nodded his head and pulled the door shut behind him. As he made his way toward the barn to saddle Samson and turn the dogs loose, he couldn't help but feel that the weight that had been on his shoulder yesterday morning and the morning before and for that matter many, many mornings for a very long time, seemed extremely light this morning. Same stuff on his nineteen-year-old shoulders; five siblings to raise, not to mention the eighteen hundred head of sheep to herd on fifteen hundred acres of land, a house, a station.......He looked out over the morning valley and the rising hues of the sun breaking through the curtains of mist hanging just below the foothills. Everything seemed brighter, sharper, cleaner. And... for some undeniable reason,...very, very peaceful.

As he prepared to enter the barn he turned and looked back at the house he had just come from. He paused to take in the view of it, looking at the windows above the porch that were Mary's and the girl's rooms. For the first time in a year he felt confident leaving the house for the day; confident that someone was there looking out for the girls, for Benji, for Stephan; confident that Mary wasn't struggling anymore on her own. He had paid attention to Mary's reaction to Srenna and he was well pleased that Mary seemed to like her, a lot. He watched the little girls interact with the young governess and saw how quickly they had placed their trust in her. And Benji; the baby was clinging to her as if she had been taking care of him all of his eight months of life. How could he not be at ease for one of the first times he could remember. He thought back over their conversation on the hill yesterday and couldn't help but wonder what this poor girl herself had suffered, losing her family, she'd said. Had she brothers or sisters as well that died when her parents died? He hoped in time she would be able to confide in him or Mary or more likely Irmani, who had a way of extracting anything she wanted from someone, especially information.

Matthew smiled at the thought of Irmani Rainga and Srenna James getting to know each other. But he needed Srenna to be acquainted with the Raingas since they were an intricate part of the children's lives. They had been like second parents to all of them, as close as any brother and sister to mum and dad, and would continue to be involved nearly every day. Jimmie and Tommy were Matthew's greatest help with the sheep and Irmani knew every detail about every one of them. Mum and Dad would never have made it in this South Pacific sheep country had it not been for them. Matthew prayed that Srenna would see them just as special as he did. Somehow he was sure she would. He had already seen real grit in this girl, coming all this way by plane and train to work for him, taking on six people she knew nothing about. And he could not forget that she was willing to stay. That thought alone gave him encouragement that they could now start putting the pieces of their lives back together, something he was sure Srenna James knew something about. He made a mental note to be sure and tell Reverend Davidson that this plan of his just might work, possibly even without a public display of repentance before the entire church.

Back at the house, Srenna did indeed take time to have that cup of coffee Matthew ordered her to drink. She sat in the quiet kitchen and thought about the plans for the day, knowing full well she had a million things that still needed catching up. Another meal for tonight and lunches for the boys, were heavy on her mind, more laundry still in baskets, and just a general thorough cleaning of the house was needed. She was still finding her way around the kitchen and the appliances. She was determined though to at least have the house picked up and something ready to eat for the boys before Irmani came this morning. She also decided to have something to nibble on when the Maori neighbor came.

All these thoughts were plowing through Srenna's head when the faint sound of Benji stirring met her ears. She had decided to make him wait just a little bit, while she prepared the nursing bottle and then she slipped back into the bedroom with a big smile on her face and a cheery welcome for the infant. He tried to be happy, attempting a smile back but his little baby tummy said he was hungry and had not eaten all night and it was well after seven o'clock.

Srenna didn't hold him off any longer then to change his very wet diaper and then settled into the rocking chair. This time she tried to simply give the baby boy the bottle first, without the security of her breast. She held him close against her, speaking to him in soft low tones, encouraging him to latch onto the nipple on the bottle. At first he fussed and fidgeted, frustrated that he could not get to Srenna. But after a few tense moments he realized the milk he truly wanted was right there, and Srenna was still going to hold him tight and safe. In the end his tummy won, and Srenna was delighted that he had gone from breast to bottle that easily.

Srenna was so grateful that Marilyn Crawford had taught her how to use the nursing bag in cases just like this one. She wondered if the woman hadn't been aware that the baby Srenna would be caring for might not be weaned. Never the less Srenna was happy this morning to see the infant content. He had fixed his eyes on her, though, always looking at her as though any minute she might disappear.

"I'm not going anywhere, little beggar," she cooed at him, kissing his blond head and hugging him gently. She heard a distinct sigh escape from the child's body, and a flood of emotions welled up in her as she finished feeding him.

She couldn't leave. She wouldn't leave. Already she knew that. Even with everything ahead of her, uncertain how she was going to accomplish everything this family needed, Srenna was sure of this.

"You've done this, haven't you God, brought me here and wrapped this family right around my finger?" she chuckled. Thinking she was speaking to him, Benji laughed back at her and this tickled Srenna to hear him and made her laugh even harder. Then suddenly as if some wall had just come down, Benji was laughing harder as well and for some strange reason neither one could stop. The more Srenna laughed at the infant's giggles, he in turned laughed harder, making her laugh until she thought her sides would split. The two of them were in the middle of this joyful competition when Srenna heard a light knock at her door and through her happy tears she chuckled, "Come in."

It was Mary, coming from upstairs and headed for the bathroom. But before she could even get past the hallway door she heard the most beautiful sound she thought she had ever heard; her baby brother's laughter. She stood for only a moment at the door listening to Srenna and Benji giggling and started laughing herself. Upon entering the room, Mary looked at both governess and child sitting there early in the morning, happy and obviously contented. She couldn't help but notice too that Srenna was not disrobed as she had been each time she had fed the baby the last few days.

"He took the bottle, without wanting to nurse!" she exclaimed, smiling at Srenna. "That's wonderful!"

"Yes it is!" agreed Srenna, still chuckling at the amused baby. "He's a smart boy, this one. I can't wait to tell Mrs. Crawford how well he took to this method. I have to admit I was a little nervous trying it."

"But it worked, and he seems happy," Mary added, smoothing the top of her baby brothers blonde head. "I'll let you two finish and I'll get something going for breakfast for the girls."

"Thank you, Mary," Srenna smiled again at the young girl. "I could not do all of this if you weren't such a good helper.

"Actually," Mary smiled back. "I was thinking the very same thing,"she finished, as she left the room and headed towards the kitchen.

Already the stirring of the girls and Stephan's impatient exit from the living room to the barn could be heard all over the house. Day four still made Srenna wonder how she would ever accomplish everything for everyone as the noises rumbled through each room and the day came to a full start. She was also beginning to feel some angst about Irmani's imminent descent upon this beautiful, but still very messy house in only a few hours. She completed the task of appeasing at least one Patton child and quickly threw on some clothes to begin the attempt to meet the challenge of the rest.

Srenna carried the happy baby she had just finished feeding into the kitchen and met the greetings of two apparently equally happy little girls. "Why, we are all in such bright moods this morning," Srenna gushed over the girls as she plopped Benji into his chair and went for another cup of coffee. Mary had made some toast and was busy preparing some eggs for everyone. The girls indeed seemed to be pleasant and even a bit excited this morning for some reason and Srenna wondered if it had anything to do with the expected visit from a certain Maori mother this morning.

"Now, why would every one be in such a gay disposition this morning, I wonder?" she joked with Lilly and Emma.

"Mani's coming!" Emma squealed, wiggling excitedly in her chair and receiving a big hug from Srenna.

"Yes, I know!" Srenna answered the child back, trying to feel the same excitement and push away the nervous jitters she was still having.

"I wonder if she'll bring Willie with her," asked Lilly, "He's such a roley poley little thing."

"And who is this,…Willie?" asked Srenna of her little nine-year-old charge.

"He's Irmani's last child, the one she had just before mum had Benji," Mary informed her governess. "He's a year old. And just about as round as any baby could be." At this description, all the girls laughed and Srenna couldn't help but wonder what shape the child truly was. None the less she laughed with the girls which once again seemed to prompt Benji into another round of baby giggles, much to his sisters' delight.

"On a more serious note, Mary, I would like to make something quick this morning before Irmani embarks upon your lovely home, something we can have with our coffee. And if we could, girls," she added, looking at both little ladies, eating their eggs, "I need you both to help me pick up around here this morning." Both girls however, seemed to not be too happy about that announcement, but one look from Mary and they both quickly agreed.

"All right, then. We'll have another contest. Let's see who can finish breakfast and then get dress the fastest. Then, let's see who can pick up and put away the most things down here. The winners will have a special treat at supper time. How about that?" she bargained with the girls.

The girls were ready for this little competition again, still wanting very much to win the affections of the young Aussie woman. Lilly knew full well, too, that now that their big brother was in good standing with this lady she would likely be telling him everything.

They also did not want to suffer the wrath of Irmani Rainga, should either one of them be found disobeying.

The next two hours flew by as Srenna and Mary busied themselves with morning chores, both determined to show the Maori neighbor that things were indeed better then they had been a week ago when the woman had last been over.

Irmani had desperately tried to come every day to check on the children, leaving her own infant at home with her oldest daughter, Nula. The short time she had to spend with them was never enough to even make a dent in the needs this hungry, messy brood had. If she could have, she would have simply scooped them all up under her large mother hen wings and shuffled them off home with her and Jimmie. However, six of her own children were still in the Rainga nest themselves. She struggled to help John and Miriam Patton's children because her hands could only do so much and her heart wanted more. Even nursing little Benji had been taxing on her while she took care of her own robust baby. When she learned of the new governess coming for sure, Irmani hoped the woman, whoever she was would have some knowledge of babies and their needs, including the weaning process. Poor little Benji was her biggest concern, as Miriam Patton had just lost any strength and will to supply the child's immediate needs the last few weeks of her life.

As the time drew near for her arrival, Srenna was fairly flitting about with more nervous energy then she knew what to do with. She had made up the boys lunches, shortly after she finished some coffee cake from another recipe she found in one of Miriam's recipe books. While she did this, she sent Mary off with the girls to dust and sweep the large living room. A quick going over the bathroom was accomplished as well and then, another thought for supper later this evening. The day promised to be a drier one, with bright sunshine and a light breeze in early in the morning. "Good," thought Srenna to herself. It would be nice to go out on the front or back porch and just sit with the new neighbor while she was here.

It was nearly ten thirty before the sound of an approaching vehicle came to Srenna's ears. She glanced at Mary, who stood up quickly and followed the girls to the front door. Srenna came behind them more slowly, with Benji on her hip. Before she even reached the door though the girls were down the steps and into the arms of one of the happiest looking women she had ever seen.

Irmani Rainga was not petite in any sense of the word. She wasn't slender either. The stout Maori woman probably outweighed Srenna by at least a hundred pounds. For that matter she probably outweighed Matthew by fifty. Her features were distinctive Polynesian, dark island skin and wavy black hair. And arms, big enough to encompass all three of the girls at once, which she was about doing as Srenna walked out on the porch. The girls had stopped her dead in her tracks halfway up the walk and she was embracing them as though the girls had not seen her in a long time. It was obvious to Srenna that this woman was near and dear to this family of orphaned children. Any qualms she had had prior to Irmani's arrival seemed to disappear in thin air.

"Where is he, where's my baby boy, that little Pakeha?" the woman gushed, as she approached Srenna, still holding Benji tightly, more for her security then his. Irmani swooped up on Srenna and without hesitation plucked the child from her arms and squeezed him, kissing the baby lovingly all over his own chubby little cheeks. Benji knew the woman for a certainty and let her fawn over him, but only for a moment. He then twisted himself around, looking at Srenna as though he was sure this time she might leave him. His whimper let everyone know he was done with greetings and he wanted his governess back. "Will you look at that, you little beggar," the Maori mother joked. Srenna waited, horrified that the woman might be offended by Benji's reaction, but Irmani handed him back to Srenna with a huge grin on her face and added, "It's high time this one latch on to something else besides my bosom." She laughed one of the heartiest laughs Srenna thought she had ever heard and all of them laughed with her as Benji clung to Srenna for dear life and buried his head in the young woman's neck.

"You have no idea, girl, how good it is to see this one happy and not wailing clear across the mountains, " Irmani smiled at Srenna. "Irmani Rainga, deary. I promise not to eat you alive, as long as that delicious smell coming from the house won't poison me."

Srenna knew in an instance, that she liked the jocular woman and she extended her hand in a proper attempt to introduce herself. " Srenna James, Mrs. Rainga. I'm so very pleased to make your acquaintance. I've heard so much about you," Srenna offered sincerely.

"Well then, you'll know to call me Irmani. No one anywhere on earth calls me Mrs., cept Jimmie when he's been drinkin' with the boys at that pub and knows he'd better get home," she chuckled.
"And look at you then, we'll have to fatten her up, this one," Irmani went on turning Srenna as though assessing the girls figure. "First easterly blows in we'll lose the likes of you. They'll be finding you

on the south island." Her tone of voice was not offensive at all and Srenna found her jocularity to be refreshing and a relief.

"Come in, won't you? I've made some cake and a fresh pot of coffee to wash it down," Srenna invited, moving towards the front door. Lilly and Emma were hanging all over their beloved neighbor and Srenna's heart was glad for them that they had this woman in their life to take some of the edge off of their mother's passing. It was so obvious the woman had influenced this home and the children in it in a way Srenna had experienced herself. It made her feel a little homesick for Daniel and Ruth Carmel who had been just such an influence in her own life when most needed. Mary had gone ahead into the kitchen and was already pouring a cup of the strong dark brew for her mother's closest friend. She handed it to the woman as she lowered herself into a chair at the table and then motioned to Srenna to sit.

"Where's Willie?" asked little Emma, seemingly disappointed that the Rainga infant had not come with his mother. Emma still hung on Irmani, leaning her head on the woman's shoulder. Without hesitation, the motherly woman scooped the child onto her large lap and hugged and kissed her.

"Well, now. If I brought that one with me, I'd have no room to squeeze you, eh?" She laughed at the little girl. "I left him with his big sis. She's getting some more practice in so she'll know what to do when her own comes along."

"She's not....?" Mary asked excitedly.

"She is." Irmani answered brightly.

"Oh! How wonderful!" Mary cried hugging the woman and looking at Srenna.

Srenna was listening to all the conversation between the girls and Irmani and waited patiently to understand what all the happy news was about. Mary seemed to notice Srenna's quietness and immediately filled her in with the details. "Nula was just married about six months ago, to Rawli Mangor. This will be Jimmie and Irmani's first grandchild!" Mary explained excited about the baby news.

"Oh! How perfectly wonderful for her... and for you!" Srenna smiled at her visitor.

"Don't have enough to do already with my brood and this one and now I get to bring my first grandbaby into this world," the jovial native laughed again.

"That's right, Mary told me you are a midwife. That should be comforting for Nula when her time comes," Srenna suggested politely.

"Comforting, if you like having your own momma telling you how to bring a baby into the world," Irmani chuckled. "None the less, she's stuck with me, eh?"

"I'm sure she'll be glad for it in the end," Srenna smiled sweetly as she cut some cake for the woman.

"In the end would be about right," Irmani offered jokingly, watching to see what kind of reaction she would get from this city bred Aussie girl. Srenna's face did get a trifle red, which seemed to delight the Maori woman even more and she patted the girl's arm reassuringly and added, "You and me, we'll be fast friends, I can tell." She looked around the warm loving kitchen and already could see the improvements made over the last four days. Whatever size this sprig of a little lady was, Irmani Rainga was a good judge of character. It was obvious just by the reaction of the children, especially Benji, that they were already counting on this young woman to meet their needs.

What Irmani Rainga hadn't been prepared for was how young she was… and how lovely.

She knew the Reverend at the little church in Castlepoint had found her through his acquaintance in Sydney, Australia. She knew the woman was experienced, five years a governess for a prominent family.

Irmani had gone to Reverend Davidson herself to see if there was anything anyone could do to help the children. He had assured her he would find someone to come, after the nanny was sent from Miriam's mother in England and had left in only four days and the others quit as well. They were all desperate, especially Matthew.

Irmani watched this young woman now as she asked the girls to help with Benji, and they followed her instructions as she showed her guest hospitality. She seemed to already have their attention. But looking at the dark haired, dark eyed girl made Irmani wonder if she didn't already have someone else's attention.

"If you don't mind me asking luv, how old might you be?" the woman asked softly. She did not miss the look she got from Mary at the sink out of the corner of her eye and immediately responded to the sixteen-year-old, "It's a fair question, you, don't give me that side ways glance." She said it in such a way that Srenna knew she wasn't angry with Mary, just bantering with her.

"No, of course not. I don't mind at all. I'm…twenty one… Just… My birthday was two months ago," Srenna offered, pulling herself up in her chair, trying all of a sudden to appear as mature as she could next to this veteran mother. Then she took a deep breath and asked her own deeply burning question. " If you don't mind MY asking,…"she started. But she never got to finish the question.

"Too old to be having any more babies, and pretty enough for Jimmie to think he can try," she laughed exuberantly, sending a pink flush over Srenna's cheeks and then uncontrollable giggles from all of them. "Ah, deary. Your ol' Mani just given ya a hard time. It's a rough life out here. Have to toughen ya up too. But from what I can see, if you haven't burned the house down, or lost one of these little ones yet, you'll do. I'm guessin' they want you to stay. And I'm guessin' Matthew's saying a hearty amen to that too," she added, winking at the girl.

"Well, we got off on a pretty bad foot the first day, but we're right now," Srenna confessed. She wondered if the Rainga woman didn't already know that and had very little time to wonder the answer.

"Know it all, luv. Not much he doesn't tell Tommy or Jimmie, or me for that matter when I threaten him," she chuckled. "He felt pretty crook, …that one did, lying to you and all. Surprised he didn't just hurl himself off the nearest cliff." At this statement Irmani could see she might have joked just a little too far with Srenna and she quickly retracted her statement in a more serious tone. "Understand something deary. No one, but no one, 'cept my Jimmie himself is as right as that boy. Like his daddy. Steady as any man on this whole island. And a lot of people know it. You've come by a right way, bringing yourself over here to take care of these babies. You mark my word on that."

Srenna looked hard at the woman she had been nervous to meet and was now glad she had. Matthew was right. She was raw. But she was genuine and true, and Srenna could tell immediately, that once again, God had plopped her smack in the middle of a place with the friends she would need. It gave her confidence as their conversation turned to more practical discussions and Srenna received the "advice" Matthew promised her she would get. She was glad for it though, and when the morning ended and Irmani announced her departure, Srenna was sorry their time had been so short.

"I'll try to arrange it with Nula to get over here, once a week, to give you a hand. We're only about eight miles up the road, passed our lane when you came in. Can't miss us. And you got the telly. Call me if you need anything. Day or night," the woman instructed. She had managed to embrace Benji again before walking towards the door and this time the youngster let his mother's friend hold him a bit longer. The memory of the woman nursing him while his mum was sick and after she passed was still imprinted somewhat in the child's mind. But none the less he kept a very watchful eye on Srenna and Irmani was glad again that the infant had found some solace in the arms of this young, but maternal woman. She was satisfied when driving away that finally someone was actually going to help these children get on with their lives.

Someone to help Matthew. That boy was dear to her. It was breaking her heart to see him struggling so, trying to be a man and still very much being a boy. This was a tough situation, even if he'd had one or two siblings, but five, and one of the largest sheep stations in the area as well. Irmani looked forward to getting more acquainted with the young governess that would be assisting him in this challenge.

But the nagging thought came back again that she had wondered about earlier. Why so young? She fully intended to ask Reverend Davidson as soon as she saw him. But she thought she already knew the answer. And it made her grin. He was a tricky one, that man. Herding his own sheep he was. And John and Miriam Patton had been two of his favorites. He would go to nearly any length, same as her and Jimmie to see to it Matthew had whatever he needed to keep his promise to his dying mother and keep his family together; ....Even if it meant finding someone to stand beside him.

Chapter 19: The First Few Weeks

It seemed as though Srenna hit the ground running anytime she truly needed to and the next few weeks were no exception at the Patton home. Once she and Matthew restarted their working relationship, Srenna found herself beginning to fall into a somewhat steady if not busy daily routine. She settled into a fairly simple schedule with the girls, Benji and strangely enough even with Stephan who if not contested pretty much left everyone to themselves. He was still painstakingly harboring his grief but was spending most of his time alone when he could. Srenna made a mental note each day to do something kind for the boy even if his response was cold and aloof.

Irmani made her weekly visits to the house, most of the time at least two to three days of the week, always with her hands full of some form of food or sustenance for the family and …of course…advice for Srenna. But Srenna didn't mind at all. It was obvious the Maori woman was seasoned in the art of raising children, taking care of her husband and had many words of wisdom to shed on each of the Patton siblings. Anything she could contribute came as a great welcome to Srenna's painfully inexperienced years. She also found quickly how much she really liked the woman and her candid personality.

As the days passed into the first weeks of Srenna's arrival, she became more familiar with the ways and means of this tight knit community and its many facets. The first trip to the market or "dairy" as the New Zealanders called it, revealed a much more laid back way of shopping then the one Srenna had been use to in the big city stores. Staples and specialties were to be had even in this wide spread rural sheep country, but Srenna knew it was still going to take some time to get use to the self sufficient ranchers that provided much of their own produce, meat and dairy products. Taking all of the children with her was quite an experience but she was determined to include the younger ones in as many outings away from the house as possible. Her presence in the Patton home was quickly the topic of conversation as the community learned of this lovely young Aussie woman and more importantly…that she continued to stay. But again Srenna didn't seem to mind when heads turned or curious tongues engaged in whispers when she entered a building.

Another key figure in all the introductions was the school director in Castle Point. The children had not gone back to school after Miriam's death and now a few weeks after Srenna arrived their session was on break for the summer. Mrs. Naples, the head of the school was pleased to see the children doing better, but concerned that they would be terribly behind when the fall session began in February. At Srenna's insistence and Matthew's agreement the children were to be tutored over their break by Srenna until going back. Mrs. Naples promised to return with books and assignments for Lilly, Stephan and Mary. Neither of the girls were disappointed, both having missed school dearly, but as was expected, Stephan showed great opposition. He lost in the end when Matthew simply told him he would attempt to catch up or suffer the consequences. Of course he had to scowl about that.

Srenna finally had the privilege of meeting the infamous and repentant Reverend Davidson, who at the prompting of his wife Patricia and Matthew's positive report came nearly on bended knee to meet Srenna and inquire personally as to how the children were faring. She found it very hard to hold a grudge against the man for having conceived the idea of fabricating Matthew's story in order to get her to New Zealand. After only these few short weeks she could not see herself anywhere else in the world then right here with the children God had delivered into her arms as well as her heart.

She could also tell in short order just by all she heard that Hamilton Davidson was a man of God not like many others. His methods were many times new and edgy. He had a congregation of mostly rugged, down to earth sheepherders and cattle ranchers. He had to move to a different drum then most parish leaders to keep his flock interested in the ways of God. Srenna read something deep and self sacrificing in the man instantly and she could see why Matthew trusted him, even when he suggested an unorthodox approach to snag some help. Even the Rainga's who attended a different type of ancestral meeting house then the Anglican fellowships held a certain respect for the hard working leader devoted to the entire community and not only his flock. Knowing he had been an acquaintance of her own loving parish leader, Daniel Carmel, she could see why the two men would have struck a life long friendship.

Patricia Davidson was as equally impressive but not at all what Srenna expected of a rural, back country preacher's wife. She too was a bit different in the fact that she was very refined and seemed somewhat out of place in this island environment. But Srenna found her extremely easy to speak too, and their first visit gave way too much discussion about big city life, the theatre, shopping and …traffic. Srenna was a bit glad to have someone to relate to where her old life was concerned. But already she could sense herself leaning far more into the beauty of this area, albeit difficult and challenging sometimes.

And what incredible challenges. Over the days that followed Srenna learned quickly how much six hungry Pattons could eat. Trying new meals along with the variety of game and fish that Matthew and Stephan provided was enlightenment to the city girl, but she plunged right into the routine of cooking in extraordinary ways, especially with the outdoor "hangi" Mary had taught her to use the second day she arrived. Again she counted heavily on Mary and now Irmani to bring her up to speed in the art of sustaining seven people and their appetites in a rural setting.

Laundry became a daily chore in some fashion or another whether washing it, hanging it, folding it or just plain putting it away, all so the routine could be repeated a few days later. She seemed to pick up quickly who did what best, the routines they had been use to and realized once again that Miriam Patton had run a tight ship even while she was ill. Srenna wondered many times if Miriam wouldn't have been one of her favorite people had she the privilege of knowing her personally. She set herself to learning as much as she could so as to encourage the children in their mother's memory.

It also didn't take Srenna James long to realize one of her new enemies at the Patton station.

It was dirt. And it was everywhere. Though the ranch boasted some of the lushes and most abundant grass, it was firmly founded in sand and dirt that seemed to come into the house in the sneakiest ways.

One thing Miriam had never done was worry about dirt. She did not worry about her floors being tracked with it or which child was capable of carry the most inside. She simply gave it the heave ho everyday and then sent her children back outside to find more. Thus she raised happy care-free children never fearful of reprimand for leaving footprints even on the rainiest of days.

And oh the rain! True to its nature, Srenna began to feel the pulse of the unpredictable New Zealand rainfall and it was the middle of spring so it was extremely heavy at times short lived as it might be. At first she became frustrated and discouraged as every other day seemed to yield a bounty of disrupted plans. But Mary was her champion there. As always Mary calmly reminded her that, "it won't last long" and indeed it did not. In the end and in short order, Srenna began to welcome the badly needed precipitation that kept the water tower full and the surrounding fields the greenest green she had ever laid her eyes on, especially when time allowed the wonderful luxury of a bath or shower.

At first Srenna found the outside shower a bit intimidating. It wasn't exactly as private as closing the door to the indoor bathroom, but it did allow one to have a relatively warm shower at the end of the day. The facility at the end of the back porch had been built by John Patton to accommodate his ever expanding family. It was easier to construct then building a shower inside. It also met with Miriam's approval as the children did not have to dismantle the bathroom inside as much, especially where Matthew and Stephan were concerned. In time the shower became completely enclosed and even had a dressing area inside its walls. When in a hurry over the first few weeks Srenna found herself finally using it while both Matthew and Stephan were in the fields and Benji was napping. Her long curly hair had time to dry in the afternoon sun before the rest of the day came to a close.

By in large Srenna found taking on the role of caretaker of the Patton children much easier, though relentless, then she had ever thought possible once she got use to their needs and their wants. She learned each one's uniqueness very quickly. After only four weeks she began to know what to expect from each child, both good and bad… with the exception of Stephan.

Reading him was just most of the time…bad. Srenna was never one to believe anyone couldn't change, but her frustration with Stephan grew and she could tell that Matthew was as equally frustrated with the thirteen-year-old. If peace was to be truly obtained in the house, they both new something was going to have to give sooner or later where he was concerned. He continued to pick fights with his younger sisters, defy Mary and Srenna during the day and tested Matthew whenever he thought he could. Benji was the only one to escape his vengeance. He seemed mildly indifferent to the baby, as though the child wasn't really there. That bothered Srenna, as Benji had become more and more bonded to her. She tucked the thought away that Stephan was for some reason even a bit jealous of him and possibly the attention he and the younger girls got most of the day. Again, Srenna determined no matter what, she was going to keep on showing the boy acts of kindness…even if it killed her.

The greatest turn of events had to be the sheep shearing at the station. Matthew had reminded Srenna that two of the most important processes at a sheep station were the shearing time and then the lamb cutting a couple of weeks later. Both were paramount to the success of the business of raising sheep. The wool was product greatly needed for commercial purposes, but the sale of the choice lambs was as equally needed as the market for mutton grew around the world.

Srenna was sure she did not mind the idea of shearing the fat wooly Romney sheep that Matthew raised on the ranch, but the mere thought of taking a baby lamb from his mother at four months for mutton left her feeling a bit squeamish. Matthew tried not to grin when she screwed up her nose and gave him a look of utter sadness when he explained it all to her.

On the day of sheep shearing, Srenna was to keep the children in the back of the house to play. Bright and early on that Monday morning four trucks arrived with the men and their equipment for shearing. Tommie Rainga showed up as well, sent by Jimmie to assist his life long friend while the shearers were there. Stephan also was part of the process. They all went to a location behind the pens where the shoots were set up to run the sheep into the holds. After a hard morning of an incredible flurry of shearing, the men all showed up on the front lawn of the house for a splendid lunch prepared by Mary and Srenna and the girls. Then much to Srenna's surprise, Matthew escorted her to the pens so she could observe the sheep's fiasco. She was amused and delighted at what she saw, how quickly and intricately the men clipped each animal. She watched each sheep run into the shoot, a fluffy ball of wool and then come out on the other side shorn and happy to be set free. As each one escaped the hold the bales grew until the four trucks were brimming with beautiful sheepskins ready to be taken to the processing plant in Tinui.

Srenna watched the process with a deep admiration for the men who came to shear the sheep. It almost seemed an art or contest with them as they intricately shorn the Romneys in record time. The six men were well known for shearing as many as 300 sheep a piece in one day. What seemed like an enormous undertaking for one person quickly became an efficient and thorough job well done.

But it wasn't only them that she watched. As the afternoon flew by she couldn't help but see a deep satisfaction on Matthew's face that they had made it this far and that he had been ready and able to help without undue worry about what was happening at the house with the children. Several times she caught him looking her way as she stood off a piece and the look on his face, the grin across his lips made Srenna feel warm inside that she had been able to help him accomplish this task.

She could also see the much deserved respect from the men as well, knowing fully that for the last four years Matthew Patton had indeed filled his patriotic father's shoes, and he had filled them well. The men did not look upon the nineteen-year-old as a boy barely out of his teens but a true man…. and one with character. It hadn't gone unnoticed by Srenna how they slapped him on the back and shook his hand.

Nor did the looks go undetected that she received at lunch time or later the looks at the pens. But again, in spite of the warm color on her face when they must have said something to Matthew concerning her, Srenna took it all in stride and knew the men were goodhearted and supportive of him. She could only imagine what types of things men would joke about with each other when working. When she finally excused herself towards what she knew to be the end of Benji's nap, she glanced back one more time at the group of men, only to catch Matthew's gaze as she walked away. She didn't miss the friendly slap on his back by one big burly shearer, probably old enough to be his grandfather. The man was grinning from ear to ear, and she unmistakably saw the deep blush on Matthew's face as he turned his attention back to the task at hand.

Srenna couldn't help but smile at the thought that Matthew had a side to him that could be sensitive about some things. Most men she had either met or had brief acquaintances with back in Sydney seemed devoid of this characteristic, too proud and too arrogant, but then most of them had not been through what Matthew Patton had experienced at such a young age.

"It was a pity," she thought to herself, that more men weren't afraid to show their emotions.

She was beginning to realize Matthew Patton wasn't one of them. He could have kept her completely in the dark about the day's events, but because he had thought to make her a part of it, she now understood all that came out of raising those sheep 365 days a year in all types of weather.

In a very short time she was beginning to see the quality and character that both John and Miriam had instilled in their oldest son. Much to their memory he was displaying that legacy now.

But she still had to wonder as she made it back to the front porch and turned one more time to look out at the pens and the continued flurry of work. He had to have some flaw, didn't he?

Didn't they all? She had seen a glimpse of him distraught and weary on the top of the hill that first day. But immediately her memory also reminded her that she had seen him broken and sorry in the fields. "Oh well," she thought quietly, "Sooner or later we'll all know what we're truly made of, eh?" She hoped it was later. No reason to spoil the ebb and flow most of the household was enjoying these last four weeks… even if Stephan was still his usual cranky self.

Chapter 20: The Shearers

The shearers were wrapping things up and getting ready to call it a day at the Patton station. The day had been a long one and already the sun was slipping behind the mountain range. They would be at the Rainga's station tomorrow along with Matthew. Tonight the sheep would be given a feast of rich grain to reward them for their endurance and their production of such bountiful fleeces. Stephan was turning them back into their pens for the night while Matthew finished his business with the men before they left. In spite of a rigorous workout everyone was in a jovial mood and again Matthew was thankful for the outcome of the shearing in comparison to the ones earlier in the year.

The men noticed it too. Hank Codders, the foreman of the group was greatly impressed with the manner in which Matthew Patton handled himself where the absence of his father was concerned. Hank and most of the men had known John Patton almost since the first year he had sheep on his land. Then at about age nine, Matthew had begun to follow his father everywhere he was allowed, including the shearing and not too long after, the lamb cutting when the choicest of the new flock were sent to the processing plant in Tinui. The boy had grown up right underneath their noses and now they saw a seasoned sheepherder, albeit a young one. They truly did respect what he and many other young men had had to face when their fathers left for war, some of which like John, did not return alive.

Still, as time was healing war wounds all over the island of New Zealand the men began to feel they could once again find some humor and light-heartedness in their everyday work. It was this mood that hung over all of them as they prepared to leave the station and call it a day.

"I think you got yourself a good turn of fleece, mate," Hank laughed, slapping his young friend on the shoulder. "And your governess ain't all that bad either, eh?" he winked mischievously at the other workers.

"Yeahr, that ones a keeper, if you ask me," chuckled Tim Harvey, the youngest of the shearers. He was near Matthew's age, two years older, the son of one of the other sheepherders in the area. He waited for Matthew to respond to his jocular statement about Srenna, but when Matthew tried to ignore the remark he decided to go on. "Better keep a close eye on that one, eh? Every bachelor on the east coast'll be fishing for her."

"Yeahr," agreed Hank, "especially when you pop off your big mouth, Timmie. They'll be lining up at the gate."

"Hey Matt, whatever happened to that little number back in school," Tim continued, "you know that rich girl? What was her name…Margi…Margi Henderson...yeahr that's it. Didn't she have it for you? Wasn't her dad some big shot over in Masterton?"

Matthew was indeed trying very hard to treat the joking lightly, but he was finding it hard not to be uncomfortable with the topic of the conversation. He could feel the color creeping up his face as he heard the jesting the men were leveling at him where Srenna was concerned and another name he wanted to forget. It was making him think of Srenna in a way he wasn't quite sure he even had a right to. Right now he wasn't sure why that was bothering him. He knew for sure why the mention of Margi Henderson made him squirm.

Tommie seemed to be the only one to notice how uncomfortable he was with the light joking and as the true friend he was, stepped in to cover Matthew's back.

"Enough of all that ribbing, you," he chided the men, giving Tim a playful shove. "This fleece ain't gonna walk itself to the plant, eh?" With that he slapped Matthew on the back and encouraged his buddy to ignore anymore statements. Hank Codders seemed to get the message simply enough and he too extended his big hand to Matthew and once again praised the young man for a job well done.

"Always a pleasure to do business with ya Matt. Your dad would be right proud of ya now, no mistaking that," Hank offered, smiling at Matthew. The feeling was mutual by the others in spite of their funning with him and with that they climbed into the fleeced filled trucks and left for Tinui.

"Well now, I think you survived that well enough, eh?" Tommie laughed as he slipped his arm around Matthew's shoulder and began walking towards the house with him.

"Survived them is what you mean," Matthew answered with a sigh of relief that they had gone and the conversation was over. He sent Stephan on up to the house for supper.

"You should have known Timmie would say something about someone as pretty as Srenna. You brought her out here. You're lucky he didn't just bloody well jump her at the pens." He waited quietly for a moment and then plunged on. "Seriously, Matt. Everything's sweet, eh?" his best friend asked with a hint of concern in his voice. "Margi...she's the past...right?" He walked beside Matthew toward the front gate noticing that as was the normal, Matthew had gone from jovial to quiet in short order, mostly because of the topic of Srenna and the issue of Margi Henderson being brought up all in the same breath.

"There never was a Margi, mate....you know that. So does Tim and Hank and everyone else for that matter living and breathing on this island," Matthew answered his friend with a slight tone of agitation. It was one memory he wanted very much to forget.

"Easy, brother. You know I know that. I guess I'm more concerned as to why you got all up in a bundle when they were joking about Srenna," Tommie responded gently.

"I don't know why. I..." Matthew hesitated. "She's my employee for crying out loud. I just wanted her to see what she helped me do today. I couldn't have made it this far without her help with the children. I thought she'd feel better about why she's here."

"Maybe the issue is...why she is here," chuckled Tommie in a good natured way.

He deeply loved his best friend every bit as much if not more then his own brothers. He had struggled right along with him all these years, through the tragedies, through the extreme changes, and especially through some of Matthew's loneliest and hardest emotions. They had confided in each other over the most private of topics, survived boyish pranks, suffered through school in more ways then one and had come out of all of this, bonded like blood brothers, Maori and Pakeha. In spite of even their ancestral differences, they neither one of them saw each other as too different, due much to the way the Raingas and the Pattons raised their children to think of others.

But this new feeling he sensed in Matthew was one that he had not yet truly seen in his friend. John Patton's son had not had time for many things these last four years, one of which was girls. Not even one of the prettiest girls in their school...Margi Henderson. She could not seem to keep Matthew Patton's head turned for very long, much as she tried.

And she did relentlessly try. She had even gotten her father Phillip Henderson, a prominent business owner involved trying to have him step in and offer help to the boy when John left for war. But like his father, Matthew's deep tie to the land John had left in his care made him refuse the man's offer to take over some of the burden of property. It was found later that indeed Phillip Henderson's true motive was to gain some benefit in all the men's property left behind while serving in the ANZACS. It appeared his intentions were to take over as much as he could while wives and young sons were vulnerable. It was then that Jimmie Rainga and a number of older land owners stepped in and formed the co-op with each other, vowing that Mr. Henderson would not walk away with any of their land they had toiled over for years. Matthew was pulled into the co-op with Jimmie and that was as they say...that.

It was also then, at the age of sixteen, only three short years ago, Matthew made the decision against his mother's approval to leave school and stay at the station all day. He struggled for a while to maintain his studies in the fields but they gradually fell to the wayside as time and work demanded more from the youth. It had broken Miriam's heart to see her oldest son become more and more burdened with the load of work he took on everyday. But he would not complain or grumble and she finally let him be about his studies.

It was this rigorous schedule that neither afforded Matthew the luxury of dating nor meeting anyone. Try as Margi did to continue pursuing him, Tommie knew that at a certain point Matthew finally confronted her and her relentless flaunting of herself to him and the whole matter seemed to come to a stop. At least until John Patton's funeral and then the girl began throwing herself at him again under the auspices of truly caring about Matthew. Once again Matthew simply brushed her off and her reputation and turned his attention to being the man of the house his father would have wanted him to be.

But this was all different. Tommie had watched closely as Matthew brought Srenna to the pens after lunch. He saw the look on his friend's face, as he tried to explain what the men were doing, the careful attention he showed her as he walked her around. Tommie could not mistake the way Matthew's face lit up when Srenna laughed at the first sheep she saw emerge from the hold, shorn and ready to run. He didn't miss the look of delight when she touched the coveted fleece in the bundles and realized how precious the work was that they were doing today. It pleased Matthew.

It hadn't hurt matters either that for the last four weeks, Tommie's mother, Irmani had gone on and on about this "little bit of an Aussie thing," as she so fondly described Srenna. He knew his mother approved of the young governess that showed up, got angry and still stayed. "She's just what they need, that one. Got some fight in her, she does," had been Irmani's assessment when she returned from her first visit. Tommie knew like everyone else in the area that if his mother approved… that was it.

Matthew and Tommie kept walking towards the house slowly, silent for a few moments. Matthew seemed to be lost in thought over the events of the whole day and Tommie was sure, over the conversation just had. But as they neared the front porch he finally felt compelled to say something to encourage his best friend.

"You know, Matt, when was the last time you just simply enjoyed something new just for the heck of it, eh?" he asked grinning slightly. He saw right away the puzzled look on Matthew's face. "It's it a fair question, mate."

"What do you mean by enjoy? I enjoy things," Matthew answered somewhat defensively, cocking his head sideways at Tommie. "I enjoy my work. I enjoy all the things the girls tell me about at the end of the day…I…"

"You see what I mean. You got this idea that nothing new is to be enjoyed. It's all the same stuff you been doing for the last four years, besides holding this family together." Tommie hesitated for only a second or two and then plunged on. "What I'm thinking is…you need to enjoy something…just for you. You haven't dated… blimey man… I'm not sure you even know how." He chuckled at that, but then painfully realized Matthew was not sharing the humor in his lighthearted joking.

"So what do you expect me to do…go in there and sweep Miss James…who by the way is two years older then me…probably only sees me as her employer…and…" Matthew started, rather irritated with himself more then the suggestion Tommie had made.

"What I expect…is for you to invite me in for supper, cause I'm bloody well famished. And then I expect you to simply and calmly enjoy getting to know who Srenna James is." Tommie took a deep breath and started to finish his pitch. "You've known her for one month. Everyday you're going to get to know her more…crikey…she's right under your nose most the time…and she sleeps right across…"

But with hand up, Matthew cut him off. "Thank you for reminding me where she sleeps, mate" he retorted sarcastically. "I'll rest so much better tonight."

"You know we could go on like this all night and both of us will starve," Tommie laughed. He was gripping his stomach in a melodramatic attempt to get his point across.

Matthew stood still and looked at his friend for a moment trying to decide if he truly wanted to be angry at Tommie or be very glad for his candidness. His dearest friend got that from his mother. In the end Matthew's hungry belly got the best of him first. Then a deep desire to be in the house with everyone waiting for him snagged him too. And…he realized…not just his family. A slow grin crossed his face as he looked at Tommie standing there with that incredible knowing Rainga attribute he shared with his mum, waiting patiently as usual for Matthew to come to grips with his feelings.

"I bloody well don't know sometimes if I should knock you out or hug you," Matthew finally said, grabbing his buddy's neck and lovingly roughing him up a bit.

"Just feed me first, eh?" Tommie laughed as they walked the path up to the porch and prepared to go in.

"I'll feed you all right. Gotta keep ya strong so you can make sense outa my life while I'm "enjoying" it," Matthew answered smartly. He was glad Tommie didn't let him slip into the moody places he went sometimes, especially tonight. They'd jumped the first big hurtle since his mum's death. He did have Srenna to thank for that and everyone else as well. As he walked through the door and was greeted by his sister's hugs and kisses, he was acutely aware of the young woman that made sure she was standing across the room taking it all in with a huge smile on her face.

Tommie was right. Matthew felt it creeping over him like a new experience. He could feel the enjoyment knowing that someone had gone out of the way to make his day easier and was waiting to hear all about it along with everyone else. He couldn't remember when he'd felt it the last time. It brought a warm glow not only to his face but inside…from somewhere deep in his chest. And he couldn't help but notice after hugging the girls and glancing over at Srenna that she was enjoying something as well. He could only wonder what was making her face glow as beautifully as it was.

He did determine not to look at Tommie. He knew his friend and closest cohort all too well and he knew for a certainty there would be a huge grin on his face and a "I told you so" look to go with it. He'd feed him first all right. And then knock the snot outa him later for being a know it all.

Chapter 21: The Invitation

With the sheep shearing behind them a full week, the goal ahead was to prepare for the lamb cutting. This was the crucial time of pulling out the choice lambs from the flock that would become prime mutton for the meat processing plant in Tinui. It was a bit more time consuming and tedious as Matthew, along with Jimmie and Tommie would separate the four month old lambs from the flock and decide which ones would be the choicest of stock. It was necessary to take the best of Matthew's and Jimmie's sheep soon before the hottest summer months drifted in and grazing became a little bit more regulated. The flocks were often taken higher into the hills in cooler fields. Matthew and Stephan would be gone longer during the day due to the distance of driving the flock to higher grazing each morning. Cutting the lambs from the rest of the flock before the temperatures changed was good.

Srenna had listened to all of this being explained the night after the shearing when Tommie stayed for dinner. He chattered most of the way through the meal, telling her this and that about raising sheep, including some of the more explicit details about sending the sheep "to market".

She tried to be enthusiastic about the information, but it was hard to hide her distaste for the idea of butchering the "poor little lambs" as she put it. Matthew had tried again not to grin too much at the expression on the city girl's face as Tommie walked her through the routine that would unfold in only a few more weeks. It didn't help at all to know that they would themselves have fresh mutton to grace their table. She made sure she was no where near the barn when Stephan provided fresh fowl for supper. After a few weeks she had gotten up enough nerve to accompany the girls to the hen house to extract eggs from under the chooks as they so fondly referred to the chickens.

Tonight, Matthew watched silently as Srenna attempted to show interest in something Stephan was sharing about the coming event. She was being every type of gracious even when his details obviously made her squirm and it was amusing somewhat to Matthew to see her trying ever so hard to listen without getting squeamish. She wanted so badly to give Stephan some desperately needed attention and interest but it was obvious that the thirteen year old was deliberately trying to unnerve his governess. Matthew was about to interrupt and save her from the conversation when the telephone gave a startling ring and it was he who jumped up from the noisy fray at the table to answer it.

In only a short time Matthew returned to the table and gladly announced to Srenna that she was wanted by Patricia Davidson and he could see the relief on her face that she was being summoned to a call.

"Hullo...Patricia...I'm so very glad to hear your voice...especially at this particular moment," Srenna gushed through the receiver.

"Srenna, dear...I was wondering if you could stand a visit tomorrow afternoon...just to check in and see how you are all faring. It's been a few weeks since we saw you last. Would you mind?" Patricia asked with a bit of pleading in her voice.

"Oh my, no...no... not at all. As a matter of fact I would greatly appreciate the company. Please do," Srenna responded with genuine desire for the older woman to pay a visit. Truth be known, Srenna was longing to get to know the women in the community more and as of yet Matthew and the children had not returned to church. Srenna welcomed any visit from Irmani but she also wanted to get to know the Reverend's wife better.

"All right then, is two o'clock suitable?" Patricia suggested.

"It is...it is," Srenna smiled through the phone.

"I'll see you all then," the lovely woman finished.

Srenna walked back into the dining room smiling and met Matthew's glance the minute she entered. He looked mildly interested at what Patricia Davidson had wanted.

"Everything sweet?" he asked calmly.

"Yes. We're to be paid a visit tomorrow and I'm glad for it. I'd like to get to know her more," Srenna explained. She stopped before making any other comment about how long the children had been gone from the Anglican Church in Castlepoint and if Matthew had any intentions of returning any time soon. It was on her mind though. She didn't want to press him. Everything had been going fairly well especially with the shearing behind them and the cutting coming up next. She was happy that things seemed a lot easier since she first arrived and though her heart missed congregating with a church, she knew the time would come when it was right.

Matthew watched as a silent conversation seemed to be going on in his governess's head. He had to look away for a while so as not to become even more amused at the way Srenna James mulled so very much over in her mind and as though it went unnoticed. He did look around the table at everyone else and realized he was probably the only one noticing.

How could he not. He was noticing pretty much every move she made, heard pretty much every word she spoke. He was a bit overwhelmed with how quickly his thoughts seemed to include her, even when he was not in the house. He found himself wishing he were back the minute he left in the morning, happier then he'd been in a long time to be home in the evening and hoping when he was there that she'd walk into the room.

Fridays were at the top of his favorite events of the week. And ... for a very good reason.

Within only two weeks Srenna had requested time to meet with Matthew during the week so she could talk to him about the children, find out what he wanted for them. He eagerly suggested Friday afternoons wherever it was he had taken the sheep to graze for that day. It was determined that Stephan, though reluctant, would be responsible for bringing her out to Matthew. He thought it would also give her some badly needed time away from Benji and the house as so far she had taken no time off. That bothered him more then it seem to bother her. The young woman from Australia appeared even more driven then he was and he couldn't help but notice how completely she threw herself into her duties and care of the children. He had made a mental note to try and figure out a way to give her some respite.

The next day brought a flurry of preparations for Patricia Davidson's visit. Srenna had become accustomed to Irmani's spur of the moment surprises on the Patton home and knew that the native Maori woman was herself hard put to keep up with her large brood at home. But Patricia was different or so it seemed still to Srenna. She and the Reverend had never had children of their own as reported by Mary, and Srenna could only wonder how clean and orderly their lives must be without the mess of numerous bodies trudging through their parsonage home.

Her first visit with the woman had left her knowing that she would enjoy her company any time just as she had Grace's. They had much in common as far as having lived in the city at one point or another. They talked about the cinema, opera, shopping and many other big city memories. But Srenna could see by the way Patricia Davidson looked at her husband that she would not choose to be any where else but right here with him, serving with him in this rural but extremely close community. It made her wonder sometimes if her mother had ever known that kind of satisfaction or if she had truly needed the continuance of the high life Srenna's father worked so hard to achieve.

But today she was just glad the woman wanted to visit them. It excited Srenna for a change of pace, even if the chores didn't all get done and Benji was a bit fussy. She flew through her morning chores as time would allow, sent Stephan on his way with his and Matthew's lunch, fed the rest and then tried desperately to quiet the baby into a much needed nap. She had only been successful for a few short minutes when the sound of an automobile came down the lane and to the front of the house.

Srenna groaned slightly as she realized she had spent a better portion of the morning working and probably looked like it. She wanted to run to the bathroom, but the door had already been knocked upon and Mary and the girls were in the garden for their usual afternoon harvest for supper.

"Mrs. Davidson! It is so wonderful to see you again...come in...come in...please," Srenna exclaimed enthusiastically as she opened the door and ushered the Reverend's wife in.

"Now Srenna dear…I told you when we first met I would have you call me Patricia…remember?" the beautiful woman responded. "We none of us have such formal titles in this community. We save all that rubbish for the Queen herself…you know… if and when she would ever grace us with her presence." Srenna found Patricia Davidson's candor to be a welcomed breath of fresh air today…especially having struggled with Benji all morning. They both chuckled at the mere thought of the Queen Mother ever gracing their small community with any visit.

"I'm sorry Patricia. I guess I'm still finding my way around all of your liberties with one another. I'm use to the stringent formalities of the big city upper crust, eh?" Srenna laughed trying to relax a bit with the woman's visit.

"It's alright luv, you'll get use to it in time, just as I did," the Reverend's wife assured her, putting her arm around Srenna and squeezing her shoulder. "Why don't you and I have a great time just chatting and catching up on how everything is going here and if there is anything either Hamilton or I can do to help." She knowingly began walking toward the kitchen as though that would have always been the place she and Miriam would have "chatted".

As soon as they entered the kitchen she found a seat and it made Srenna suddenly realize that this woman had probably frequented this home for many years. She and the late mother of this brood of children had been close in a way much different then that of Miriam and Irmani Rainga. What little Srenna knew about Miriam Patton was that she was indeed a woman of poise and at the same time rural fortitude. It would be no small wonder then that the two women would strike up such a close friendship over the years.

In short order Patricia Davidson had caught up on all the news about the Patton station and the success of the first shearing since the children's mother had died. She was relieved in every way to see the house and the children doing as well as they were in comparison to the condition of everyone six or seven weeks earlier. She had witnessed Matthew's and Mary's complete frustration trying to deal with the enormous responsibility of commandeering this energetic brood and as well, dealing with their grief. She watched with great pleasure at the way the girls responded positively to Srenna after only a few weeks of being here.

It was this condition in the home that made the suggestion she was about to make a little easier then she thought it might be.

"Srenna, I have a confession to make about my visit today," she began gently. She picked up her cup of tea Srenna had given her when they first began to talk and moved to the stove to fill it with more. "I hope what I'm about to bring up will be well received and considered…for all your sakes, eh?" she smiled at the lovely young governess, as she returned to the table.

Srenna waited wide eyed and wondering what it was that the Reverend's wife would need to discuss with her and at first she felt a bit apprehensive that perhaps there was something she had done or not done to the woman's liking. But Patricia Davidson recognized immediately that she had caused Srenna some worry.

"Oh no dear…no…there's really nothing wrong. Don't go fretting any," Patricia quickly assured her. "Anyone can see that you have definitely filled a void here in such a short amount of time…why…none of us could have hoped for more then what has happened for this family when you came." Her words calmed some of Srenna's anxiousness but the girl still waited with baited breath concerning Patricia's thoughts.

"Please Patricia. I really do want any input you can give me, any suggestions or comments concerning the children, especially Stephan as I've yet to break through his icy exterior," Srenna begged.

"Yes… well that will be a challenge, that one will be," laughed the older woman. "What I came to talk to you about today beside seeing how you and the children are faring may be a bit underhanded even for me, but I assure you…sometimes we women have to be a little crafty to get the men in our lives to see a certain way. Do you know what I'm talking about?" she asked of the young governess.

A smile crept across Srenna's face with a sudden understanding of exactly what Patricia was eluding to. "Yes…actually. I do. When I first arrived Matthew and I had…well…words…or more like I had words with him and well…we were quite at odds with each other for a few days…until…" she began.

But Patricia was also grinning and cut her off. "Until you buttered him up one side and down the other and made him feel better about what he'd done, eh?" she chuckled.

"You knew about that?" Srenna questioned with a puzzled look on her face.

"Your little trip up the mountain to settle matters with Matthew was his first account to Hamilton after you'd been there," the Reverend's wife smiled. "There's not much that goes on in this community that Hamilton doesn't know and what he doesn't know he finds out...from Irmani Rainga." At that comment both woman laughed at the thought of the forthright Maori midwife and her tie to the countryside and the families that lived there. "You know of course that we'd be around much more if we didn't know that the Rainga's were right up the road and keeping an eye out for all of you. Truth is... the children would never have made it this long without them and now it's clear to see that they have you as well and none too soon."

"But that's not really what you came here to discuss, eh?" Srenna gently responded trying to bring the focus back on the subject she was dying to know about.

"No actually, but I do know that you seem to have Matthew's full attention where the children are concerned according to Hamilton and Irmani and that's why I'm going to ask you for your help on a little matter of my own," Patricia began.

"I don't understand. What could I possibly help you with?" the young woman asked with a slight frown on her pretty face.

"Well...Hamilton and I both agree that...well...Matthew and the children have been out of church for a very long time...very long," she started quietly. "I know that the first time they return might not be easy for them by any measure, the memories and all." She hesitated and watched Srenna's expression to see if the girl was following her. She felt a little relief to see Srenna nodding her head in agreement. "Hamilton feels that if Matthew had the support and encouragement he needs to resume the fellowship that he might make the decision to come back. And we both think that encouragement would come best...from you." Patricia stopped and waited to give Srenna a chance to absorb all she'd just said. She needn't have waited very long.

"I completely agree with you...about the family needing to go back. I've wanted to talk to him for a couple of weeks now...but with the sheep shearing and ...." Srenna began rambling quickly about her own pent up thoughts on the subject. She stopped suddenly when she realized how much Patricia was grinning at her exuberance. "I'm sorry. I get so carried away some times."

"No dear. Do not be sorry… especially concerning this," Patricia assured her. "They have been away long enough and they need their church family to support them every week. Jimmie and Irmani…you…can't do it all."

"No…of course not," Srenna answered with a look of frustration.

Patricia could tell that the girl was holding something back and patted her arm lovingly.

"Darling…since you've been here have you had a break at all…taken time for yourself?" she started and then as quickly held her hand up to stop Srenna from responding in a way that the older woman knew all too well would be coming out of the girl's diligent mouth. "I'm not talking about a bath…even if you do get one of those a week. I'm not talking about your little meetings with Matthew…Ah! Yes! I even know about those too," she chuckled as Srenna attempted to defend her hard work and dedication towards this young family. "Hamilton and I want the community to share this load. We can't have you going and burning yourself out like a low candle, can we? Or Matthew."

"I suppose I know what you're getting at and actually I was thinking the very same thing myself… at least a bit," Srenna admitted, sighing heavily. "I miss church. I'd like to get to know more people in the community and…"

"Of course you would and you can do that best on Sunday and when we have fellowship times, eh?" her visitor answered candidly.

"But how do I bring it up to Matthew. That IS what you are wanting me to do, eh?" Srenna questioned the woman with a mischievous smile on her face. She stared sideways at Patricia and waited for some formidable advice from the seasoned woman.

"My dear…In only six weeks you have managed to come into a home falling apart both with normal needs and grieving needs. I am again highly impressed with what you've accomplished in such a short time. I am sure you will figure out a way to convince Matthew Patton to return to church. After all… he does still love God in a great way in spite of all that's been dealt him and his siblings. And I am certain you love your Heavenly Father as much. So…" Patricia hesitated as she stood to leave, "Between the two of you…God that is…I believe there will be a way to bring it up and discuss it with Matthew. And if all else fails…feed him. That works every time."

"More honey?"

"More honey indeed."

Srenna stood from her chair and hugged the woman she was already beginning to respect incredibly and began walking with her towards the front door. She felt a new determination to take on the goal of returning this young household back into the stream of fellowship one way or another. As she and Patricia said their goodbyes and the car drove away she was thankful that Benji had slept quietly that afternoon after all. The girls had stayed busy in the garden during the visit as well and Srenna was sure God had appointed this time for some well needed direction and encouragement.

Now all Srenna James had to figure out was how to get Matthew Patton's full attention on the subject and encourage him that returning to the Sunday morning service was a necessary step to his family's full recovery. This was something she thought she should do without Mary's involvement or foreknowledge. Srenna would be meeting with Matthew tomorrow as she normally did on Fridays. She would have to think fast. Sunday was three days away. Her thoughts already went to plans for supper, something special for his lunch tomorrow and anything in between.

"Feed him indeed," she pondered in amusement as her thoughts seem to naturally lean towards her wiles to "get his attention".

Srenna James just didn't know how little she had to do at all to get Matthew Patton's attention.

Chapter 22: He Leads Me

It always amazed Srenna how fast her morning flew by, but none as fast as the Friday mornings before she rode with Stephan to take Matthew his lunch and spend some time talking to him. She was becoming more and more excited to have a chance to communicate with him on a weekly basis concerning the children's needs, the house and her many responsibilities to him. Since assuring him she would stay and asking him to be open and honest with her, Srenna noticed him loosening up, becoming more comfortable with her presence and contributions to his home, to his siblings. The events of the last few weeks were becoming more and more positive and productive where this young parentless family was concerned.

She was beginning to understand each child as an individual. She also wanted to understand Matthew better, what he liked and how he could be encouraged in his grueling day to day schedule.

When Mary had shared that her brother loved to write and Srenna gave him the journal, she had hoped that some day soon he would open up enough to let her read some of his poetry or writings, but she knew that was probably far down the road.

She turned her thoughts to finishing the sandwiches she was making when the girls came in with Benji in Mary's arms. Mary and the girls had played with him while keeping him up in the hopes that he would nap even better this afternoon. Everyone was hungry now and Srenna snatched the boy out of Mary's arms so she could sit down and feed him before leaving. He was finally engaging in a bottle instead of the nursing bag and Srenna. He had developed a healthy appetite for the goat's milk and readily drank the bottle with no fuss. But the infant still watched Srenna closely as though at any minute she might simply disappear if he closed his eyes. None the less as was hoped his baby eyelids became heavier and heavier till he slept and sucked till the bottle was dry.

Srenna quietly stood up and carried Benji to his crib, a sleepy burp escaping his satisfied belly. She had to giggle at the grin on the tired child's face and marveled at how much just this change in him had brought peace back into the house. She checked his diaper and laid him gently into the crib. His adorable little mouth still appeared to be sucking a bottle in a dream where no bottle went dry.

Srenna watched him for a moment as she had been now for six weeks and was amazed at how strong the bond was with this infant. Even Grace Havilland's new baby had not captured her heart like this poor little motherless boy. She had felt no maternal urge when her own mother had given birth to her twin brothers when she was five and Srenna gladly gave her mother much space while the boys were growing older.

Memories of the boys, the quickness of losing them, losing her mum and dad, tried to flood her thoughts, but she snapped herself quickly back into the room and the sleeping baby here and now. She also saw the time on the clock on the wall.

"Oh! I'd better hurry," she thought to herself. She left the room and rushed to the kitchen to find Stephan impatiently pacing the floor, waiting for her. "I'm sorry! I'm sorry!" Srenna offered penitently. "Did you eat your lunch?" she asked, hoping he could do that while she used the dunny.

"More like he sucked in his lunch!" Lilly snickered, laughing at Stephan, who immediately stuck out his tongue at his most annoying sister.

"I've eaten, let's go, we're late!" he snapped, walking to the hallway door.

"All right. Here. Here is your brother's lunch and mine. I'll meet you outside," she responded, a bit flustered with the thirteen-year-olds impatience to reach the fields. But in spite of his exasperating grunt he walked out and headed for the front gate where Bear was tied and waiting.

Srenna looked at Mary who was calmly washing the lunch dishes and started to say something to her when Mary cut her off gently and commanded softly, "Just go. I think I can handle it."

"Yes, I believe you can," Srenna gratefully admitted. With that she literally ran into the bathroom, splashed some cold water on her face and checked to make sure her long hair had not completely fallen apart from her braid during the morning chores. She was satisfied she wasn't in too much disarray and headed for the front door.

Stephan was waiting at the front gate stomping some unsuspecting ant hill to kill time. Srenna headed down the walk and waited for him to mount Bear. "Are we ready now?" he questioned with a great deal of sarcasm in his voice. Srenna was still unsure how to respond to him as she took the boy's hand and put her foot in the stirrup. He pulled her up and she settled herself on the horses back behind the saddle. She decided to respond calmly with an "All ready" to him. She made a mental note though to bring him up when she talked to Matthew along with the other delicate subject she wanted to discuss.

They headed for the more rolling hills where Matthew had taken the sheep that morning; the hills that nestled up to the higher pastures. When he was beyond the fields above the pens, Srenna couldn't see him. The sheep were tiny dots from the porch and yard. She had felt surer initially being able to see him closer, but she was becoming more secure at the house through the day. The extra comfort was knowing the large bell at the side of the house could be heard even past the point he was today if anything happened or he was needed.

She and Stephan rode for about ten minutes, unable to speak at all because he was still in a hurry and it was all Srenna could do to stay on Bear. She was extremely grateful when Stephan came to a stop and she saw Matthew a short way off. She waited for Stephan to continue approaching his brother but instead he offered help for Srenna to get down. As she dismounted he seemed even more impatient, even agitated as he saw his brother coming towards them.

"Tell Matt, I'll run the edges, make sure everything's right, eh?" he muttered quickly and then just as Srenna stepped away from Bear, he pulled the horse around and trotted away.

Srenna watched the teen leave in what seemed to be great haste and failed to see Matthew coming up behind her.

"I'm starved," he chuckled playfully, grabbing the basket from Srenna and reaching for one of the sandwiches she had brought for him. As he walked back in the direction he had come, Srenna turned and rapidly walked to catch up with his long legged strides.

"Hullo to you too!" she laughed as she grabbed the basket back and jokingly slapped his hand.

"Sorry," he mumbled with a mouth full of food and the same satisfied and dimpled grin of his baby brother.

"You're just like your brother," she giggled.

"Not like that one, I hope," he retorted looking back at the disappearing teenager. "Where's he off to in such a bloody hurry anyway?" There was a little edge of concern in Matthew's voice.

"I don't know, "Srenna answered thinking of her own concern with his earlier disposition.
"He's been antsy all morning, impatient, moody."

"Was he rude to you?" Matthew asked with more concern. He'd been getting more and more tired of butting heads with Stephan over little things, chores and manners, his sisters. He looked down at Srenna's face and could see she was holding back "You've come up here so we could talk, so we could discuss the children," he reminded her. He stopped dead in his tracks and waited.

Srenna took a few more steps and turned to face Matthew. His blue eyes seemed to bore through her till she was sure he was reading her mind. But before he could say anything more Srenna gave in and reported from start to finish, Stephan's behavior that morning and a few others besides. She was frustrated with the boy and still did not know what could be done about his attitude.

Matthew looked down at the ground, shaking his head in his own frustration. He was trying to think of something to say to reassure Srenna he would take authority and do something about Stephan. But the truth was he didn't know what to do and before he responded with an angry solution short of horse whipping the thirteen-year-old, Srenna smiled calmly at him and offered her opinion.

"He's all bottled up and ready to blow, Matthew. Has he ever even really cried?" she wondered out loud.

"No. I don't think so; At least not that I've seen. You know, maybe he has at night or off by himself, but not even at the funeral." Matthew's face softened at the thought of the enormous grief his younger brother must be feeling and "bottling up" as Srenna put it.

"What do you think I should do?" he asked with a real desire to receive Srenna's input. "I can't just let him keep snapping at the girls, flipping off at you or defying me."

"No you can't," Srenna agreed. "But Grace Havilland always said "there must be order in the house with a lot of love and little chaos," she smiled at Matthew. Again her light response seemed to lift the brevity of the issue a bit off of him "Let's eat," she instructed Matthew, "and we'll figure out something."

He took the basket from her and like a perfect gentleman, offered his arm. With a whimsical bow he announced, "You're table Miss, right through here." They had come to a small grove of trees not too far from the flock and there was the picnic blanket Srenna had searched for earlier, spread out over the lush grass under the shade.

"Hey, I looked all over for that this morning, you," she scolded.

"Oops, I guess I must have had it all along," Matthew laughed, taking yet another playful swat at his hand as he reached for a cookie in the basket. He sat it on the blanket and was going to help Srenna sit but she dropped to her knees before he could and she began removing the contents of the lunch.

Matthew was beginning to realize that unlike the first week Srenna had been here when he felt somewhat as though he were walking on eggshells, he was finding her surprisingly easy to talk to now, to joke with and especially to ask of her the things he needed her to do. She seemed so easy going and steady. He could see where her five years of experience as a governess had help to ground her. But there was something he couldn't quite put his finger on where she was concerned. As he looked across the blanket at her fussing over the lunch she had made he couldn't help but wonder what might make this seemingly well put together young woman…vulnerable. He could tell she was holding back in some ways and yet in others was very open and honest, trusting. But he sensed in her a part she was not quite ready to share. Even in discussing Stephan's grief or any of the rest of the children grieving she was extremely careful not to divulge many details about her own tragic past. He secretly hoped someday soon he would be able to hear her story and understand this brave young governess and all she had been through. He knew from Hamilton Davidson's report that the young girl had overcome much to be as far along as she was today. He was extremely grateful for that.

They ate silently for a while, Srenna taking in the view of the mountains from this new spot, and Matthew trying to focus his attention on his sheep and not the company he sat with. His glances her way did not go unnoticed. She was also trying to read him and his mood now that his belly was full. He had relaxed a bit since the beginning of their conversation. She really had wanted to bring up Mrs. Davidson's suggestion, her invitation for the Patton family to return to church this Sunday.

It had been over three months since Miriam's funeral, six weeks of that since Srenna had arrived. She agreed with Patricia the day before that the children needed to get away from the house, however, she really wanted Matthew to be sure, to be ready. To attend the Anglican Church the children had grown up in meant Matthew would walk in as the head of the house and sit in the pew his father and his mother had occupied together for fifteen years. Though his mood seemed lighter these last few weeks, she wasn't sure how much he was still struggling with adjustments and the ever incredible responsibilities he had inherited. She was also not sure yet whether he could or would swing into another display of grief such as the one demonstrated on the hill the first day she arrived. She struggled for a few moments wondering if and how she could bring it up when she glanced over at Matthew and saw a knowing look on his face.

"What?" she asked him realizing all this time he had been studying her. She felt a warm glow of color creeping into her cheeks.

"That's quite a war you're waging over there all by yourself. Mind if I join in?" His whimsical tone eased Srenna tremendously and with great determination she quickly began her speech.

"Mrs. Davidson, Patricia, she made a suggestion yesterday. She thought it would be lovely if we..."

"Came to church on Sunday?" Matthew broke in looking away from Srenna and out across the field. He was trying very hard to appear serious, but he began to impishly giggle as Srenna gasped and threw a piece of cookie at him.

"You knew, all this time, you knew!" she scolded again, throwing yet another piece.

"Of course I knew," he laughed, "Where do you think the honorable Reverend Davidson was while you two were visiting, eh?" Matthew laid back on the blanket rather pleased with himself that what Srenna had been agonizing over discussing with him, he already knew.

It was her mood that began to swing. She found herself almost a bit agitated that she had worried so much about approaching this subject with him. Matthew suddenly realized when he looked over at Srenna that maybe he had upset her. She was looking out at the hills and appearing to be not so amused.

"I'm sorry," he said simply, rolling over on his side with his head in his hand. "I didn't mean to joke about it. I know you must have wondered…if it was too soon…if it would upset us." He waited for a moment for some response, some indication that she wasn't angry, but she continued to look out over the scenery. "Look, Srenna. All we can do is try. I think we can at least try. It it's not time we'll come home, simple as that," he stated very seriously. Again he waited.

This time Srenna turned to face him and saw such an earnest expression on Matthew's face she instantly decided how she would respond.

"Good!" she answered pertly and calmly. Then before Matthew could even draw his next breath, she picked up another cookie and began breaking it into pieces, throwing each one at him until both were laughing so hard Srenna thought her sides would split.

"You'd better start cleaning the crumbs out of your hair now, you," she giggled.

"My hair," he chuckled, as pieces were retrieved and thrown back at her.

"All right! Stop!" she shouted, jumping to her feet. She began brushing the crumbs off her hair and blouse and Matthew stood to shake himself off as well. He couldn't remember when he'd laughed so hard or felt like he had anything to laugh about. But as he picked up the blanket to shake it off, he sighed a different sigh; one of relief. Then he suddenly remembered Stephan and his dilemma with him. As though understanding that Matthew was about to bring up the sullen boy, Srenna smiled at him and simply suggested, "No more problems today, eh? He'll still be here tomorrow." She waited to see if she saved the light moment that needed to last a little longer and was relieved when Matthew grinned and picked up the basket.

"Let me ride you home, Miss James," he offered courteously as he gave her his arm as any proper British gentleman would.

"I'd be very grateful, Mr. Patton," she answered him in her best British lady like voice. She took his arm and they walked to the edge of the trees. Matthew gave a loud whistle from his lips and

Samson came trotting up to both of them from the nearby patch of grass he had been grazing in. Matthew lifted himself into the saddle first with basket in hand and pulled Srenna up behind him. She gripped Matthew firmly around his waist as Samson was a bit taller and broader then Bear. "Could you just walk him?" she asked over Matthew's shoulder. "I'm afraid there won't be any bones left in my bum after Stephan's ride," she chuckled as Matthew turned the big horse down the path. Looking back over his shoulder only inches away from her face he answered her as politely and as seriously as he could without laughing.

"Anyway you want it, Miss. We don't want you to go breaking your bum, eh?" He couldn't however stop the grin from crossing his face.

Srenna slapped him playfully one more time and then quickly recovered her grip as Samson side stepped down the hill. But Matthew didn't mind the slap. He was grateful to Samson at the moment and was glad they were walking all the way back to the house. And slowly.

Later that evening at the dinner table Matthew waited till everyone had almost finished eating and watched each one of his sisters and his brother to read their mood. Aside from Stephan's still apparent bad one, the girls seemed gratefully cheery. The two youngest recounted their day for Matthew, all the games they played with their little brother on the blanket in the yard. He acknowledged Mary's meal she had prepared with only miniscule help from Srenna when she returned.

Matthew looked down at the other end of the table where Srenna sat smiling encouragingly at the young man trying everyday to fill his father's seat and shoes. She nodded at him as if to coax him to bring up the subject of church and his decision to try and go back. He took a deep breath as he scanned the very full table one more time. Then he cleared his throat to get everyone's attention.

I have something I'd like to discuss with everyone," he began, "something I hope we all can do as a family again." All eyes were on him now and he fixed his gaze on Srenna's face for a moment.

"Go on," she encouraged him.

"We've been invited to go back to church this Sunday, if we all feel like we're ready," he stammered, suddenly very nervous.

"Church!" Stephan lamented. But his response was quickly drowned out by his sister's excited answers of, "Oh could we?" and "Oh, yes let's" and "that would be wonderful".
Matthew looked at Srenna and the relieved smile on her face but she motioned her head towards Stephan and her concern for his adamant disapproval. He had the hugest scowl on his face and was slumped in his chair wishing someone would for just once listen to anything he had to say.

Matthew heaved a deep sigh. He didn't want a battle with his brother nor did he think this was the time to confront him about his attitude today and the last few days for that matter. He hoped he was right as he took yet another deep breath and began as calmly and firmly as he could make his nineteen year old voice sound. "You can stay home if you'd like, Stephan, for now."

Srenna and the girls became stone silent and looked first at Matthew and then at Stephan. Stephan was in shock and somewhat deflated since he had fully expected Matthew to dictate his going. He seemed almost embarrassed that all eyes were on him waiting for a rebuttal of sorts or some negative response. But Matthew had caught him off guard.

"Can I be excused?" he snapped, standing up at the table but not away from it.

"Yes you can," Matthew answered him keeping his eyes fixed on the boy. "But Stephan, if you stay home, you stay here…till we get home. I won't have you mucking about while we're gone. You decide." Matthew picked up his cup and finished his tea, hoping beyond hope that no furry was about to unfurl at the cheerful table.

But Stephan was too aware that everyone was expecting him to blow and instead he defiantly and sarcastically retorted to his brother, "I'll think about it!" He left the dinner table , went thru the kitchen and then they heard the back door slam. Srenna wanted to rush after him, not sure if to correct him or console him, but Matthew motioned to her to stay. He continued to drink his cup and tried to listen to the girls about the return to church only a few days away.

But Srenna couldn't keep her mind off the angry boy outside, trying hard to reason his anger towards a God he hated at the moment, even though she pretended to listen to the happy plans being made. She uttered up a silent prayer for Stephan and wondered how the boy could be consoled. As she did her eyes met Matthew's and she almost could hear his own silent cry for God to send the peace

Stephan needed. He smiled reassuringly at Srenna, already very aware of how much she wanted to fix it.

"Give him some more time, eh?" Matthew suggested out loud as the girls began clearing the dinner table.

"Yes,... more time," Srenna smiled, hoping they were indeed right.

After all the evening clean up was done and bedtime loomed over the house, the girls came to Srenna. She had just barely put Benji down for the evening. Srenna knew just by the way both girls came up to her in the living room and hung on her, hugging her that they were up to something.

"Play something for us, please. Anything before we go to bed," Lilly begged. She was always attempting to incorporate one more thing, one more request, even one more dilemma to stay the sentence of bedtime each night. For days now the children had been trying to get Srenna to sit down and play the beautiful black piano in the corner, especially since they learned that Srenna could play. She had been so busy attempting to catch up in this dear despairing home, she had simply walked pass it. The pleading in Lilly's voice and her dark blue eyes begging Srenna were no match for her resolve.

"All right, all right! I'll make a deal with you. Up those stairs and into bed immediately..." Srenna commanded, chuckling at little Emma who was already at the stairs nodding her head in complete compliance. "I'll play when I know you're there!" She waved her hands at Lilly towards the hallway door. Then she followed the girl to the stairway and opened her arms for hugs.

Lilly grabbed Emma's hand and pulling her up the stairs exclaimed to Srenna, "We're going, we're going." As the girls disappeared, Mary also hugged Srenna and announced her own willingness to retire. Matthew had gone to his room a while ago and Stephan had snuck up to his over an hour ago.

"Good night Mary," Srenna smiled at the extremely strong girl who she had quickly come to count on completely in a few short weeks.

Srenna stood at the hallway door and within only a few moments heard Lilly's resounding announcement, "We're in." She chuckled at the little echo that followed from the five year old who would not be left out. "Yes! We in." She moved across the living room to the baby grand, a splendid gift from John Patton to his endearing wife on their tenth wedding anniversary. As Srenna sat down and opened the cover that had remained closed for far too long she hesitated at the thought of what she was about to do. Would this bring repair to this healing household...or would it be too soon a memory to relive. But that quiet steady voice in her heart whispered gently in her ear, "It's time. Let the healing waters flow."

Srenna placed her fingers on the silent keys and offered up a prayer as she recalled the song she had first learned in the Havilland's home. Grace had blessed her with lessons in an attempt to give the girl some refining for her love of music. It was about to pay off, now, when she needed it most. As she moved her hands across the keys and played the hauntingly sweet lullaby, she was unaware of the affect she began to have throughout the house; unaware that two little girls lie silently still as their eyelids drifted into sleepy dreams of their mother playing for them somewhere in heaven. She was unaware of the hot tears of a rebellious young boy, too old to show emotion, too grieved to keep it hidden forever. She was unaware of the grateful tears of an exhausted sixteen year old, too young to be a mother and too determined not to try.

But Srenna was even less aware of the ear of a young man pressed against his door, listening to the melodic strains. His own hopeful tears were falling freely down his cheeks, his hand clutching the book Srenna had brought to him on the hill. His tears were so mixed, fresh sorrow for his lost parents, and yet a sudden welcomed wave of hope and not despair. The despair had been washing away over the last few weeks but now like a torrential rain it seemed to be gone completely, with every measure, every note. It was being replaced with "We'll be right".

He remembered his mother's last prayer, "Send Matthew an angel". He was sure now he was hearing one. So much so he crawled onto his bed, curled up like a tired little boy and for the first time in a long time he closed his weary eyes and fell deeply and peacefully asleep. He never remembered hearing the end of the sweet lullaby Srenna was playing, nor did anyone else in the house. They never saw her own tears either; tears of determination, tears of hope. Even tears for her own memories. They missed the prayer that left her lips at the end of the song as well.

"Please Father, help me help them."

Chapter 23: The Return to Church

There had to be one more shoe somewhere in the endless pile of things in Emma and Lilly's room; only one more little black shoe to go with the already well guarded black shoe in Srenna's hand. She crawled around on hands and knees looking for anything promising under Emma's bed, closet or pile of dirty clothes in the corner.

"Ugh! Emma! How long has this sock been under this bed, you?" she grimaced, pulling a well soiled sock out instead of the badly needed shoe.

"Three years!" taunted her sister, holding her nose jokingly, provoking looks of fury from her sibling's face.

"She's only five!" grumbled Srenna, as she threw the sock in another pile and then went into the closet for another look.

"I found it!" exclaimed Emma proudly, holding the prized shoe up in the air.

"I don't care where child, just put them on and go downstairs with your sister," Srenna ordered, laughing at the proud youngster and handing her the other shoe. "On your feet and go!" she added again, giving her five-year-old charge a playful swat on her rear and pulling herself up on the bed. She smoothed her deep blue dress out after crawling about on the floor and watched as Lilly grabbed her little sister's hand and headed for the stairs.

"Front porch and no further!" she ordered as a quick after thought. She breathed a sigh of relief that at least those two were ready for church, and chuckled as she commented under her breath, "two down and only five to go, not too bad!" She stood and walked to the door nearly running into Stephan as he came flying out of his bedroom and headed down the stairs. He was almost dressed…shirt hanging out and jacket in hand. "At least he has his shoes," she quipped making her way down behind him. "Keep an eye on your sisters please," she added. Stephan grunted his disapproval but agreed to take charge as he caught Mary's threatening look when he came through the living room. She was holding Benji in her arms, still dressed in her robe. Mary passed the infant to Srenna and ran for the stairs to throw her church clothes on. She had finished dressing her squirming baby brother so Srenna could assist the girls in the hunt for the elusive shoe. He looked adorable in his little dress pants and shirt, his baby curls forming an angelic crown atop his head. Srenna kissed his cheek and tickled the boy, breathing a giggle into his ten-month-old ear.

"What a handsome little man you are," she cooed, wondering how he would take to his first time in church this glorious Sunday morning. But Srenna had very little time to contemplate that thought as the door at the other end of the living room opened and Matthew stepped out of his room. He was fitted out in his father's best Sunday suit that Srenna had feverishly altered for him the last two nights. It seemed even at nineteen Matthew had sprouted a few inches over the last year and had need of the suit left behind by John Patton.

Matthew stood for a moment looking at Srenna with Benji on her hip and all he could do was stare. She watched his face as he assessed her appearance in the lovely blue outfit that she had not worn until today. When he simply continued his gaze at her, she began fussing with the dress, wondering if there was something wrong with it.

"Is it…is it too much, too dressy…I can wear something…"she began. But Matthew suddenly found his tongue and cut her off with a smile of approval and a hearty answer.

"No…it's beautiful…you look…" he stammered uncomfortably. He knew what he wanted to say but before he could Srenna grinned at him and crossed the room.

"Look at you!" she exclaimed, tugging at the sleeve of his jacket and smoothing the lapel. "It's a perfect fit, if I do say so myself," she finished proudly.

"Thanks to you. A couple more inches and I wouldn't have needed the pants shortened," he grinned down at her. He allowed his gaze to wonder down Srenna's slender frame until it came to rest at her feet and then with a boyish chuckle he jokingly commented," I hope you're not planning on going to church barefoot. That would be the Rainga's church meeting."

"Ugh!" she grunted again, handing Benji to his big brother and hurriedly rushing across the living room to her own door. "I'll only be a minute, and watch that he doesn't spit on you," she added grinning back at Matthew. She quickly went to the old wardrobe in the corner and grabbed her dress shoes. As she slipped them on she took one more look in the mirror at the dressing table. Srenna suddenly realized how she really felt this morning, a feeling she hadn't had very often in her young life. She had never given much mind to what others thought of her, their comments or looks or even stares when she entered a room.

But today she cared. Today for some odd reason... it mattered. It made her feel different in a new way. She realized everyone at church would be seeing her, many of them for the first time, the Patton children's governess, their caregiver...Matthew's employee. All these thoughts began tumbling through her mind in a way the usually confident and outgoing girl had never felt before. Fortunately those thoughts were cut off by a comforting voice.

"You look fine...really," Mary's encouraging voice assured her. She had come to the bedroom door with Benji now on her hip. She grinned at Srenna and added, "Matthew's getting everyone else in the car."

Srenna took a deep breath, a bit embarrassed that Mary had seen a moment of struggle with nervous thoughts, but once again the oldest of the Patton girls wisely stated, "You're fine. We'll all be fine; even this little wiggle worm!" handing him back to Srenna, heading for the door. "Let's go."

Srenna hugged the baby boy as if to find some strange comfort from him and followed his sister out to the car. Matthew stood with the front door open for the ladies and waited for them both to crawl in, Mary first and then Srenna. He handed Benji in to her after she smoothed her dress and settled herself next to Mary. She suddenly remembered the first time Matthew Patton had helped her into the truck the first day she arrived and how nervous they had both been. Now she felt such ease around him it seemed as though she had been at the station for a year and not just six weeks. She did however feel a warm glow come over her as Matthew handed Benji in to her. That was interrupted quickly by Stephan's impatient and usual annoyance, mostly because he was wedged into the back seat with his younger sisters.

"Can we go!?" he lamented loudly, as Matthew hurried around the car and hopped in.

"Yes we can! He answered looking at his younger brother with a tiny bit of reproach in his voice.

Secretly Matthew didn't care how annoyed his brother was, how anxious anyone was or hard today might be. He was going back to church! He hadn't known how much he missed it until they had firmly decided to go. Now that the car was on its way up the road and headed towards the church in Castle Point he was truly excited. He glanced at Mary hoping she was okay after all and her eyes told him she was. Then he glanced in the rear view mirror at the girls and saw that they were occupied with the crayons and books that Srenna had given them to keep them busy.

Stephan was leaning against the window looking out with his usual bored and disinterested expression. But Matthew turned his eyes passed his sister in the front seat to the lovely young woman holding his baby brother. He felt a bit concerned. He could sense some of her nervousness. And small wonder. Good, loving church as it was, he knew all eyes would first be on them and their return, but then they would be curious about this mysterious governess from Australia. He knew by now that Srenna's deeply devoted love of God had been deprived of church since arriving at their home. Yet in her unswerving patience she had not pushed, nor pressured him to go until Matthew thought they were ready. Now he wondered…was she?

But Srenna had some of her own senses heightened right now. She caught Matthew's glance and smiled reassuringly at him, not so much as saying she was alright but that she would BE alright. In a wordless understanding he grinned back. To finalize the moment Mary looked at both, putting a comforting hand on their arms. But the moment was sealed with a laugh from everyone when a delighted squeal came from Benji at the sight of a field of cows. Matthew felt as though the car might just burst wide open with joy at that moment.

"Only my Heavenly Father could've done that," he thought with a silent prayer of thanks. He remembered also what his father would have probably said, "The joy of the Lord is my strength." It most certainly was.

The drive to St. James Anglican Church took only a short twenty minutes. The lovely white building was located on the east coast of New Zealand's North Island, just outside of the cozy little town of Castle Point. It sat up on a green tufted hill with gentle rolling land, open in some spots and wooded in a few others. The parsonage sat a bit further away, perched on a bluff overlooking a sandy beach below. A short distance up the beach one could see the shoreline giving way to jutting cliffs and rocky precipices, typical of the New Zealand landscape.

Every time Srenna saw a new view of the remarkable country she felt awestruck by its incredible beauty and contrasting scenes. So far she had not ventured this close to the seashore as the market in Castle Point had been as far as she'd gone. But today she reassured herself that they would not go down to the beach and she was far too busy concerning herself with the children and meeting everyone there.

They had arrived just as the singing had begun. Only a few others were still lingering around the steps and at the double doors. Matthew found a place to park and then quickly exited to help Srenna and Mary out of the car. He turned to look at the building he had called church his whole life and took a deep breath. It seemed, so did everyone else.

"Are we ready for this?" he asked, looking at Mary first, and then each of the others till his gaze fell on Srenna. He saw her smile softly as she jiggled Benji in her arms and suddenly he felt surer then he had in a long time; sure that they were all together, that they needed to do this and they could. He grinned and turned to move towards the door when he felt a little hand slip into his. Looking down at his side, little Emma, his "Little Bug" grinned up at him and stated soundly, "We ready!"

This brought a much needed round of laughter as Matthew led his brothers and sisters to the steps, Srenna close behind him. Several people moved quietly and quickly to receive the children with glad hearts and hugs and encouraging slaps on Matthew's back as the usher showed them to a row towards the back of the church. Many heads turned when the congregation realized they had entered and moved into the pew. Everyone smiled, many curiously examining the young dark haired woman who held the baby and slipped in after the children had and before Matthew did. But no one noticed as much as Reverend Davidson as the two young people stood side by side in the pew. The lovely girl cuddling the curly blonde headed baby as though she had always loved him and the tall handsome youth fitted in his father's church suit made Hamilton remember another first Sunday; the one which he'd finally convinced John and Miriam Patton they were loved by God and forgiven as sinners. They had finally come that first Sunday morning only a few weeks after the birth of Matthew. They had been part of his flock ever since.

He felt as though a strong memory was being played out at that moment, and as then, he stared and watched the boy look down at the girl with the baby, and grin at her as they sang a familiar hymn; grin as if to say, "We'll be all right."

It took all of Hamilton Davidson's resolve to speak when the song ended without bursting with unspeakable joy and unfailing hope.

"Matthew, I can't tell you how wonderful it was to see all of you filling up that pew again. And this little nipper. Great job, Miss James, great job. It appears you have things a bit more in order, at least with the younger ones," Reverend Davidson chattered on, giving a sideway glance at Stephan who still seemed disgruntled and impatient with the whole morning.

Matthew looked over at his younger brother standing by the door waiting for a quick exit.
"For the most part, we're sweet," he smiled at the Parish leader and then looked down at Srenna still near his side. It had not gone unnoticed by either he or Mary how many of the women had been curious about the lovely young woman with the Patton baby in her arms most of the morning. She had undeniably been the brunt of gawks and whispers along with what Matthew was sure were speculations on how his family was doing. For the most part they were all received, Srenna included, with resounding compassion and heart felt joy. Many of the men and women had contributed in various ways to support Matthew and the children before and after John and Miriam had died. Many reassured again today to be of "any assistance whatsoever", encouraging the boy that he and the children were in their thoughts and prayers.

Matthew resolved before Reverend Davidson's message was even over that they would be back from now on. He hadn't realized how much he needed them, needed the fellowship; needed the message. Several times this morning as Patricia Davidson moved Srenna from group to group introducing her to different people Matthew had looked for her from across the room. He found himself watching her protectively wanting to make sure she was not overwhelmed by all the introductions and attention. He realized quickly how gracefully and skillfully Srenna moved among the people, how at ease she became after only a short time. He caught her eye several times and she smiled reassuringly, indicating that she was alright. There was a deep satisfaction that the older women who had known his mother well, seemed to readily embrace this stranger from Australia. The day almost appeared to be going quite nicely without insult or injury.

Almost.

Just as Matthew began gathering his young family and herding them towards the car, an undesirable voice came up from behind him; a voice he had hoped to avoid, not just this morning but as far as he was concerned…for the rest of his life.

"Why…Matthew Patton! You weren't planning on sneaking off without at least a "Hullo Margi, how are you", eh?" came the crooning sound from a girl who had slipped up beside Matthew and slid her arm through his.

Everyone stopped and turned, Srenna included, looking at the beautiful pristine blonde girl who suddenly and rather unabashedly accosted Matthew. Srenna saw the look on his face go from a warm blush to an irritated cringe, especially when he saw everyone watching him and this forward display of unwanted affection. He forced himself to not simply yank his arm free but he did slip it away and then turned to Srenna and suggested to her in a quiet and controlled tone, "Why don't you get everyone in the car and I'll be right there."

He seemed to Srenna to be embarrassed and yet his eyes told her he needed some privacy. Without a moment's hesitation, Srenna received Matthew's instruction with her usual grace and poise, motioning to the children to "Come along everyone." They all followed her, a bit disappointed that they weren't going to hear the conversation between their brother and this seemingly brazen young woman.

"He'll let her have it, I bet!" said Stephan, suddenly interested in something for the first time this morning. He was walking backwards peering over his sisters to watch his brother's reaction to his old schoolmate.

"Stephan, turn around and stop gawking. Let Matthew alone!" Mary snapped at her younger brother.

"Yes, Stephan, it's rude to watch," Srenna agreed, "Come on now, in the car, the lot of you."

She hustled them all in, but as she prepared to climb in she couldn't help but steal a glance back at where Matthew stood with the girl. She had only to look once to see that he was indeed, "letting her have it" or at least something unpleasant.

Srenna crawled in and began praying immediately that whatever was occurring just then would not rob Matthew and all the rest of them of the wonderful morning they had just had. She made herself not look again as much as she wanted to and was relieved when the car door opened and Matthew slid in and nonchalantly asked everyone in a surprisingly chipper tone of voice, "Everyone ready to go home and eat?"

Resounding yes's and "I'm starved" and "Let's go" seemed to clear the air that only moments before threatened to be taunt and uncomfortable. Srenna chuckled at all of them and added." It's lucky for you, Mary and I made dinner last night!"

As Matthew pulled the car out onto the road leading home he looked at Mary in the back seat with a slight grin and then shifted his gaze to Srenna who held his baby brother in her arms and had his baby sister leaning against her side between them. He knew he saw a question in her eyes concerning what had just taken place. It was unmistakably noticeable. But he simply grinned his endearing dimpled grin, the one she had already come to know meant, "She's sweet, everything's right." Srenna returned his grin with hers and sighed a deep sigh, glad on one hand that the morning was over and yet as always wondering what the rest of the day would hold in store.

Chapter 24: The First Kiss

As God would have it, the week following the first visit back to the close knit church seemed to bring with it some measure of marked peace in the Patton home; at least where most of the Patton's were concerned. True to his intentions Matthew made a point of finding some way to give Srenna some badly needed time off and a family meeting with the children found a speedy vote on the decision to make Sunday afternoons hers exclusively. The announcement was the real highlight of the children's day as they proudly made it to her just moments after the dinner meal. They all shot down her attempt to argue her way out of it and Matthew sealed it with an adamant order that she would indeed let them take care of things the remainder of the day so she could slip away and do whatever her heart desired. Matthew even offered to take his mother's coveted lounge chair out into the trees or down by the nearby river so she could get completely away from the house. In the end she lost and they triumphantly prevailed. They were all pretty pleased with themselves.

Her decision was to take up Matthew's offer and the chair was carried to the grove of trees behind the house just before the path to the river. He in turn took the opportunity to do something else he had been thinking about for weeks now. As soon as he was sure Srenna was comfortable in her little "time off" spot, he slipped something out of his back pocket and handed it to the young woman who had just showed him how much she trusted him and respected him for the last six weeks. It was one of his journals.

Srenna was delighted that he actually thought enough of her to let her see the writings that were so private and so personal to the nineteen-year-old. He said very little about it and Srenna assured him quickly that she knew she would enjoy them. With that said he walked back to the house and hoped that he had done the right thing in opening himself up this way. It was indeed a new thing for him as only his father and mother, maybe Hamilton Davidson and in desperate moments Tommie, had ever really heard his deepest thoughts. He couldn't explain why he needed to do this but he did. He needed to know how Srenna James would perceive his innermost thoughts.

Srenna found herself completely lost in his thoughts, many of them not unlike her own over the past seven or eight years. One entry in particular peaked her interest. It was a poem written by Matthew that was apparently not finished but none the less started. The beginning phrases caught her attention immediately when she realized the lines might actually be describing Matthew's feelings over the events that had transpired in the last few years.

> Lord when the darkened clouds obscure my sun
> And all my world has seemed to come undone
> I've only but to keep my eyes on you
> I'm in my Shepherd's gaze
>
> And when the angry waves crash from the sea
> And threaten to surround and frighten me
> I've only but to lift my arms to you
> I'm in my Shepherd's gaze
> I can feel you watching

Srenna mulled over the words in her head for a very long time. Images of the children, of Matthew and all they had gone through for the last few years made her emotions run high. For a little while she found herself tearfully praying for them, for herself so she would know what she could do further then she had. Her heart was still troubled for Stephan and his unresolved anger and grief. All morning in church and then at home he had defiantly sat with arms crossed and such a look of misery on his face. He couldn't wait to be dismissed and even after the announcement that they would all chip in to take care of clean-up he managed to disappear.

Srenna had watched Matthew's reaction to his brother's insubordination and could see how easily the boy vexed his older brother…and everyone else for that matter. But Matthew didn't let it go any further after the successful return to church that morning and how elated he was to be back around old friends.

Srenna suddenly felt her spirits lift as she thought back over the morning, especially after the service when she was introduced to so many people. Numerous times she had caught Matthew's eye as he watched her across the sanctuary and then on the church steps. To her surprise she had found she too was watching more then usual to see where he was and what he was doing. What surprised her even just now and more and more these last few weeks was how much she was thinking about everything Matthew Patton said and for that matter…did. The incident with Margi and Matthew earlier that morning had caught her by surprise when it kept her wondering what had really happened.

It did not go unexplained, thanks to Lilly's quick little tongue and Mary's attempt to soften the explanation. Srenna found herself completely privy to Matthew's past relationship with the girl and for some odd reason after Mary's rendition found some satisfaction in finding out the girl was never a love interest where Matthew was concerned. She did however wonder why Margi Henderson still found any interest in him at all as the two seemed worlds apart and Matthew made it quite clear he was not going to tolerate her brazen displays of affection…especially not at church!

Further and later accounts from Mary also brought her up to speed on the attempts by Miss Henderson's rich father to swallow up as many of the vulnerable stations as he could while husbands and fathers were away at war. Once again, Srenna found herself gratefully aware of just how protected Miriam, Matthew and the children had been, in the constant care of the Rainga family. She increasingly respected them and was growing fonder and fonder of the couple for all they had done and was still doing for the Patton family after the loss of their parents.

Routine became an even more welcomed visitor as the next couple of weeks passed. October had slipped quickly away the first couple of weeks Srenna had arrived and now November had flown by. She suddenly found herself thinking strangely enough about the Christmas holiday that loomed ahead of all of them as December's first week arrived. She made a mental note to speak to Matthew about how he wanted to handle what would be the children's first holiday without their mother.

Before she ever had a chance Mary gave her the agenda that had usually transpired over the years, beginning with the church festival at the end of the week. It sounded as though the whole church and half the more of the community, Maori, Pakeha or otherwise would attend the festivities at the Anglican Church after the Sunday morning service. It was one of many annual get-togethers that Castle Point recognized over the years; this one being one Hamilton and Patricia Davidson had birthed in an effort to bring all races into one joyful celebration.

"There will be yard games and food," Lilly described to Srenna, her eyes bright with anticipation, "and dancing…and the boys will play rugby and we'll have cricket matches and…."

"All right Lilly…enough. Give someone else a chance to talk for a change," her older sister retorted, a bit annoyed at her sister who relentlessly was cutting her off as she tried to tell Srenna what needed to be prepared. "Beside the horse race in February it's probably one of the most wonderful times of the year," Mary finished, sounding a bit melancholy.

Srenna heard the bittersweet tone in the young girl's voice as she was sure Mary's memories of her father and mother were invading her thoughts. She watched the girl's face for any signs of tears but Mary only grew a little quiet and thoughtful for a moment. Then a quick scan of the other two sitting at the kitchen table revealed much the same mood beginning to overtake the one that had been predominant only minutes ago as Lilly rattled on.

"You know what I think we should do?" Srenna quickly intervened. "Do you remember when you felt sort of sad when I first got here and we knew Matthew and Stephan were feeling badly too?" She prayed a quick prayer that her idea was not too easily forgotten. And it was not.

"We made cookies…mommy's best!" piped little Emma, looking so proud that she had gotten the answer before anyone else.

"We did indeed, Little Bug…and…." Srenna began.

"We put them on Mum's favorite dish!" added Lilly, grinning from ear to ear.

"We most certainly did!" Srenna finished, smiling hugely at Mary and seeing the cloud lift off the older girl's face.

"We could make some of Mum's favorite dishes and take them for everyone to enjoy," offered Mary, then to Srenna's surprise added gently, "It would be as though she were there."

Srenna watched carefully at the reaction from all of them at this suggestion but was delighted to see some measure of resolve from all three of the girls as they discussed there mother's contribution to the festivities they would attend. She hoped with all her heart that this was an indication of how much of the holiday season would be easy or hard concerning her young charges. She was glad the discussion had occurred before approaching Matthew about the family's plans for the rest of the events.

So Miriam's best dishes were duplicated for that next Sunday, her hot candied potato salad and delicious fruit pie were lovingly prepared from scratch on Saturday and ready to be rewarmed in the oven at the church and parsonage. The girls made cookies again like they had for their brothers to cheer them up that first week Srenna had come. It hardly seemed possible to her that only eight weeks had passed by. Already she had formed an irreversible bond with each of the girls and Benji was never far from her side. She still struggled wondering how she could break Stephan's icy exterior but she was more determined then ever to find a way.

And then there was Matthew. She had become acutely aware as of lately of just how much he was crossing her mind during the day. She found herself wondering when he would be in if he went back to the barn or pens after dinner. She instinctively woke every morning knowing full well when he was ready to leave for the fields. And their Friday afternoon meeting was becoming the anticipated highlight of her week and not just to discuss the children. She and Matthew had begun sharing more and more what was important to them both as well as what was important to the children. Sometimes in the midst of these discussions both would stop and nearly blush for how comfortable they'd become with each other's presence. A definite friendship was being forged and it was unlike anything either one had ever experienced before. She felt as though she could say anything to him and he to her. As the holiday crept up, it gave Srenna pause to wonder how close they both truly were after only two months.

She was about to find out.

The voices in the car on the way to church on Festival Sunday were sometimes deafening…but Matthew restrained himself from putting any damper on them. They could be crying, he thought silently as he tried to pick out the different conversations going on all at once.

Several times he glanced over at Srenna who was trying to listen to all of Lilly's chatter while being sandwiched between both he and the lovely young governess. As much noise was being raised in the back seat between Stephan and Mary and little Emma. Benji was adding his baby babble to the noise and every now and then actually contributing what sounded vaguely like a real word…to which everyone was made to stop momentarily and attempt to interpret.

Matthew had to smile as he drove down the road leading to Castle Point and the church by the sea. He honestly had thought by now that his world would have come to an ugly end with his family being dispersed anywhere and everywhere. But no such thing had happened. His grandmother seemed to have simply forgotten that she had sent a governess and he was sure the one she sent would in no way let her know she had defected. All right by him! He did however wonder when or if the Headmistress Baxter would swoop down on them at the end of her school session and demand something…anything. He wondered too how long before Family Services would try, if at all to intervene. He quickly shook that thought out of his head and continued to watch his little family enjoy the drive to church.

It was tradition for all to come clothed in casual garments so they could participate in the yard games and competitions planned for after the service. Hamilton Davidson kept his sermon very short and sweet, reminding each one of his parishioners how grateful he was for them this holiday season and the strength and beauty they showed one another during the year. He encouraged all to determine to make the next year an even brighter and better one for one another in as many ways as they could. That said, he prayed over the festivities waiting for everyone outdoors and the congregation was dismissed to begin the exciting chore of having the greatest of fun with families from all over the community.

As a tremendous array of island foods of all types and tastes were set out, others from the area churches and fellowships began showing up. The Rainga's arrived to share in the annual party as they had done for years as the Patton's friends. Many of their own congregation at the Maori meeting house also showed and Srenna was amazed again at the closeness of two diverse cultures and pasts coming together to fellowship and enjoy each others good company.

As the afternoon flew by Srenna tried to follow each of the children as they participated in races and games. With the help of Irmani and Patricia she was able to do more then she thought she would have been as each woman fawned over Benji. She was glad for the opportunity to just have fun. She had temporarily felt some measure of homesickness a few days ago while thinking about Reverend Carmel and Ruth, Grace and the family and even Mrs. Crawford, the people she would have been spending Christmas with this year had things not changed so abruptly.

But it was mid afternoon when she was watching Matthew attempt to sack race with little Emma while sitting on the blanket with Benji that she was acutely reminded where she "was" and why. She thought for sure her heart would burst as she watched big brother and little sister forget all their sorrows for a time and laugh with pure joy as they tumbled to the ground. Mary and Lilly were laughing with some of the other girls and discussing plans to return to school after the first of the year. She watched Benji crawl with a vengeance trying to discover everything within his reach and wondered when she had not loved this baby boy. Her heart even turned to her daily thoughts of Stephan and hoping soon there would be a way to reach the heart that seemed to still be breaking.

It astounded Srenna that only eight weeks had gone by. Only three weeks remained before Christmas day. So much had been accomplished and still so much to do to keep up with this energetic and ever changing family. And then her thoughts turned where they had been turning without fail as she once again watched Matthew entertain his "Little Bug". As if knowing her thoughts were tumbling one over another he looked up and over at her and caught her gaze as he had been doing now for several weeks. And for several weeks now his attention had made her cheeks blush and her heart beat a little faster each time he did.

She hadn't much time to enjoy that sensation as several musicians rallied around the dance area to begin some good old fashion dance tunes. Lilly and Mary ran up just as they started and with Patricia's assurance that Benji was in watchful hands, pulled

Srenna to her feet to entice her to the make shift dance floor. She could barely resist the two and found Emma running up and slipping her little hand into Srenna's with a grin and a beg to "dance with me!"

Srenna laughed joyfully at the first sounds of the light hearted Gaelic music the instruments began. But she couldn't help but look around for Matthew and was greatly surprised and a bit disappointed to see him disappear into the line of trees beyond the church.

"Where is Matthew going? The dancing is just beginning," she asked of Mary.

For a brief moment a slight cloud came over the girl's face as she responded with somewhat of a matter of fact tone. "He won't dance…not Matthew."

"Why ever not?" Srenna inquired, suddenly concerned for him, as he had only moments ago been in such a good mood.

"Mum and Dad use to dance in the yard nearly every night when we were little," she explained and then added looking in the direction her brother had disappeared, "I suppose it's just still too hard for him to remember that, eh?"

"Maybe Mary. I hope he'll be all right," Srenna responded with concern and disappointment that he had gone off by himself.

"You know Matthew. He'll go somewhere…have a long talk with God…and then come back. No worries. He'll be sweet." Mary smiled at Srenna and continued to pull her into the group of dancers. Srenna tried to keep her mind on the light steps to the songs and enjoying the girls frolicking to the music.

That only lasted a little while though and then another thought began to plague her mind. She couldn't remember the last time she had seen Stephan and to add to her "worries", the ones she wasn't suppose to have, she and several others could tell that an infamous New Zealand rain cloud was beginning to cover the sky in the close distance. Much as she hated too she could see that their day of fun and games would probably be coming to an end…and soon.

Srenna pulled Mary off to the side of the dance area and suggested to the girl that she was going to go look for both Matthew and especially Stephan and that she wanted Mary to start getting things rounded up and to the car.

"I'll only look for a few moments, Mary. Perhaps Matthew went to look for your brother as well," she suggested to the oldest sister, setting off in the direction she had seen Matthew go.

Not far into the line of trees Srenna found a path that very quickly led her passed a cozy and quaint gazebo and then continued on away from the church and parsonage. She was surprised to find it open up above a backdrop of the beach and open sea. She nearly turned and ran back up the path when she realized how close she had come to the path leading to the waters edge below. What made her hesitate was the quaint but beautifully landscaped cemetery above the bluff. It was surrounded by a lovely white fence and something about it intrigued her to take a closer look. Once inside the fencing it didn't take very long for her to find what she knew had to be there.

Srenna stood for a quiet moment as she gazed down at two headstones nestled side by side in the lush green grass. She recognized the names on the stones right away and felt almost as if she had intruded in what was a very sacred place for John and Miriam Patton to share. Several trees blew gently in the wind and sparrows sang overhead in their branches. All around her she could feel a hushed peacefulness but in spite of that another unwelcome emotion was attempting to flood her senses. She couldn't remember when she had ever been in a cemetery, especially when there were no gravesites for her dear family lost at sea. The thoughts that began to overtake her made her turn to make a speedy retreat. She however was not prepared to come face to face with someone she would have rather never encountered...ever!

"Why...Miss James...what a pleasant surprise to see you here," gushed the beautiful Margi Henderson. Srenna noticed right away that the girl was blocking the exit for her retreat and looking quite pleased with the accomplishment.

"Miss Henderson...I didn't hear you come up. I was only just getting ready to go back and finish packing up the children. It looks like it could downpour any moment. I had hoped to find Stephan... and Matthew," Srenna began moving towards the gate in the hopes that the obstinate young woman would indeed get out of her way. But Margi Henderson had Srenna James right where she wanted her; or though she thought.

"Oh... don't worry about Matthew. I walked him back when we were finished catching up. You know, we have so little time to spend any more with one another what with all the tedious work he must do," the girl gushed.

Srenna could feel the color rising in her face whether due to anger or the mere thought of that person being any where near Matthew and alone. She found herself wanting nothing more then to just slug the girl and get it over. But being the lady she was she took the deep breath she needed and then simply began to walk to the gate with every intention of simply pushing the girl out of the way if need be. But Margi saw that Srenna was not going to stay and fight. She moved ever so slightly so that Srenna could pass and then turned to get what she thought would be the last word. She was wrong again.

"You know, given time Matthew and I will have a chance for a life together. You know what they say…patience is a virtue," Margi grinned, her arms crossed.

Srenna thought she might be able to just keep walking, but suddenly something rose up in her; something she remembered hearing and reading in the Bible as a child. She whipped around and stared hard into Margi Henderson's face and responded with a sure voice, "I also heard this one too," she began, "and the truth shall set you free."

"Why I'm not sure what that one has to do with the other…Miss James," Margi snickered.

"It has everything to do with it …Miss Henderson. Matthew has not nor will he ever be interested in you…and I pity you if you have not gotten that by now. Certainly everyone else has," Srenna stated firmly and simply. And then she simply walked away. She prayed the whole time as she headed back to the wooded path that she would not be followed and thoroughly bashed by the girl… but no such thing happened. Instead, much to her relief she nearly ran full into Matthew as she turned at a fork in the path leading back to the gazebo. She tried desperately to pull herself together so as not to let on that she had just confronted the troublemaking young woman he seemed so greatly to despise.

"There you are," he began quickly and with a bit of relief in his voice. He knew immediately though that something had upset Srenna and a look of concern spread across his face and in his eyes as he grabbed a hold of her arm. "Are you all right?" he asked peering down into her face and pulling her closer towards him. "Where were you?"

"I went looking for Stephan ...and you," she started hesitantly. "I wondered off a little too far and I saw that it was going to rain any minute...so I..." But before she could finish her sentence true to it's nature the weather cut loose and it began raining...and hard!

"Come on you...we'll have to make a run for it!" Matthew yelled as he began to run pulling Srenna with him. They headed as fast as their feet could fly back up the path and within a few moments they were up and into the gazebo. Both were winded, but laughing so hard at their fiasco that for a moment they simply stood in the middle of the gazebo and stared out at the downpour all around them.

"Oh... I do hope the children got in out of this," Srenna moaned, looking at Matthew and then added right away, "And where do you suppose Stephan has gotten too?"

"I can't help you there...I gave up looking for him an hour ago...but no worries...Mary and the children are sweet. They're in the fellowship hall with Irmani. I came back out to look for you...Miss James," he laughed, grinning from ear to ear.

"For me, you say. I came looking for you...sir. We had no idea where you went, you," she laughed in playful response. They both laughed so hard Srenna could barely keep standing. She ended up against one of the posts to steady herself and Matthew came along side her leaning against the rail. Both watched silently for a few moments as the rain fell until Matthew remembered that Srenna had appeared to be upset when he found her.

"All jesting aside...Miss James...you looked as though something or someone unsettled you. Are you alright, truly," he asked with genuine concern. He leaned a tiny bit into her as he asked, wondering as well if she were cold as she always seemed to be when it rained. She was indeed shivering. But she was not answering. "Srenna...what happened out there, wherever you were?"

Srenna hesitated for a moment...not sure how much if anything of her conversation with Margi she should share. "I went a little farther then I thought and ended up at the cemetery. I was going to head right back but I ran into ..." she hesitated again and then slowly finished, "...Margi Henderson." She watched Matthew's face and was not surprised at all to see the immediate irritation in his eyes. He turned his head away momentarily shaking it with anger and then gazed back down into Srenna's face.

"She had better not said…" he started with great anger in his voice. But Srenna cut him off shaking her own head adamantly.

"No…no really it's all right actually. I think I handled her quite nicely…if I do say so myself," she grinned trying to reassure the young man leaning over her.

"Really?" he questioned, with a puzzled look on his face. "And how exactly did you…handle it, eh?"

"By speaking the truth," Srenna advised him lightly. She could see that he was waiting to hear what that truth was so she went on. "I simply told her you were not and never would be interested in her…" And then Srenna added quickly… "according to Mary." She waited to see what Matthew's reaction would be to her rebuttle of the outspoken and vexing young woman.

Matthew stared for a moment at the slender young woman standing very close to him in the gazebo. He looked at the face that had been predominately imprinted in his mind since the first day he'd seen her. He then imagined without much difficulty at the conversation that must have transpired between the two women. That wasn't hard at all as he himself had suffered her wrath that first day, but the image in his mind of Srenna "telling" Margi anything brought him to hardy laughter.

"What…you?" Srenna gasped, as Matthew continued to chuckle uncontrollably. He tried to compose himself before suffering her wrath again.

"I don't suppose there's anyone I could tell off for you…eh?" he giggled. "Anyone who thinks they have your fancy?"

"No!There isn't," she responded smartly. She was feeling a little reproved, but she couldn't help laughing a bit herself as she remembered what she had said to the girl and how good it had made her feel.

"Come on then. No one has ever turned the head of Miss James …or thought they have?" he asked with a sudden desire to hear an answer to a burning question on his heart. He had stopped laughing and was beginning to seriously wait for her response.

Srenna began to feel the deep blush that had been coming to her face on a more regular basis lately. She looked away for a moment and took a deep breath. "There's never really been anyone…you know…not that I have truly been interested in."

"You're going to try to tell me that Srenna James did not leave a string of interested young men in her wake back in Sydney," he kidded with her.

She hesitated for what seemed to him to be an agonizing amount of time. Then his heart nearly skipped a beat as she started slowly, "Well...there was one gentleman...a friend of Frank Havilland's, a business associate actually." Srenna looked up into Matthew's face and saw the expression that told her he might not want to hear what she had to say after all. But again Srenna went on with the truth, and quickly. "He was quite an ass really...wanting to kiss me after only one date and I really didn't want him too and well...I had to push him away and then I told Grace and Frank threatened to never do business with him again and..."

But Matthew had heard all he needed to hear. He stopped Srenna's string of explanation with his hand up and then pointedly asked her, "And so... tell me...if you can. How would a gentleman know if Srenna James WANTED to be kissed, eh?" He waited with bated breath for an answer.

Srenna not only felt the warm glow on her cheeks but a warmth all over her as Matthew leaned a bit more over her, waiting for her response. She thought for a second as to how to answer him and then lifted her face to meet his gaze directly. "I suppose if two people knew each other, really knew...each other...then the gentleman would...just know... that she wants him to kiss her...and he would risk it anyway to..."

But before she finished Matthew had made his decision to indeed risk it. Hoping upon hope he was right and that the risk was worth everything, he leaned over Srenna's face and met her lips with a kiss. It was a gentle kiss...the first one. And when he felt her kiss back he tried again, this time with more force. He could feel her lean willingly into his frame as he leaned over her and put one hand around her back and held her face with the other. She so easily fell into his embrace that it startled both of them at how quickly they responded to the flood of emotions filling their senses; until they heard the sound of footsteps and laughter!

Before either realized who it was Matthew instinctively pulled away from Srenna and even took a step back away from her. She however was still reeling from the effect of Matthew's kiss and simply stood there for a moment. That was until she heard the anger in Matthew's voice as he addressed the company that had just joined them.

"Where have you been?! We've been looking everywhere for you!" Matthew started angrily.

Srenna turned her head towards those that had run up laughing and saw Stephan and one of the boys from church standing on the edge of the gazebo. They were snickering under their breath and looking at Srenna and Matthew as if they had just been privileged to see everything. Srenna could feel the color rise up on her face so hotly that she momentarily turned her head away to try to regain some composure. But the tone of Matthew's voice brought her back to attention as he moved in on his delinquent brother and she wondered if things were about to get ugly.

No answer had come from Stephan and once again Matthew began grilling the boy as to his whereabouts over the last couple of hours.

"I've been around. What's your problem anyway, mate?...I was..." he began sarcastically.

"Stephan we were just worried...." Srenna offered in a quieter tone hoping she might be able to defuse the anger between the two brothers. But Matthew once again held up his hand to her...this time with great anger and frustration.

"No Srenna...not this time. This time he's going to answer me...right Stephan?!" Matthew ordered whipping his head back to his younger brother and moving even closer. The other boy immediately left, running towards the church. Stephan looked as though he might also take flight, but not before he yelled at Matthew with venom in his voice.

"I don't have to answer to you. You're not Dad!" he spewed out.

"What did you say, you!?" Matthew got close enough now to his brother that Srenna did the only thing she could think of as she had often times intervened in fights between William and Thomas.

"Stop!...both of you. This will get us no where!" she exclaimed, getting a bit angry herself with the whole incident and stepping closer to the boys.

"You're right Srenna...it won't. We'll deal with it when we get home!" Matthew stated flatly and firmly to Stephan, staring into the boy's defiant face and squaring off with him. Then as a final attempt to regain some control over the moment he ordered his brother, "Get to the car, you! And not another word or so help me I'll sick Irmani and Jimmie on you and half the county if need be." He pulled himself up to every bit of his six foot frame and stood over Stephan with an threatening expression on his face that the boy had seldom seen on his older brother's countenance. He hedged for only a second and then scowling as hard as he could moved off the gazebo platform and began heading up the path towards the church.

Matthew turned away for a moment, away from Srenna and her burning stare at him. She had kept silent ever since he had quieted her. He wasn't sure he wanted to see the reaction on her face to the way he had just handled everything. He hated it when she disapproved of anything remotely having to do with him. But still he turned. He wasn't too surprised to see her big dark eyes simply staring at him as though any moment she might start crying.

"Srenna…I…" he began, moving towards her.

"No Matthew…really…you're right. We can't handle this right now. It would be better at home…so we'd better just get going," she answered flatly as she moved towards the steps and the rainy path.

"Srenna…wait…please," he attempted, as he reached for her arm in the hopes of stopping her and smoothing the moment over. But she was down the step quickly and running into the rain before he could stop her. He felt more frustration then he had in months, especially in lieu of what had just transpired between the both of them only minutes ago. This thought made him even angrier at Stephan and more determined to have it out with his brother when they got home. So whether he liked it or not he followed close behind Srenna through what was left of the New Zealand downpour.

Chapter 25: Let Not the Sun

The drive home was anything but happy. True to its nature the rain had stopped as abruptly as it started but the gloomy little cloud that had overtaken the picnickers was obviously still hanging over the car. It didn't take long for the girls to figure out that something had happened between Matthew and Stephan. Srenna's unusual quietness was a tip off as well. She scurried to round everyone up and into the car, Stephan included and then instructed everyone to sit back and take a rest for the drive home. Matthew disappeared for a few moments with Jimmie and she could only guess what the two spoke about.

When Matthew joined them in the car he seemed more composed but very quiet. The only buffer of the trip was when little Emma, sitting between Srenna and Matthew, leaned into her big brother's side and he immediately put a gentle arm around his "Little Bug". Srenna felt a measure of comfort that in spite of everything that had just happened…she knew in her heart of hearts that Matthew was doing the best he knew how. She, however, could feel the glare from Stephan in the back seat directly behind his big brother…and if looks could kill…Matthew was a dead man driving.

Once home Srenna immediately began the chore of undoing the day…the leftover food…dirty clothes and dirty children, and one extremely tired little boy. Benji's first big outing and longest day away from home had left the child fussy and exhausted. Srenna tried desperately to console the weary infant and lay him down for a short nap while she ran through the rigors of cleaning up. Matthew and Stephan both disappeared, Stephan to his room as ordered by Matthew and Matthew to the fields to bring in the sheep.

"And hopefully to pray." thought Srenna to herself.

She was able to get most of the clothes rounded up, dirty dishes washed and Lilly and Emma into the bathtub after a light supper, all before Benji woke, fussier then ever. Mary took over where the girls were concerned promising to get them both safely into bed earlier then usual. When nothing seemed to placate the baby boy Srenna took him upstairs to see the girls, hoping they could perhaps entertain him for only a while.

"He's not very happy Mary. I don't know what's wrong with him," she explained to the boy's sister. "Maybe today was just too much for him, all the passing around he got."

"You could try something Mum use to do with the younger ones when they'd fuss and not want to sleep," Mary offered.

"Anything…just give me any idea and I'll try it," chuckled Srenna, bouncing the wiggly baby.

"Well…Mum use to take the little ones into the shower with her. The water's warm enough after all day in the sun. It relaxed Lilly every time. Emma too," Mary suggested. "It couldn't hurt you either." She grinned at that statement as she smiled at her frustrated governess.

"Why Mary…Are you suggesting I need a shower after being out all day?" Srenna joked with the girl.

"Yes! I am. To relax you though…not because you smell," Mary laughed.

Srenna hugged the girl and walked out of the room with the full intention of taking her advice. She went downstairs and grabbed up a few towels and a robe and headed for the shower on the back porch. She wasn't too worried about running into either Stephan or Matthew as one had not come out of his room and the other was still hiding out in the barn. She quickly entered the dressing area and removed Benji's clothes first and then hers.

The first streams of warm water coming from the shower head seemed to frighten Benji a bit, but Srenna gradually worked the little boy under the flow of water and over her own tired and frustrated body. It felt nearly as wonderful as if she'd drawn a bath and crawled in. She washed the baby's hair and spoke to him in quieting tones as his fussing began to soften some and he began to relax in her arms. Within only a few more minutes she actually had the child giggling as she encouraged him to play in the water. She was glad Mary had suggested this idea and was sure it would become a new routine to unwind and get the boy ready for bed some nights

Srenna was nearly ready to end the shower as she could feel the water becoming slightly cooler, so she turned the nozzle off and prepared to wrap a towel around Benji. But suddenly she heard a noise above her. At first she thought only that a bird had possibly landed on the edge of the shower and she swept her eyes around the top of the roofing. The sun had only just begun to set and still some light could be seen through the small cracks in the top of the ceiling against the house.

But it was what Srenna saw next that sent her into a frenzy of screams, for as quickly as her eyes panned the edge of the roof she saw two eyes peering through a crack big enough to see what had been going on inside. And that crack gave way to the owner of the eyes!

"Stephan!" Srenna screamed. Again she let out another round of screams as she grabbed her robe and threw it around her and Benji, who by this time was joining her in the most incredible screams she had heard from the child yet.

Srenna came out of the shower and dressing room in just enough time to see the back side of a young boy running into the line of trees off the edge of the house. Mary almost collided with her as did Lilly and Emma when Srenna turned to run into the house. She was still trying to pull herself together, robe and all when Matthew rounded the end of the porch with a look of pure fright on his face. He stopped short of running into all of them fully expecting to see someone either injured or under attack.

"What in the bloody hell happened out here!" he yelled. He looked first at Srenna realizing it was her scream he had heard first and then Benji's shrieks as he sprinted the distance from the barn to the back of the house. One look made him blush and turn his head for a second when he fully comprehended that Srenna was standing there in her robe holding a very wet and crying baby. She was desperately grabbing the robe around her body and all he had to do was look at her face to know something horrible had just occurred. He looked at Mary's angry face and addressed her quickly, "What happened here?"

"I think Stephan was peeping!" she answered her brother angrily. She looked over at Srenna who was feverishly trying to console Benji for having scared the boy to death when she screamed.

"Srenna…is that true? Was he looking through a crack?" Matthew asked, feeling his temper starting to over take him. He had just barely resolved himself to talk to Stephan before bedtime as Jimmie had suggested and now seeing how disturbed Srenna and Benji were, he was just simply ready to kill his brother. "Srenna!"

"Y…y…yes!" she chattered, beginning to feel the effects of the early night air and a very long day. "I'm sure it was him. He jumped off the roof at the end of the house and ran into the woods…that way," she advised Matthew. She was angry to be sure. But she could see that Matthew was ten times angrier then she could have ever been.

"That's it! He's had it now!" Matthew snapped angrily as he headed for the end of the house with the intentions of hunting his younger brother down and throttling him.

Srenna handed Benji over to his sister quickly and pulling the robe around her securely went after Matthew calling desperately to him. "Matthew! Wait! Please wait! Let's talk about this first before you go off and do something you regret later!" she yelled at him.

"Regret?!" he yelled back, turning towards her. She had never seen such anger on his face since she met him and it nearly frightened her to see that he was quite capable of losing his temper in some fashion even if it was with Stephan and even if she was herself completely livid with the boy at the moment. But Matthew turned again to continue following his brother into the woods.

"The only one that will be regretting anything is him when I'm done," he nearly screamed over his shoulder.

But Srenna wouldn't stop going after Matthew. She ran to catch him at the end of the yard and grabbed his arm. With all the strength her slender form could muster she stopped him in his tracks and whipped him around. "Will you just wait a minute and talk about this…please?" she begged. She was nearly in tears now wishing upon wish that they were back in the gazebo enjoying the splendor of their kiss they shared earlier that afternoon. Now it seemed everything was wrong and she was tired. Mostly she wanted to stop Matthew from doing something hurtful to Stephan even if at the moment she herself would pummel the thirteen-year-old if she could. But it was precisely that knowledge of her own temper that made her plead with Matthew to calm down and think.

Matthew looked down into Srenna's face and with almost as much frustration as he had felt before she came to the station he felt irritated and helpless where Stephan was concerned.

"I give up Srenna. I don't know what to do with him. He disrespects me, he taunts his sisters to death and now this…this is the last straw!" he snapped with despair in his voice.

"I know…I know…I'm angry too right now," she offered leaning towards Matthew and putting a comforting hand on his arm. "which is precisely why we both need to cool off and truly figure out what should be done. Besides…he's got a great lead on you. You'll be hard put to even find him at this point, eh?" she suggested in quieting tones and hopeful words. "If we wait…I'm sure sooner or later he'll come back…you know him and his stomach…and where is he going to go anyway."

Matthew stood for a moment looking off into the trees wishing that his eyes could somehow see beyond them and detect his contentious brother. But try as he might it was no good. Then he looked down at Srenna who stood patiently beside him, hand still upon his arm. He suddenly realized her hair was dripping wet and she was shivering some from the early night air. It was getting dark quickly and he knew he would never find Stephan now.

"You need to get inside…before you catch a chill," he said softly, still looking very frustrated but wearing an expression of surrender…at least for the time being. He took Srenna's hand and started leading her barefoot frame towards the house. But before they reached the porch, Srenna pulled up on him and stopped. He turned to see what it was she wanted.

"Matthew…are you going to be all right?" she whispered gently. Mary had taken the children inside but Srenna still wanted to settle the matter with him on how they would deal with Stephan.

"Am I going to be all right? What about you? And Benji. I can still hear him caterwauling in the house," Matthew whispered back loudly. He was really having a hard time understanding how Srenna could be so calm right now. She seemed to have pulled some great reserve of control out of no where while he felt totally out of control. So he did the only thing he knew to do when he felt that badly. "I'm going back to the barn," he announced angrily. "I can't be here right now. I need to think about what I'm going to say to him or for that matter how I'm going to keep from beating the snot out of him!" He let go of Srenna's hand and began walking around the edge of the house.

"Matthew…wait…" she started desperately, trying to follow him.

"No! You go in the house. I can't have you being sick." Then in a softer tone, "I'll be in later," he ordered gently but firmly. He waited only long enough to see if she would heed his directive and something in her knew she'd better. She turned immediately and headed for the back door. Matthew watched for only another moment till she disappeared into the house and then shaking his tired head walked back to the barn.

No one said a word to Srenna as she walked into the house. The girls were strangely quiet and Mary had somehow gotten Benji a bit more subdued. At the sight of Srenna, though…his softened whimpers became fussy cries again.

"Let me take him Mary and I'll just rock him till he goes to sleep. He needs to know I'm all right," the young woman suggested as she reached for the weary boy.

"Are you?" Mary asked with grave concern. There was still much anger on her face as well.

"I will be. It's your brothers I'm most worried about right now, and who will survive tonight," she joked sarcastically, though at the moment she felt very little humor about any of the end of the day.

It took her almost an hour to settle Benji but finally the infant succumbed to exhaustion from the tiring day. The security of Srenna's arms as well as her soothing voice finally lulled the child to sleep. Several times she thought she too would fall into a deep slumber sitting up but she was able to lay the baby boy in his crib at last and tip toe out of the room. She then went on the search for everyone else. It took only a moment to know that dear Mary had rousted the girls into bed and had also turned in for the evening. A quick stop at Stephan's door revealed an empty room.

Something …or someone made Srenna enter and stand in the middle of the floor. It was already well past eleven o'clock in the evening and still there had been no sign of the incorrigible youth. Srenna was sure that Matthew had not come in as well when she had stopped at the front window and seen the light in the barn still burning. Now she stood here wondering what it was going to take to bring back the peace that had begun to return to this home. She was still angry to be sure because of Stephan's antics but more importantly she knew that the critical point of a possible permanent fracture between this boy and his siblings was very…very close, if not already here.

It was this thought that made Srenna shut Stephan's door and lock it. Again some directive… or unction made her cross the room and sit down on the floor with her back against the wall in the corner. In the dark she was easily unseen. Reason told her to sit…pray… and wait.

She needn't have waited very long.

Within the half hour she heard the first noises coming from outside on the porch roof. Then just as she had suspected quiet footsteps crept across the shingles and the window was pushed opened. First one leg entered and then the slight frame of the thirteen-year-old she knew would return sooner or later. When the other leg was well in and the boy attached to them crossed the room to lock his door, Srenna stood in the darkness and quickly walked to the open window. Before Stephan knew anyone was even there Srenna closed it and stood in front of it.

"Before you even think to unlock that door and escape, you, consider the fact that your brother, who I might add outweighs you by at least 60 pounds, is more then likely waiting for you downstairs and he is much…much angrier with you then I am," she whispered loudly so not to rouse anyone sleeping in the rooms next door. She stood looking at the startled boy with her arms crossed and felt as though she were looking more at a frightened deer then a young boy.

"I…I…was just going…" he began, stammering nervously, looking down at the floor. Even in the shadows Srenna could see how embarrassed he was to even look at her directly.

"You were going where…to bed…to sleep…maybe to get something to eat?" she asked him angrily. "What you're going to do is sit…down!" The tone of voice and the direct order was unlike anything Stephan had heard her use so far even when she had let him know early on that she was not afraid of him. He crossed the floor quickly and miserably and sat on the bed, but not without his arms folded and a deep scowl on his face.

Srenna stood looking at the boy for a few moments wondering if at anytime she would have exactly the words she needed to confront him on his actions at the shower, but nothing came. She went to the lamp on his stand and lit it, turning the wick down low till only a slight glow of light filled the room. Then she began to pace the floor in front of him which seemed to make him even more nervous. Then with utter exasperation and her hand over her forehead Srenna went to Stephans' surprise and sat right next to him on the bed. She thought he might actually jump and run but her hand on his arm and two quick words made him think again. "Stay…you!"

Again, Srenna waited, hoping that that still small voice would give her words of wisdom and frustratingly again…nothing. At least not words of wisdom. Just one word came slamming into her mind as well as her heart. "Listen," it said. She thought a moment back over the last few months at the flurry of events that had catapulted grief and confusion around this young family…around this miserable boy sitting next to her and the things he had been doing and saying and this evening's infraction…when suddenly a thought even stronger then that one word gripped Srenna's heart with a fervor. This was not just a boy sitting next to her… and while all of the world had been unraveling around him…he had slipped from boy to young man…and that… without his father.

Srenna thought for sure she might start crying. The mere thought of the loss of her own dear father at Stephan's age had been devastating to her. Even now the thoughts threatened to undo her. And she was a girl. Revelation after revelation began to overcome her, not with standing, his seeming contempt for Matthew's authority in the family. Part of her wanted to simply get up and run rather then confront these issues with him and possibly expose her own buried grief.

But Srenna found she was unable to move. For what seemed like forever she and Stephan sat frozen beside each other until finally one burning question entered her mind and then crossed her lips. "You resent Matthew…don't you Stephan?" she asked cautiously and quietly. She waited with bated breath for the teenager to react. His reaction was to turn his head away. She was sure there were tears brimming in his eyes.

"Stephan…Are you upset with Matthew because of your father?" she asked in another way.

"I don't know what you're talking about," the boy spewed out angrily. Srenna knew she had hit a nerve.

"I think you do, eh?" she plunged on. "Matthew had to spend so much time with your father before he went to war, didn't he? And extra time when he came home to visit. And probably they spent a lot of time together when you were younger because Matthew helped…"

"Matthew thinks he's just like dad!" began the hot confession. "He thinks he's the big man around here, has all the answers and all the orders. Well he isn't and he doesn't!" The end of that statement came with obvious hurt and open jealousy. At first Srenna was stricken by the hate she thought she heard in the boy's voice… but something calmed her…quieted her from getting upset with the distraught youth. He was indeed crying even though he was doing his best not to let her see. She remembered many times she had been in this same position and had not wanted the world to see how vulnerable she was. Great pity for him overwhelmed her and again she fought her own urge to begin crying. Then, when needed the most, now that the boy was open and at least speaking some truth about his feelings, Srenna heard what she needed to hear.

"Stephan…I know it feels that way. God knows I literally hated the other girls when their parents would come to visit them at the school I grew up in. I never told anyone because it made me feel like a monster…a horrible person," she confessed.

"Where were your parents?" came the question she knew she would have to answer and secretly hoped she might not have to. But she was there now and she knew she could not back out of this moment and at the same time, hope to accomplish anything with and for this boy.

"Didn't you know? My parents died too when I was about your age," she offered gently.

"How did they die?" Stephan went on, looking inquisitively at his governess.

Srenna hesitated for a few seconds and then took a long deep breath before answering his painful question. "They died in an accident. I was with them and survived," she added looking off towards the window and wishing she could escape from the rest of the conversation. But she pressed on. "One day they were there and the next…they weren't." Srenna had to stop there as she began to feel as though she might lose control of her own emotions in front of Stephan and she was sure she did not want to do that.

"Look, Stephan. Your brother isn't to blame for what your father did or didn't do with you or any of the other children. He's been doing the best he knows how. He should have never had to do most of what he's done but he has…so all of you could be together," she explained. "I'm absolutely sure that there have been times when he wishes he could be free to do things he should have been able to while he was a teenager and he couldn't and do you know why?" she asked cautiously. There was no answer from the boy but he was openly crying now, still looking away.

"He loves you, and Mary and the girls and Benji. That's why. And there isn't anything he wouldn't do to make sure you are all together and healthy and cared for and…"

"Well he hates me now, eh?" he sobbed, "Especially after what I did. And you probably do too!"

"No! No! I could never hate you…I'm angry with you and what you did was wrong and for sure you're going to be punished for it…but Stephan…" she spoke softly, her arm circling the boy's shoulders whether he wanted her to or not. "We could never hate you. You are a part of this family. I know your mum and dad would tell you the same thing." She waited for awhile and then went on. "I'll bet you at one time or another Matthew did something that made them angry with him and they had to punish him…I'm sure of it. I know I did." At that statement she chuckled slightly and that simple little change in emotions suddenly seemed to puncture a hole in the sad little cloud hanging over the room. Then in all seriousness she continued her thoughts. "I bet you wish you could ask someone some questions, about…you know…things…things you're wondering about…not sure about…about girls and changes you're feeling…maybe…" Srenna awkwardly stumbled over her words.

"Well not a girl…not you!" Stephan answered with a bit of disgust in his voice.

"I didn't mean me…and just for the record your sister wouldn't want to either. But you could talk to Irmani, eh?" she jokingly suggested and then laughed at the thought. Surprisingly Stephan laughed with her.

"I'd bloody well rather be whipped before I'd talk to her about…you know…anything," he adamantly stated. Still Srenna could tell the boy's icy exterior was melting as he chuckled at the thought of Irmani Rainga explaining anything about girls too him.

"Well…then…might I suggest that your brother would be the best person to ask and I know he'd tell you whatever you want to know," Srenna suggested.

"What does he know? He's never even had a girlfriend or dated or anything as far as I know. Can't count that Margi Henderson. Good lot he'd be able to tell me," Stephan scoffed.

"Is that what you think...that your brother doesn't know anything about girls, eh?" she grinned, raising a knowing eyebrow. She heard Stephan's chuckle. Then she couldn't believe what she heard come out of her mouth next. "Did you know Matthew kissed me in the gazebo this afternoon...during the rainstorm...and right before you came running up?" She watched the teenagers face for any reaction.

"Matthew kissed you!?" he gasped loudly. Srenna immediately put her finger to her lips and shushed him.

"And quite nicely too I might add," she said softly, looking off over the room and remembering the moment quite well. The very thought of it made her heart begin to beat a bit faster and as usual her face to flush. Then she realized Stephan was staring at her full in the face and she really blushed.

"Did...did you want him too?" Stephan asked carefully.

"Yes actually...I did...but you know that is precisely what I'm talking about," she began quickly as she stood and started heading towards the door. "Your brother can answer these questions much better then I can...I think...although Stephan I can always tell you what girls like and don't like or how we want to be treated. You can always ask me those kinds of things." She stood at the door for a moment and waited to see if there were any more responses from him, but the boy suddenly hung his head down looking at the floor and once again looking miserable. She wanted to get back the moments of laughter they had just shared but she knew that still fresh in the boy's mind was his violation of her privacy.

"Look Stephan...you're still going to have to be disciplined for what you did...and God knows what Matthew has in store for you, but as for me...I'd be happy if you'd just say you're sorry," Srenna offered. She prayed hard and heavy that no lapse into his old contentious self was taking place...but to her delight he raised his head and sheepishly responded.

"I am sorry. I shouldn't have been up there and I wouldn't blame you or Matthew if you punished me for a year," he mumbled despairingly.

"Well...apology excepted...and maybe a year of cleaning the shower once a week wouldn't be such a bad idea, you, and patching all the cracks as well, eh?" she chuckled at him, with her arms crossed, trying to look firm. Her grin gave her away and Stephan knew he'd come out of this much, much better then he should have. He was however still uncertain as to his fate where his older brother was concerned. There was still an expression of concern on his face. Srenna prepared to leave the room but before turning the door knob she encouraged the broken boy. "Why don't we both believe that your brother is trying to do the right thing, and that both of you can figure out this part of growing up together. Right now you need to get some sleep. I know you've got to be tuckered out. I know I am."

Srenna opened the door slightly and then turned as an after thought, "Good night Stephan. No worries…I know she'll be right." For a brief moment Stephan actually looked her eye to eye finally without malice or aggravation. Then much to her surprise in a completely different tone of voice he answered her.

"Good night Srenna. I'll start cleaning the shower first thing tomorrow," he announced.

"All right then. I'll see you in the morning."

Srenna pulled the bedroom door closed quietly and stood for just a second before walking to the stairwell. She was ready to take the first step down to go to bed when a soft deep voice spoke gently to her.

"Careful…I don't want you to trip and fall."

The voice belonged to Matthew, sitting on the third step down in the darkness of the stairway with only a single light wafting up from the living room. She saw his tall frame hunkered against the wall, his long legs taking up several more of the stairs. He reached his hand up to pull her onto the step beside him and she found herself sitting close to him in the darkness of the shadows. Even after positioning her body next to him he still held onto her hand. She could see his face in the shadows and it was clear he had been crying. She could only squeeze his hand as her own tears threatened to spill over again.

"How long have you been here," she asked quietly.

"Long enough," he answered.

Srenna sat perfectly still and waited some more.

"I missed that one, eh?" he started miserably, his voice quivering a bit. He threw his weary head back and closed his eyes still gripping Srenna's small hand.

"Matthew…" she whispered soothingly, leaning against him. "You're never going to get them all… None of us will…Not even Hamilton or Irmani or Jimmie…not your father or…"

"I get your point, Miss James," he admitted, "but still…I should have seen this one coming. I should have.

"Maybe we both should have…but what's important is… we know now. We know he hurts for not having had his father like you did…and nothing is going to ever change that, except God." Srenna waited for a moment and then plunged on. "Somehow he's going to have to let you and maybe Jimmie fill that void. After all it's not like you've had your dad all these years either," she added trying to encourage Matthew.

"I never realized until tonight how young Stephan was when dad left to go to war. He was such a scrawny little nipper…barely nine…and when I was thirteen he was …" Matthew stopped there, fully understanding now how resentful and grieved his brother must have felt for losing their father at a time when a boy so greatly needed one. "I was so busy trying to be the man of this house I forgot what it felt like when I wasn't."

All this time Srenna felt as though she needed only to listen to Matthew, just as that quiet voice in her head had told her to just listen to his brother. She knew he was feeling as though he'd failed somehow and yet she also sensed he was receiving revelation from God this very moment. There was a deep quiet over the whole house as he spoke.

"Do you know what I did when I was Stephan's age?" he asked looking over at Srenna's face and grinning mischievously.

"No…what did you do?" she whispered.

"I stole a car…Tommie and I did." He waited to see what reaction he had stirred out of Srenna. Even in the darkness of the stairwell he could see her dark eyes widen. Then he shook his head and chuckled lightly. "Thought I was a saint or something, eh? John Patton's incredibly stable and dependable son. It was even my idea…yeahr… that's me…juvenile delinquent extraordinaire. Surprised?"

"I…no…I mean…" Srenna stammered awkwardly.

"It's all right. I got saved in all the hoop-la. Been a little more accountable since then. But to be sure it was my coming of age event." Matthew was grinning slightly as he recounted the details of his adolescent years. "Know what Dad did when he picked me up at the jail?"

"I can only imagine. And I don't even want to think about what Irmani or Jimmie did to Tommie," Srenna giggled softly.

"Well…we made a brief stop at the house just long enough for me to feel horrible when Mum looked at me, grabbed up a few days worth of supplies, loaded up Bear and Samson and off we went into the bush," the young man remembered out loud. "I'll never forget that time alone with Dad," he reminisced softly. "Instead of yelling at me he took me fishing and hunting and talking…lots of talking. We slept out under the stars for three nights and went places I didn't even know existed on this island. When it was all over I was so repentant I nearly ran to the front of the church next Sunday morning and cried out my sins to God." Then another thought crossed his mind. He grew very silent for a few moments and Srenna again felt as though she should simply sit and let him speak when ready. But she was definitely praying to an end. It was really no surprise then when Matthew finally asked the next question.

"Do you think you, Benji and the girls would be all right by yourselves for a few days…especially if I get Tommie or Jimmie to move the sheep for me?" he inquired of her while still holding her hand. She could almost feel the hope in the grip of his hand as well as the idea on his lips. "I know what I have to do…for Stephan…for me."

"Yes I do…and it's really for all of us, eh?" she responded heartily. Even as tired as she was at this moment she felt an incredible surge of encouragement.

"You think he'll go for it, going bush with me?" Matthew asked with a tinge of doubt in his voice.

"I think he has no choice in the matter if he wants any reprieve at all, eh? You might want to remind him he'll be getting out of scrubbing and patching the shower for a short while, see if that doesn't persuade him," Srenna chuckled softly, as she began to stand. Still Matthew had not let go of her hand and she gently attempted to coax him off the stairs and down to the living room. He finally gave in and followed behind her. She tugged at him in an exaggerated motion as though it was quite a chore to get him to move but before even making it into the middle of the room he stopped dead in his tracks and pulled her around to face him in the subdued lamp light.

"Was I wrong this afternoon?" he asked timidly, remembering the great risk he had taken to express his true feelings of affection for Srenna today in the gazebo.

Srenna stood for a moment gazing up at Matthew's face and the look of genuine hope that he had not been out of line when he kissed her. She grinned at him just a bit mischievously and looked at him with a side ways glance. "Now I thought I did a very good job of letting you know if you were or not, eh? Besides…I thought you heard my conversation with Stephan…especially the end…"

"You mean the part where I did "quite nicely". I believe that's what you said, eh?" he joked, grinning from ear to ear and moving away just in time to miss her playful swat.

"You bugger….you heard everything," she gasped in a loud whisper. Matthew was laughing now but not so much that he couldn't grab her hand and pull her to him. Before she had the chance to rebuttal any further he had her in another embrace in the middle of the room.

But Srenna had no more rebuttal, only gladness that the day had somehow again ended on the happy note it had started out on. She was thankful that Matthew had a plan to help Stephan, all of the children were safe and sound asleep in their rooms and at the moment she was precisely where she wanted to be. When the kiss ended, it was Matthew that turned her around toward her bedroom door and playfully pushed her in the direction of badly needed sleep.

"Good night Miss James," he finished politely, as he too headed for his own room.

"Good night, Mr. Patton," she responded with equal formality as she moved to enter hers.

Both knew however as tired as they might be…sleeping was still going to be a rare commodity tonight after the events of the day played out in their dreams.

Chapter 26: And When the Mountains Quake

"If we get this line of fencing done, then I can go over to Miki's house, eh?" Stephan asked his older brother as he strained to hold the roll of stakes Matthew was driving into the ground. He was referring to his lifelong friend, Mikanu Rainga, one of Jimmie and Irmani Rainga's eight offspring. The last couple of days had seen him and Stephan reuniting and spending some badly needed "boy" time together. It had been far too long since any of the children had just gone and played beyond the Patton borders. The girls were generally happy just occupying each other, but it had been determined by Matthew and Srenna, with Irmani and Jimmies encouragement that Stephan needed to be "set free" on occasion.

Now Matthew looked at his brother, attempting with all of his thirteen-year-old might to lend him the help Matthew so badly needed. He grinned slightly, looking away from his brother so as too try and maintain any semblance of authority, especially since only a week ago Stephan was still greatly rebelling and continued to grieve in his own unique angry way. Much of both of those aspects had changed drastically since Stephan's infraction against Srenna. Her gracious and merciful confrontation finally brought things to a head with the distraught teenager. It hadn't hurt either that both Matthew and Srenna had shown Stephan considerable unconditional love and forgiveness for his antics. That Matthew had truly stepped in as the father figure he had to be and sequestered Stephan away for a few days in the surrounding mountains for "man to man" talks put the final touches on a new beginning for the boy. The time spent with his younger brother brought an indelible mark of healing to the whole family.

"She's sweet, if we can at least get to the gate," Matthew finally agreed.

The trip up the mountain began with some resistance and doubt, but by the second day when Matthew took his brother to the mountain top where his father had left him for a while he knew he had done the best thing possible for Stephan and very likely the only thing that would bring an end to the teenager's incorrigible grief and a much needed bridge between the two brothers.

An encounter with God had indeed taken place with the boy while he was alone in the same location John Patton had taken Matthew. Stephan was not the only one to receive respite and revelation from a loving God who had been watching over them both since birth. While waiting for his sibling beside the cool mountain stream flowing down the slope Matthew took the time not only to pray for Stephan but himself, Mary, the girls and Benji and last but not nearly least…Srenna. His obvious feelings for her over the last few weeks had reached a crescendo of sorts. Since their first encounter of affections for one another Matthew had found his thoughts tumbling over the next time he would be near her or with her. So true to his nature …he prayed. He knew he'd better. His feelings were new to him, stronger then any he could ever remember, even a little frightening. And it was one of the topics John had made sure he discussed with his young son when he slipped into his mid-teens. But Matthew Patton trusted the God he'd loved since his own encounter on this same mountain top. He knew the very thing he needed to do was what he was doing for himself, for his brother.

When the walk-about was over and the boys returned home, very little was said. Not much was needed to be spoken as the rest of the household noticed the marked difference in Stephan immediately. However Matthew did take some time to pull Srenna aside and report to her that Stephan had in fact had a visitation with his Heavenly Father and had made some great strides in making peace with the earthly one he had lost.

Now only days later Matthew watched with deep relief at the changes that had almost immediately followed after their trip. He had also been learning to show more lenience towards Stephan instead of just gruffly ordering him about. The balance of expecting more from him and then giving more back was beginning to pay off and Matthew began remembering how it was that his father had shaped his behavior at that age. Just seeing some evidence that Stephan was starting to heal from the pain of losing their parents was all the pay off Matthew needed.

Stephan stood up and stretched for a moment from holding the heavy roll of fence stakes and wire he was balancing for Matthew. He watched as his brother marked off the next spot for the post and began digging the hole for it.

"I think this is our hottest day so far. Miki and I were going to go to the swimming hole if it's good with Jimmie…and you of course," Stephan suggested, adding the last part of the statement as an after thought. He watched his brother's face for the hoped for response.

"No worries. I wish I could go with ya though, but I promised Mary and Srenna I'd watch the girls and Benji so they can go to that ladies thing, whatever the blazes it is," Matthew grinned, not really annoyed at the thought of taking care of any of his younger siblings for the evening. "Maybe I'll take them all back to the river and throw them in for a while…right after Srenna leaves, eh?" He chuckled at that statement knowing that his brothers and sister's governess was a real mother hen when it came to letting her little flock out of her sight. But he had to agree with Stephan. It was hot. And the air was eerily still for a mid December summer day.

Several times during the morning he was acutely aware of the intense quiet, even from the birds or the lack of them. The sheep seemed to be aware of it as well, almost agitated, edgy. A couple times he had to stop what he was doing and go after a few groups of his Romneys that neither Duke nor Duchess or any of the other six dogs seemed to be able to corral and return to the field. Samson and Bear jolted a few times as though having been bitten and then seemed to be all right. The feeling seemed to hang in the air but not as if a storm were brewing off the coast. It had thoroughly rained the day before, so Matthew knew it wasn't that which hung over them this late afternoon. He couldn't quite put his finger on how he himself felt. It seemed as though something was coming. He didn't have long to find out what it was.

Matthew dropped another post into the hole he had just finished and straightened and stretched his muscular six foot frame before he helped Stephan move the roll up to the post. But he never got a chance. The first sound he heard was the subtle sound of the dogs whining as though something or someone was frightening them. He heard them only long enough to turn and look at them wondering quickly why his pack of border collies would feel threatened. Samson and Bear were close to them and both horses were doing a side step. Then he heard the dogs begin to bark as though an ominous intruder was on their backs. But it was the next sound he heard that struck an instant fear in Matthew's heart as the sound of thunder came rolling towards him and Stephan.

But it was not thunder from any angry sky. The thunder was rolling across the ground, coming at them with the speed and intensity of a hundred trains all at once. Before Matthew could whip his head back around to warn Stephan, the ground under his feet began to rock and reel. He only had time to look at his brother's terrified face before the first jolt of the ground sent both boys collapsing to the rumbling dirt.

"Earthquake, Stephan!" he shouted over the roar. "Drop the roll!" he ordered his younger brother. He was only approximately ten feet away from Stephan but he might as well have been a hundred. He could do nothing but stay on the ground and ride out the furry of the trembling ground beneath his body. He could see the sheep scattering and both horses were running in a frightening circle mindlessly trying to escape the unseen enemy. At one point Matthew could see Stephan roll and hit his head on the ground. Both felt like it would never end, when in all actuality it lasted only three minutes. When Matthew was sure the earth had ceased moving he half crawled, half stumbled to his younger brother's aid and pulled him up in a sitting position.

"Are you all right?" Matthew cried, putting his arms around the frozen teen. He began checking Stephan all over especially his head and was greatly relieved that only dirt covered his brother's face and no bumps or blood.

It was Stephan who made the next important declaration. "The girls, the house! We need to get down there!"

Matthew stared at his brother in amazement at how fast his mind had riveted towards the concern for his family. "You're bloody well right! Let's go!" He stood up feeling as though the ground still might be moving but knew it was only his legs that were shaking. Looking around for the horses, he saw Samson a little way off, but no Bear was in sight. He gave his usual shrill whistle, hoping his horse would faithfully come to him now. The frightened animal did indeed come but when he got to Matthew he pranced as though his own legs were still unsure of the ground beneath him.

"Ho, boy….easy does it, mate," Matthew crooned to the black stallion, brushing his neck with his hand while taking up the reins. Samson flipped his head several times letting the boys know he was greatly disturbed by what had just happened, but the animal calmed under Matthew's gentle and reassuring hands. "Come on Samson, you gotta get us down there, eh?" Before the big horse could argue that point Matthew had mounted him and once again encouraged his faithful steed to quiet and obey. As soon as Samson stopped sidestepping, Matthew gave Stephan a hand up and before the teenager could settle his bottom on the back side of the horse Matthew shouted, "Hold on!" With a fervent kick to Samson's side they were all three off towards the house.

When the first rumble hit the house all of the girls were either around the table or at the counter. Benji was still fast asleep in his crib, much to Srenna's satisfaction. But in only a split second that satisfaction turned into terror.

Mary knew first and then Lilly, as the nine-year-old instinctively pulled her baby sister to her side and then shoved her under the table. Emma began to shriek immediately at the movement of the floor under her and the deafening sound of the quake beneath the house.

Mary turned to Srenna as she saw the utter look of fear on her governess's face. "Under the table, quick!" she yelled over the roar at Srenna. But much to her dismay as she herself flew under with the girls, Srenna clung to the counter and turned her frenzied eyes towards the bedroom where Benji could be heard wailing in utter terror. Mary knew what was going to happen next without a doubt.

As if to defy anything the earthquake could do to house or human, Srenna hollered over the noise, "I have to get Benji!" With that she stumbled across the room gripping anything she could to keep her footing as the floor reeled under her.

"No Srenna…don't…wait!" Mary cried, but it was no good. The young woman was bound and determined to reach the baby before anything could happen to him. Before she even made it to the front room she was on the floor, but true to her stubborn intent she simply kept going on all fours.

Srenna thought she would make it. The sounds of the terrified infant drove her on, even when the windows in the front of the house burst, shattering glass everywhere. She fell to the floor, covering her face and head with her arms and then kept going. She had barely made it through her bedroom door when the ground ceased convulsing under her. With shaky legs she stood and ran the remainder of the distance across her floor and into the nursery.

The crib had danced itself clear across the little alcove room and had come to a stop against the other wall. Benji was on his knees howling as though someone had thoroughly thrashed him, but even as Srenna lifted him from the crib and began to console the frightened child, she knew he was physically unharmed. She was hugging him to her bosom and kissing his face when Mary and the girls came wobbling into the room. Emma was still shrieking and Lilly was so pale Srenna thought for sure that the child would pass out. Before anyone had time to think about how they felt, Mary ordered everyone outside in the yard.

Srenna followed the order without question. As they passed through the living room both Srenna and Mary could see that everything in the once clean and neat house was now in complete chaos. Everything that had been on the walls was not, and glass was everywhere. Even the piano had moved a few feet across the floor and come to a stop against the wall.

Once outside on the grass Mary began to access any visible injury to Lilly and Emma, but thankfully there seemed to be known. It was Srenna she gasped at when she glanced at the young woman holding her baby brother and saw the blood on her arms.

"Srenna! You're cut!" she cried as she reached for Benji and called to Lilly to take him. But Srenna nearly knocked Mary away determined not to give the infant in her arms over to anyone.
Mary calmly addressed Srenna thinking she might be in a bit of shock for what had just happened.
"Lilly stay here with Srenna and Emma. I'm going back in the house for the first aid kit." Lilly pulled Emma with her and came over protectively to Srenna seeming to understand that her dear governess was very upset at the moment, as was her brother. She put her free arm around them both and started quietly shushing Benji…and Srenna.

"She's sweet," spoke the youngster in what she hoped sounded like a grown up voice. It was in fact quivering quite a lot.

But Lilly tried to encourage everyone some more. "It's just the "shaky land" remember Emma. Remember the story Matthew told us the last time?"

"The last time!" Srenna gasped, looking at the little girl with pure horror in her eyes.

Lilly was about to explain what she meant by that when Mary returned with the kit and over heard her proclamation concerning the earthquake they had felt last year. She saw the expression on Srenna's pale face and quickly tried to console her.

"We had a mild one a year ago, nothing major, no damage. It's not out of the ordinary to have tremors and shudders every now and then…not here. There hasn't been a really bad one since 31," she offered reassuringly trying once again to get Srenna to let go of Benji so she could attend to her cuts. This time the sixteen- year- old forcefully removed the baby and handed him to Lilly. Srenna watched with great concern as Lilly moved a little ways away and Mary led her to the steps of the porch.

"Here…let me look at this now…see what you got, eh?" the girl crooned softly. Srenna still was greatly preoccupied with Lilly and Benji…only until Mary found the first piece of glass in her arm.

"Ow! Mary! Please try to leave me some of my arm, you!" Srenna shrieked clenching her teeth at the shooting pain as Mary extracted the sliver form her flesh. There were four in all, each bleeding somewhat, but in short order and as if she had been doing it all her life, Mary had her cleaned up and bandaged. It wasn't until they were done with that chore that anyone said anything at all about the boys

Both brothers felt the fear in their hearts as they rode the distance down into the valley where the house was hopefully still standing. Along the way Matthew had to dodge fallen trees and sink holes where the ground had opened up and created crevices. Just that alone told him that the quake had been a major one. He couldn't remember when they had felt one quite as hard as this except the earthquake in 1931 that leveled the city of Napier north of Castle Point on the east coast. He had only been three and Mary just born when it hit. Since then only minor jolts had frequented their area, most of them short and tolerable. New Zealand was the land of tremors, but Matthew knew this one had more then likely been a destructive one. He just hoped his father's careful building of the house after Napier had indeed paid off.

And it appeared to have done just that. As the boys topped the last hill leading into the homestead both were heaving great sighs of relief as the house stood before them apparently in one piece for the most part. They were also hugely glad to see everyone they had left there this morning standing in the yard. From the top of the lane they could hear Benji's cries of fear, second only to Emma's own pitiful crying. Mary had Emma and Srenna was bouncing poor little Benji in her arms. Lilly clung to whomever and whatever she could, choking back her desire to join Emma in much crying and trying desperately to behave grown up for her baby sister.

Matthew brought Samson to a grinding halt and bounded off of him before the horse had a chance to move. Stephan was close behind him through the front gate.

"Is everyone all right?" he cried grabbing Mary and taking Emma out of her arms. He cradled the terrified child in his arms kissing her face and shushing her at the same time. He looked first to Lilly, hugging her and smiling at his middle sister. He saw the relief on Mary's face as she looked first at Matthew and then at Stephan.

"I think we're all in one piece, though a bit shaken up, eh?" she tried to joke. But Matthew could read her tone and knew she was fighting hard to keep it together.

He turned finally to Srenna who was still trying to quiet the frenzied infant, pacing back and forth. Matthew was not prepared for the utter look of terror on Srenna's face. The color was drained from her face and he wasn't so sure she might not be about to pass out. He knew the instance he caught her eyes that she was at least about to fall apart. As yet he had not seen anything like this in the young woman he had come to know as steady and seemingly fearless. He noticed right away that she was bandaged on both arms. He immediately put his arm around her shoulder, lowered his face against hers and breathed a worried question into her ear, "Are you all right?" He glanced over at Mary for any indication as to what had happened in the house. But Mary only came to him and began taking Emma out of his arms. She handed Emma to Stephan and whispered to her older brother to join her a few steps away.

"You'd better talk to her Matthew. I'm not sure what happened in there, aside from the quake. She tried to get to Benji. He was in his crib. She wouldn't get under the table," Mary explained.

She had an acute expression of deep concern for the woman who had been holding them all together for the last two months. Mary was hugely concerned for Srenna and her reaction to the earthquake.

Matthew didn't hesitate at all after Mary's report. He walked up to Srenna and tried to take Benji from her but he could feel her grip on the child and had to speak to her in a gentle but firm voice. "Let me have him Srenna. He's all right, eh?" Matthew spoke low and soft into her ear. She loosened her hold on the boy and kept quieting him in spite of Matthew taking him in his arms. Matthew motioned to Mary to come and take Benji much to Srenna's obvious dismay. But before she had a chance to dispute Matthew's action he had caught her hand in one of his, slipping the other one around her waist and began leading her a short way from the children. When they were far enough out of ear-shot, Matthew turned her towards him and looked down into her face. She was however gazing passed him to the children, in particular to Benji.

"Srenna, are you all right?" Matthew quizzed her, now more concerned then ever with the paleness of her face and the fear in her eyes. He could tell she was not even hearing him and was keeping her eyes fixed solely on Mary holding Benji. "Sren.... I have to know if you're okay. Look at me...look at me..." he whispered as he turned her face with his free hand.

But Srenna James wasn't even close to being "okay" at the moment. She looked at Matthew only because he was forcing her gaze at him and when she saw his deep look of concern she felt herself slipping far into a fear she had not felt in a very long time.

"Oh....Matthew...I...I...couldn't get to him. I couldn't...he was crying and everything was crashing..." The words were coming out in sobs now, but before she could say much more Matthew pulled her into his strong arms and held her tightly. He felt her cling to him as though to let go would mean to simply collapse, so he held her some more, quieting her as though she were little Emma in his arms.

"It's over. The quake is over and we're all good. The house is still standing," he held her for a few more minutes as he looked passed her towards the children. "Srenna, I need to know if you're going to be all right." Matthew bent his face down to her and tried to get her to look at him again. She had stopped crying and was beginning to pull herself together a little. She was even a bit embarrassed that Matthew was actually seeing her cry for the first time and for something such as this.

Suddenly, as was usually the case, Srenna pulled herself up and away from Matthew's grip as though something had snapped her to attention. She glance at him and then the children and then back at Matthew. "Oh Matthew, I'm so sorry. I didn't mean to…"

But Matthew cut her off with his hand before she could finish her apology. "Not another word, you," he smiled, wiping some of the tears off her face. "This had to have been your first earthquake and it was a buggar, this one." He grinned at her trying to ease some of her fear and embarrassment. In a more serious tone he asked her again, "Will you be all right while I check some things out?"

"Yes…yes…of course. I should be over there with the.…" she stated as she attempted to move back towards the children. But Matthew stopped her yet again.

"Srenna, any minute now, the Rainga truck will come barreling over the hill and Jimmie will be descending upon us by orders of her Imperial Highness the Irmani. If she could come herself she would have been here by now. But you can be sure she'll send Jimmie to make sure all the children have their arms and legs still attached to their bodies." Before he could even finish the jocular image of their neighbors coming to their aid, the Rainga truck indeed came flying over the top of the hill and rushed down the drive to the front gate. Tommie was with him.

"Bloody hell, mate. Are you all in one piece?" Jimmie yelled as he ran up the walk to the children and was met with the need for more hugging and reassuring. Matthew squeezed Srenna one more time and with his arm around her waist he led her back over to where everyone stood. He could feel her body still trembling a bit but knew she was holding it together now for the children. As soon as she came up to Mary she reached out for Benji right away. He fell into her arms and buried his face in her neck, still slightly fussing.

"We're sweet. Don't know where Bear got off to. I haven't had a chance to check the house, the beams and all. I'm guessing the power is down too, eh?" Matthew answered his dear neighbor. "Irmani must have everything under control over there to send you, eh?"

"Yeahr. No worries, mate. Everyone's good at the Rainga station. Now let's go have a look see and make sure nothings cracked or damaged, right?" Jimmie instructed the boys as he and Matthew moved towards the house and Tommie and Stephan began walking the outside parameter.

Srenna began to walk with them but Matthew turned and gently instructed her to stay there in the yard while he and Jimmie checked the house. She wasn't terribly happy letting Matthew out of her sight or with being in the yard much longer either but she turned back to the girls and gathered them all around her.

"I'm sorry Mary, that I got so upset," she apologized. But Mary already had her arm around Srenna's shoulder and squeezed her as if no apologies were necessary.

"I guess we're use to them some, quakes and tremors. This is the "shaky land" after all," quipped the sixteen-year-old. "You'll have to have Matthew tell the story about how New Zealand was born. He loves telling it." She walked Srenna and Benji over to the porch steps and sat down pulling Emma who had given up her hold on Stephan onto the step beside her. Lilly squeezed her way in next to Srenna and leaned heavily against her governess for comfort. Srenna put her arm around the dear child who usually showed as much bravery as was possible in a nine-year-old. Lilly was not feeling too brave at the moment though.

"We'll be all right, all of us. The house just needs to be cleaned up a bit and we'll be good. Like it never happened, eh?" stated Srenna, more for herself then the rest of the brood around her.

"Yeahr, we'll make it all right," Mary agreed, about to add something that she wasn't sure Srenna would want to hear. She decided to wait.

Inside the house, Matthew was getting the first glimpses of just how soundly built his home was. His father had painstakingly built the structure to withstand a fairly descent jolt. However the contents of the house were in a bit of a shamble. Glass from the windows was everywhere and nearly everything that had been on the walls, mantel and tables was now on the floor. But all in all they had faired well. Matthew walked through to the kitchen, in even more disarray and unplugged all the appliances. He went on through the house looking at the walls, floors or ceiling for any cracks or noticeable damage. There seemed to be none.

Jimmie came in from the upstairs rooms where he examined everything and announced the good news that everything was good as gold as well. He had checked the lavoratory for busted pipes but they were lucky there too. Satisfied that things were tolerable inside, they met Stephan and Tommie in the back of the house.

"It looks like the pipes even survived this one," Matthew breathed a sigh of relief. He walked to the water tower and was greatly relieved to see only minor damage to the huge barrel and pipes running from the side. Only minimal water was dripping from a few of the pipes coming down out of the bottom of the tank, but it appeared none was leaking in or around the house itself. They continued to walk around the house checking the foundation for any structural damages, but were gratefully relieved to see that John Patton's careful and patient construction of the home was paying off now. Matthew uttered up a gracious prayer of thanks under his breath as well to the One he knew had been watching over all of them this afternoon.

Before they rounded the house Jimmie stopped Matthew. "Gonna go on to the meeting house Mate, make sure the Ancient's didn't slide off the mountainside," he joked about the Maori community hall. He knew others would show up soon when they'd had a chance to secure their own homes.

Matthew answered also, "I suppose I should go over to the church, make sure the Reverend and his wife are good." Jimmie could hear the hesitation in his voice though and slapped the boy on the back.

"No fault in staying here with your family, Matt. None at all," the gentle man suggested. He could see that Matthew was worried at the thought of leaving just now.

"I'm a bit worried about Srenna. She was pretty upset. Never been in one of these before," he explained. But he knew he would not be at rest either till he knew if Hamilton and Patricia were safe.

In short order all the men came around the house and announced much to everyone's relief that it was in adequate shape. Matthew broke the news to the girls that there was a lot of picking up of things and plenty of glass to clean. Before he could go on though, Jimmie made a suggestion.

"Clean up the glass, Mate, close the storm shutters over the windows, but I'd leave everything on the floor for now, until…" he began and then stopped when he saw the look on Matthew's face. The boy was trying to get Jimmie to stop what he was about to announce and quickly looked at Srenna who was still clinging desperately to Benji.

"Until what, Jimmie?" she asked, realizing the big man had been cut off by Matthew's expression. She waited for a moment looking at the big Maori man and when an answer seemed not in the coming she glanced at Matthew who had turned his back so as not to be caught grimacing. "Until what…you?" she asked of the young man, who had scooped up his baby sister again and was consoling her some more. "Someone had better answer my question, before there's some more shaking up of things," Srenna threatened.

"That's just it Srenna," Mary began carefully as she scowled at her brother and Jimmie.
"There's still going to be some "shaking up" more then likely…aftershocks…eh?" She watched Srenna's face for the reaction she was sure she would see and there it was. What color had begun to come back into the lovely cheeks, drained in an instance.

"After shocks!?" Srenna exclaimed. She looked at Matthew in horror and felt nauseated at the thought that at any minute the earth beneath her feet could begin rolling again.

"There's always after shocks, to be sure, but they probably won't be as bad. I'm sure the worst is over," Matthew offered quickly. He added right away, "They won't last very long, promise."

"You can promise something like that, eh?" Srenna asked sarcastically.

"Well… all I'm saying is that after that jolt…" Matthew started, but Jimmie cut him off.

"Look mate, we'd better keep the sheep out in the fences tonight, get 'em down out of the hill. Keep your livestock out tonight too. Then we can go check on everyone else…make sure they're all right." Jimmie looked at Srenna cautiously, worried that she might hedge at the thought of Matthew leaving. But the girl suddenly pulled herself up straight and finally realized the brevity of the event.

""Jimmie's right, Matthew. You'd better check on the Reverend and his wife and anyone else you think might need your help," Srenna suggested, not really sure she wanted him to leave after what she was just told. But she was suddenly and acutely aware that everyone, not just them had been affected by the earthquake and may not have faired as well as they had. She felt badly that she was showing fear, especially when Matthew needed her to be brave and in control. She took a deep breath and bolstered herself to take charge and take care of her brood.

Matthew could see the change in her demeanor and the determination on her face to tackle this head on, so he smiled slightly at her and then thought to offer a solution for help. "I'll leave Stephan here with you, if you want …he can…."

But a loud disapproval came from his brother at the thought of being left behind. "I want to go!" the boy lamented.

"It's all right Matthew. Take him with you. He needs to go. We'll be all right, won't we Mary?" Srenna asked of her oldest charge and helper.

"What about your arms, are they bad?" he asked with great concern.

"They barely hurt. They're only scratched. Mary did a great job cleaning them up. Really."

"Yeahr. We'll all be fine. I know the drill Matthew. We'll be good till you get back," added Mary, encouraging her brother not to worry about them.

Matthew heaved a big sigh and looked first at Mary and then at Srenna who was doing everything within her power to keep her earlier fear hidden. Benji was finally settling down in her arms, Emma had even stopped her sniffling, and Lilly had discontinued any leaning on either one of them.

"All right then. Srenna, Mary. I'll only check on Reverend Hamilton and the church and anyone between here and there. Keep the girls off the second floor for now. Mary… get their stuff for tonight. But Srenna have them sleep in your room. That's why Dad didn't build over the two end rooms. Your's and mine are the safest rooms in the house, Sren. I'll even move Benji's crib in next to your bed, eh?" he suggested as he turned to head for the house. He changed his mind suddenly and walked back to Srenna. He knew full well he had better not try prying Benji from her arms again, so he gently took her by the shoulder and began walking her with him away from the children. Once again, Matthew turned her to face him and gazed full into her face trying desperately to read her condition before he left.

"Are you sure you're going to be all right, because if you're not I won't go. I'll stay in a heartbeat if you tell me too," he confessed. He waited anxiously for her to break again…but it never came. She had steeled herself to do what she must and he could see she was not going to admit anymore defeat or fear this evening.

"Go Matthew. Really. If the girls get too undone, I'll load them up and we'll go to Irmani's, eh?" she suggested smiling faintly and looking over at Jimmie and Tommie. "You can stop there on your way home and see if we're there." Jimmie nodded his head at Matthew in approval of that idea and the Rainga's headed for their truck and began the drive back to their fields.

"Yeahr, all right. Do that if you need," he began with some relief. He then proceeded to tell Srenna that Mary would know what to do about cooking and the icebox and other issues concerning the earthquake. He then looked full into Srenna's face one more time and then bent to kiss her cheek without thought or concern of anyone seeing him. When Matthew was convinced she was ready to take over he continued to enter the house and ready the crib next to her bed. Everyone followed gingerly as they came into the living room and saw the mess. Srenna could see the fearful expressions on the girl's faces and immediately spoke up in her best encouraging tone. "She'll be right girls. We'll get it cleaned up tomorrow. Tonight we can have a picnic on the back porch, eh Mary?"

"Yeahr. Everyone can have their own flashlight, what do you say?" Mary suggested with as much enthusiasm as she could muster.

"Oh, how lovely. Yes could we?" Emma squealed, for the first time not showing the incredible fear she had earlier.

"You help me find them and Lilly can help Srenna with Benji, all right?" Mary suggested taking her little sister by the hand.

Matthew looked at each one of his siblings one more time and then again at Srenna before calling to Stephan and heading for Samson still waiting at the front gate. Things seemed to be under a little more control now. But his heart was still struggling with leaving them all there and venturing out into the community. His head however told him he should go, especially as much help that had been given to him and his young family. He knew he needed to reciprocate to his friends if they were in need. As he and Stephan rode back up the hill to the fields where they'd left the shaken flock he said out loud to his brother, "We won't stay out long, eh?"

Stephan could feel the pull in Matthew's decision to go. He quickly and quietly added, "Only a little while." With that they passed under the sign at the top of the lane, the sign that still hung ever so firmly to the two unmoved and undisturbed posts. He stopped Samson for a moment and turned to look back at the sign his father had strung across the gate posts nearly thirteen years ago. He remembered something then that his father had told him the day that he and Jimmie had driven the tall posts deep into the ground as

Matthew looked on. He was six at the time, but he remembered it as though it were yesterday.

"They have to be driven down deep Matty," John Patton explained to his young son. "The only way they'll stay strong. Just like us. We gotta go deep if we're gonna stand against everything, eh?"

Matthew looked back on the house and then across the land surrounding it. Then he offered up a prayer out loud, one that Stephan could hear.

"Thank you for driving us deep God; deep enough to stand."

Chapter 27: The Shaky Land

All in all two more tremors shook the ground that evening, none nearly as bad as the first but definitely bad enough to unnerve the littlest ones again. It was all Srenna could do to keep her wits about her each time and after the first aftershock she made sure the girls and Benji were within Mary's or her reach at all times. They tried to enjoy a makeshift picnic off the back porch, far enough away from the water tower and a little bit close to the house. A quick fire was started and some soup cooked over the hangi. Bread and cheese and cookies were added in the attempt to appease Lilly's and Emma's anxieties. Srenna, along with Mary's more seasoned experience of the whole ordeal tried to make light of the shaking ground by pulling the girls into a huddle with Benji squeezed between them and holding on to one another during the short endurance. Neither one lasted more then a minute.

By bedtime Srenna was reasoning with herself that they should indeed go in and go to bed. She remembered what Matthew had said to try and encourage her about the way his father had built the rooms so nothing was above the downstairs bedrooms. She wasn't so sure this made her feel better.

In the end when darkness crept in all around them she was finally certain, especially with Mary's gentle prodding, that they should all have a slumber party in her room. The girl's were, of course, ecstatic about that idea as they had been with the flashlights outdoors, so Mary slipped away to retrieve blankets and pillows and pajamas for the evening. While the girls were getting ready in Srenna's bedroom, Mary took one of the battery powered lanterns and began picking up some of the frames that had broken in the front room. She had barely started when Srenna came to the door and stood watching the girl try to salvage one in particular. Something in Srenna felt Mary's heart as she looked at the picture of her family cracked and broken.

"It's all right for tonight Mary, even the glass," she began, walking over to the sixteen-year-old and putting her arm around her. Mary was close to tears and suddenly Srenna realized it had been the oldest Patton daughter who had shown more bravery this afternoon then even she had.

"Oh Mary! What would I have done this afternoon and evening without you," Srenna whispered into the girl's ear. She pulled Mary's head down on her shoulder and felt a slight sob escape from her body. A few sniffles followed and then both were hugging each other, Mary clutching the picture as if letting go of it would mean losing it.

"You know, I have an idea," Srenna thought out loud. "Let's take the picture in the room with the flashlights and have the girls tell us about the picture, you know…tell a story about it…for Benji. It will keep their minds on something else and hopefully tire them out as well," she chuckled.

She and Mary walked back into the room where Lilly and Emma were entertaining Benji in his crib. The boy was beginning to get sleepy after having been so rudely awakened from his afternoon nap. So Srenna had the girls curl up on her bed and showed them the picture of John and Miriam and all the family at the river. The girls loved the idea of telling a story and gradually everyone began to yawn and blink in the fashion of sleepiness. It wasn't much longer before Lilly willingly crawled down under the crib with her blankets and pillow and was soon breathing deeply. Mary followed close behind her and snuggled up next to her on the floor.

It was dear little Emma who fought the thought of sleep for fear the ground beneath her would rumble her awake. Try as she might Srenna could not convince the child to settle down except to keep her in the bed, cuddled up beside her. Even then Emma's usual inquisitive five year old chatter kept Srenna wide awake and wondering herself when the next tremor would shake the house. But it did not.

Srenna thought she might nearly be able to finally rest when the sound of the truck that Matthew and Stephan had come back for earlier pulled up to the house. In short order both were inside and much to Srenna's relief, Matthew's six foot frame was leaning over her next to the bed.

"What is this Miss James? Why... I do believe you've a bedbug beside you that needs a good tickling," he whispered as quietly as he could so as not to disturb the others. But Emma's giggles had to be stifled quickly as a squeal of delight attempted to escape her lips.

"Hush you! They'll all be awake again," Srenna whispered frantically putting one hand over the child's mouth and slapping the other playfully at Matthew.

"Shhhh...." Matthew hissed into Srenna's ear causing even more giggles to come out of Emma.

"I'm going to send both of you to sleep in YOUR room, eh?" she threatened them both, hoping Benji indeed would not be aroused out of his slumber. Then she suddenly thought to ask where Stephan was.

"I sent him to get his things out of his room. He'll be right down," Matthew assured her as she made account of each and everyone of her charges. "I'm going to do the same and then I'll be back." Srenna watched him leave the room and then turned to Emma, attempting to quiet the little girl again.

Only a few moments passed and Stephan entered the room and without saying much he found a spot on the floor at the end of Srenna's bed. She would have asked the boy if he was hungry or had eaten, but she knew full well had he an empty stomach she would have known about it. Instead by the time Matthew came back in the room, Stephan had nearly fallen asleep.

Again Matthew came to the side of the bed and this time sat on the edge next to Srenna. Emma was curled up in her arms. Before Srenna could ask or Matthew could answer, Emma had something to say. "I want Matthew to sleep next to me," the wiggling child begged. Her pleading tone made both Matthew and Srenna simultaneously shush her one more time.

Matthew looked at Srenna for approval and saw the nod of her head, and even in the dim light of the little lantern light on the stand he could read the look in her eyes that said tonight she needed him close by.

"I doubt that I can get around the bed without stepping on Stephan..." he joked with his favorite baby sister... "so...I guess..." he began as he started to swing his frame over Srenna and Emma, "I'll have to..." he chuckled quietly, pretending to possibly smash them both in the process... "crawl over both of you," he finished as he plopped himself down beside Emma and stretched his long legs down the bed. He pulled the blanket he had brought with him over him and snuggled for a moment with Emma, who was finally happy to settle down now that her big brother was safely home. She started to say something but Matthew cut her off. "Shush, you, if you want me to stay." That said the little girl began to finally nod off.

Until the room began to shudder.

"It's all right everyone! It's not that bad," Matthew calmly proclaimed as he heard the sounds from under the crib from Lilly grabbing Mary or Mary grabbing Lilly. Stephan was elated at that one, realizing by now that they were only baby quakes compared to the one earlier this afternoon. Benji never stirred. But it wasn't only Emma that buried her face against her brother. At the first jolt of the bed, Srenna found herself reaching for Matthew with the first sign of fear she had shown all evening. His strong arms went around both of the girls and it was over before he could say another word.

"All right, everyone?" he asked of his siblings. Each let him know they had survived that one and they began to drift off to sleep again. But not Emma, or Srenna who still clung to Matthew without shame or humiliation.

"How can one ever get use to all this shaking about," Srenna whispered over Emma's head. The little girl was dually upset by the bed trembling, even if only for a moment. Matthew hugged her tight and decided it was time for a short story to try and quiet the child one more time.

"I think you both need to hear the story about "the Shaky Land" before you go to sleep," he suggested in his low deep voice.

"Oh yes! Please can we?" Emma burst out almost at an outside voice.

"Will you tell her the story so she'll shut up?" came an irate answer from the end of the bed.

"Shhhhh!" came the duet of shushing from both Srenna and Matthew.

"Please just get on with it before the ground rolls both of you out of this bed...or I do!" said Srenna with clenched teeth.

Matthew was trying hard not to laugh at her annoyance but he knew as well he'd better heed her order or sleep alone with a five year old tonight.

"Well then…here goes," he began. "Not too long ago when the ocean was bright and blue and quite empty, God decided he wanted a brand new piece of earth covered in more beauty then any one had ever seen before. So one day he reached deep down under the waves and stuck His hand into the sand below. He began to stir it up and push the sand up with all His might. The sea began to rumble like thunder and the ground God was pushing up trembled in His hand. With it he formed rolling hills and waterfalls and rivers from the sea water. He pushed harder and made breathtaking mountains and volcanoes that stood like majestic towers. The ground was so clean and rich that everywhere forests and fields began to grow with the greenest of grass and pasture. He loved it so much that he reached his other hand in and pushed up another bit of earth and formed the same incredible land just a little ways off, this one with snowcapped mountain peaks and lush tropical gardens tucked all around the base of them. More waterfalls and crystal blue rivers and lakes came forth when the waves from the sea spilled over the new earth."

Matthew hesitated for a moment peering first down at his little sister and then full into Srenna's face as she stared at him wide eyed and captivated by his story. "From up in heaven where God was looking at this beautiful land he'd just created He wonder what He would call it. It had to have a name befitting of what He saw and as He gazed across Heaven itself, He was sure this little piece of ground He'd created was His favorite of all times. Then God looked back at the glorious strip of land and from where He was way up in Heaven He could see the lovely puffy white clouds begin to float across the land He'd just pushed up out the sea. So He decided to name the new islands Aotearoa, meaning "long bright world". God loved it so much He sent first the Polynesian people called the Maoris because they loved and respected the islands and took good care of them. Later God decided to let some of the white men or Pakehas in the other parts of His world come too. Especially the ones who loved the lands and mountains and agreed to take special care of this incredible place along with their brother the Maoris. In time they learned to live together under the mountain ranges and long green fields and raise something else God loved very much."

"Sheep!" came a little voice from under the covers between Srenna and Matthew.

"Yeahr…sheep. God loves sheep almost as much as He loves you!" Matthew chuckled quietly into his little sister's curls.

"But why must the ground keep shaking?" asked Emma peering up at her favorite brother. "Yes   please…Why?"   added Srenna.

"Well…He loved the land He made so much that he decided that every now and then He should push more of it from out of the sea. And so…. He does. The end." Matthew waited to see if truly this would be the end…the end of the evening, the end of the chatter and hopefully the end of the shaking. Emma began to argue the silence but Matthew cut her off with his finger against her lips and gently instructed the child, "To sleep, you…now." No more was heard from her after that.

For several minutes there was actual quiet and Matthew thought perhaps even Srenna had dozed off, but then her soft voice spoke across the inches that separated their faces from each other.

"Will it last much longer, the aftershocks?" she whispered.

"Only a few days most likely and they'll get shorter and easier."

"Is everyone good?"

"Everyone's good. There was only minor damage to the church and none to the parsonage. A lot of mess, like here, but really, for a 6.9 earthquake we faired quite well," Matthew offered encouragingly. "Ray Benoit over by the church has a short wave. It hit hardest just beyond Masterton in the mountains. Don't know how much damage was there. We'll hear the next few days."

"How long till the electricity is back up?" Srenna asked, wondering how much longer she would have to rough it with all the children.

"Can't say about that, but we'll be right. It'll be a new challenge for the little ones, but a good one. Maybe getting their minds on Christmas coming up will help. Keep them outside and busy," Matthew suggested.

"Christmas. I can't believe it's time for that and so much to do," Srenna pondered quietly.

"Well…not tonight, Miss James…not tonight, eh?" he whispered as he stretched his legs one more time, yawned and closed his eyes. There was no response from the young woman laying only inches away from him and separated only by one tiny little five year old. He thought for sure and gladly so that Srenna had finally closed her own eyes and slipped into badly needed rest. But he was wrong. He opened one eye to find Srenna instead wide awake and watching him.

"Close your eyes Srenna. Go to sleep. And that's an order," he playfully commanded her. She was ready to argue his instruction but was caught by his fingertips gently pressed against her mouth to stop her. "Sleep," he repeated and closed his eyes. He remembered falling asleep with his hand brushed against her face and that's where it stayed as they both finally succumbed to the weariness of the day's events.

Chapter 28: The Holiday

The busy events of the next two weeks hardly gave way to any further concern with the after shocks or minor tremors following the earthquake. The surrounding sheep community had been most fortunate and greatly spared of any significant damages or injuries. The epicenter had much to do with the sparing of most towns and structures. Hardest hit had been those located directly in the mountainous area beyond Palmerston North. After a few days of cleaning up glass and repairing some of the family belongings the Patton children along with Matthew and Srenna moved on to more immediate concerns, that of Christmas. It was only around the corner and along with the anticipation of all the celebrating was the grand invitation given to the family to join the Davidsons for a holiday on the beach the week after. Now that time was upon them and Srenna was not completely excited about it.

Christmas had come and gone. Last week had been comfortable in spite of heightened emotions for the first holiday spent without John and Miriam. Matthew and Srenna had agreed they would keep it low keyed and expect anything from the children. They were prepared to let the children even cry if need be and then help them through it, but all in all it went fairly well. In preparation a few remarks were made about how mother or father would do things and when said, Srenna made a point to follow up on it as close as she,

Mary and Matthew could. They even got some support from Stephan who seemed to find some solace in trying to accomplish some of the things his father would have done to prepare for Christmas morning. Numerous times during the morning festivities and then during dinner Srenna caught Matthews glance and his grateful look of happiness that his family was going to be all right. She found herself wanting more then anything to see that peace in his eyes and on his face. It was beginning to be a daily goal to see even the smallest effect she had in helping him and supporting him.

For a short time that morning she felt a few of her own twinges of memories of her family and missing them all these years. She had spent Christmas with Reverend Carmel and his wife for several years after her family had died and a few years with the Havillands. But this year she felt differently. As she watched the children open the presents they had either made or bought with meager allowances and monies earned doing special chores she felt more tied to the sweet faces she was enjoying then she ever had since the last Christmas with her family; especially little Benji and his first Christmas experience.

His continuous shrieks of delight actually lightened the mood at precisely the right moment. He oohed and aahed at every package opened and found great sport in crawling through the piles of wrapping paper and boxes. Everyone agreed that Emma and Benji would be the center of attention, since nine year old Lilly already had given up her belief in the infamous Santa Claus. They all took delight in trying to make it as great a Christmas as they could for little Emma who spent most of the day hanging onto Matthew as much as she could. Srenna watched him as he held her, hugged her and showered her with affection and attention, doing his best to keep her happy. But more then once Srenna found herself wondering how he was really doing and if he was giving everything he had into making the day as painless as possible for the rest of them.

They had decided to draw names for exchanging gifts, but each of the older children had rallied around, finding things to make or buy little gifts for each other. Srenna was amazed at their creativeness to give gifts. She was once again reminded of how endearingly and lovingly Miriam Patton had taken care of her offspring and how much both parents had influenced the children. Srenna herself had purchased or made something for each one of them, including Matthew. For Emma and Lilly she had sewn each a little handbag to put drawing and writing paper in. There were pockets for pencils and crayons, and their names were embroidered on the fronts. For Mary she had made a beautiful dark green skirt to go with her new blouse Matthew had bought her. Mary had not so much grown taller as she had grown shapelier much to Matthew's dismay and to Srenna's knowing eyes. For Stephan, the hardest of all, Srenna had gone to Matthew for any ideas. In the end they pooled their money together and bought him a new saddle for Bear. Benji was the easiest, receiving little toys and new clothes for the fast growing infant who was nearing his first birthday.

Srenna thought Matthew would be hard to give a gift to as well but over the last few months she was surprised at how quickly she had come to know his likes and dislikes, his moods, even a lot of his needs. She was constantly aware at hard he worked, how little he complained and how much he still gave at the end of a long day. Her first gift when she came had come in the form of her own journal book that she had purchased before leaving Sydney. She had no idea she would find a young man at the other end of her trip that thrived on writing. She never hesitated one moment when trying to make amends with him that first week by presenting the book to him on the hillside, especially after Mary told her about his passion. But now after almost three months of serving him as the children's governess Srenna found herself wanting to give him something special. Little did she know he was also wondering just what to give as a gift to this extraordinary woman he knew he was falling in love with. Neither one knew they had confided in the same person to help them; Mary.

And Mary was loving it. She watched them both attempting to figure out what would be the appropriate gift for each one, suppressed a chuckle when first one and then the other would press her for any ideas, and then found great delight in having the final approval for the gift chosen. She was watching them both as their affections for one another unfolded right before her happy eyes.

For Matthew it was a set of beautiful pens and writing pencils in a carved box made from the rich wood from the Kauri tree used across the islands. His full given name, Matthew Lucas Patton, was wood burned on it, thanks to Jimmie.

For Srenna it was a new album of classical piano, something he would have thought to buy for his mother, as the two women shared the same great love for music. He also finally bought a new needle for his mother and father's old phonograph to ensure her being able to play the endearing concertos. The quieted player had been brought out of storage where it had been put after Miriam's funeral. But now Matthew felt it was time to incorporate the use of the music machine coveted by his parents to bring culture and beauty into their home. Matthew's hope was that Srenna would keep gracing them with her own music at the piano, something they all agreed they missed terribly. She had made it a familiar habit to play a little in the evening when everyone was winding down and getting ready for bed, just as their mother had for years.

She played some that day too, after they returned from dinner at Jimmie and Irmani's house. Srenna hadn't known a time when so many people had sat down together at one table to eat, but somehow that day they managed to feed the seven of them and the Rainga's ten all at once. Loud as it was she couldn't remember either when she had been so happy. She thanked God many times over during that day for bringing her into this circle of beautiful and boisterous children and friends.

But today, seven days later on this warm, sunny day when she should have been thrilled at the idea of beach fun, Srenna was trying hard not to show her emotions. The drive to Castle Points' beautiful shoreline should have been a pleasant and joyous one, but Srenna was having a hard time trying to join in the excited chatter about what everyone was going to do when they got there. All week long she tried to dismiss the knot in her stomach and the impending holiday they would all be sharing with Reverend and Mrs. Davidson at the beach. Sunday after Sunday she had been able to overlook the fact that they were only a stones throw away from the parsonage perched just above the shoreline and the sloped path down to the frothy waterfront. Church had kept them all preoccupied for numerous weeks now but Matthew and the children were looking forward to a much needed day of fun and relaxation.

Srenna had tried to think of a way to stay behind, perhaps keeping Benji with her so they could enjoy the day unhampered by his care. But none of them would have it. Matthew pushed that idea away and assured her that they all needed to go after all they'd been through together over the last few months. She finally gave up trying, even after the excuse of not having a bathing suit. Mary had given her one, which fit perfectly and looked very smart on her, but she pulled on a pair of her shorts over the suit and hoped no one would press her to get wet. Her plan of action was to cling to Benji most of the day so as to avoid the water. She had a very foreboding feeling though that she might not be successful, especially with this bunch. There was no escape however and she wasn't about to spoil the children or Matthew's fun.

When they arrived and piled out of the car, Matthew began handing out this and that from the car for everyone to carry down to the beach. The Davidson's were waiting and overjoyed that the children had come. They made great sport of hearing all about the children's Christmas festivities including the full glass of cranberry juice Benji pulled over on himself at the Rainga's. That sent him into the sink for a thorough bath. There were still hints of red juice in the infants blond curls and everyone had another good laugh about it, everyone but Srenna. She took a deep breath as they began the walk down the path to the sandy beach. It was beautiful, she had to admit, and the sun felt good on this summery January day. She never forgot to thank God that she lived in a part of the world where the climate was mostly warm and in spite of the abundance of rain, the weather was pleasant much of the time. Even this was not enough though to calm her jitters and quiet her heart as they drew closer to the beach.

The children were totally unaware of anything. They dropped their load and before Matthew could say a word to them they were running to the waters edge. He looked at Srenna as if to apologize for their impatience but she suddenly found some reason to be preoccupied for a while. She forced a laugh and motioned to Matthew to "just go" to which he gladly ran after all of them. Before she had even shifted Benji to her other hip Matthew had caught up little Emma and swung her high into the air. He then swung her feet over and into the tumbling waves much to her screaming delight. Srenna watched him for a moment as he played with the youngster and then turned away. She felt a strange heaviness coming over her and she didn't like it, so she did what she had grown very good at doing for so many years now. She got busy.

Reverend Davidson had followed the children to the water as well, but his wife Patricia stayed behind helping Srenna to organize all the Patton belongings that had come on the trip. Blankets were laid out for everyone to set on and Srenna put the baby on one as soon as she could. He however found his way off of it immediately and proceeded to try sand as a snack.

"You little beggar, you!" she exclaimed, both women laughing at the screwed up expression on his disappointed face.

Srenna began to feel a bit more relaxed when she realized just how much she would be preoccupied with him and she glanced back at the children frolicking in the waves.

"We are so glad you could all come today, Srenna. The children needed this very badly and truth be known, so did we," Patricia Davidson laughed. She was much different then Ruth Carmel, a slender attractive woman in her early fifties. The Davidson's and the Patton's were good friends for nineteen years. Hamilton Davidson had taken a shine to the young John Patton and his wife when he first learned of their arrival in New Zealand's sheep country. He learned quickly that John had strong convictions that were being acutely tested at the young age of twenty. Hamilton had convinced them that they needed the love and support of a strong church family and with persistence the Patton's finally showed up only a couple of months after. The Patton's had welcomed Matthew into the world shortly after they arrived and John's hands were very full. They fell into the much needed fellowship of Hamilton Davidson's unique parish of farmers and sheepherders. They stayed for the next eighteen years until both were laid to rest in the picturesque cemetery on the bluff just beyond the church.

Patricia watched the children with great delight remembering each one of the children's first experience in the salty waves. "He'll be going in the water sure as anything before the days over, mark my words. It's a Patton tradition, a sort of baptism if you will, "she chuckled knowingly, looking at Benji.

"Surely not!?" Srenna gasped, noticeably upset by the notion that this baby she held on her lap would enter the choppy waves in any capacity. "He's much too little, eh!?" she added, looking at Patricia Davidson with noticeable horror on her face and deep concern in her voice.

"It's alright, dear. No worries. Matthew learned how to swim right here in this spot when he was
barely two. He'd never let anything happen to this little nipper," the woman consoled Srenna. She sensed a tone of something beside just concern for the baby. Fear, she thought to herself. She heard fear. It made her wonder as she observed the edgy girl. Srenna watched the others with most of her reserve gone now especially while she thought at any moment Matthew might come up and snatch the child from her arms and carry him away to the sea that Srenna hated so

much. She realized that Patricia was watching her with some concern and quickly tried to recover her poise and control.

"I'm sorry. I didn't mean to sound so harsh or….critical," she apologized to the woman and then tried to excuse her behavior. "I'm not very fond of swimming. I didn't want to tell Matthew or spoil the children's excitement about coming. I hope you understand."

"Well of course I understand, darling. It's quite alright. You don't see me running in, eh?" her companion chuckled lightly and patted the nervous girl on the leg.

"Really? You don't like swimming either?" Srenna asked in amazement. "But you live right here next to the ocean. How have you dealt with that all these years?" she questioned her.

"Honesty, luv," she smiled at Srenna, leaning towards the girl with a grin on her face, "And a few threats as well."

Srenna laughed at the lovely woman and her forthright way of putting things. She felt a little better that she had told her but wasn't quite ready to tell her why. Patricia Davidson somehow knew that and refused to press the girl for anymore information.

Patricia studied the young woman's face sitting across from her not only to see if she was relaxing but simply because of the unusual beauty of her face. It wasn't hard to see and really a bit obvious to trained eyes that Srenna James, in spite of her city bred appearance wasn't quite "Pakeha" or white as the Maoris so fondly referred to their English neighbors. The Reverend's wife could see that in only the short amount of time Srenna had graced the north island she had favored the sun instead of burning as most Pakehas did. It gave her cause to wonder about Srenna's heritage.

"You've taken quite well to the sun on our island paradise my dear," Patricia began carefully. "I myself burn within moments if I'm not careful. Have you always darkened so beautifully…so naturally?"

She watched for any reaction in Srenna's expression, but only a distant stare off over the sea was present on the girl's face. Then ever so quietly Srenna offered the answer Patricia was looking for.

"My father was part Ginny, you know… aboriginal," Srenna began. She in turned looked at the dear woman's eyes to see if she could read her reaction to Srenna's candid reply. Then she plowed on with more explanation. "My grandfather was English but my Grandmother…she was full blooded Ginny." Here the girl hesitated as she slipped into a difficult memory. Patricia could tell that the conversation was beginning to make Srenna uncomfortable so she quickly determined to soften the edges a bit.

"She's sweet, luv. There are so many people here half and half we don't even think about it in these parts." That said she decided to change the subject for Srenna's sake and hoped that at some other time the young woman would confide in her more about her past.

For a good while Srenna and Patricia sat on the blankets and enjoyed one another's company and covered all the news about the children's Christmas and plans to go back to school at the end of January.

Srenna had felt very fortunate to have found so many dear friends in this tight community and this woman was one of them, along with Irmani Rainga. She couldn't help thinking though how unique each one was. Irmani was raw in many respects, earthy and definitely bound to her Maori beliefs. They did include a faith in God in her own way and the ways of her people, but much differently then those of Reverend and Mrs. Davidson. But not once had Srenna ever heard or seen any judgmental attitudes in any of them concerning their differences. Even though the Anglican man and his wife had been parish leaders for over twenty-five years they had readily excepted the Rainga's as vital and special people in the area and most definitely in the lives of the Patton family. Srenna found that to be a breath of fresh air from the old ways she had seen in Australia between the white race and the Aboriginals.

Nearly an hour and a half had passed while the two women talked and laughed. Trying to keep the energetic infant out of the sand and playing with the toys Srenna had brought proved to be a feat worthy of two sets of hands. And Srenna was completely engulfed in his play when she heard footsteps coming up to the blanket. She wasn't too concerned as she had begun to relax more as time went on, but that quickly disappeared when she saw the approach of Stephan and Lilly and the look on both of their faces.   It wasn't good.

Srenna knew the minute she looked at them that they were up to something. Every hair on her body stood up as Lilly went behind her and Stephan positioned himself directly in front of her. But before she even had time to protest loudly or Patricia had time to stop them Stephan had grabbed Srenna by the hands and Lilly was pushing from behind. With sickening strength she could feel herself being pushed and pulled to the waters edge. She tried to protest but the words were choking in her throat and all she could do was shake her terrified head adamantly and try to dig her bare heals into the sand. As they pulled her closer she felt a sudden surge of stricken energy. Angry energy. She felt as though neither one of the children, who were in their minds, just playing with her, even existed at the moment. She fought them and she fought them hard. And then the scream came, one word at first. "NO!" It came franticly and then again. And then she heard a familiar voice, one with authority, one with deep concern, yelling at both the kids to "STOP!" And stop they did.

The next thing Srenna knew she was crying and trying to run up the beach to the path, away from all the eyes looking at her in dismay at what had just happened. The voice had been Matthew's. He quickly glanced at Hamilton and then at Patricia both motioning to him to go. He started after Srenna as quickly as he could after telling the children it would be all right. His immediate concern was her.

Once she started up the path she never looked back, feeling both upset and embarrassed by her reaction to an innocent attempt to engage her in their fun. It only made her feel worse and all she could think of was getting away and falling apart. She found her self heading towards the cemetery so she wouldn't see anyone. But Matthew was close behind her and caught her at the fork in the path leading to the parsonage and the other way to the cemetery.

"Srenna! Wait! Stop and tell me what's wrong," he yelled ahead at her. But this only made her pick up her pace, determined to get away, even from him. He was not about to let her though, and he finally caught her, grabbing her arm and trying to stop her. So upset was she, that she literally shoved at him, pushing him away temporarily. Again he reached for her arms, both this time and attempted to pull her into his to calm her.

But now she was completely out of control, her body wracking with sobs as she felt the confused pain of old memories she had kept buried and new horrible feelings for what had just happened. She still fought Matthew as though he were attacking her, even though reason told her he wasn't. He wouldn't let go and his strong arms won against even her resolve to escape. Then she collapsed and Matthew lowered her onto the ground still holding her in his embrace, trying to console her as though she were Emma or Lilly after a nightmare or injury. He held her for a long time, gently rocking her and holding her head against his bare shoulder. He could only think to say, "It's alright, you'll be alright," and even this seemed to be too little in the wake of what just took place. He wasn't sure what he would get from her or out of her once she calmed down, but he did know right now all he wanted to do was hold her, quiet her.

The sobs began to ebb a little as Srenna's energy was drained. Matthew could feel her body tiring and going limp in his arms, but still he didn't press her for an explanation. He had rested his head against her ear and was still whispering to her when the crying stopped suddenly and Srenna sat up and pushed him a bit away. He kept his arms around her as much as he could, afraid that she had simply gotten her second wind and would attempt to dart away, but she looked at him with horror on her face.

"Oh, Matthew! I'm so sorry!" she cried, the tears streaming down her face again, fresh and hot. "I've ruined everything for the children. They must be horrified at my behavior. I should never...." She wept bitterly.

"Stop, Srenna, don't worry about the children. They'll understand if you'll just give them a chance, if you'll just tell them why it upset you so much.....If you'll tell me," he quickly interjected gently. He held her far enough away to look at her face, to try to read the pain and fear in her eyes. "Tell me what just happened. I wouldn't listen to you before, but I am now," he added, remembering the conversation they had had when they got the invitation to come today. "You tried to tell me and I didn't hear you."

Srenna looked into the face of this young man who kept surprising her with his ability to read things, to see things and she knew she wasn't going to be able to walk away without telling him why she loathed the sea. But she wasn't sure herself what really made her feel the way she did. She just knew that the sea was her enemy, or it felt like it was. Even living near it she had stayed away as much as she could. She had refused to be on a ship or enjoy anything remotely having to do with it all these years, even at the gentle prompting of Reverend Carmel to find closure. But now here she was, and with someone she had promised to be honest with, someone she had begun to care about deeply, and his family. Srenna began weeping softly again and covered her face with her hands in utter dismay.

"Srenna, I can't help you if you don't tell me what's wrong. I can sit here all day and hold you and I would if I thought it would help...but it won't, eh?" Matthew whispered softly up against her face. "Tell me what happened to your mum and dad… Can you?" he said, much to Srenna's surprise.

She looked at him again and saw a knowing look in his eyes. She realized all of a sudden that all this time, all these three months, not once had Matthew ever pressed her about her own loss of her parents. He knew they had died when she was only twelve, he knew she had grown up at the girl's school, but she wondered now if he had any idea what she had truly been through. He waited patiently for her to decide to trust him even more now then she had already over the last few months. He felt her body relax a little and she looked down at her lap before taking a deep breath. She shook her head a few times and looked out at the water below them.

"I didn't realize how much it still hurt. How much it still affected me," she cried softly.

"Did your parents drown?" Matthew asked quietly and carefully. He hesitated for a second and when she began to cry harder he plunged ahead, asking more. "Were they on the ship that sunk in the Sydney Harbor?" he pressed her gently.

Srenna couldn't answer but shook her head in a despairing nod and once again Matthew pulled her into his arms and against his chest, taking the new tears along with her painful response. His own memory went back to the year he was ten and he heard his mum and dad talking about the Bella Ava sinking after being struck by a science sub. He remembered how few people had survived and one of them was a young girl found swimming towards shore. He started putting two and two together and realized all of a sudden that he very well might be holding that brave little girl in his arms this very moment.

"Were you on the ship with them?" Matthew asked softly, rubbing his face against her hair.

"Yes," she sobbed, the tears coming with no promise of ever subsiding.

"You got off some how, didn't you? You were found in the harbor, rescued from the water," he offered remembering the article in the paper his father had brought home.

Srenna could only nod her head against Matthew's chest. She wanted to stop crying. She'd always been able to gain control, except the day when she had run into the alley, the day Reverend Carmel told her she was leaving Sydney. And now…

At that point it was all the information Matthew needed to hear. He was more concerned that Srenna was spent, emotionally drained. As the tears began to lessen and her body began to relax in his arms for the second time, he decided he would ask nothing more. He simply held her and rocked her just as he'd seen her do when little Benji cried fitfully, needing nothing but safe arms. He could only imagine what horror this incredible girl had endured, what enormous pain she had suffered at the loss of her parents. And here she had been rallying all of them, caring for them with great tenderness and genuine love.

At that moment Matthew was sure his own heart was breaking for her. He hurt just thinking about her being left alone, waking up without a family. He looked toward the path leading to the parsonage where he knew his dear brothers and sisters had most likely been herded for lunch by Patricia Davidson.
He was gratefully aware how blessed he'd been to have them, for all of them to have each other to get through the death of their mother and father. There were tears welling up in his eyes now, tears for all of them, for all they'd been through and all God was bringing them through together. He knew unlike he'd never known before that God had surely brought Srenna to him, to the children, not just for them and their needs, but for hers as well.

Matthew heaved a heavy sigh and for some strange reason it brought Srenna's crying to an end. He waited for a moment or so to see if she was indeed finished or if she had fallen asleep in utter exhaustion. But she moved her hand against his chest and began wiping the tears from her cheeks. He kissed the top of her head reverently and breathed into her ear, "Are you alright?"

She tried to lift her head away from him but she was drained. Matthew cupped her face in his hands and looked at her with tender concern. He wanted her to stay in this place as long as she needed to and not just shut down for their sake. He also didn't want her to feel any guilt at all for having broken down and reacting the way she did. But he could see that her strong resolve was already kicking in and as usual Srenna James was bolstering herself and indeed getting back her control. She wouldn't look Matthew full in the eyes. She pushed herself back from him enough so that his close embrace was broken and she was able to sit back on the sandy path. Matthew took a deep breath thinking he might press her now to tell him more but she was already pulling herself together with strong determination.

"I'll be alright, really. I….I need to let the children have this day Matthew. It's so important to them…and you and I can talk later and…" she rambled quickly, attempting to stand. She made it to her feet, but as soon as she attempted to straighten up, the ground beneath her felt as though it were sliding away and Matthew caught her just before she lost her balance. He braced her for a moment and bent to look in her face. But she was still trying very hard not to catch his gaze.

"Srenna, don't… you know you can tell me…." He encouraged her firmly. But she cut him off quickly.

"I know I can. I know I probably should. I just…I'm really sorry right now and a bit embarrassed and I…." she babbled word after word. As she spoke, she tried smoothing her hair and wiping her tear stained face with the back of her hand, fussing like Matthew had seen her do a thousand times when she was flustered or upset.

This time though he wouldn't have it. With almost an air of frustration he shook his head at her and grabbed her by the shoulders. "Srenna, stop. You have nothing to be embarrassed about, certainly nothing to apologize for. You obviously needed to get this out of your system. You were so worried about Stephan never crying and now I'm wondering if you ever did," he said with just a little edge of sarcasm. He noticed right away that Srenna looked as though she would begin crying again and he felt badly for his tone of voice. "Look, …all I'm saying is…you need to stop thinking you have to be strong all the time. You're part of us, …our family… and the rest of the family is strong when one of us hurts or is scared or whatever it is. That's the way we've always been, the way mum and dad taught us, showed us." He pulled her to him gently, hoping she would come without resistance and when she submitted to his arms again he couldn't help but think about the kiss they had shared in the gazebo a couple of weeks ago during the rainstorm. It had been a huge chance he'd taken then, hoping he was reading her correctly. He wasn't disappointed when she succumbed to his attempt and realized with great relief that he wasn't the only one struggling with strong feelings. She had kissed him back with definite fervor, much to his delight. He only wanted now to reassure her that his feelings for her were growing stronger every day and he would do anything to help her, support her, love her.

She did know. She needed his love, his incredible strength and uncanny sensitivity. His firmness.

All of it. All of him. And right now her emotions were so raw she wanted to feel anything but the grief she felt. She offered her face to him and he took her lips quickly. He too wanted only for the moment to help her feel assured; assured that he did care and would hold her for as long as she needed. But as easily as they fell into each others embrace, Matthew felt himself easily losing control of his senses. He kissed her for just another moment before he gently but firmly pulled back from her lips and put his mouth against her ear. He barely breathed loud enough for her to hear him, "I'd better stop. I don't want to, but I'd better."

Srenna felt so many things just then that she wasn't sure what to do. Still feeling somewhat embarrassed by all that had happened she pulled away from Matthew in some confusion and took a deep breath. "It's alright Matthew, I... I think we'd better see if the children are okay, and I'll try not to spoil the rest of the day, I promise." She began to walk down the path towards the fork to the house, and all Matthew could do was follow in frustration. He knew he couldn't just let the day go unresolved, but he did agree that the rest of the matter would have to be dealt with later.

"Look...Srenna, ...if you want me to explain to the kids why you were upset, I can, ...you know... before they come back down to the beach. If you'd like to have some time alone too... before talking to them...you can wait here and I'll go get them," he offered graciously.

Srenna was ready with an answer before he barely finished. She had completely pulled herself together and even smiled lightly at Matthew responding in an even tone, "Maybe I should, so they won't think I'm still upset."

Matthew nodded at her and looked out over the bluff so she wouldn't see the frustration on his face. He began walking past her and answered over his shoulder as he headed up to the parsonage, "I'll give you a little while. We'll be down in a bit." With that and one more look back at Srenna, he kept going, praying as he went that maybe God would do what he had not been able to; praying also that he would indeed be able to explain to the bewildered children what had taken place. But more then anything he was praying that God would help him to know how to help Srenna reconcile this incredible and crippling fear and pain he had witnessed today; that they had all witnessed today. As he approached the house and saw the children sitting at the picnic table, he felt the intense presence of the Shepherd who had always led him, always been there for him in even the darkest hours of his life. He knew he had never been left or forsaken, not even when he'd stood at his mother's bedside at the hospital and watched her slip into heaven. He also was fully aware that the woman waiting now on the path, the one that had just poured herself out to exhaustion, the one that had taken his young brood of siblings and brought order back into their lives, and the one who had willingly and passionately kissed him twice now, was his future wife. And that made Matthew more determined then ever to help her be freed of this demon, whatever it was. He stopped and looked back briefly and then turned towards his brothers and sisters who were waiting anxiously to be reassured that this dear woman they also loved was going to be alright.

Chapter 29: The Painful Truth

The children did come back to the beach later. All of them, even little Emma agreed that they wanted Srenna to tell them what had happened to her family when she was a little girl. Matthew tried to share some of it with them before they met her on the hill but he really wanted her to be able to talk about it. Stephan and Lilly felt awful when they knew why Srenna had been so upset with them, but Matthew assured them that she wasn't angry with either of them.
Reverend Davidson prayed for all of them before they went down and Patricia Davidson stayed at the house with the baby.

Srenna waited for them to return with some anxiety about what to say to the children. She loved them all so much and reacting the way she did was absolutely no reflection of how they made her feel. She was still very shaken by how brutal her feelings had errupted after all this time. And embarrassed. She knew Matthew was right when he encouraged her not to shove down all her emotions concerning her family's death. But she wasn't sure how it could be reconciled either. Even now after Matthew had tenderly held her while she cried, she dreaded any attempt at all to come to grips with the ocean below her. She was standing on the hill at the fork in the path when she heard Matthew approaching with the children and it was all she could do to stand still and not run again.

But when they got close enough to see her and then close enough to touch her an unexpected thing happened to keep her from running. The four children stood for only a moment looking at Srenna as though they were waiting for her to have a chance to explain. She barely got the beginning of an apology out of her mouth to Stephan and Lilly for having gotten so emotional when Stephan, who had not cried for several months after his mother's death, stepped next to Srenna and put his arm around her. Then as quickly as he had moved, Lilly threw her arms around Srenna's waist and began to cry. Before Srenna could react, Mary and Emma had joined in on the hug and tears were flowing freely on everyone's part. Matthew stood there for a few moments and watched his little orphaned family hold their governess while she and they cried together. He looked at Hamilton Davidson and knew the parish leader was praying quietly under his breath as the group ministered some more healing to one another. It had so far been Srenna bringing most of the healing or at least the avenue for it to take place for the children, but here he was watching John and Miriam Patton's children ministering to what was at one time a devastated little girl who had gotten too strong for her own good. He smiled at Matthew, who just stood there astounded that his siblings had so much to give back to her. It wasn't until Mary motioned to him to join them that he moved to the group and threw his arms around all of them.

After awhile, Hamilton gently suggested to everyone that they go and sit on the blankets so Srenna could tell them as much as she felt she could. Matthew kept his arm around her as they moved to the blankets that had been left on the beach. As they approached them, he felt a shiver run up and down Srenna's body and he squeezed her reassuringly and smiled down at her. "She'll be right, Srenna. Only what your ready for and nothing else," he promised her.

As soon as everyone had gotten comfortable on the ground, Reverend Davidson took the initiative to begin the conversation for Srenna and asked encouragingly, "Can you tell us what happened that day Srenna, the day you lost your family?" He also smiled lovingly and supportively at this young and very brave girl. He had known some of the details just by what Reverend Carmel had shared with him about this remarkable young woman and all she had been through. It was because of those comparisons to losing her parents that they both had felt Srenna James would be the perfect person to minister to the Patton family. But now Hamilton Davidson was beginning to see a much bigger plan on God's part. "Just like God," he thought to himself as he watched Srenna's face for any sign of struggle. For a very long moment she could only look out over the beautiful turquoise waves and wonder where and how to tell everyone her story.

In the end she did, relaying the account in minimal amounts. She stopped several times to cry again, the children hugging her and holding her each time. Matthew sat behind her almost as if to gird her up and numerous times simply pulled her back into his arms while the others embraced her. He watched little Emma carefully for any signs of too much information, but the five year old who normally wanted to behave like the baby in the family amazed him with her desire to help Srenna.

It was Stephan that surprised him the most. Matthew saw the genuine concern his thirteen-year-old brother showed the woman he had fought so hard to resist over the last few months. There was something definitely softening in Stephan's will as Srenna poured out the heartbreaking details of that horrendous day nine years ago. Matthew could see the revelation in Stephan's eyes when the boy realized that his governess did truly understand the grief of losing his parents. He looked at Srenna with more compassion then Matthew could ever remember seeing in his younger brother. Mary and Lilly both behaved as though Srenna was now the frightened, distraught child and they were the mothers as they held her hand or patted her leg. The whole experience lasted for nearly an hour and in the end pretty much exhausted everyone.

But in the end when the tears were spent for at least that moment everyone assured Srenna they loved her and cared more about her then playing anymore. They also all agreed that they would come back to the beach another day, when hopefully Srenna could face her fears and memories with more resolve. But she wouldn't hear it. She begged them to go back to their fun. Matthew realized it was important to her that the children's lives resumed as much normality as possible. He agreed that the children should try to go back to the water and enjoy the day as well. After tears had been wiped away from eyes and hugs and kisses had been shared they did. Reverend Davidson went with them and soon Mary, Stephan, Lilly and Emma were jumping in and out of the waves with him.

Matthew stayed behind, determined to not let Srenna out of his sight for the time being. He knew that something had been broken loose in her, but was still not sure how or when she would be ready to go farther with the pain of the memory. She was trying to watch the children but he could also tell it was still very hard for her.

"Would you like to go up to the house for awhile?" he asked quietly. "You and I haven't eaten anything all day. I guess I'm a bit hungry."

Srenna gazed over at Matthew and saw the slight grin on his face that she had come to find endearing in him. He was trying to be subtle, gentle and she could tell he was still greatly concerned with her state of emotions. "I suppose you are you poor thing, after missing lunch. We'd better go see if this brood left anything to eat," she answered grinning back at him in a feeble attempt to lighten the already charged day. With that she stood and prepared to walk back up the path one more time. Matthew was on his feet before she could move ahead of her though and caught her arm.

"Srenna," Matthew said, looking at her deeply and still smiling cautiously, "Whatever happened today, it's good. She'll be right, eh?" he asked, hoping that what he read in her eyes was her own glimmer of healing. He knew she had had enough for one day, but he also knew by now that this incredible resilient girl was quite capable of coping to what he knew now to be a fault. He didn't want to just let this day be buried deep inside her ability to survive. He was already praying quietly for wisdom to know if there was anything else he could do to facilitate her making amends with the memory.

But Matthew tucked another thought away. It was a determination that somehow he would find a way to help Srenna reach that resolve, and soon. It suddenly struck him how close the river was to the back of the house, that Emma could easily wonder off and that Benji would soon be walking and exploring as well. It quickened his heart to do something, anything to make sure Srenna's apparent fear of the water was not a hindrance, not only to herself …but to his family. He knew her surprisingly well after such a short time. Srenna James would be "right" indeed, even if she really wasn't, all for the sake of the children. How like his mother she was. But after what he experienced with her on the sandy path he wasn't about to let this one slide. He didn't know how he was going to bring it up again, up to the surface….but he knew he would.

Srenna smiled back at him as his arm went around her shoulder and they walked together up the path to the house. "You're right Matthew. She'll be sweet. I guess I'm going to have to practice what I've been telling the children all along and trust God to heal me." She let him guide her along the path to the parsonage and neither of them said anything more.

Srenna suddenly thought about Matthew kissing her again and how safe she had felt in his arms as she fell apart. She knew in her heart he was falling in love with her and she with him, but it didn't really surprise her at all. Ever since the day they had gone back to church and he had fixed his eyes on her in that blue dress she had sensed it for sure. Then, the kiss in the gazebo. As each week passed her own feelings were becoming stronger and stronger. Now she was as sure after today that he would do anything he had to in order to help her find closure, to help her heal.

What she couldn't get out of her mind... was the nagging thought of how he would do it.

Chapter 30: Still Waters

From somewhere deep in her sleep Srenna smelled an expected and comforting aroma she had
come to know every morning. Even though another hour of sleep would have been greatly welcomed after the always hectic and consistently busy day before, Matthew's faithful pot of early morning coffee roused her awake. She knew he would be leaving soon to run the sheep up to the grazing fields so she pushed herself away from her pillow and sat up. She immediately glanced over at the baby's crib with a silent prayer, but all hopes of little Benji still sleeping were dashed when his sweet baby's head popped up and his little baby hand reached thru the slat towards Srenna. One quiet little word slipped from his lips to her, "Mim" and melted Srenna to the bone. She sighed and looked at the angelic face peering at her wide-eyed and wanting and all resistance was gone. "How am I to ever discipline you, you little beggar?" she grinned with her facescrewed up in fun with him. He then sat up and still reaching out his baby hands to her, she stood and crossed the short distance to his crib while pulling on her robe and plucked him up into her arms. He clung to her neck still sleepy as she kissed the top of his curly blond head good morning.

"You'll have to wait this time for what you want, little beggar, until I've said good morning and have a great day to your brother."

Srenna moved quickly to the bedroom door and slipped into the hallway leading to the kitchen. She nearly ran full into Matthew as he came thru just about to leave.

"Hold up you two, what are doing up with the sun?" he smiled as he reached for Benji. The boy came willingly to his big brother and Matthew gave him a big squeeze and buried his face in the baby's neck until the child giggled with delight.

"Quiet you! You'll have the whole lot of them awake and wanting breakfast at six a.m. Then I'll be forced to ban you both to the hills," Srenna tried hard to sound stern but it was no use trying to stifle the giggles coming from both of them and making her laugh as well. None the less, Matthew suddenly relinquished the boy back to Srenna with a wink at Benji and a devilish grin at Srenna.

"He's wet... and he really wants to spend the day with you," he laughed, squeezing by both of them, not quite quickly enough to miss Srenna's playful swat of his shoulder. Indeed all the giggling and neck kissing had produced a wet baby. Srenna followed Matthew into the living room, stopping at her bedroom door. She was about to tell him as she had for weeks now to have a great day and she would see him at supper. Beating her to it he turned and asked her quickly, "You think Mary would watch everyone at noon so you can come out to the low field? I have some things I want to go over with you and I'm going to need to go to Masterton on Friday." He saw the puzzled look on Srenna's face knowing they usually met together on Fridays to talk about the children and matters concerning the house and the station.

"Of course. I'm sure she wouldn't mind at all," Srenna replied."Is everything alright?" she questioned with just a bit of concern in her voice.

"Yeahr," Matthew smiled reassuringly. He leaned to kiss her gently and then walked to the door. He had just placed his hand on the knob when he hesitated and turned toward her for a moment. Srenna still seemed puzzled by his request but Matthew gave her another grin and waited. She suddenly realized he was waiting for her, waiting to hear her say what she had been faithfully saying to him for over three months now.

It was her turn to grin as she gave a little chuckle and once again said, "Have a great day Matthew and I'll see you at noon."

He finally seemed satisfied that he could leave and stepped through the door, closing it quietly behind him. This time though instead of crossing the yard and heading towards the stock pens, he walked around the side of the house to the outside door leading to his room as though he'd forgotten something.

But Matthew had forgotten nothing as he opened the door and reached for the things Mary had left for him the night before. He just hoped that Benji's unplanned need for immediate attention had indeed sent Srenna back into her room to attend to the child. He moved quickly towards the barn to saddle Samson and after securing his bundle to the back of the saddle, he let the excited dogs out of their stalls and began walking on to the pens to release the hungry sheep. Matthew threw open the gates and told the two older dogs," Low fields today, mates." Without missing a beat the two dogs followed ahead with the others close behind and began to lead the flock down the road. When they reached the low field gate Duke jumped up and pushed it wide open while Durango and Duchess stood their ground on the road challenging any stray trying to defy them. But they didn't. The sheep liked the low field and the gentle part of the river to graze beside. Matthew brought up the rear on Samson and closed the gate after going through it. It promised to be a beautiful day, the sun already burning off the early morning mist. As he rode along in the solitude, hearing only the bleating of his sheep and the occasional barking commands of his dogs, Matthew began to wonder if he was right in what he'd planned on doing later. He'd made a promise to Srenna to never deceive her again after that first day she'd come to their family, after she came out to make peace with him. Yet here he was planning what was beginning to feel a bit like an ambush.

As quickly as that thought crossed his mind he suddenly and vividly recalled what had just happened a few days earlier at the beach. He had come to know Srenna as brave and resilient, strong; already bringing so much healing and needed peace into his and the children's lives. To see her so terrorized and grief stricken when Stephan and Lilly had pulled her towards the water made him even more determined to carry out his plan. He had to, he told himself, for her, for him, for all of them. He just hoped God was in agreement with his plan and Srenna wouldn't hate him when it was over.

The morning flew by for Srenna as she followed her daily routine with the children. With Mary's help she prepared a lunch for all of them ahead of time. Thankfully it was not laundry day, as all of her day was consumed by that event twice a week. While the girls went out to the garden to pick some fresh vegetables for the evening meal she managed to get most of the sand from their beach excursion and the daily accumulation of dirt swept off the wood floors and woven rugs. Little Benji slept peacefully in his crib in her room and she hoped the infant was tired enough to give her the time she needed for her household work. Stephan had done his chores around the house and was finishing the work Matthew had asked him to do. She came out on the front porch sweeping away the last remnants of grit off the edge knowing full well new sand and dirt would find it's way back in by bedtime. Something was nagging at her since Matthew had left, even though he'd seemed happy and positive, even jovial this morning. She was anxious to get out to the field and find out what he wanted.

But she pushed her feelings away as the girls came around the corner from the garden. Each one carried a large bowl bearing the harvest of the picking. Even little Emma proudly displayed her half full bowl while Mary stopped behind her to pick up what she had dropped along the way. Srenna followed the girls into the kitchen with the vegetables and pulled out a colander to wash everything. "Mary, can you get these cleaned and ready to cook later when I get back?" she asked the sixteen-year-old. "Emma and Lilly can play with Benji in the living room or front porch now that I've swept all the sand on the north island back outside," she added, laughing at the new dirt and sand tracked in by the girls already.

Mary grinned and took over at the sink, ready to respond gladly to Srenna's request, when both of them heard the sound of a waking baby and his familiar whimper, letting everyone know he had rejoined the world from his nap. "I'll get them their lunch if you want to feed him before you go," Mary smiled.

"I'd better or he'll be fussing for you all afternoon," Srenna answered, grabbing his bottle from the stove and slipping quickly out of the kitchen. Upon opening her door she found a happy baby bouncing up and down, ready to leap into Srenna's arms to escape his crib. She changed the little nipper's diaper as quickly as she could and then sat down in the rocker with him. As she had been, she tried simply giving the weaned youngster his bottle while snuggling him close to her breasts. He gazed up at her with his deep blue eyes with such a look of contentment and gratitude that Srenna was almost disappointed to hurry and leave him with Mary. It had taken a while to wean the poor forlorn child away from the natural memory of his mother's breastfeeding. He had been so distraught by his base needs that Srenna's attempt to allow him to suckle and then take the special bottle brought quick comfort and much needed nourishment. Srenna knew it was why he had bonded so quickly and so strongly to her those first few days she arrived. Her love for him was unlike anything she had experienced with Grace Havilland's children.

She looked towards the doorway where the sounds of happy giggling and chatter were coming from the girls in the kitchen. The sound of Stephan coming up the steps of the house whistling a cheery tune filled her thoughts with amazement at how quickly God had brought healing and restored peace and joy into this devastated home. It also made her suddenly realize as she glanced at the clock on the bedside stand that it was time to go meet Matthew.

Stephan hollered her name as he walked towards the kitchen door and she anawered back letting him know where she was. "It's time to go," the energetic thirteen-year-old stated, poking his head through the door and looking at his watch. "I'm starved!" he added.

Srenna grinned at his impatience to head out to help Matthew where only a month ago he really resented his older brother's position of authority. But now that Matthew was giving him greater responsibilities and showing Stephan how much he needed him, the boy was coming to grips with some of his early angry reactions. "Mary has your lunch. I'll be right there," she responded, as she rose with Benji still finishing the last of his bottle. She laid the infant down on her bed for a moment and closed her door. He continued to drink and watch her as she pulled off the blouse she had worn all morning to clean in and she grabbed a clean blouse from the wardrobe. She quickly checked herself in the mirror on the dresser to make sure her long dark hair was still somewhat braided before picking up the satisfied baby, with empty bottle in hand and raced to the kitchen. She handed him over to Mary as she asked his sister, "Please would you burp him for me just in case....?" She and Mary knew full well the happy baby might still spit up even yet as he continued to adjust to the milk.

"I will," grinned Mary, "We can't have you smelling like fresh lilies and sour milk to go meet Matthew." As soon as she had said this she turned away from Srenna so the young woman couldn't read anything on her face. But she wasn't fooling Srenna at all.

"Mary," Srenna said her name slowly, "Do you know what Matthew wants to talk to me about?" The girl continued to pat the boy and kept her back to Srenna. But she managed to get a desperate look in Stephan's direction and for once he fully cooperarted with his older sister.

"We'd better hurry," he said as he grabbed up the sack of sandwiches prepared earlier and headed for the front door. Srenna had the distinct notion that both of them knew about Matthew's request to see her this afternoon. Mary finally turned back to Srenna and smiled, "Can't we help the two of you spend a little quality time together?" Srenna gave Mary an exasperated look and then spoke to Emma and Lilly, "Mind your sister til I get back."

She hurried to the front door to catch up with Stephan who was already waiting on Bear, his horse. He gave her the stirrup and reached his hand down to help her up behind his saddle. She had gotten use to riding this way to go out to the fields but was determined to someday ride by herself as she had done earlier in her life. As they rode along Stephan ate his sandwich that Srenna handed him but she decided to wait until she got out to Matthew.

In no time at all Bear had made his way to the gate and they both saw Matthew waiting next to a grove of trees, leaning and looking out over the vast grasslands dotted with the sheep. "There you both are," he said walking towards the horse and its riders. He grinned his dimpled smile that Srenna had come to know as the boyish way he would try to reassure her in any number of situations. For some odd reason he had realized his request would set Srenna to speculate all morning long what it was he wanted and in fact at the sight of him waiting she felt her heart begin to beat a little faster.

"Sorry we're late," Stephan apologized to his older brother, "but you know Benji has much more pull then either one of us," he added jokingly. He winked at him as Matthew lifted Srenna down from Bear.

"Do I get lunch, or am I still in trouble for a wet baby this morning?" Matthew questioned with a forced look of repentance on his face.

"Stop it, both of you. I swear you'd think you were both the babies and neglected beyond belief," she giggled as she shoved the sack with the rest of the sandwiches at Matthew and shook her head in playful despair. Matthew seemed pleased that he had made Srenna laugh and looked up at Stephan to give him some instructions for the afternoon.

"Run the edges, make sure everyone's not too far out." Stephan nodded and turned Bear around to head into the field. Srenna suddenly realized Samson was nowhere in sight but before she could ask, Matthew answered her, "I left Samson to graze and I thought you and I could walk while we're talking," he smiled again at Srenna and then pulled out a sandwich, handing it to her, knowing full well her morning had probably kept her from her own needs. "We can eat and walk, can't we?" he asked as he began to move towards the trees where he'd been standing.

Srenna caught up with his stride and Matthew slowed down to keep her beside him and his six foot frame. "I don't mind it, especially out here," she answered, her eyes sweeping the breathtaking view around them

"Good," Matthew added with some relief that she seemed to be less nervous about meeting with him. "I want you to get more and more familiar with the area," he began to explain, "and more comfortable, more sure of it." Srenna felt comforted by Matthew's desire to tie her more firmly to the land beyond just the immediate surroundings of the house and yard. It comforted her as well that he was sure that she would stay and was growing in her commitment to taking care of his brothers and sisters. Her feelings for him, for his needs, were deepening with every week that passed. The fact that his displays of affection towards her were growing with more regularity made her realize that his own feelings for her were also growing.

As they walked along the path where the tree line ran, she realized these meetings had been affecting her for some time now. She had been learning more and more about this remarkable young man barely out of his teens, and how he'd had to grow up incredibly fast since the first day his father had left for war. If that hadn't been enough, the death of both his parents had affected him greatly. She and Matthew's common knowledge of grief and loss seemed to bond then together, giving them a common goal to keep the children moving forward and most of all keep the family together.

"I want to know everything I should Matthew, so I can help the children and you," she answered him looking at the view ahead of her.

For a few moments neither one said a word. As they walked and ate they took in the pristine beauty of the New Zealand countryside. From somewhere off through the trees Srenna began to hear the sound of the river running. She thought nothing of it as they continued on for a short distance until the path came to an opening in the line of trees.

"I'm glad you feel that way," Matthew spoke with a sudden tinge of anxiousness in his voice.

Srenna felt a shiver of realization run through her as Matthew stepped through the opening in the trees they had been following. As Srenna watched Matthew pulling his boots and socks off of his feet she looked at what appeared to be a sandy entrance into a quieter, deeper area of the river. But her intuition was not nearly quick enough for what happened next. Before she could even turn to escape back through the trees she felt Matthew's gentle but sure grip around her waist and then found she was being pulled towards the frightening waters of the river.

"No Matthew! I'm not...I can't..." but her words went unheeded as Matthew fought her surprising strength and resistance, but neither one was a match for his determination to take her in. He finally scooped her up and over his shoulder and pulling off her shoes as he went, stepped into the warm summer water in spite of her struggle to free herself.

"Matthew, stop! I can't, ...please, ...please don't make me...!" She twisted herself as much as she could, pounding his back and trying hard to make him let go of her. Once he had walked into the calm waters up to his thighs he lowered Srenna back over his shoulder in an attempt to put her in.

But she wrapped her arms around his neck with tremendous strength. He tried to calm her as he moved farther into the river but her panic sent her legs wrapping securely around his waist and clinging to him even tighter. She was shaking uncontrollably and Matthew could feel her trying desperately to hold back sobs of fear as she struggled with the memory once again of that horrific day her whole life changed. He calmly whispered in her ear, "It's alright, I've got you." Srenna closed her eyes tightly and buried her face in Matthew's neck. She was now beyond the point of any desperate attempt to free herself from his strong arms and his even stronger resolve to bring her face to face with this crippling fear. His resolve was immoveable and again he breathed calmly and quietly into Srenna's ear, "Shhh... I won't let go, I promise. Not until you're ready." She had been so panic stricken it had gone unnoticed that

Matthew had moved even farther into the river and the water was now up to his chest. But he needed her to trust him, even if only today she realized that his word was good and he most certainly would not let go or let anything happen to her.

All Srenna felt was the paralyzing water engulfing her, surrounding her, slapping against her arms, her back. She could hear the sounds of the grating metal of the ship as its hull slipped into an unforgiving sea. The sounds of screams and panic everywhere were fresh in her ears. The painful memory of her father's last words came ripping through her heart as she remembered him ordering her to swim, swim away, swim away from everyone she loved.

This time, however, was different. This time instead of waking painfully from the nightmare, she was acutely aware of something even stronger, aware of someone speaking to her in soft, low tones. All the time she had been fighting him, Matthew had been gripping her firmly, with his face pressed against hers. He waited patiently as Srenna spent herself with sobs of sheer terror and grief, just as she'd done a few days earlier. He could feel her body begin to tire and then relax as her crying began to subside and she finally lay in his arms like a small child after being consoled from a nightmare or injury. He could only imagine the horror of that night when Srenna's father made the painstaking decision to throw her off the side and beg her to swim away from the sinking vessel.

"Why did he throw you over Srenna? Why would he do that to you?" Matthew whispered into her ear. A lone sob wracked her body again and for a moment Srenna fought back the answer she had known all those years. Her father had ordered her to jump to save her life. He knew she was a good swimmer. He had taught her himself, and well. He knew her better then anyone. He knew she could make it. But he also knew his daughter would not obey him and leave him. She would have followed him to find her mother and brothers. He did the only thing he knew to give his daughter a chance to survive and try to save the rest of his family as well. The revelation of this truth brought another round of tears as these thoughts washed over her even as the river washed around her. Yet there was something more, something even Srenna couldn't quite bring herself too.

And still Matthew held her.

"You knew how to swim, didn't you?" Matthew asked gently. "He would never have thrown you over if he knew you couldn't make it. But he did. He knew how strong you were." He could still feel a few light sobs escape from Srenna but he thought the worst of it was over. Her arms had gone limp as well as her body and Matthew cradled her in his arms like he would have Emma or Benji or even Lilly. He then began to carry her to shore.

"You're not going to make me swim?" she asked in exhausted surprise.

"Maybe some other day. I think you've had enough for one day," he answered, kissing her face. "Besides, if you conquer everything in one day then I have no excuse to get you back in my arms tomorrow. I'll even make a deal with you," he bargained. "If you promise to swim for me soon then I'll promise to dance …with you." Srenna was too tired to respond to his offer. As Matthew carried her out of the water and onto shore she wasn't even mildly surprised that a blanket had already been spread out on the grass. He dropped to his knees and set Srenna down in front of him. Another blanket laying there was quickly unfolded and wrapped around her. She had started to shiver again but the sun warmed blanket and Matthew's brisk rubbing of her arms quieted them before she knew it. When he was sure she was warming up, Matthew pulled his shirt off over his head and reached for a towel lying beside Srenna. He also began briskly rubbing the river water off of his arms and hair.

All the while Srenna huddled under the blanket trying not to think anymore about what she had just been through and at the same time, trying to make sense of what she was still feeling at the moment. She knew Matthew cared deeply about her, maybe even loved her, but right now she was sad, angry, confused and still unsure about letting go of this fear and some other unknown idea. Matthew wasn't sure at the moment how she truly felt other then cold. He settled himself beside her and putting his arm around her began rubbing her arms again. Smiling cautiously at her, he asked, "Are you getting warm enough?"

Srenna lowered her face into her drawn up knees for a moment and then tilting her head, looked at Matthew. She saw the look of anxious hope on his face, hope that when she regained complete composure and some strength again, she wouldn't haul off and hit him, as he knew only too well already she could probably do. The anxious look gave way to a desperate boyish grin as Matthew moved behind Srenna on his knees and began to rub her very wet, braided hair with his towel. As he blotted some of the river water out of it, he leaned into her and quietly, and somewhat seriously stated, "I had to do this, Srenna, for you, for the little ones, for my peace of mind."

"You had this all planned, Matthew Patton. Didn't you?" she asked in what she hoped sounded like an angry voice. But it didn't come across very angry.

"Planned enough," he replied, trying not to sound pleased. He reached behind him and grabbed a bag on the blanket and placed it next to Srenna. She opened it to find a change of dry clothes, but before she could even react, Matthew stood up and grabbed another bag of his own clothes. He pointed to a clump of bushes close to the blanket and still grinning walked towards the trees. "Boys on the left, girls on the right," and with that he disappeared into the line of trees they had come out of.

Srenna stood up slowly, her legs feeling a bit shaky. She steadied herself and stepped behind the bushes, quickly pealing her blouse off and then her summer slacks. The bag held everything she needed to completely change and this was enough evidence to know that Mary had indeed been in on Matthew's plan. She hurriedly dressed and picked up her wet clothes, stuffing them into the bag on the ground. When she came out of the bushes, Matthew was already collecting up the blankets and their shoes. He handed Srenna hers and sat down to put his on, but she only stood there, looking beyond him to the river they had just come out of.

Matthew saw the look on Srenna's face. He knew he would be naive to think this battle was over for her, but for now he knew she had at least come face to face with it and hopefully wanted to put it to rest. He wanted more then anything for her to have peace about her family's death. He stood up and gazed at the magnificent New Zealand mountain range on the other side of the river. He then glanced back at Srenna still trying to size up what he had made her do and what she still needed to face.

Matthew came up behind her and with his fingertips he gently tilted her face to make her gaze rise above the river's edge. "Look past the river, Sren. See that? Look at all that's just waiting for Srenna James," he began. "She wouldn't have even gotten this far if she hadn't been strong enough, strong enough to keep fighting, to keep going, to keep living. That's what got you here, to us, to this."

Srenna was very aware how close Matthew was as he spoke again into her ear, the words she had heard many, many times in her waking, her sleeping, her quiet moments with God. Now she heard

His voice again, only this time distinctly coming from this young New Zealand shepherd boy.

She watched as he began moving towards the path leading home and gazing one more time at the breathtaking line of mountains beyond the river, she turned to follow him. He stopped to let her catch him and held onto her as she bent to put her shoes on. As she straightened up she still felt a little wobbly in the knees, but Matthew steadied her immediately and smiled.

"All right?"

She answered only with a nod of her head, scared to death that even one word would resume her crying. But Matthew held his arm around her securely and began to lead her back to the gate. Neither one said anything more on the way. He let her process all that had just happened. He didn't need to know what she was thinking at the moment. That she seemed to trust him was a relief. That she had possibly left some of her fear of the water behind in the river was a small victory. That she did not appear to hate him or clobber him gave him some hope that tomorrow would bring more healing, for her, for him, for all of them. He however could never have known what he had just stirred up.

He was about to find out.

He rode her home in silence and still he did not press her or push her to talk. She leaned her face against his back on the way and there was some small measure of comfort in that. What he didn't know was the process that was taking place in Srenna's memories, the ones that had been buried even farther then the one of the angry sea swallowing up her family. There was one hidden deep inside of her that she had kept at bay for nearly nine years. As she struggled with the mere memory of that horrific accident in Matthew's arms, this one came swelling up from the bottom, unleashed, like a growing monster a small child imagines they see in the dark. As she and Matthew approached the house it was beginning to overtake Srenna in a way even she could not have known would set her off the way it was about too.

As they reached the front gate some foreign strength came over her body. It made her dismount before Matthew could even reach to give her a helping hand down off of Samson. And as she hit the ground every muscle in her slight frame was commanding her to walk as quickly as she could to the front door. Her conscious mind heard Matthew's voice behind her asking in complete surprise at her abrupt dismount if she was alright. She never stopped to answer. This thing, this inescapable thought going off in her drove her up the steps, through the door and directly into her room. Some blur of events happening around her could have been Mary trying to intercept her, Matthew following her into the house in utter surprise at her actions, and possibly even Benji's whimpers at the sight of her.

But it did not matter. Before she could rationalize her actions she was through the bedroom door, had slammed it shut and was falling into her bed, curled into a fetal ball and numbed by the entire afternoon.

Matthew stood in complete confusion with what had just happened. It was Mary holding Benji on her hip and staring first at the door and then at her brother that spoke first.

"What did you do?!" she asked Matthew loudly, with great concern for Srenna.

"Just exactly what I told you I was going to do!" he answered, frustrated and suddenly very scared. He had felt only a few moments ago that what had happened at the river had been a good thing and now….he was sure he had probably done the worst possible thing he could have to attempt to help Srenna.

Mary could see the agony on her older brother's face. She knew how much he cared about the girl on the other side of the door. She knew he would never do anything to hurt her. Her next question came in softer tones and with equal concern for Matthew and how he felt right now.

"Do you want me to talk to her, make sure she's alright?" she suggested putting her hand on Matthew's drooping shoulder.

"I don't know…maybe…maybe not…I don't know," he answered, with real despair in his voice.

Mary moved quietly to the door and knocked lightly. When no answer came from the other side she put her mouth up against it and softly spoke into the wood. "Srenna…may I come in?" Still no answer. Again Mary spoke, this time with more firmness. "Srenna…we're worried about you. We just want to know if you're alright. Please…let me come in," Mary pleaded, hopeful that indeed Srenna's voice would sound from the other side and beckon her in.

An answer did come from behind the door. "Please leave me be for awhile…if you would…I don't want to talk right now." The tone of her voice told both Matthew and Mary she was crying.

Mary looked at her brother's bewildered face. She wished she knew what to say to him to comfort him. He himself looked as though he were near tears and even as she formed some semblance of encouraging words for him he was already turning away and heading for his room as well.

"Matthew...I'm sure if we give her just a little bit of time, eh?" Mary offered, as she followed him towards his room. But it fell on deaf ears as he too walked into his room and shut the door behind him. She stood there first looking at Matthew's door and then at Srenna's and her heart felt incredibly heavy. She was uncertain what, if anything she could do right at the moment to alleviate the sadness that had just covered the house in a shroud. She wanted to cry as well, but a little hand suddenly grabbed at her face and she was acutely aware that all this time she had been holding her baby brother. Looking into his face just now she saw even an expression of bewilderment in his little eyes.

"Come on you, let's go get supper ready... at least for the rest of us...even if those two stay hold up all night," she whispered into his curls. She hugged him reassuringly, even if she didn't feel much reassurance right now. Then as an afterthought she made a suggestion to the infant, almost as though an inspiration had just overtaken her. "I think you and I should rally the others and start praying. What do you think, eh?" she smiled at the boy. Then, as though it were something natural Benji seemed to know, he folded his baby fingers together and laid his head against Mary. With a soft murmur escaping his baby lips that no one could have understood Mary felt her heart lighten, some undeniable peace following.

"Exactly," she agreed, as one single tear slid down her cheek.

It was going to be a long night.

Chapter 31: From God's View

The smell of coffee the next morning only made Srenna roll over in her bed and wonder through sleepy thoughts how she would get through the day. She really had hoped when she woke that some of the anger she had felt last night would have softened, but the memory of what Matthew made her do at the river still sent floods of emotion over her, most of them not good. Even her words with Mary, who had delicately come into the room before retiring, were strained and painful. She had not been prepared at all by what they tried to do at the river to help her face her stifled memory.

All these years, even Reverend Carmel had never been able to get her to deal with the nightmare of that day the ship had sunk, taking her family with it. She was strong indeed, to have spent the last nine years burying the pain. But the trip to the beach was what truly caught her off guard and she knew Matthew was right. This was their life, his and the children. They lived on an island, a small one as well. Their home was Castle Point. And now it was hers too. They all loved the beach and the beautiful memories they had made there with their mother and father. They could not have ever known that the emerald sea could hold such deep horror for Srenna. The thought of them all right now wondering if she would be angry enough to leave made her feel such confusion, that she wished she could simply stay in bed all day and not face anyone.

But it was Matthew she wanted to avoid the most right now. When she came out of the river and returned home with him she even surprised herself when entering the house and going to her room. She wasn't even sure what came over her as they rode Samson back and she had time to mull over the events that had just unfolded. Matthew would never hurt her, she knew that. But to have someone make her face the day that had changed her entire life, was more control then she thought she wanted to give away. Even now as she thought about him forcing her into the water, she could feel the anger rising up in her. She didn't want to face that day, remember what she was doing when the ship was struck. The memory of her last moments with her father, why he had come looking for her, the knowledge of where she should have been and wasn't, all those thoughts flooded over her now in waves greater then the river or even the angry sea could produce.

But she hadn't lost complete control of suppression as she rolled back to her other side and listened for the front door to close. When it didn't at the stroke of six o'clock, Srenna wondered if Matthew was deliberately waiting, with the faint hope that she had forgiven him and decided to meet him before he left. But after several minutes of her lying perfectly still, she heard the quiet close of the front door and then Matthew's footsteps descending the steps and heading for the barn. It wasn't until her ears detected the sound of the border collies being set free and the sheep being released from the pens that Srenna finally rolled out of the bed and made a dash for the bathroom.

She had spent most of the night crying. Several times she was sure she had heard his door open and then heard nothing. She wasn't sure what he was doing. But she was sure he had to feel very miserable by her reaction to his plan. It made her remember the first day they had met. She had been so temperamental with him then. But this thought also made her feel confused and irritated, mostly with herself.

She wasn't surprised then when she looked in the mirror behind a closed and locked bathroom door, and saw how red and swollen her eyes were. Srenna splashed cold water on her face for a few minutes, but not even this seemed to take the edge off of the way she was struggling this morning. She turned from the mirror and decided to just return to bed and wait for Benji to wake up. She decided to submerge herself in work today and simply not talk to anyone about what had happened when she and Matthew returned home yesterday.

But that was not going to be the path allowed either. As she stepped out of the door, she nearly slammed into Stephan, who immediately began apologizing.

"I'm sorry Srenna. I didn't know anyone was up and in here," the startled boy began. "If you want I can…"

"No, Stephan, that's okay. I was just finishing," Srenna answered him quietly. "Do you want some breakfast before you go out?" she offered. She really wanted him to say no but she would never have let him think so. But she could see the look on his face that said it all. He remembered all too well how angry he had been a few months ago after his mum had died. It had been Srenna's relentless care for him that had finally melted him not too long ago and made him realize how much she cared for all of them. Now it killed him to think he had been a party to making her so angry that she would lock herself in her room and not even come out for supper. The last few months and all the changes had been hard on all of them, but their lives were beginning to feel somewhat normal again. Right then he would have done anything to turn back the clock and never try to pull Srenna into the surf at the beach. But he and Lilly had. He was confused by Srenna's emotions. She had told all of them when they came down from the parsonage that she wasn't angry with them. But now….he didn't understand why she was mad about Matthew trying to get her into the water.

"I'm not that hungry," he told Srenna, as he walked past her and into the bathroom. He turned to say thank you to her, but she had already left the hall and he heard the bedroom door close before he had time to react.

And that was pretty much the way the morning went. Benji woke hungry as usual and almost as if in a mindless mode, Srenna got the boy up and went through the routine of preparing them both for the day. When she came into the kitchen, Mary was starting breakfast as she had done for months on end. She said good morning to Srenna and looked at the young woman quickly, catching a soft and sleepy "morning" from her.

"Are the girls up?" Srenna asked wondering where they might be at nearly eight o'clock on a Wednesday morning.

"They are …but… I told them to stay quiet upstairs until breakfast was ready," Mary explained, hoping as Stephan had that Srenna was in a little better mood this morning. She could tell just by looking at the young woman that it had been a rough night for her. For that matter it had been rough for all of them.

Srenna knew it too, as soon as Mary called the girls to the kitchen. Both dear little girls came into the room with such dismal expressions on their faces at the sight of Srenna that she thought for sure they would begin crying at any moment. She hated how she was making everyone feel. This had become a house of joy again, laughter, happiness, fun. Now because of her she saw faces that wondered what they had done, wondered if she would be all right.

It was more then Srenna could bear.

"Mary," she started quickly, as she turned from the counter and handed Benji to his sister. "I need to get out of here for a little bit. Go for a drive or something. I need..." she tried to go on. But the tears were coming again. She could not believe there were so many. But she knew she needed to do this...alone...away from the children."

Mary tried to reach for Srenna, but before the girl could put her arm around the distraught woman, Srenna had pulled away and started for the hall. "I'm just going to go for a drive, maybe go see Irmani, I... don't know...I...

"No...I think that would be good...But you'll have to take the truck... remember. Stephan is...." But Mary never got to finish that last thought. Srenna had grabbed the keys off the hook by the door and without even stopping to get her handbag she was out the door and headed for the barn. She knew she would have to use the station truck since Stephan had been working on the family car. She had driven it before and was not even the least bit concerned about driving it now. Right now she needed to escape; escape to something. She wasn't sure to what. But the last few weeks as she and Matthew's feeling for each other were becoming stronger and harder to resist, it seemed the sometimes rough Maori mother was the only one who understood the struggle going on in Srenna's heart. What she didn't know was the wise old woman knew even better what struggles Matthew Patton was having.

Srenna turned the truck down the road and headed for the Rainga's sheep station eight miles away. There was still some mist hanging over the lower spots in the hills and valleys along the way, not unlike the mist that seemed to have settled over Srenna's heart and mind and for that matter this morning, her body and soul as well. It wouldn't have mattered if Srenna had known that Mary, desperate to help her dear governess and new friend, had called Irmani the minute the front door had closed. It wouldn't have mattered either if Srenna had known that Matthew saw the truck leave the gate from his position in the fields and had ridden home to find out why it left. He would have gone after her had it not been the firm persuasion of his sister and the quiet voice in his head that told him to "Be still and know that I am God".

So he did. He got still. And the children got still with him, and many prayers went up for a young woman that morning after she left; a woman they all had come to love dearly in such a short time. She was the young woman Matthew knew he would go to the ends of the earth for, do what ever was needed to help her, even if at the moment, it meant doing nothing at all...but pray. When they were done he encouraged the children to keep praying for her and that she would be all right.

But it was less then all right that Srenna James felt as the truck pulled into the Rainga lane and came to a stop in front of the house. She sat there frozen even now uncertain that she wanted to be there looking for Irmani. But she never got a chance to convince herself to leave. Before she had time to react the passenger side of the truck had opened and the big Maori woman had climbed in. Without a moment's hesitation she simply looked at Srenna and spit out two words.

"Drive, you," she ordered, motioning with her hand to pull away from the house.

Srenna only gazed at the demonstrative woman for a second knowing full well by now that any resistance would only lead to more rebuttal, something she truly did not want right now...so she drove. Irmani gave her one word directions for a while until Srenna could no longer stand it.

"Where on earth are we going?" she questioned as the truck wound and turned up the roads leading higher into the hills. Eventually they began the ascent up into the higher altitudes, places that Srenna had only so far seen from a distance when looking around the sheep station.

"You'll see when you need too," was the only answer she got. Irmani kept her silence for a long while until they came to a dead end in the last road they turned onto. Srenna brought the truck to a stop and looked at her navigating friend.

"Now where, eh?" she questioned becoming a little irritated with all of this.

"Out. We walk the rest the way," came the answer. Srenna was not sure she wanted to hear that but had no time to argue with her as the woman left the truck and began walking away. Srenna barely had time to think as she hopped out and panted after the stout middle-aged mother. She was too out of breath to make any more inquiries and for what seemed like an agonizing amount of time they continued up a path leading even farther into the elevations above them. She was astounded that the older woman could set the pace she was, with Srenna huffing and puffing behind her as they climbed higher and higher.

Finally Srenna could stand it no longer. She came to a complete stop and tried to shout at the woman. Her sides hurt and her heart was pounding. She could barely get the one word out.

"Enough!" she gasped, trying to catch her breath.

"Oh, it's enough all right," Irmani announced, stopping as well and turning towards the young woman she had come to love greatly over the last few months. She began walking back to Srenna with a knowing look on her face, one that Srenna had seen before in such a short time, one she was sure was going to be followed by a definite opinion from the wise motherly woman.

But she was greatly mistaken.

"The rest of this journey is yours," Irmani began. She swept her hand in the direction she had just come from.

"What do mean?" Srenna questioned still rasping with the need to breathe. She wanted to cry but she was too out of breath for even that effort.

"You came to get an answer from me, some great insight about why you're feeling the way you do right now…and what to do about it. I don't have it. It's up there," she stated flatly, pointing once again to the path beyond her.

Suddenly Srenna knew what Irmani was asking her to do, but she felt frozen in her tracks. To move up the mountainside meant she would be alone…alone on a path she had fought so hard to leave behind her for all these years. To stay meant to possibly jeopardize everything she had come to love over the last three short months. She stared hard at the path in front of her not wanting to look at Irmani.

"How far up must I go?" she asked softly.

"You'll know when you get there, luv," was the only answer she got.

For some odd reason, Srenna could not even look at the woman standing in front of her and off to the side just a bit. She suddenly felt a strange pull, an unexplained urge to find out what was up the path that had caused Irmani to bring her here. Without another moment of hesitation Srenna walked past her and began the rest of the ascent beyond her. She followed what seemed to be a well worn but very private path leading up through the trees and then only rocks. A few times she had to pick her footing carefully as the incline became narrow and rockier. But still the girl went on, something prodding her curiosity, almost a sense of intrigue at what she would find wherever it was she arrived. It seemed the path would never end when suddenly it led her between two large rocks and into a small open area just beyond them.

Srenna found herself standing in front of an incredible and panoramic view of the entire valley before her. She caught her breath as she realized she was looking down at the area she had come to know over the last few months. Not too far away off to one side was the layout of the Rainga station. But it was the image directly in front of her that caught her eyes and fixed them firmly on what she saw. There in front of her and far, far below in the most beautiful view she would ever remember was the home she had come to know and beyond any doubt...love. It seemed as though someone had painted its loveliness and warmness with a great deal of creative care. She was looking directly down at the Shepherd's Gaze. The station spread out across the lushly carpeted hillside of the valley. The house, even from this distance, had a welcoming luring aura about it that made Srenna suddenly realize why she needed to be here at this moment... at this time. It seemed as though she was looking at some great heavenly blueprint.

It was then that the flood gates opened unlike anything they had done the day before or certainly even on the beach. Srenna crumbled to the ground beneath her and wept into her hands as though her heart was broken. She knew at that precise moment that God himself was very likely at this spot, just as he had been with Moses at the burning bush and she did not want to look anymore for fear she would simply disintegrate into thin air.

But her heart did spill out of her mouth. "Oh Father... I shouldn't be here. I should have never made it off that ship. I should have...." She hesitated. "I should have died that day...with the rest of them...I disobeyed my mother...If I hadn't gone up on the deck we might have been together...Daddy could have gotten all of us off...we would..." But Srenna could no longer go on. Her guilt she had buried so deeply for so long was completely exposed, finally spoken. All that had spilled out of her hurt so badly she felt as though she were near death right now, that at any time God would simply strike her and it would all be over. She huddled on the ground, face covered and waited with a greater fear then the one that had surrounded her that unforgettable day. Yet as she sat there on the hard ground, face still covered, she neither found herself struck ...or disintegrated. Instead a quiet voice in her head and her heart began to fill her senses, beginning with her sense of touch.

All around her Srenna began to feel a warm sensation as though someone had just wrapped their arms or a soft blanket about her. She then became acutely aware of the sounds of the mountain top she was sitting upon. The birds were the first thing she heard, each melodic song distinctly unique. The sound of the breeze, clear and unfettered by any noise from anywhere blew away thoughts in her heart and her head that had been shrouding her with despair and pain. The trees, though few up here, were rustling ever so quietly and it was this sound that made Srenna realize the incredible hush that had settled over this mountain balcony. Then the smells, clean, clear lovely green smells, the wind carrying subtle aromas from the flowers over the hillsides to her. It was this that finally afforded her the courage to look up again now that she supposed God would not evaporate her for her guilt. Once again, before her, lay the breathtaking view of the Shepherd's Gaze below her. She watched the scene below realizing that at this very moment while she was perched here at the top of the world that everything she had come to know and love the last few months in that house was waiting in desperate concern for her return.

Then she heard another sound, this one as true as any she had ever heard in her life. She heard HIS voice, her Shepherd's voice. Clearly as though He were standing over her or all around her as the case might be, she heard him say, "I love you more then anyone ever will. I had a plan for you, a hard one, but one only you could fulfill for me. That plan lies before you, below you and all around you. THEY are my plan for you. They have need for someone as strong and determined and as stubborn as only Srenna Adelaide James can be. I made you that way. It was that same child that had to drink in everything she could for as long as she could that day on the ship, not because she was disobedient or bad, but because I made her inquisitive and adventurous. It was meant to be for you to survive. I made you strong. I made you a survivor. It was my plan for you. Nothing that happened that day was your fault or could have changed anything that happened. Forgive yourself. Look Srenna…Look below you at my love for you. That is where you belong. I will be there with you, always."

For what seemed like hours Srenna sat curled up in a huddled ball looking out over the valley below her. It was after all that time that she began to realize this must be what God saw when He looked down over the balcony of Heaven and watched his children below. She was awed by the revelation that He must not have ever missed any of her movements, any of her steps, the imminent swim for her life, the encounter with an angel, Mrs. Crawford, Grace, Reverend Carmel and Ruth. The thoughts of all those that had encompassed her life since that day and now others, Matthew, Mary, the children, Reverend Davidson and his wife…Irmani…who waited now below for her…hoping for her to find the badly needed forgiveness and closure concerning the loss of her family, all these came flooding over her as she sat in silence drinking in the revelation God had meant for her to know all this time.

Srenna's thoughts began to turn towards the children in the house below and the young man who would undoubtedly be in the fields with his sheep. She could make out the image of the woolly animals far below on the other side of the station. She imagined Matthew's face as he watched for her return for suddenly she was sure that he would know by now that she had taken the truck and come looking for Irmani's help. Her heart began to swell at the mere thought of how much Matthew had been through and how strong and true he had been for so long. The memory of that first day at the train station came flooding into her mind as she remembered the look on Matthew's face when she turned to face him for the first time. She could not forget either the sound of his voice as he spoke her name for the first time and another incredible thought swept over her. Reverend Carmel was right. She was only now getting it. She heard his voice. She heard Matthew's voice ringing in her ears as though she had only just heard it for the very first moment; her shepherd's voice. Not the heavenly one but the earthly one God had fashioned for her… to be ready for her.

But she remembered again how angry she had been with him yesterday. He had struck a nerve in her at the river, stirred up the most painful thoughts she could have ever remembered. He had pushed her, hoping his attempt would have a positive affect on her. Instead she had retreated in anger and withdrawal. Now a new fear was creeping into her mind. A new lie to replace the old one she had carried in her memory was beginning to take shape. Maybe Matthew would be too discouraged with her to keep trying. It was that incredible thought that sent her up to her feet and nearly running down the side of the mountain path she had climbed up. It was no small miracle that she didn't simply tumble the entire way down until she came back to the spot Irmani had been sitting to wait for her. The native woman stared desperately at her young friend's face and knew something had occurred while Srenna was gone. She held her tongue for one of the few times in her life and allowed the girl to begin.

"Irmani…It wasn't my fault…my family dying…not making it off the ship…God showed me that…and how much He truly loves me…how He planned all this time for me to be here…with Matthew…the children…but what if …" she started to argue.

"That boy has loved you from the first moment he laid eyes on you at the train station when you came off of the steps." Irmani announced, finally cutting off the rambling girl.

"What do you mean?" Srenna asked staring wide-eyed and surprised at the remarkably wise and outspoken Maori woman.

"I mean…he was there all the time, when the train pulled in, when ya got off of it. When he saw you come down those steps, he nearly turned and ran. Then he couldn't move. He watched ya from the end of the building like some nervous love struck boy …didn't know what to do. He was scared out of his mind you might be there meeting someone else, not be the new governess." Irmani hesitated for only a few seconds watching Srennas' face as she disclosed Matthews' flood of emotions that first day.

"When he saw no one claiming you and finally worked up enough courage to approach you he was all mixed up inside. He knew he'd lied, he was sure you'd hate him for it, but…." She waited smiling.

"He needed me." Srenna finished the thought looking towards the road they had come up, her mind quickly sending her to the fields where Matthew would be right now.

"He did! So much so, he'd rather suffer your wrath then let you walk away. But make no mistake, Srenna James, he would've laid down his life right there on the train tracks to make things right. That's the Matthew Patton I know; the Matthew Patton I helped bring into this world. He'd never do anything to hurt you or dishonor you. But he will push, just like his daddy, if he thought you needed it. Truth is…you needed it. You need him. You need each other. Those kids need you both." Here the Maori woman hesitated and then quietly went on. "There's something you need to know about John and Miriam and why I brought you here, why Matthew is as intense as he is sometimes, why he just might understand how you feel about your guilt. And why he has pushed himself away sometimes. I know you know what I'm talking about."

Srenna could not even imagine what she was about to share with her, but some intriguing anticipation seemed to hang over both of them as Irmani Rainga began a story about two of her most beloved people she had ever known.

"I'll never forget the day we first laid eyes on John and Miriam Patton. Jimmie and me…we'd been around Pakehas before, but never as lily white as the two of them…and young…oh my, were they young…and scared and Miriam so full of baby. She was so homesick for England. Didn't understand that one for awhile…not till after Matthew was born right into my hands, he was."

Srenna watched the older woman's expressions as she unfolded this tale about the two people she would never meet and yet thought she knew so much about.

She was dead wrong.

"Jimmie and I…we took a liking to them right off. John was a hard worker…rugged farm boy from the other side of the world. We thought it was a bit strange he'd brought Miriam with him to start the station from scratch. Most men send for their wives after a few years…you know… till they get settled. But there she was and nearly ready to drop with child. Wasn't till she was near her time she confessed something to me."

"What was it?" Srenna asked in a reverent tone, as though she was asking for some deep dark secret to be revealed.

"They weren't married," was all Irmani said and then waited to see what reaction she got from the proper young woman. When she saw Srenna's eyes widen in disbelief she plunged on.

"John and Miriam loved each other more then any two people I'd ever seen....except maybe ol' Jimmie and me," she chuckled, "but apparently that love spilled over just a little too much for proper English folk and Miriam found her self very pregnant. John had planned on asking her mother, Madelaine Brewster if he could have her blessing to marry Miriam, to make things right and then send for her after he got a house built, got the sheep station going...but when old lady Brewster found out her refined young daughter was knocked up...she was determined to handle the problem the only way a distinguished headmistress saw fit. John found out by the grace of God that Miriam was going to be sent away for an abortion. He managed to spirit Miriam away and they made it here."

Srenna looked off over the hillside in front of her and began to imagine how frightened Miriam must have felt at a time when she should have been elated about having a child. Then it struck her hard that that child...was Matthew.

"Did they ever get married?" she asked hesitantly. Her tone wasn't judgmental but concerned.

"Oh sure," chuckled the woman as she recounted each detail. "Jimmie brought John up here same as I did you just now and showed him the whole of the valley and all that was his for the working...and how blessed he was to have everything he did. Told him right out he'd better marry Miriam Brewster and get ready to build a home for his family." Irmani stopped for a moment and waited for Srenna to take everything in. "We weren't the only ones though what got our hands on the two of them. Hamilton Davidson got wind of their arrival in short order and being the genuine man of God he was, he came after them with all the force of a flock of angels..." she laughed. "He loved on them same as we did ...'cept his had a message of how much God loved them both in spite of all that had happened and everything that still needed to happen. Wasn't too long before he led 'em both right up to the throne of God and got 'em both "saved and forgiven". They got married right after all that and then here comes Matthew. You would have thought that would have been the end to that story but John still felt so guilty about Miriam being estranged from her mother...well...he tried several times to send a message to Madelaine to let her know they'd made things right and that she had a grandson. Wasn't until years later when Mary was about eight and old enough to be going off to boarding school, if you believe in that rubbish, that Headmistress Brewster came swooping in with all kinds of sweet. Seems she thought she could actually convince Miriam to feel bad enough to hand over Mary so she could go to the old coot's school in England."

"All the way there, away from everyone?" Srenna gasped in disbelief.

"Yeahr…all the way there. John was so angry he sent her packing. Worst of it though…she never acknowledged Matthew the whole time she was here…as if he didn't even exist. It was obvious to them both she couldn't stand to be reminded why she'd lost Miriam. She could barely look at Matthew. He tried to be nice to her, but the old woman treated him as if he'd truly been a bastard child. It broke Matthew's heart for a long time. He felt guilty…blamed himself for having been born under the circumstances…was a real pain in the bum for a while…that is till Hamilton got a hold of him the same as he got John…with God's help, eh?" she laughed. "Matthew found what his mum and dad found…forgiveness and truth…that none of what happened was his fault. Now you wouldn't happen to know anything about that, right?" Irmani grinned watching Srenna's face for a reaction.

Srenna felt the incredible healing of her own truth she had just received. Then she remembered how firm, yet gentle Matthew had been with her, not once judging or ridiculing her for her fear of the water and her memory. She remembered vividly the feel of his strong arms around her, making her stay and face the horrifying memory of her family's death and her fight to survive. She had never realized how determined she had been all these years to stuff it as far away, as far down as she could. Even coming to New Zealand, away from Sydney, away from familiar surroundings revealed to her a desire to never have to look at that harbor again. "Take care of someone else Srenna," she had told herself. "Stay busy, help someone else." All this time she had still been kicking, still been swimming.

Tears were welling up in her eyes now, tears of regret for even having been cross and angry with Matthew at all for what he had meant to do for her. She knew now that Matthews' intention was to help her find her own peace in her life, just as she had intended to bring peace to him, to his family.

All this time, Irmani sat patiently next to the girl, watching her face, her struggle, and then her revelation. Irmani knew even with her Maori beliefs in God that He had spoken intensely to this brave but sometimes strong willed child.

"It's all right to be weak Srenna and you are not to blame for your family going down with that ship," she reminded her, and that sent a flood of relieved tears down Srennas' face and sent her into the large woman's loving arms.

Irmani cradled Srenna as if she were one of her many children until the tears were spent. Again Srenna felt like a wave had caught her just as it had yesterday in the river. This time this one seemed to be waves of gratitude for all that had been given her. Then as suddenly she felt her feelings for Matthew rushing in, this wave larger and stronger then any in her whole life. Her thoughts of him, how much he must love her to risk everything to bring some healing to her, consumed her.

She loved him! She had to tell him, reassure him and let him know she wasn't angry with him. Srenna came up from Irmani's arms so quickly the older woman thought something was horribly wrong.

"What girl, what is it!" Irmani exclaimed wildly, jumping up from the rock she'd been sitting on.

"Irmani, I have to find him. I have to tell him I'm all right! I love him!" she laughed, wiping the tears away and giggling like a silly school girl.

"Well, right you do! I knew that!" the woman laughed with her, relieved and thrilled as she watched Srenna head for the truck. The two woman made the trip back to the truck in record time and in even less time Srenna pulled up to the Rainga house and sat looking at her dear friend.

"There's something else I need to do," Srenna announced as though an after thought came to her.

"Whatever it is, you'd best be doing it quick, eh?" Irmani stated, as her eyes caught the darkening sky off to the east. "It's gonna rain," she added with a hint of concern in her voice as she crawled out and peered back in at Srenna.

"Thank you!" Srenna smiled gratefully at Irmani, her heart feeling both light and full at the same time.

"Don't mention it, you. Now go!" Irmani ordered in her best motherly voice. She waved her out of the driveway and as an after thought she yelled to Srenna as the truck pulled away. "Call me when you get home!" Srenna acknowledged with a wave of her hand as she turned the truck onto the road.

But she didn't intend to go home just yet. Such a feeling of release was still flooding over her she felt like she just might be able to do something she hadn't been able to do in many years; face the selfish sea that had claimed her family. Maybe even truly lay to rest her disobedience that day and how she felt she had contributed to the loss of them.

When she reached the turn in the road that would lead her home she hesitated. Srenna knew Matthew would still be in the fields with the sheep and the drive to the little parsonage above the beach would only take her roughly twenty minutes. It was only lightly raining, so she quickly decided to head for Castlepoint and the shoreline. But even as she drove east she began to sense a strange foreboding feeling, overwhelming even. She could see how intensely dark the sky was ahead of her and the light rainfall was becoming a steady downpour even before she had gone halfway.

Srennas' common sense told her this was no ordinary rainstorm. She could feel the wind beginning to pick up as well so she quickly decided to turn the truck around and head for home. As she retraced the miles back towards the station she realized how difficult it was becoming to see the road in front of her. She started to feel a knot in her stomach as the truck began the winding trail around the foothills towards Shepherd's Gaze. She was still a bit unsure following some of the curves the dirt road had to offer, so she slowed down as she came to the bend at the highest point leading into the valley.

But her decrease in speed wasn't quick enough, nor her reflexes fast enough for the chain reaction that took place in the next few minutes. In one sickening moment Srenna felt a blast of wind hit the truck from the side, sending it sliding into a dizzying spin and off the road. But the truck didn't stop there. Before she even had a chance to scream, Srenna felt the truck begin to tip in an agonizing angle in the now muddy slope beside the road. She finally let out a terrifying scream and cried loudly the only word that would form on her lips, "Father!"

Almost before she drew the next breath, as quickly as the truck had been sliding, it came to a sudden stop against a large rock on the passenger side. Although it was at a dangerous tilt, it had indeed wedged into the mud and rocks around it. Srenna uttered up a desperate fearful prayer, "Help me Father."

She felt frozen to the seat whether by fear or common sense that told her if she moved around too much, the truck might keep going down the muddy slope and begin to roll.

"What am I going to do?" she whispered to herself. She could see now that the rain was washing out the road off to her left side from where she had just come. It appeared the whole area was becoming a potential mudslide and now she began to fear staying in the truck was even a greater concern.

"Tell me what to do," she prayed. Almost immediately she felt as if something or someone was pulling her, a surge of adrenaline rushing through her body. In one quick movement she pushed the truck door open and jumped from the seat into the muddy ground above the running board. Her feet sank up to her ankles in the mud but with another surge of strength Srenna pulled them out and fought her way up the ten feet the truck had slid down. She fell several times but each time the same voice she heard all those years ago told her to "keep going". Matthews' deep blue eyes, his loving smile and the faces of the children loomed in her mind as she reached the road and a little steadier ground. She looked down at the precarious looking truck and was dumbfounded she had even made it out. With that realization she uttered up a grateful prayer of thanks for her deliverance. The rain was pelting her though, as well as the wind and Srenna knew she must get out of the storm. She also knew she was still four or five miles away from the house and most of it was downhill. But the Raingas' house was even farther, so with great difficulty she began walking down the road in the direction of home, her home. Her life WAS there, with Matthew, with the children. She was more determined now to get there and without looking back she kept walking, even though she slipped here and there when a gust of wind hit her. She came to the next curve and descent in the road and gingerly took a few steps. But the gravel was as slick as any ice could have been and before she even completed the third step Srenna felt her feet slipping from underneath her. At the same moment she felt a sharp stab in her ankle and found her self on the ground. Just as the truck had previously done she began sliding off the side of the road. Grabbing desperately at anything she could Srenna tried to break her fall and once again she cried out for help.

When she came to a stop less then a moment later she was already thirty feet or so down the hill. It was a tree trunk that had stopped her and at this point all Srenna had the energy to do was curl up against it, bury her head in her lap and cry.

Chapter 32: To Find the One

Matthew ran the distance between the stock pens and the barn as quickly as he could and was still thoroughly soaked before reaching it. He had seen the ominous clouds flying in and knew from experience that a summer easterly was crashing in from the Pacific with a vengeance. He had sent Stephan ahead with the dogs and both horses and fully expected to find his brother already on his way into the house. He also expected to see the truck parked in the barn indicating to him with great relief that Srenna was back safely from her visit with Irmani. He had been praying all day that Srenna would be able to get past the pain of her own family's tragic death. Like the healing path of the Patton children, Matthew wanted Srenna to find hers and complete freedom and restoration. He had hoped his mothers' dear old friend would be able to help.

Stephan, however, was still there, as was Mary. And no truck was to be seen. Samson and Bear were still saddled and all Matthew had to do was look at his brother and sisters' face to make him ask in a frightened voice, "Where's Srenna?" He waited for only a few seconds and before either could answer he grabbed up Samsons' reins and led the large black horse to the doors.

Mary finally found her tongue and feverishly answered Matthew, "Irmani called fifteen minutes ago, said Srenna was going to call her when she got back. When she didn't call, Irmani got concerned that she might've gone somewhere else first"

"Where first and why in this?!" Matthew asked feeling his heart pounding out of control.

"I'm going with you," Stephan added quickly leading Bear behind Samson.

"No!" Matthew answered his brother abruptly. Then he noticed the painful look on the boys' face. Only a few months ago he had fought Srennas' presence in the home, her position, her care, her determination. Now Matthew could see how much she had even affected Stephan, how much he cared about her. Matthew softened the rest of his order to his younger brother. "I need you to stay here with the girls and the baby. Can you do that? Please!"

Stephan looked at Matthew and nodded his head immediately. "I'll take care of things here. I'll call Jimmie and Irmani too."

"All right. I'm taking Duke with me. If she's between here and the Rainga's, he'll find her," Matthew stated as he grabbed his slicker and hat off the hook by the barn doors. Mary let the old dog out of his pen and he sensed his masters' dilemma and bounded after Matthew. Then without another word to either one of his siblings he went back through the doors and into the wild wind and rainfall. It was all Mary and Stephan could do to keep the rest of the dogs contained in their pens.

As Matthew followed the drive up through the gate he realized he would see the truck at least halfway up to the highest point if it was there, but much to his dismay it was not visible. Surmising this he knew he could save some time and left the road, going through the trees. Samson's footing was surest of all the horses his father had ever had and Matthew trusted the strong bred stallion to carry him safely now. Duke seemed to know they were on the hunt and Matthew yelled only once to him, "Find her boy! Find Srenna!" The old dog seemed to shed ten years and became the vibrant and energetic leader he'd been since Matthew was seven years old. At the heed of his masters' command to "Find Srenna" he set off up the hill in front of him letting everyone and everything know he was coming!

And it was that sound that came to Srennas' ears as she laid huddled against the tree crying out once more in her life to be saved. She was beginning to shiver uncontrollably in the drenching rain and her ankle throbbed. She was covered head to toe with mud but the driving downpour was soaking her and at the same time washing away the mud. But all the misery in the moment couldn't drown out the glorious sound of a dog barking and Srenna stopped crying. She began yelling as loud as her frozen lips could yell. "Here! I'm here!" she screamed. "Help me, please help me!"

The cries had barely hit the windy air when Duke came rushing up to her and nearly knocked her over with all his might. Srenna grabbed at the dog but to her despair, missed him before he darted away.

And then another glad sound came to her ears. It was a voice calling out her name, a voice she needed to hear just then more then anything else. It was Matthews' voice, loud and strong, coming closer, following the sounds of Duke's relentless barking. She heard Matthew again as Duke appeared beside her. This time letting his owner know exactly where Srenna was. Finally looking up through the pouring rain towards the road, she saw him.

"Matthew!" she sobbed.

He bounded off of Samson and checked the footing on the edge of the hill. It was soft and ready to give way under his feet. "Hang on Srenna! I'm coming down." he yelled.

Srenna was able to grab the Border collie this time and he seemed to knowingly position himself between her and the slope to protect her from mud and rain. Matthew took his rope from his saddle and securely tied it around the horn. He breathed into the faithful horses' ear to "hold up" and then threw the rope down the slippery hill towards Srenna. With great caution he carefully lowered himself step by step to the tree where she was huddled. Once there he dropped to his knees and before Srenna could even breathe out his name he had pulled her into his slicker and sat holding her, soothing her cries. Without thought or hesitation he smothered her face with kisses and then finally kissed her so soundly that Srennas' sobs were silenced. They clung to each other for dear life, interrupted only by Dukes' exuberant barks and attempts to get in on the hugs as well. Matthew freed one arm from around Srenna and pulled the dog into their embrace exclaiming to the excited animal, "Good boy, good ol'Duke!" Srenna reached for him too, breathing her own grateful thanks to the old boy.

"I've gotta get you out of here," Matthew finally said remembering suddenly the whole hillside was becoming muddier and slipperier as each moment passed. "Are you hurt?" he asked as he began looking her over as though she was one of the children.

"My ankle. I think I sprained it," she answered, still trying not to cry. "Can you stand at all!" he asked, beginning to get up and lift her as he did.

"I think I might be able to," said Srenna, with resolve to get out of the mud and up the hill.

"Well, I can't carry you in my arms up the hill so we'll do piggyback. Think you can hop on?" he suggested as he pulled off the slicker and put it on Srenna. He then tied the end of the rope around his waist and squatted low enough so Srenna could lean over him and put her weight on his back. "Arms around me, Miss James, and hold on tight," he laughed as Srenna clung to him the way she had in the river. He straightened up and reached one arm over the other to get a good grip of the rope. His first few steps were unsure and he felt like he might send them both pitching, but he found some solid footing and tugged on the rope.

"Now Samson, hey!" he yelled at the stallion who had been waiting patiently till his master gave him a command. Knowingly, the big black horse began to back up even before Matthew shouted again to him to pull.

Srenna held on with every ounce of strength left in her body, trying not to slide off of Matthews' back. She also tried to ignore the shooting pain in her ankle or to hinder him as he held onto the rope. The thirty foot incline seemed like three hundred to them both but miraculously no more slipping or falling occurred and finally they topped the slope, and made it to Samsons' side. Srenna slid off of Matthew onto her good foot but before she had a chance to even put weight on it Matthew had lifted her up onto Samson's back and was pulling off the rope. He wound it around the horn and grabbed the horses' reins. Without a moments waste, except to praise the faithful horse for a job well done, Matthew told Srenna to hang on, yelled at Duke to follow and started leading Samson down the road. The rain had not let up at all and was even becoming heavier, the wind stronger.

"Where are we going?" Srenna yelled, wondering why Matthew was headed back towards the truck and not the house.

"Samson will never make it back down now," he answered back. "Pull the slicker over your head!" he ordered.

Srenna could see how miserably soaked Matthew was walking in the rain without anything but his hat to protect him, yet he determinedly led Samson down the slick road. A little way down it he suddenly veered off to the left and into a small grove of trees. Srenna was grateful and surprised to see a little house, like a cabin, no bigger then the whole of the kitchen or living room at the station. It was invisible to any passerby who wouldn't have known the path was there. The front of the cabin had a small porch and overhang and Matthew literally led Samson up under it. He reached up for Srenna and pulled her into his arms before her bad ankle could even hit the ground. Again Matthew thanked the brave horse and opening the door, he stepped inside the cabin with Duke close behind him.

He carried her across the tiny room to a small table and a few chairs. Srenna's eyes quickly swept the little cabin's interior. It was simple in comparison to the house, yet immediately she caught glimpses of a woman's touch. Lacy curtains graced the windows and across the floors were woven and sheep skin rugs. There was a bed in the left hand corner barely large enough for two people, but a lovely quilt covered the mattress. One overstuffed chair sat in front of a stone fireplace. The kitchen on the opposite side of the room boasted a sink and counter and an old wood burning stove was off to the corner. There were only two rough hewn cupboards hanging over the counter. At the farthest end of the room was a loft with a little ladder leading up to what must have been another make shift room years ago. Srenna was amazed that as devoid of any luxuries as it was, the cabin had a feel of a loving person, …a person she had come to recognize and appreciate though she had never met the woman.

"Whose cabin is this?" Srenna asked looking at Matthew intently as he placed her in one of the chairs at the table.

"It was Mum and Dads' first house when they came here from England," he explained as he pulled the wet slicker off of Srennas arms. She shifted just enough for him to pull it out from underneath her and hung it on a hook at the door. He stood looking at Srenna for a moment and then he also scanned the room as if seeing it for the first time in a long time. Srenna saw the look on Matthews' face as he slipped into what must have been deep memories of his mother and father and their inseparable love for each other.

"Were you born here?" Srenna asked reverently, remembering suddenly what Irmani had just shared with her only a while ago.

"Yeahr," Matthew answered softly, smiling as he looked at Srenna. She was glad there was no pain in his eyes or on his face and the room seemed suddenly very important to her. She watched him as he walked around the room lovingly drinking in what had been his first surroundings as a baby, and probably a small boy.

"How long did you live here?" she quizzed him, still speaking quietly and hoping she wasn't prodding him too much.

But Matthew seemed willing and wanting to share it all with her. As he walked to an old trunk at the end of the bed he answered easily, "Until Mum was expecting Stephan. Mary was born here too. Dad started the big house then." As he finished this bit of history he pulled out some clothes and a few blankets from the trunk and walked back to Srenna. He realized she had begun to shiver again and was wrapping her wet arms around her. They were both soaked to the skin and he knew he needed to get them out of the wet clothes they were wearing and into the dry ones fast.

"Here," he said, handing Srenna a large shirt and one of the blankets. "It's not one of your prettiest outfits but it's dry and it should cover all the necessary parts, eh?" he grinned.

"Very funny, you," she laughed, slapping his hand and adding, "And what's going to cover all your necessary parts?

"Dads' old pants," he quipped back at her and with that he moved to the door. Duke tried to follow him but he told the old dog to lie down.

"Where are you going?" Srenna asked with a sudden change of tone. Matthew heard the fear in her voice and quickly came back to the chair. He bent over Srenna and tipped her face up, kissing her softly and reassuringly said, "I'm not going anywhere. I want to take Samson's saddle off him and put him in the lean so he'll be a bit more comfortable. It'll give you a bit of time to change. Yell at me when you're done." With that he crossed the room, opened the door and stepped back outside into the storm.

Before he had closed the door, Srenna began peeling off all of her dripping wet clothes. She gingerly removed her mud caked shoes and socks and suddenly realized how awful she must look, how muddy she was. But to her relief at least the shirt was indeed long enough to cover her slight frame. None the less she wrapped the blanket around her as well for she was beginning to feel the real effects of the soaking rain she had been pelted with this evening.

"All finished!" Srenna yelled. She was relieved how fast Matthew came in from the porch, having already changed only into his father's old pants. They fit him far better then John Patton's shirt fit Srenna. Matthew placed his wet boots and clothes by the door and crossed the room to the stone fireplace. Fortunately dry wood and matches were in the kindling box on the stone floor and Matthew started a roaring fire in no time. Neither one of them said anything for several moments while Srenna huddled under the blanket trying to get warm. He busied himself with getting some water from the pump into a kettle and placed it over a hook in the fireplace. He waited only a few minutes before filling a basin with some of the warmed water and came back to the chair with a towel and washcloth. As though this was as normal a service for him he kneeled down in front of Srenna and first washed her face with the wet cloth and then lovingly and reverently pulled the blanket away from her slender legs to gently wash the mud from her feet. He was so gentle, Srenna watched in amazement as though Jesus himself were kneeling to wash his disciple's feet at the last supper. When Matthew was done he dried them with the towel.

"Now… let me have a look at that ankle," he finally said. He carefully picked up her foot but as cautious as he was she still winced, drawing in a sharp breath. "Sorry," he said screwing up his own face, feeling the pain with her. Matthew carefully felt the bones for any fractures and was relieved that everything seemed to be in one piece. It was swollen though and Srenna was obviously in pain. "She's sweet, not broken, but definitely sprained and I know it's got to be hurting you," he smiled caringly at her. "Let's get you off this hard chair and into the bed and then we can elevate it. That'll help some." He stood up and once again lifted Srenna, blanket and all and carried her to the bed. He put her down just long enough to pull the cover back and still holding on to her ordered, "In you go, Miss James. Maybe you'll finally stop shivering." Matthew pulled the quilt back up over Srenna after she relinquished her blanket. He pulled the end up away from her sprained ankle and rolled the blanket, placing it under her foot. Having finished trying to make her as comfortable as possible Matthew sat down on the edge of the bed and asked her sympathetically, seeing the pain on her face "Hurts pretty bad, eh?"

"Yeahr," she answered, suddenly feeling the weight of the day falling heavy on her. Tears began to well up in her dark eyes again as words just began tumbling out of her mouth. "Oh Matthew, I'm so sorry. The truck, it slid off the road and started to tip and I didn't mean to be angry with you and I just wanted to get home and tell you…"

But she never got to finish. Matthew put his arms around her and holding her to him for a moment he quieted her and with his face against her ear whispered, "You're safe now. I've got you." His feelings for her were overwhelming, unlike anything he'd ever felt in his life and like the torrential rain outside he sensed himself losing control and knew he'd better do something to calm himself. He knew if he did not his love for her would fuel his desire for her.

She felt it too, but this time she knew that Matthew was struggling and trying to be honorable and respect her. This time it was Srenna who pulled away gently, saying only, "Matthew," in a low voice.

"I know, I'm...." he started, but Srenna interrupted him quickly.

"Don't you dare say you're sorry," she whispered firmly and looking him in the eyes. Even her looking at him right now was sending a flood of feelings through him, but before they could overtake him again, he stood and walked to the kitchen area.

"I think I can at least offer you a hot cup of tea. Mum kept stuff up here for us, just in case," Matthew explained as he took the kettle from the fire and going to the cupboard he made two mugs of tea. He then gathered all their wet clothes from the room and moving the chairs closer to the fire he laid them out to dry. Srenna watched in silence as Matthew moved about accomplishing the tasks of taking care of her. She wondered how many times this young man had had to do the gentlest of caretaking of his mother while she was ill and dying. Still in all of this he had kept his sense of humor, an acute love for life, and his brothers and sisters. Many men twice his age would have given up or grown bitter by the hand God had dealt them. But not Matthew. And she loved him dearly for it.

Matthew was finally satisfied that the tea was strong enough and not too hot to drink. He glanced over at Srenna who seemed to be temporarily distracted and quickly grabbed a flask in the back of the cupboard. He thought it might still be there; rum his father had always kept for his tea. It was a well known fact that John Patton was not a drinker, never joining the locals at the pub or boozer. He had made a promise to his dear wife and a deal, which included a hot cup of tea on a cold night with a shot of rum, after a hard day. Matthew smiled as he remembered his mum bringing up the supplies to the cabin, including the small flask.

"What are you grinning about now, you?" Srenna asked suddenly, bringing him back from the past. He had just poured a shot into Srennas' mug and he looked over his shoulder to see if she had seen him. He set the flask in the sink and turning towards her with both mugs he could tell she was still shivering in spite of the blazing fire and the quilt pulled up around her. He knew she was in a lot of pain too and he wanted her to sleep. He needed her to sleep. He sat down on the bed and handed Srenna her mug. She began sipping it immediately and could feel the warm and welcomed liquid run through her cold body quickly.

"Oh, Matthew, I think I might finally get warm, "she sighed gratefully, seeming not to notice anything unusual. She had nearly finished the mug when she looked up at him as he sat quietly drinking his. "It's wonderful tea. I don't believe I recognize it though. Certainly not black tea, some special island brand, eh?" she questioned, finishing the mug down to the last drop. Matthew tried not to grin at how fast this refined city bred girl had guzzled the rum tea and as he took the cup from her he wondered how long it would take for the affects of it's potency to hit her. He had only to wonder as long as it took him to walk back to the sink. He could hear her speech becoming quieter and duller and before he could return to the bed he saw her begin to list to one side. He reached her just in time before she toppled over on the bed and gently pulled her down and under the quilt. He vaguely heard her comment in a whisper "the best tea ever" as he heard her sigh and then heard her deep even breathing. He tucked the quilt up around her, making sure she was covered and checked her ankle one more time. For a few minutes he painfully remembered another who he had faithfully cared for each night after coming in from the fields. Memories of his dear mother lying in the bed after the baby was born, threatened to wash over him when Srenna suddenly shifted in her sleep. Matthew snapped back to the moment, stroking her face and brushing a curl off her forehead. He leaned over and reverently kissed that forehead just as he'd done every night after his mum went to sleep.

Tears brimmed in his eyes and he suddenly felt very tired himself. He could hear the storm still raging outside, but inside in this little cabin of memories a deep peace suddenly filled it. He stood, picking up the other blanket off the table and dropped to the sheep skin rug beside the bed. As he had done many times as a young boy when he and his dad had spent nights here, Matthew rolled up in the blanket and listening one more time for the comforting sound of Srennas' restful breathing, he uttered a prayer of thanks that he'd been able to leave the fold and find the one. It was his last thought as he drifted off to sleep. He never even noticed Duke curl up protectively next to his boy, a satisfied dog, sure as any dog could be that he'd also saved the young girl sleeping safely in the bed above them.

Chapter 33: The Wrath of Rainga

Bang! Bang! Bang!

Three deafening pounds on the cabin door brought Matthew out of a deep dream-laced sleep and to a full upright position next to the bed holding Srenna. He looked around the room a bit bewildered until he suddenly remembered the flurry of events the night before. Duke barked instinctively at the sharp raps on the door and stood ready to protect those he loved. Matthew had just turned himself around and looked at the awakening girl lying in the bed when the banging began again, this time followed by the loud and unmistakable voice of Irmani Rainga.

"Matthew Patton, if you're in there, you'd better open up this door, you!" she yelled franticly and even a bit angry.

"Whoever is making all that noise at this hour of the morning?" mumbled Srenna, pushing her head up from the pillow. She saw Matthew standing next to the bed, shirtless and barefoot and then realized she was wearing even less under the quilt. She remembered quite suddenly what had led up to her being in this condition when she moved her leg and felt the reminiscent pain in her ankle.

"I'll give you one guess who it is," Matthew answered anxiously motioning to her to stay put as he moved towards the door. Fortunately before he could reach it, the stout Maori mother had swung the door wide open, just missing Matthew and Duke as they jumped out of the way.

"Where is she, eh? Where is that deary. Poor little thing?!" Irmani gushed, as she pushed Matthew aside and rushed to the bed.

"I'm just fine myself," Matthew laughed," Not a scratch on me, if you were wondering."

"Hush you!" she snapped, fawning over Srenna without even looking at the boy.

"Give it up, mate," Jimmie Rainga chuckled as he came in the door. He knew full well that at that moment his wife of thirty years was not to be reckoned with and was the person in charge in that cabin.

All this time, Srenna was painfully quiet and a bit embarrassed by the abrupt arrival of the couple. Her being only partially clothed and in bed, and Matthews' appearance as well eluded to different circumstances then were real.

"I'm alright, really," she finally offered to Irmani, who had been literally checking the girl's arms and face for any injury. "I sprained my ankle, that's all," she added.

Irmani pulled the quilt away from Srennas' leg and saw the swelling in her ankle instantly. She quickly stood from the bed and looked at both Matthew and Jimmie and briskly barked at both of them, "Out, the both of you. I can't help this one with the two of you standing here gawking. Go on. Get your clothes, you, and get dressed…outside!" she finished commanding. Her waving hands told Matthew he'd better go without another word.

He looked at Jimmie for support but the big Maori man was obediently gathering Matthew's clothes from across the chair. He then took the boy's arm and firmly said to him, "Get your boots mate and I'll help you get Samson saddled." Matthew turned only for a second, looking over his shoulder at Srenna on the bed. She caught his glance and tried to give him a reassuring smile as Jimmie pushed him out the door.

As soon as the door had shut Irmani gathered Srenna's clothes and handed them to her. "Get these on and we'll get you home in your own bed. I'll be able to do something about that ankle when we get there," the woman instructed more gently as she walked to the sink. Srenna obeyed quickly and silently and began dressing. She watched Irmani gather up the mugs and towels and straighten the room, but she failed to notice the intuitive woman as she sniffed the mugs before putting them in the sink. She knew John Patton's flask of rum had been pulled out of the back of the cupboard last night.

"Slept well, did ya?" she asked Srenna.

"Yes, actually, I did. I couldn't stop shivering for anything, until Matthew made the best tea I think I've ever had," she explained to Irmani as she gingerly pulled her slacks up and wiggled them on.
"I was in a lot of pain, but amazingly I fell asleep. I was exhausted, I suppose, after everything," she rambled on trying to read Irmani's thoughts about what took place last night. Irmani crossed the room and sat on the bed beside her. She put a strong motherly arm around the girl and hugged her, glad that Matthew had indeed found her, and in spite of the rum tea had obviously taken the best of care of his charge during the night.

"I suppose you were, luv," she gushed, squeezing her again and smiling with relief on her face "Now, I'd better get one of them in here to carry you out to our truck," she finished as she stood and went to the door.

"Irmani," Srenna spoke softly.

"Yes luv," Irmani answered looking back at the disheveled girl, her hair falling all over her face, her clothes dirty and wrinkled from all that had happened to her.

"Nothing happened last night," Srenna offered, holding the woman's gaze firmly. "He was a perfect gentleman."

"Of course he was, luv. Told ya he would be. Best I remember my own words, eh?" Irmani admitted. With that she opened the door and shot out in her best commanding voice, "Well, come on then, you! Get in here and carry her out! She's not going to walk home, is she?"

Both Matthew and Jimmie stood at attention when she passed them and then Matthew walked back into the cabin immediately to retrieve Srenna.

"Are you alright?" he asked, wondering what had been spoken to her during his absence.

"Are you?" she grinned, reaching her arms out for help to stand.

But once again, Matthew simply scooped her up in his arms and grinned back answering her jokingly, "I'll live. It's not the first time I've suffered her wrath." He kissed Srenna's cheek before reaching the door and descended the step off the porch to the Rainga's truck. Irmani was standing with the door opened and motioned Matthew to put the girl on the seat. He carefully deposited Srenna down and reassured her he'd be right behind on Samson.

Jimmie had closed the cabin door and was climbing in the driver's side when Irmani followed Matthew to the end of the truck. Before he could do anything else his mother's closest friend boxed the side of his ear.

"Ow! What was that for?!" he exclaimed, surprised by the woman's action .

Irmani looked at the boy she had known now for nineteen years. She knew he had a good heart, a strong will and more determination then ten men. But she also knew how passionate he was, and how equally passionate Srenna was.

"You and me, we'll talk later, eh?" she answered, "Now get on that horse and get yourself home!"
With that, the gruff spoken woman put her hand lovingly on the boy's cheek and patted it once letting him know in her own strange way that she didn't know whether to swat him or hug him as he had experienced many times in his life.

Matthew climbed onto Samson who had been patiently waiting next to the porch and quietly followed the truck out of the trees and back down the wet road towards the house. Matthew's mind was flooded with thoughts as they drew closer. So much happened last night. So much still needed to happen. So much that could happen. One thing was sure. He had revealed his true feelings and desires again for Srenna last night when he found her, when he got her safely to the cabin. But he wondered to himself… what if? What if she hadn't been injured? What if she hadn't fallen asleep? What if … what if… what if, kept rolling through his mind. Just as he saw the truck turn the corner into the lane leading to the house, Matthew realized that he and Srenna had also turned a corner. A huge corner. The reality of his true feelings for her was tugging at his heart even as they approached the house and the children came running out at the glad sound of the Rainga's truck. It made him wonder what was about to unfold in the weeks to come, or for that matter, the next few days.

Chapter 34: God's Balcony

Opening even one eye seemed for some odd reason to be a great effort for Srenna as she peeked from behind sleepy eyelids. She realized the moment those eyes finally focused that instead of the usual shadowy sunrise she was accustomed to waking to every morning, bright sunshine was escaping her lacy curtains at the end of her bed and sending golden streams of color across the room. It seemed peculiar to her…only until she stretched her legs and felt the shot of pain through her propped ankle. Then a bevy of memories of the day before came flooding over her senses ten times more then that of the insistent sunlight. She had been rushed into the house when they returned with her to the frenzied questions of the children and of course the frantic cries of little Benji when he saw his "Mim". Before she could protest over the fuss she had been bathed, fed and tucked into her bed, ankle propped and iced and was given strict orders to rest until Irmani returned. Now she moaned slightly and turned her head towards the bedroom door just in time to see a familiar grin spread across a welcomed face belonging to an even more welcomed young man sitting in the rocking chair next to her bed.

"Hullo, you. Won't you get it if Mother Rainga finds you in here?" Srenna smiled, holding her hand out for Matthew to take.

"She left, otherwise I probably wouldn't even be in the house, let alone in your room," he chuckled as he took hold of Srenna's hand and squeezed it gently. He was surprised that the grip of her hand allowed her to pull at him, encouraging him to leave the chair and settle on the bed next to her.

"And the children, Benji...Is he napping?" she whispered suddenly wondering if the baby was in the nursery at the end of her room.

"He is. But the girls have him upstairs on Lilly's bed. They are in charge, or something like that." Matthew leaned over Srenna and brushed her curls away from her face and then kissed her forehead lightly.

"And Mary. I know Irmani will have instructed her to keep me quiet for now and undisturbed, you," she giggled.

"Am I disturbing you, Miss James? I come bearing sustenance and...oh yes...more ice," he laughed. He reached for a fresh towel of ice for her ankle and what appeared to be some form of food. Srenna actually felt a slight pang of hunger once her sense of smell kicked in.

"You know...I am actually a bit hungry after everything. Except what little bit I ate this morning before being put to bed I...I've barely eaten anything since yesterday morning," she remembered.

"Well then...It is my humble duty as a gentleman and head of this household to make sure you eat everything I brought you," he answered her as seriously as he could muster. He wasn't very successful though so instead he just kissed her. "Now...I'd better prop you up," he suggested as he sat up and pulled her with him. She grimaced only slightly as she slid her legs along with the rest of her body into an upright position. Matthew placed her pillows behind her back gently and fluffed them until she seemed comfortable...or as comfortable as she could be under the circumstances.
"Good, eh?" he smiled hoping she was not in too much pain from the injury she had received the previous day.

"Yeahr. She's sweet. My ankle only feels half the size it did last night," she joked as Matthew moved to the end of the bed with the makeshift ice bag. He turned back the cover that had been keeping her legs warm during the morning and Srenna could see that her ankle still resembled the color of...well... several colors, not withstanding...purple, blue and even a bit of green. She sighed heavily wondering how she would ever tolerate the amount of time it might take to heal.

Matthew seemed to have read her mind or at the very least the discouraging expression on her face and quickly propped the ice on the swollen ankle. Before she had time to say another word he returned to the edge of the bed and picked up the tray of food he had set on the night stand.

"Eat and we'll worry about how everything will get done while you're healing," he ordered her as he propped the tray on her lap and steadied it for her.

"Matthew, I simply can not stay in this bed for very long or…" But she was cut off before she finished the thought.

"You're going to let me worry about that, and Mary and Stephan and yes…even Lilly and Emma. It's not going to kill any of them to pick up the slack while you recuperate, eh?" he stated adamantly. He waited for the rebuttal he expected from the girl he'd come to know as extremely determined and as equally stubborn. But much to his surprise she simply stared off across the room with a look he was certain he had not yet seen on her lovely face.

"What is it Sren? What are you thinking right now?" he asked softly, trying to read the mood she had just slipped into. Thoughts of the events of the last few days stirred in him heavily and he wondered if that was where she had drifted off. Hard as it was though…he waited.

"Irmani took me to the mountain top," she answered, looking full into Matthew's eyes and waiting to see if he understood what she meant.

"Oh," was all he could say. But that alone gave her reason to believe he knew exactly where she'd been taken. Then he added, "It's what we all refer to as "God's Balcony". It's where Jimmie took Dad and he took me and…"

"You took Stephan," Srenna finished.

"Yeahr."

Srenna turned her eyes toward the window, catching the streams of bright sunlight dancing between the curtains fluttering in the afternoon breeze. "How different today is then yesterday or the day before and the one before that," she began. "I thought I'd never get use to this unpredictable weather here and all of a sudden I understand it." She looked back into Matthew's face realizing all this time he was waiting patiently for her to speak, to offer any idea of what happened to her up there on God's ground, what great revelation had been given her that would send her rushing to the foreboding sea she had so greatly loathed only days before. He continued to wait.

"Matthew…I wanted to go to the beach because I thought for sure I could finish making peace with myself…with my memories…my guilt. Then it started to storm and well…" she drifted off discouragingly.

Matthew heaved a big sigh and caught up Srenna's hand in his strong one. He looked at the small hand…small in comparison to his and frowned ever so slightly. "What guilt Srenna? What could you possibly feel guilty about concerning your parents and that horrible day?" He watched her closely and cautiously to make sure she wasn't headed for the reaction he had gotten at the river, and the one at the beach. She saw his deep blue eyes filled with concern for her and all that had been dredged up over the last week.

"Matthew…I'm alright…really I am," she spoke reassuringly. She stared off again towards the window but this time not to drift off into the memory but to explain it and what God had spoken to her. "He loves us so much Matthew, so very much. He told me that up there. I heard Him! He spoke as clear as I am speaking to you right now. Maybe it was only truly in my heart but it might as well have been out loud." As she spoke one lone tear rolled down her cheek. But Matthew could tell it was not a tear of sadness but of heart-felt joy that the burden she had been carrying with her all these nine years was finally rolling away. The light in her eyes as she recounted her episode on God's Balcony made his own heart swell with gratitude that she had found the peace she needed in the end.

"What else did he tell you Srenna? Did He tell you how much we love you…how much I love you, how much I need you?" Matthew asked holding her hand tightly. His own tears threatened to spill over as he waited for her answer.

"He didn't have to tell me that silly…I already knew that," she teased him lovingly. She was about to move the tray away from her lap so as not to spill it but Matthew was way ahead of her and placed it back on the stand. But before he had a chance to take the next step Srenna threw her arms around his neck and clung to him as though her life depended on it. As he held her he listened to the rest of her story. "It wasn't my fault, my family dying. There was nothing I could have done. If I'd been with my mother and the boys I would have died too. But God told me he had a plan for me. And do you know what it was…what it is?" she whispered into his ear.

"I sure hope I do," he smiled, clinging tightly to her.

"Daniel told me I would know…when I heard my Shepherd's voice. Well I did and I know I want more then anything to be right here with you…the children…Irmani and Jimmie…and…" she hesitated.

"And what?" Matthew asked pulling back for a moment with a puzzled look on his face.

"And all twelve hundred sheep," she laughed, grabbing his face and kissing him soundly.

Matthew pulled away from her when the kiss was complete and with his forehead against hers he breathed a statement that sent her heart beating as though she had just been running.

"I suppose then…I should ask you a very important question…Miss James, while I have you captive in your bed and unable to flee," he jested lightly, grinning his endearing grin at her and taking both her hands in his.

"Ask me what?" she inquired, her dark eyes widening.

"Who would I inquire of as to my intentions of courting you Miss James…with the express purpose in mind to marry you after an acceptable waiting period," Matthew asked with as straight a face as he could keep. Srenna's response was a loud gasp, throwing her arms back around his neck and then kissing him soundly again. When she was done reacting, Matthew could only respond one way. "I take it that you are agreeable with this request," he laughed.

"Of course I am, you, and as for permission… well…" she thought for a full minute, "I believe you would need to ask Reverend Carmel and Ruth. They are after all the ones that got me here. And God of course. I think Daniel and Hamilton knew all along that this would happen and that you and I…" but Matthew gently cut her off with a kiss to stop her rambling and presented her with yet another question.

"Srenna…we are going to need a chaperone if I'm to court you proper and I intend to court you proper. Any ideas, eh?" he teasingly asked, as he kissed her lightly on the lips. But that inquiry was fully answered when a little head popped into the doorway and Emma turned to shout at the rest of the household.

"He's kissing her again!"

Matthew buried his head against Srenna's shoulder and they both began to laugh with hearty joy. "Come here you, Little Bug," he ordered his baby sister. She came, throwing herself playfully into

Matthew's opened arms and both he and Srenna hugged the child between them even as they had done the night after the earthquake. She looked up at both of them waiting with anticipation for the next kiss, but instead got hugs and kisses from them both.

"I believe this is your answer…Mr. Patton and there are four more where she came from…not to mention the Rainga clan…all ten of them and of course Hamilton and Patricia and…"

"Enough! I shall never be allowed another moment of privacy with you until we're quite married and then…" he joked, tickling his sister and blowing kisses on her neck. At that statement whether she fully understood or not Emma's eyes grew large and one word came out of her mouth.

"Oh!" She was off the bed and out the door before either Matthew or Srenna could react and all through the house her five-year-old feet flew announcing to everyone everywhere, "They're getting married! They're getting married!"

Within moments the room was full of children, including Stephan who had just come back from the pens. For several moments the flurry of conversation revolved around Matthew's request and Srenna's reply and their plans they had not yet made but wanted the children to be involved with. Even Benji who had awakened moments before sensed the excitement in the air. It wasn't until Matthew noticed how quiet Srenna had become that he remembered that she was probably weary from all the events earlier.

"All right! Everyone out!" he ordered firmly but lovingly to his siblings. "If Irmani comes back and finds all of us in here she'll string us up, injured people excluded." He himself stood and prepared to end the festivities that had been going on in the room so Srenna could rest some more. The children moved towards the door disappointed to leave, whinging and whining that there was so much to talk about. But Mary also knew that Srenna was tired and as the motherly thing to do rallied all four of the children out the door. Matthew lingered behind for only a moment.

"I guess I'd better make a trip into Tinui to wire the Honorable Reverend Carmel with my request, eh?" he smiled at Srenna bending over to kiss her one more time.

"You needn't do it right this minute, Matthew. It can wait until tomorrow," she offered, knowing full well that he too had to be a bit weary.

"No…it can't wait. If I'm going to court you and you are going to continue to live in this house while I do…then I want it to be right…you deserve to have it right," he explained seriously.

Srenna remembered then the story that Irmani had shared with her yesterday about John and Miriam and she suddenly realized why this was so important to Matthew. She smiled at him reassuringly and nodded her head in support.

"All right then. It will be right. And we certainly have enough chaperones, eh?" she chuckled, pulling him down to her level for one more kiss before he left. He then placed the forgotten tray of food on her lap and gave one quiet little order.

"Eat. I'll be back later to check on you. You'd better be resting." He stepped toward the door and then turned to look back at Srenna watching his exit. He nearly gave in to the urge to walk over to the bed and scoop her back up into his arms. Her dark eyes were fixed on his with a knowing look and a slight grin warmed her lovely face. She had her own one word order for him.

"Go. The sooner you leave the sooner you'll be back," she suggested, grinning mischievously at him. She heard a slight groan escape him not unlike that of the children at their departure and finished the command with a gentle motion of her hand towards the door. He lowered his head like a disappointed child but then remembered what it was he was leaving to do. As he turned to close the door behind him he reminded Srenna once more, "I love you…and I want to spend the rest of my life with you."

He was finding it difficult to close that door but Srenna once again swept her hand towards him and then added, "I love you…and I can't wait to spend the rest of my life with you either." Then to end the conversation on a lighter note she finished it all with, "so go…go…before Sam Mathers closes the wire office." She grinned from ear to ear, heard one more groan from Matthew's lips and then watched as the door closed behind him.

For several minutes Srenna sat in silence looking once again at the curtain stirring in the afternoon breeze and the sun still dancing across her room. It was as though her every sense was heightened, just as they had been on the mountain top. She doubted that any sleep would come to her the rest of the afternoon from all the excitement. She tried to consume some of the delicious sandwich that Mary had made for her and the cookies Lilly and Emma had included on the dish for her. In the end she drank the tea and found herself oddly tired again. Before she knew it her head was indeed nodding. So she pulled herself down on the pillows and closed her eyes. All she remembered was the beginning of a thankful prayer that slipped from her lips.

"Thank you God. You've given me so much…so very much…I could never begin…" but that was as far as she got with her praise. She succumbed to the rest her body still needed and for the first time in a long time was privileged to dream about the handsome young man who had just requested her permission to court and marry her. She knew all too well it was the same young man she had seen in her dream the very first day she arrived…waiting for her…motioning to her on the far shore of the frothy waves she was engulfed in. Even in her dream her heart knew an undeniable peace that she had made it to that distant shore and found that boy.

Chapter 35: The Telegram

It might have been one of the hardest things she ever had to do. She was sure it was, especially after only the second day of being confined to bed and knowing all the things that needed to be done, Srenna was ready to scream if she had to be confined to bed one more day. But the children, along with Matthew had been given strict irreversible instructions to keep the young woman at bay and in bed or at the least on the sofa in the front room. These direct orders came from the one woman none of them would even think to cross or defy and Irmani Rainga made absolutely sure that her instructions were carried out to the end. Never knowing when the stout Maori mother of the North Island, or so she thought, would embark upon them assisted in their efforts to discourage Srenna from disobeying and getting up. But their work was certainly cut out for them and a new side to the usual easy going governess was displayed for the whole household to see.

"I'm not being cranky," she had snapped at dear Mary during one of her moments of whinging and complaining about being bedfast. Mary simply fluffed her pillows again, brought her some more tea and left a good book for her to read. All the while she was smiling at the thought that Srenna had a childlike side of her that gave Mary some cause to chuckle at the usually well controlled young woman. But Mary also understood what Srenna was feeling as she herself had been confined to bed while sick at one point in her childhood. It made her wonder how Srenna dealt with her long convalescence after the loss of her parents. It did help matters some as well that Mary had listened to her mother's insistent complaints about being confined to rest while she was ill.

After a few more days Srenna was released from her sentence when Irmani was convinced the ankle had completely regained its ability to support even her slight frame. But even in that she was given orders to "take it slow, none of your usual running here and running there to get things done."

Easier said then done.

"There's so much to do, Mary, so much!" Srenna declared to her closest household advocate. "There's only two more weeks left before you all return to school, clothes to get ready, Emma to get enrolled…"

""Relax…Srenna…take a deep breath," laughed Mary, hugging the dear woman who would be her sister-in-law at some point in the hopefully near future. Mary was trying not to be overly excited as well about the events over the last week or so and those quickly approaching. She had been out of school for far too long and a tiny bit of angst was creeping over her. But on the other side of this thought was the deep desire to return to her classes, her friends and her plans for graduation this next school year. Srenna was right. There was a lot to do.

"Matthew and I are going to take Emma to the enrollment day and make sure she knows what will be happening. I can't believe she's going to be gone all day. She's just a baby," Srenna sighed. She was beginning to realize how empty the house would be for the first time since she arrived in October and already she felt a bit strange for the changes that would be overtaking the house at the end of January.

"Look at it this way Srenna," Mary began. "You'll have all of us out of your hair for six hours five days a week. Think of all you'll get done, eh?"

"Maybe…maybe not, now that my Benji entertainers will be gone, not to mention my extra sets of hands," Srenna suggested discouragingly. Still she was very happy for the children that they seemed to be ready to resume their classes and more of their normal routines. It had been a long journey back to some semblance of the children's life before Miriam and John had died. Even now there were the unexpected moments of memories popping up here and there. Time and time again Matthew, along with Srenna's help, had stopped everything to help the children deal with raw grief still hidden beneath the mundane schedule of everyday life. Srenna was beginning to understand how easy it had been for her to bury her feelings and "survive" by throwing herself headlong into her work. But she and Matthew resolved to do everything they possibly could to make sure that did not happen with any of the children.

It appeared that life was going to move right along this late Monday morning with its usual day by day expectations, not withstanding the many plans needing immediate attention. This included Daniel and Ruth Carmel's ecstatic approval of Matthew's proposal to court Srenna. The wire arrived two days after he popped the question and they both felt as though a whirlwind of emotions was swirling about them, all of this lending in part to Srenna's adrenaline rush. For the time being she really did want to concentrate on the children and assuring their return to school was a smooth one. Hard as she tried, that was not to be the case.

"Mary, let's finish that list of things we absolutely must get in Masterton for you and the girls. We can go on Thursday. Irmani said she would watch Benji," Srenna rattled off, almost without missing a step with what she was doing at the counter. But as she began the next round of instructions to Mary they were both startled by the sudden pounding on the front door.

"Who in the world would that be at this time of the day?" she asked Mary with a concerned look upon her face. Anyone they knew would have simply hollered and walked in.

Without answering, Mary walked past her and headed for the front room with Srenna in close tow, only after looking outside on the porch at the girls occupying Benji in his chair.
By the time she entered the room Mary had opened the door to Sam Mathers, who for the second time in a week was gracing their doorstep.

"Gidday, Sam. What brings you out here again so soon, you?" Mary addressed the mailman. It was not his scheduled day to deliver mail, but then neither had it been a few days ago.

"Gidday, Mary…Miss James…I thought I'd better be bringing this out to the station straight way. It's for Matthew and pretty important to be sure," the older man began with concern both in his voice and in his eyes. His gaze swept the room at the two young woman and then the girls who had entered the room when they heard Sam's voice from outside. Lilly was holding Benji on her hip and both girls seemed to be aware that the envelope he held was something very important.

"He's in the south fields today, he and Stephan. Can it wait til he comes in for supper?" Srenna asked, becoming slightly anxious for the expression on the man's face. But it was his answer that sent a cold chill over her and a sheer look of horror from all of the girls.

"No miss…I think not. It's from Madelaine Brewster, the children's grandmother. I shouldn't be telling ya this…but…she's on her way here," Sam whispered, as if to keep the news from the little ones.

Srenna stared in complete disbelief until she felt a little hand slip into hers and looked down at the fearful eyes of Emma. The expression on the child's face gave reason to believe that even though the little girl had never even met her maternal grandmother she had heard enough. Srenna looked up then at Mary who seemed to be equally frozen by this news.

Suddenly something kicked in and Srenna reached for Benji and barked out an order to Lilly. "Go ring the bell," was all she had to say and the nine-year-old ran to the end of the house and began pulling the rope as hard as she could. Then in an attempt to lighten the moment and the grueling wait for Matthew and Stephan to make the run home once they heard the bell Srenna ushered everyone into the kitchen and tried to dutifully offer Sam a cold drink and some lunch. She purposely busied Mary with preparing the man a glass of lemonade and a sandwich as she could easily tell Mary was barely holding it together.

It seemed as though Matthew and Stephan would never get there. They actually made it in record time for being nearly four miles away. Both said little except to wonder what was happening at the bustling homestead now. The actual words out of Matthew's mouth as he mounted Samson were something to the affect of, "What in the name of the Queen Mother has happened now!" That said they had both raced down the south fields above the house praying all the way that no new catastrophe had occurred. Matthew was not prepared for the news that awaited him.

Both he and Stephan nearly jumped the gate when they arrived in front of the house, neither one stopping when they hit the porch and entered the front room. Voices were heard from the kitchen, sending both racing through the hallway door and out of breath when they finally came to a stop in front of the table. Sam was about to take another bite when Matthew flew through the door, but in an instance he was on his feet and holding out the wire in his hand.

"For you…I thought for sure you'd want it right off. It came in around an hour ago. Stopped everything to bring it," Sam announced and stood looking at Matthew with great concern. Everyone knew it was necessary for the wire officers to actually know the content of the telegrams coming in and going out. A few days earlier Sam had had the wonderful pleasure of sending off the request to the Carmels and then the joyful duty to bring the response everyone was hoping for. Now he was obviously vexed by the disturbing news he was delivering to the Patton home.

"Thanks Sam…I do appreciate you bringing it out so quickly," Matthew answered trying desperately to be optimistic. Before he opened the envelope though he stole a glance at Srenna. That was all it took for her to walk to his side and slip her arm through his to give him moral support while he read the telegram. He took a deep breath and quickly scanned the letter to himself first. Srenna waited with bated breath until he finished. She could immediately feel the change in his demeanor as she felt his body clench. "Lilly, would you take your sister and brother upstairs for a little while please?" he requested gently but firmly.

"But I…," she began to protest, but before Matthew had a chance to snap at her, Mary grabbed Lilly and Benji and called to Emma to follow. The fear in Emma's eyes made Srenna want to scoop up the little girl and console her but she knew Mary was doing the right thing to remove them all from the room for the moment. She followed the children to the door and hugged Emma before encouraging her to follow her sisters.

In only a few moments Mary returned and stood next to Sam. All the while Stephan stood stone cold against the wall by the door. He wasn't about to leave the room and one look at his face gave Mathew reason to not even try suggesting it. Srenna returned to his side and wondered out loud if everyone should sit down. As they situated themselves around the large kitchen table, Sam nervously announced that he would show himself out.

"No Sam…please stay," was all Matthew could say.

Sam took a seat at the end of the table and sat watching the faces of this dear young family he'd known all their lives. He wished with everything he had that the telegram bore happier news.

Matthew began reading the wire haltingly.

"Have left port of England on this 8th day of January aboard the cruise ship Tavinier to travel to New Zealand…stop…Will be arriving in Wellington approximately eight days…stop…Will be in Masterton soon after…stop…Please be advised of legal documents pertaining to custody of your sisters…stop….Please prepare them for travel immediately as my length of stay can not be more then a few days…stop…Have made all arrangements to return with the girls to boarding school for further education and care…stop…Madelaine Brewster."

Matthew finished the wire and sat frozen in his chair. No one could look at each other but instead stared at it still clutched in his hand. Then as if some great force of determination had shot through his body, mind and soul, he slammed the telegram onto the table and stood up from his chair. Looking around the table first at Mary and then Stephan and finally resting his eyes on Srenna's large dark eyes, Matthew stated firmly without any quiver in his voice at all, "She is not doing this!"

"What can we do, eh?" Mary answered with much quiver in hers. "She's got legal papers."

Matthew looked again at Srenna and now she could read some measure of fear in his deep blue eyes. She was praying so hard so quietly and yet the fear began to envelope her as well. But she did think of one thing as an idea popped into her mind.

"Matthew…I could wire a lawyer friend of mine in Melbourne. He would know what we might be able to do," she offered desperately.

But Matthew suddenly grinned slightly and he reached for her hand and squeezed it tightly.

"I should have thought of that…Why didn't I think of that?" he rebuked himself.

"Think of what?" Srenna asked, puzzled by Matthew's sudden turn from worried to nearly bursting with excitement. As he spoke he walked to the telephone on the wall and grinned back at his sister, who by now was figuring out what he was talking about. "Would someone please tell me what you're so happy about all of a sudden," Srenna begged.

"I'm calling my father's lawyer…in Masterton…that's what. I don't know why I didn't think of it sooner except…I've just been so preoccupied," Matthew explained as he picked up the receiver. That made Srenna jump from her chair and stand next to Matthew as he dialed out to the operator for the law office in Masterton. Within minutes the kindly woman on the other end had put Matthew through to the law firm in Masterton where his father had received business and legal help numerous times in his life. In no time at all Matthew had heard what he needed to hear on the other end.

"He wants me to come yet this afternoon. Said he'll see me at 2:00," he announced to everyone in the room as he hung up the phone.

"I'm coming with you," Srenna stated flatly and firmly. He wasn't about to argue with her. "Can you be ready in 15 minutes?" he asked looking down into her determined face.

"I'm ready now, you!" she smiled as she tore off her apron. "Just let me grab my handbag from my room." She never even waited for his response and was at the front door before everyone could rally themselves there. They were about to head for the car after Srenna spit out some orders to Mary, when Srenna noticed three little sets of eyes peering from the hallway door.

"Wait, Matthew," she started, pulling at his arm as he and Sam prepared to walk out. Matthew turned and saw Lilly and Emma standing in the doorway with tears about to spill over. Little Benji seemed to understand something was wrong and even his baby mouth was screwing up into a possible deluge of cries.

"Come her you three," their big brother motioned holding his hand out to them and then bending to take them into his arms. He hugged them all tightly and then looked into their big blue fearful eyes.

"Are we going away?" Emma asked softly as she clung to Matthew and stared wide-eyed at him.

"No…no…Not one of you is going anywhere without all of us together," he assured his sisters, smiling first at one and then the other. Srenna had come to Matthew's side as did Mary and Stephan and for a moment there were hugs tightly given to all, even ones from Sam.

"We're only going to talk to a man that is going to help us with Grandmother's visit," he explained. Then he added, squeezing first Emma and then Lilly, "No worries girls, she's sweet. You listen to Mary and Stephan now…you here?"

Both girls nodded adamantly and Mary put her arms around both of them and motioned Matthew and Srenna off.

"Call Jimmie and Irmani. I want one of them here till we get back, eh?" Matthew ordered quietly. Mary nodded her head and Stephan was already headed back to the kitchen and the phone.

Nearly ten minutes of the forty minute drive had gone by before Matthew or Srenna said anything at all to each other. When she crawled into the front seat Srenna slid across to sit next to Matthew immediately. Before they had even passed under the station sign Matthew reached for Srenna's hand and pulled it onto his lap. She felt very quiet and only this because she wasn't sure what to even say. But her prayers were as loud as any silent ones could be flying up to God. It wasn't until they had come out of the other side of Tinui and saw the sign to Masterton that Matthew broke the silence.

"I should have done something about this long ago, Sren...I should have," he began. "I guess I thought we could go on like this with no one contesting the affairs of the children."

"It's not like you haven't been busy seeing to their care Matthew...their affairs have been taken quite care of, eh?" she quipped, "by you."

"And you," he smiled down at her quickly. Squeezing her hand he turned his eyes off to the landscape around them. "I could never have gotten this far without your help." He kissed the side of her head and then put his arm around her.

Srenna wanted to cry. She was scared and she knew for all his appearances of trying to hold it together...Matthew was scared too. She wondered to herself if Madelaine Brewster could indeed do anything at all about taking the girls away to England and what kind of fight was ahead of them to keep it from happening. All of a sudden the joy of the courtship, the future plans of a wedding...even preparations for school had taken a back seat to this more immediate crisis. The rest of the trip was spent in prayer first from Matthew and then from Srenna as they continued to drive the remainder of the way into Masterton.

In short order Matthew was pulling up to a brownstone office building. Both seemed to simultaneously draw a deep breath and after squeezing her hand one more time, Matthew hopped from the car and came around to help Srenna out. His hand in hers, he led her up the stairs to the front door and into the lobby of Philip

Cramer's law office. The secretary smiled when she saw Matthew and spoke to him as though he were an old acquaintance.

"Matthew Patton. I wish we were seeing you on happier terms but it is good to see you none the less," the woman declared, beaming at Matthew. "Mr. Cramer is all ready for you. He's cleared his calendar for the remainder of the day so he could see you. Canceled all his afternoon appointments."

"I'm very grateful for that Mrs. Harvey," Matthew answered, shaking Selma Harvey's hand and smiling back. Matthew had visited the office once or twice while with his father when he was much younger. Mr. Cramer had been to first his father's funeral and then sadly enough to Miriam's. Both times he had assured the boy that if ever in need of anything he was to call. Mrs. Harvey led them to the door into the office. One slight knock brought an immediate response from the other side to enter.

"Come in…come in. Matthew…it's good to see you…good to see you." Philip Cramer stood and rounded his desk reaching for Matthew's hand in a vigorous shake and smiled at the young woman at his side. "I am guessing that this must be the lovely Miss James the whole of the countryside is squawking about, eh?"

"Mr. Cramer…I'd like to introduce Srenna James, our governess for the last three months and one of the reasons why we are doing as well as we are, that is up until now, sir." Matthew couldn't hide the worried look on his face even as Philip Cramer grabbed Srenna's hand in an equally sturdy handshake.

"Miss James…yes…it is good to meet you and…well both of you come…come and sit. Let's see what this ruckus is all about, eh?" the distinguished man suggested as he walked back around his desk to his chair after motioning to Matthew and Srenna to take the chairs in front of it.

"Now the telegram…you did bring it with you?" he began, to which Matthew immediately handed over the wire that had arrived only a short time ago.

Mr. Cramer studied the piece of paper Sam Mathers had delivered for several minutes while Srenna and Matthew sat and clung to each other's hands. They both watched his facial expressions as he read it once and then read it again. They held their breath waiting for his first response to the news from Madelaine Brewster. It was his deep breath and sigh that finally sent Matthew over the edge and asking the burning question on both their minds.

"She can't really do this, can she?" Matthew asked, almost in a whisper. Srenna could hear the raw fear in his voice. She watched his face and held his hand tightly. Neither one of those actions went unnoticed by Philip Cramer.

Another deep breath escaped the lawyer's lips before he began his answer. "Matthew…if your grandmother brings papers to New Zealand from England…the good news is they will have next to no validation here in this court system, per say." That said he saw an immediate reaction of relief on both his visitor's faces. He quickly went on.

"However, the bad news is that she can come here and contest, in family court, the present and future welfare of any of the minor children…which in this case is all of them," he announced bluntly.

"She doesn't want all of them," Matthew retorted angrily. "She's only interested in the girls and that only because she's still carrying a grudge against anything male in this family for what happened to her daughter." His voice was bitter and Srenna could feel the tension in his hand and see the hurt on his face.

"I understand that. Your father was concerned about that. He did make provisions for all of you in the event that something happened to him. I told you that after his death. He even made sure that Jimmie and Irmani Rainga were guardians ad litum in the event that your mother needed help." At this explanation, Mr. Cramer hesitated for a moment to give Matthew and Srenna a chance to digest what he had just spelled out.

"If that's true Mr. Cramer…then why is there any problem at all. Wouldn't the Rainga's then be the guardians in the event of the death of their mother?" Srenna inquired.

"Not necessarily, unless it had been included in the event of her death…unfortunately, John did not foresee Miriam following him to the grave any time soon. He did not modify the will in any way to encompass the welfare of the minor children still residing at home. Jimmie Rainga is your executor over the station until you are twenty one Matthew. Other then that your grandmother could make a case of you not being suitable for the raising of five children at your age…especially with a 1500 acre sheep station to oversee." The kindly man stopped at this realizing he had just dumped a tremendous amount of unsettling information on the young man. He however still could not dismiss the strength and fervor in which Srenna was clinging to Matthew's hand for moral support. As Matthew began to stare off at the window as he was accustomed to do sometimes when trying to absorb any news at all, Philip Cramer decided to take a risk.

"Matthew…the truth is…the court would be likely to award her custody of the girls for one reason alone," he began.

"And pray tell what would that be…that she would be a more fit model or example for Mary and Lilly and God forbid Emma?" he snapped angrily.

Before the lawyer could attempt to answer Matthew's snide remark Srenna interjected a question burning on her own heart. "Mr. Cramer…isn't it enough that Matthew has hired me…a woman… to help him take care of the children and the home?" she asked desperately. She held her breath for his answer.

"Miss James…how old are you, my dear?"

"Why, I'm twenty one sir…and I've had five years of experience in the field of taking care of children with a very prestigious agency in Sydney," she responded hopefully.

"Twenty one…quite single and I might add…very becoming. I'm sorry dear but the court will probably look upon you as a flight risk at your age…someone who will want to be married in a few years or less, start a family of her own," the man offered. But Srenna saw his expression. She saw a knowing look in his eyes. At least one he was hoping he knew. All the time he spoke he watched both Matthew and Srenna for any sign of reaction from either of them concerning what he was suggesting. He saw both of them look at each other as though holding a great secret.

"What if we were married, Matthew and I? Would that make any difference?" Srenna started hesitantly watching Matthew's face as she asked.

"Well…I believe it could add some stability and solidness to your case. Especially if the Raingas are still willing to act as a support system," he answered her slowly. "You would also need to request custody of the children, become their legal guardians."

"And what kind of cost are we looking at to do all of this?" Matthew inquired hesitantly.   "Rough   figure Matthew…approximately $1500. There'd be know charge on my part of course, not after what your father did for all of us in the war but the court cost…the fees for each child…a home study would be done to make sure you can financially support and care properly for the children…."

Srenna could see the droop in Matthew's shoulders and the discouragement on his face as Philip Cramer went on. She had heard enough.

"Mr. Cramer…is there somewhere Matthew and I could speak to one another in private for just a little bit?" she questioned, her heart racing with the thoughts whirling in her head. She turned to look at Matthew while still squeezing his hand and saw the look in his eyes when she made her request.

"I think that would not be a problem, Miss James. I need to speak to my legal secretary for a while and you are welcomed to stay in here and discuss whatever you need to until you're done." Philip Cramer stood to leave and then as an after thought turned to face the young man and woman sitting in his office. "It's been my experience Matthew that the apple generally does not fall far from the tree. You're your father's son. John Patton would not stop until he figured out a solution to this problem, and one that would indeed keep his family together, eh?" With that he walked to the door, grinned at both of them and exited.

For what seemed to be forever, Matthew sat holding Srenna's hand, but looking off towards the window. She wanted several times to begin the much needed conversation with him but something urged her to hold her tongue. Finally, and a bit abruptly he stood and walked to that window, leaning against it as if the weight of the whole world were on his shoulders again. Srenna took a deep breath and rose to stand next to him. She quietly slipped her arm through his and simply leaned as well as held him, her head rested against his shoulder. She resumed clinging to his hand, weaving her fingers tightly through his own. Once more Matthew could feel the distinct smallness of her hand compared to his, but he now also felt the strength that seemed to pulse through her fingers and send encouraging unspoken words straight to his heart.

"I wanted this to be right for you. You deserve to have it right," he started quietly, still peering out the window.

"Matthew…" Srenna said almost in a whisper gazing up at him and sighing.

"No…I mean it Srenna. I know what has to happen if we're to contest her at all. But it hardly seems fair…to you. All of this has been so much to ask of you…from the very beginning…" he rambled almost despairingly.

"All right…enough, you!" Srenna interrupted sternly. "You make it sound like I was hogged tied and forced to come here or that I somehow had no choice in what I wanted to do or…" She stopped then and waited but when there was no rebuttal she went on. " Matthew…I love you. I love the children…all of them! I can not even imagine any of them being gone or sent away. For crying out loud…I'm struggling to send Emma to school in two weeks. I'll bloody well not stand still for her leaving to go to the other side of the world…or Lilly or Mary!" At this statement she was near tears and for the first time since Matthew had come to the window he looked down into Srenna's big dark eyes and smiled.

"I don't think Grandmother has a clue as to what she's about to walk into, or in this case … "who" she's walking into." With that said he pulled Srenna into both his arms and held her tightly.
"Srenna James…I love you with all my heart. I have ever since that first day. I know that sounds crazy but I guess then I am. I'm a crazy man."

"Then that makes me a crazy woman…because I love you and I know I must have that first day or I never would have stayed," Srenna admitted. They both laughed at the memory of that first day only three months ago that now felt like a lifetime ago.

"Then…will you stay now…Stay with me…Marry me!" Matthew whispered into her curls.
Then almost as an afterthought he added, "I promise you will be properly courted the rest of our lives."

At that Srenna laughed at him and he looked down in a bit of surprise at her reaction.

"Yes…I will marry you now, but Matthew…you have been courting me from the very first day, eh?" she grinned up at him.

"How so Miss James?" he asked her with a puzzled expression, especially since his memory of that day was how at odds they were with one another.

"The flowers on my night stand…the way you helped me into the truck…the way you would look at me from the other end of the table…the shearing day...our walks."

Matthew smiled at all those reminders of his growing affections for this woman he now held…the woman he had just proposed to…the woman who had just excepted his proposal.

"Srenna…do you have any idea what we have to accomplish in the next twenty four hours or less," he suddenly exclaimed, pushing her back away from him and earnestly looking into her excited eyes. "And the cost of all of this. God's got a big miracle to work."

"Yes…He does! Or as it were, I think, He already has," Srenna grinned mischievously, "So …shall we get on with this and let Mr. Cramer know what we are contemplating," she suggested still grinning and still clinging to him.

Matthew grinned back somewhat encouraged but still concerned about the enormous need they would have for filing the guardianship papers. But he walked to the door and let Mrs. Harvey know they were ready to resume their discussion. In no time at all Mr. Cramer entered and took his seat, waiting with bated breath to hear what he hoped would be the answer to this family's ordeal.

This time it was Matthew who spoke and this time with resolve and hope in his voice.

"Mr. Cramer. It would appear that after having requested Miss James to allow me to court her for a proper amount of time that she has in fact agreed to forego the courtship…in some respects…and has accepted my proposal of marriage…immediately," Matthew explained with a bit of delight in his voice and even more on his face.

The smile on Philip Cramer's face spread ear to ear as he looked first at one and then the other of his young visitors. "Then it would appear Mr. Patton…Miss James that you will have a very strong case in court…of which I will do my best to get set up as soon as possible." He then gently turned to the matters of filing costs at which Matthew nearly slipped back into a stage of discouragement. But before that could even take hold of him…Srenna squeezed his hand tightly and turned to address Mr. Cramer.

"Sir…I don't think the cost is going to be any problem what so ever," she started as she turned her gaze back to Matthew.

"$1500 Srenna…that's a lot of money…more then I have sitting around," Matthew interjected sadly.

But Srenna seemed to not even waiver at his remark nor did she appear to be at all discouraged. Instead, she reached into her handbag and pulled out a banking book and pen.

"Mr. Cramer how would it be if I signed a check over to your law office and you can fill it in when you know what the exact amount is?" she suggested. Then quickly she added. "The check is good on my account at the First Bank of New Zealand. I assure you I had my account transferred here recently and Mr. Barnes at the bank can…"

"I'm sure that will not be necessary young lady…not if you say it won't," he responded firmly.

"Srenna what in the blazes are you doing or talking about," Matthew finally reacted. The whole time she was speaking to Mr. Cramer he simply watched and listened in complete confusion. But as he saw her begin to write out a check indeed he became concerned. "That's far too much money for you to just write off all at once and…besides how in the world…" But Srenna stopped him before he had a chance to finish the sentence or the burning question on his mind.

"Mr. Cramer…I have a huge confession to make to my future husband…one I would like for you to be a witness too if you would," Srenna began, smiling at a very bewildered Matthew and beaming until she thought she would burst.

"Why my dear girl I would not mind it at all," he chuckled lightly sitting back in his chair.

"Srenna…what…?" Matthew asked again.

"Dear Matthew…I was going to tell you this at the appropriate time…whenever that might have been…but it seems to be very necessary at the moment…so…here I go." Srenna took a deep breath and then began her incredible announcement. "As it were…I need to let you know that you just proposed to a very wealthy woman…Oh and I haven't been spending any of the money you've paid me over the last three months…actually I put it in a trust fund for the children because you see I've had no need of it…you've taken care of all my needs and…"

"What did you just say?" Matthew asked in a faint whisper. The expression on his face was pure shock…even disbelief…Srenna wasn't sure which one.

She calmly repeated herself knowing full well which of the things he was dumbfounded by.
"You're about to marry your family's very…wealthy…governess."

"How…what…how is that possible?" he stammered.

"Matthew…just before I received your letter in Sydney I received a visit from my grandmother's lawyer. She left me her estate…all of it." Srenna said slowly and gently.

"Do you mind my asking, Miss James…how much exactly is "all of it"?" Mr. Cramer requested inquisitively not so much as to be nosey but to understand the brevity of her news.

Srenna glanced at Philip Cramer first and then back at the man she loved. His eyes were fixed on her with an absolute look of surprise in them. "Well...there's the estate home of course in Melbourne and then...my grandfather's insurance money and also his finances after his business was sold and..." She suddenly stopped when she saw both men nearly ready to jump out of their seats and with one more sigh, finished her sentence "Roughly one million dollars."

Srenna waited. She watched Matthew's face for a reaction but he truly seemed in shock for what she had just proclaimed. There was dead silence for several moments as first one then another looked at her and she at them.

"Well...someone say something and quick...I have a wedding to plan," she finally broke in grinning.

At last Matthew seemed to shake himself from the incredible news Srenna had just shared. First he laughed and then he looked around the room as if he fully expected to see God simply standing in the room watching the whole scenario unfold. Then he grabbed Srenna's hand in his and squeezed it so hard she nearly winced. But before she had a chance to do that Matthew had pulled her up and out of the chair and was squeezing her entire body...and crying.

"He knew all the time...God knew. He knew it would be you that we needed. Srenna..." Matthew wept into her hair. She held him and peered over his broad shoulder to see Philip Cramer wiping away a few tears of his own. She held Matthew tightly. Without shame he began kissing her face until Srenna and Mr. Cramer began to laugh at the young man's reaction.

"I take it Matthew...that you are all right with this news, eh?" the lawyer chuckled.

Over Srenna's shoulder Matthew grinned broadly and still holding her in a bear hug responded to the man's question with tremendous fervor, "Like the woman said sir...we have a wedding to plan! Is there a phone we can use...we have some calls to make."

For the next hour things seemed to be almost a blur as a call to Hamilton Davidson was made and a resounding yes was heard on the other end by the joy-filled parish leader. It was decided that the next afternoon would be absolutely possible as well as necessary if Matthew and Srenna were to be married before Madelaine Brewster hit land. Then a call to the children and deafening screams over the receiver were heard at the happy news. Irmani jumped on the phone and yelled something to the effect, "it's about time" and then let them both know how much she had to do before tomorrow.

When all the calls were finished and both Matthew and Srenna were ready to leave, Philip Cramer assured them both that he would work to prepare the needed documents for a court hearing. He advised Matthew that both he and his new wife would need to return as soon after the wedding to sign papers for the filing. With that said, they bid Mr. Cramer goodbye, only after inviting he and Mrs. Harvey to the ceremony tomorrow afternoon.

Once out on the street and back in the car Srenna and Matthew sat staring out the window for several quiet moments. He slipped his hand over Srenna's and finally began to speak.

"I don't know what to say Srenna...I'm happy...blimey...I'm about to explode. And yet I know you wanted..." But Srenna cut him off quickly.

"I want you! I want the children! Matthew...I don't need a big fancy wedding...we'll do what we can and then get on with our lives together. That's what God intended...that's what will happen." Srenna leaned her head against his arm and then as an after thought added," And anyway...who said I can't have the wedding I want!"

Matthew laughed at the determination in the voice of his bride-to-be. It was just like her to make the best of any situation...even this expedited one. But part of him still felt badly...remembering the circumstances in which his own parents found themselves in and the kind of wedding they must have had.

"What about a dress...flowers... anything for that matter?" he started, a little discouraged again.

"You let me worry about what I'll wear and I'll let you worry about my flowers, eh?" she laughed lightly. Matthew kissed the top of her head and started the car. Then she added, "There is one little thing we'd better go find before we go home."

They stared at each other for only a second and then in duet exclaimed, "A ring!"

Chapter 36: The Wedding

At this precise moment Srenna was remembering a favorite philosophy of Grace Havilland's. It was that a household must run on a lot of love and a little bit of chaos. It was certainly the case this morning as she listened to the noises throughout the house. She wondered if any time soon they would all return to the peace and somewhat organized environment she had helped to re-establish over the last few months. That seemed to be quite an impossible feat this day…her wedding day.

"Wedding!" Srenna exclaimed to herself under her breath in the late morning hours of this exciting and yet nerve-racking day. She stood around staring at the room that had been hers exclusively for the last three months and only briefly thought about the fact that as of today all that would probably change…tremendously. Srenna stared at the wedding gown hanging on the wardrobe door where Mary had hung it to let out the wrinkles from the box it had been packed in.

Only last night had Srenna finally opened the package given to her by Grace before she left Sydney. She knew when she drove home with Matthew that it was time to open the mysterious box. She was not the slightest bit surprised when the contents exposed the lovely gown that she had admired one time when she and Grace had gone shopping. It was just like her dear friend and employee to do something that spontaneous. Mary's eyes had nearly popped out of her head when she saw the beautiful dress Srenna would wear after all for her expedited marriage to Matthew. They both cried and both agreed that Matthew would probably stare in utter disbelief that all this time Srenna had the gown under the bed. They agreed, along with the girls and Irmani that it would be a surprise kept until Srenna walked into the church at three o'clock to take her vows with Matthew.

The chaos was already in full swing when Matthew and Srenna arrived back at the house and in no time at all orders were handed out by her Highness the Imperial Irmani. It was decided that Matthew and Stephan would reside at the Rainga home that night and she would arrive bright an early the next day to do whatever needed to be done to get the Patton entourage ready. Nula was left to organize the Rainga clan even in her rounded state of expectant motherhood. Jimmie had the privilege of getting the boys ready and …well…Tommy was in charge of making sure Matthew didn't head for the hills as he was accustomed to do at times. He did however manage to show up that night around midnight at Srenna's window encouraging her to meet him out on the side porch. He dutifully stayed in the grass below the porch and promised Mary he would not come any further. Leaning against the tree in the side yard was the unmistakable form of Tommie, following his mother's orders to keep Matthew in tow and bring him back if he strayed too far.

But Matthew never intended to abuse the sanctity of the eve of his vows to the young woman standing on the porch in the New Zealand moonlight. He simply and painfully missed her after all that had been decided earlier that day. They spoke for only a few moments, Srenna assuring him again that everything would be wonderful, and that she loved him more then breathing. They both admitted there would probably be little sleep that night and then kissed one more time before Tommie escorted him back to his truck and they disappeared up the road.

Bright and early the next morning Irmani arrived to begin her contribution to pulling together three girls, one baby and the incredibly stressed out young woman who would become the wife of her best friend's son by this very afternoon. Dresses for the girls were quickly decided from their best Sunday clothes. Bathes for all and hair freshly washed and shoes cleaned and polished, were the frenzy of the morning. Srenna was ordered to stay downstairs no matter what she heard upstairs and she resolved to follow that direct decree…as much as was possible. Instead she busied herself getting Benji bathed and tried quieting the little boy for an early nap since he would be up most of the afternoon and off his usual schedule. She had barely gotten him to sleep when a soft knock was heard on her door and Irmani poked her head in.

"Can I come in, you?" she asked quietly.

"Yes of course," Srenna smiled at the dear woman. She stood by the bed as Irmani entered and closed the door behind her. The stout Maori mother set down on the bed and patted her hand next to her indicating without question that she wanted Srenna to join her. Without hesitation Srenna sat. She could tell undeniably that Irmani for all her take charge bravado was trying to keep her emotions in check at the moment. For one of the few times since Srenna had met her she seemed at a loss for words. Several times she and Srenna's eyes met and then both simply smiled and gazed off at something on the wall or something not even there. But finally the older woman took a deep breath and started what she came in for.

"I feel like I'm sitting here with Nula all over again. And that's only been a year and a half," Irmani began softly. That statement alone threatened to send Srenna into a fit of premature wedding tears. She quickly grabbed the woman's hand and squeezed it for moral support, both for her and for Irmani.

"You have no idea how much that means to me, 'Mani," Srenna acknowledged her, using the endearing nickname the children called her.

"No...I think I do, and I hope you know what you mean to me...to all of us." Irmani wiped a tear straying down her round cheek and pulled herself together in order to finish her loving speech. "This has been a room full of love in the past. I helped bring three babies into the world thanks to this room...well...maybe the cabin had something to do with all the little Pattons running around." At this thought both woman enjoyed a light moment of laughter. "It's known too much sickness as well, too much sadness...but now..." She trailed off at that statement putting her motherly arm around the young woman beside her. "It's for you and Matthew to fill it up." Srenna heaved a big sigh at the thought of the days to come as she began her married life with Matthew.

"I think you should know something about this room...what we did before you came," Irmani started sweeping the room with her free hand.

"What did you do?" Srenna asked with a look of puzzlement on her face.

"Well...Jimmie and I, and the Davidson's...we all felt it would be a good idea to rearrange things a bit differently, change the look in here a tad bit. We convinced Matthew that the bed that his mother had been in for so long, sick and dying, should go. We painted the room and got new stuff...you know...to brighten it up before you came," Irmani explained in almost a hushed reverence. "This is...will be yours and Matthew's bed...your room."

Srenna looked around the room as if seeing it for the first time. She was a bit surprised that all this time the room had not been left the way it had been before Miriam's death. "I guess I figured it to be the way she would have liked it," Srenna pondered gently.

"She would have...she would have wanted you to be comfortable...at ease. That's the way the woman was with everyone...always caring first about everyone else. You're both so alike in that respect it's uncanny. I'm as sure of this as I am anything that when Miriam prayed that God would send Matthew an angel...she really meant a wife...and one up to the challenge." Again the Maori woman hesitated looking for the next words of hopeful wisdom she wanted to relay to Srenna. At this moment Srenna's thoughts were overwhelmingly making her think of the next few days to come and all this little family would be going through. She wondered how she and Matthew would have time to...well do anything. Her thoughts apparently were louder then she assumed for the wise woman sitting next to her hugged her hard and simply stated in her open and candid way. "No worries, Srenna. She'll be sweet. You and Matthew will find a way to fit in all your loven' you'll be doing in the hoopla of this family and all it's "stuff". Just hold on to one another no matter what and the rest will get figured out...trust me, eh?" she laughed quietly. Her jocularity gave Srenna some peace of mind that she and Matthew would indeed "figure out" what was to come in their lives together.

"Now, you, we have exactly two hours and we have to be at that church and ready to shove you down the aisle at that boy. I suppose we'd better find a way to prop him up, eh, so he doesn't pass out cold when he sees how beautiful you are in that dress over there," Irmani laughed again. She patted the girl's hand and stood to leave. "Come on then. Let's get some food into that skinny little body of yours so you don't go floating away." The two women walked silently out of the room, closing the door carefully, both hoping the sleeping baby boy would stay that way until the last minute.

"Two hours…" Srenna thought quietly to herself. "In two hours I will be Mrs. Srenna Adelaide Patton." She walked next to Irmani, the stout Maori woman still hugging the girl she had come to love as much as her own. In slip and robe she entered the kitchen where the girls were eating a light lunch and giggling over all the plans of the day to get ready.

She knew she'd better eat or suffer the consequences

It was indeed a good thing that Irmani Rainga slipped a word to her son and Matthew's best man before the wedding started. Her exact words to him were, "If you love your brother, be prepared to catch him." When the doors to the sanctuary swung open and Jimmie stood there with Srenna holding onto his arm, (it was decided that Jimmie would in fact give Srenna away in the absence of her own father) it mattered little that Mary walked in first. In front of him was the most beautiful bride Matthew was sure he'd ever seen or would ever see again in his life. He stared in utter amazement at the full length pearl white gown enveloping the woman he was about to marry. The only color came from the bouquet of wildflowers he had picked early this morning and had delivered to the house by one of the Rainga siblings. There was an indescribable flush of color on his breathtaking bride's face. He felt Tommie's hand against his back as his dear friend and brother, steadied his tall frame. The look on his face as Srenna and Jimmie walked up the aisle to where everyone waited was priceless astonishment.

Jimmie grinned at both of them and took delight in answering Reverend Davidson when he asked "Who gives this young woman to this man." Once passed into Matthew's able hands he took his seat next to his wife, wiped the tears from his eyes and silently thanked God in his own way that things had come to this after all. He remembered another wedding in which he stood with a young, scared couple trying to right their wrongs and start a new life together in this rugged sheep country. Now Jimmie watched as that boy born to that couple nearly twenty years ago stood with his bride and vowed "to have and to hold her".

Though it seemed a blur in some sense to Srenna she absolutely would never forget the light in Matthew's eyes and the smile on his face as she stood there with him and exchanged the vows that would tie their lives together. It was only Matthew she could see in front of her holding her small hands in his strong ones, trying desperately not to crush them in his excitement and enthusiasm. Several times Hamilton Davidson spoke one or the other's name to bring them back to attention, patiently repeating what he had just asked, grinning as he too remembered the vows spoken by John and Miriam at this exact place twenty years ago.

When the simple rings they had found at a jeweler the day before were exchanged and the vows were sealed, Hamilton ordered Matthew to kiss his bride and turned them around to present them to family and friends who had rallied for the ceremony. There was nearly as much commotion then as was the evening before when they returned home to begin the feverish plans. The children, Benji included had kept their silence during the short ceremony, but they were making up for it now that congratulations were all around.

Somehow…it was everything Srenna could have hoped for. Aside from missing Daniel, Ruth and Grace being there she was not the slightest bit disappointed for not having her courtship time to prepare a wedding…thanks to Grace. By five o'clock the frenzied party moved to the fellowship hall where Patricia Davidson and her flock of faithful woman in the church had literally thrown a meal and cake together in wonderful celebration of this event. It was unbelievable to Srenna the time that had passed when Matthew, with Irmani's prodding, finally suggested that the children were getting tired and the evening was getting late. In short order the Patton car was filled with weary but happy souls and the return to the station was on its way.

Some buzzing conversation was still heard now and then from the back seat, but Matthew, Srenna and even Mary seemed fairly subdued on the trip home. Benji fell into a deep sleep as was his habit on any ride in the car but much so after the constant handling of the church ladies attempting to give Srenna a break. Now she cradled the infant as though she were protecting him from imminent disturbance. Several times she and Matthew glanced at each other quietly, smiling at a full day ending and only beginning to understand what they had just committed themselves too. It was a much more tired crew that pulled into the lane and up to the gate, ready to try and end the hectic day.

Once inside and in the nursery, Srenna laid the tired boy in his crib fully dressed, determined to not wake him after the events of the day. She slipped quietly from the room only pulling the door mostly shut and fully expected to see the other children lingering around the front room. Only Mary stood there waiting for her.

"I've sent them to bed," she smiled at Srenna with a sparkle of knowing in her eyes as though she had a secret of some kind.

"He's waiting for you at the end of the porch," she grinned. "Wear the blue dress, the one you wore to church the first time. He said to tell you he has a promise he needs to keep." With that she put her arms around Srenna and hugged her warmly. Tears were in both their eyes, happy tears to replace all those sad ones shed in months past. As they released each other's grip, Mary kissed Srenna's cheek and whispered in her ear "Sister". She turned and walked to the hall and stairway leading upstairs.

Srenna stood for a moment trying to compose her self with all the emotions of the day flying around her head and her heart. She turned back into the bedroom quietly and retrieved her deep blue summer dress she had worn the first day they had all returned to church, the first day everyone had met her, the first time she had seen Matthew fully looking at her without fear, without doubt and with new joy, new laughter, new hope in his eyes.

She slipped out of the wedding gown, putting it carefully across her bed, and pulled on the blue dress. She slid her feet back into her white slippers and again stole out of the room silently so as not to wake Benji.

As she opened the door onto the front porch she felt as though she was stepping into a place she was sure she wanted to go yet her heart was pounding as it had when Matthew held her on the beach, when he held her in the river. She had been terrified both those times to face her memories, now she was sure she needed to make this one come true. And it was. At the end of the porch by his room stood Matthew leaning against the corner post with his back to her. He immediately turned at the soft sound of her feet approaching him.

She moved slowly towards him and stopped a bit away. "Mary said you wanted to see me?" she said with a slight question in her voice and in her eyes. But looking at him and seeing him take in all of her beauty she knew he was and had been "seeing her," hearing her, knowing her unlike anyone ever had before, except God himself.

She stood waiting until he reached his hand out to her and when she took it he led her around the corner of the porch beside his bedroom door.   There on the table that sat outside was the old phonograph.

Matthew turned to Srenna and with a grin on his face and his eyes laughing he said, "I owe you a dance." The promise had been, she would swim for him, if he would dance with her. True to his word as always, Matthew bowed low to Srenna, "May I have this dance, Mrs. Patton?" he asked, extending his hand to her, stilling grinning his boyish grin. "I'll even be fair and take off my shoes," he laughed, kicking them off.

Srenna giggled and gave him her hand willingly and replied, "Yes Mr. Patton you may. And so will I," she giggled as she too removed her shoes.

Matthew placed the arm down on a record and a beautiful waltz John and Miriam had danced to many times began to lend its lilting tune into the clear evening air. Matthew led Srenna down the steps and into the grass. Taking a hold of her waist and hand he moved the two of them across the yard in a perfect three quarter time to the dearest song he could remember. It was as though his best kept secret was this all along.

Srenna could only wonder if four beloved parents and God himself weren't peering over the balcony of heaven watching their son and their daughter join in this beautiful dance as they began their lives together. As thy twirled in rhythmic time, every sorrow, every pain and sadness was falling away like broken chains. They seemed to glide effortlessly across the grass as if it were in fact the clouds…Heaven's clouds.

Srenna was sure all of Heaven was watching them just at that precise moment for the joy that was pouring out all over this blessed homestead. But Heaven wasn't the only audience the two of them had as four glad-hearted children watched from Mary's window. The memory of Mum and Dad dancing in the New Zealand moonlight full of love for one another was now being played out before them, new and unrestrained, free and beautiful.

As the song came to an end Matthew pulled Srenna closer into his arms letting her know every word, every vow he had spoken this afternoon before God and man, had been meant with all his heart, mind, body and soul. He had known from the moment he had seen her, he could never love anyone else like he loved her. He turned her one more time as the song came to an end. Then pulling her back into his arms he bent his face and kissed her again as he had at the wedding, this time lingering, unrestrained.

Matthew pulled away first looking beyond Srenna's image in front of him and then whispered into her ear, "We have an audience." She hid her face against Matthew's shoulder and giggled. Before she could turn to look, Mary had whisked everyone away and closed the curtain.

Matthew was laughing now as well and then almost as if on cue a light rain began to fall on both of them. He grabbed Srenna by the hand and they both ran for the cover of the porch, still laughing and giggling. Once Matthew had lifted the needle from the record and turned off the beloved Victrola, he gazed down at Srenna, suddenly overwhelmed by even looking at her.

"Srenna, I told you we could wait...you know, til..." he began to remind her. But she cut him off with her finger against his lips.

"Until what Matthew? Until we can get away by ourselves...until I'm sure I love you enough...until...." She trailed off as she leaned up to kiss him and reassure him. He was assured all he needed to be so he began leading Srenna to his door. When he began to open it, he turned one more time to say something but again she cut him off. "Well Mr. Patton. Aren't you going to carry me across the threshold and into our home?" She had a mischievous grin on her face which made him even more determined then ever to hold her, so swinging her up in his arms he entered that room, entered the beginning of the rest of their lives together, entered the promises they had made to each other to have and to always hold, through anything, through everything; even the inevitable decent of Madelaine Brewster.

Matthew pushed the thought of his grandmother out of his mind as quickly as it had crossed it. He closed the door with his foot, shutting the world outside and looked into Srenna's deep warm eyes. For the moment she was all that mattered to him, all he could see, and certainly... all he could think of.

Chapter 37: The Landing of the Brewster

"Please make sure they each get three new outfits for school, Mary. After you're done with shopping you can take the girls to lunch." Srenna was scurrying to get Mary and the girls out the door bright and early this morning. They were to head for Masterton to do the clothes shopping for school. All her plans had been altered since the infamous telegram had arrived three days ago. Between the wedding, the drive back into Masterton the next day to sign papers requesting custody of the children, trying to clean in anticipation of Grandmother Brewster's arrival...well... Srenna felt like her head might simply spin off of her shoulders. Getting some of them out of the house today would help. Mary, as well as Lilly and Emma, looked like they needed a tremendous distraction.

Srenna wrote a check for Mary and instructed her to cash it at the First Bank of New Zealand so she could indulge the girls and help herself at the same time. It had taken the children by surprise when she explained to all of them how rich she was. They were speechless when she and Matthew filled them in the night before after they returned from the Rainga house for the day.

Srenna was the first to be surprised the morning after the wedding when she and Matthew woke to a quiet house and found themselves quite alone for the better portion of the day. Matthew had arranged for all of the girls and Benji to go to their neighbors for breakfast and lunch, leaving the noisy house in a state of exquisite hush. It gave them much needed time to discuss their plans, enjoy their first morning together as man and wife, and then drive into Masterton to finalize the paperwork for court. Srenna couldn't help but notice Matthew watching over his shoulder the whole day in anticipation of his grandmother's descent. However, she wasn't completely unsuccessful in distracting him. They were both extremely thankful for what time they had before the chaos of life had come crashing back into the house.

Now this morning it was inevitable that within the next day or two Madelaine Brewster would be here and Srenna was beginning to feel the anxiety of the visit. Once she rallied the girls to the car and got Benji situated in his playing pen Stephan had built she threw herself into the business of cleaning the house. Stephan had been sent to shepherd the sheep for the day with Mika Rainga. Matthew was trying desperately to repair a leaky pipe in the outdoor shower. He disappeared again after lunch when Srenna went to put a tired baby down for a nap. She was successful in getting Benji quieted quickly due to the little boy's frenzy of activity in the last two days. His eyes fluttered shut almost as soon as his curly head hit the mattress.

Srenna walked through the solitude of the house and for a moment just stood in the front room looking around. How could it be possible that she had only been walking through this room and the others about her for a little over three months? It felt more like three years. The room was so familiar to her. She walked across the floor to Matthew's door...well... what used to be Matthew's door and was now simply the study. Only yesterday when they returned home from Masterton, Matthew had removed his belongings from the room and moved them into Srenna's room, now their room. It felt a little odd last night for only a little while until she and Matthew fell asleep in each other's arms finally exhausted for all the events of the last few days...not to mention the last week or so.

Srenna took one more peek at the study that would remain as an office for Matthew and a guest room for anyone coming to visit. She had cleaned and primped the room for Grandmother Brewster's visit on the off-side chance that Madelaine would want to stay at Shepherd's Gaze and not at a hotel in Tinui or Masterton. Srenna wasn't sure which one any of them hoped for but she wasn't about to be rude to the woman and really hoped for the best once the formidable woman got there and Matthew and Srenna reasoned with her.

Satisfied that there was really nothing more she could do to make the room comfortable, Srenna headed for the kitchen. She was determined that she would be as organized as was possible before Miriam's mother embarked upon this well-used home. The children had been very co-operative the last few days due in part to their fear that the woman just might be able to spirit them away. But the truth was they were all determined to do what ever they had to in order to convince their grandmother that they were better off all together in Castle Point and not split up in two different worlds.

Srenna pondered heavily the request that she and Matthew had just made to family court to become the legal guardians of all the children. It was no doubt a tremendous responsibility; one she was sure would come under grave scrutiny. But it had to be done. Once and for all the fate of the children needed to be determined so they could all get on with their lives together. They had already been through so many obstacles together, Benji and then Stephan, the earthquake, grieving and healing with one another, she and Matthew. Srenna was certain beyond a doubt that whatever crisis arose, they could get through it as a team…albeit a young team. She prayed once again as she had been doing nearly nonstop now for days. She knew deep down in her heart that every step they had taken had never gone unseen by their heavenly Father and Shepherd. She trusted that now more then ever.

Her thoughts had completely distracted her when she felt two strong arms wrap around her waist and Matthew hugged her from behind. "You sir are wet!" she exclaimed as she wiggled free from his embrace and turned to push him away playfully. He stood back away from her with a boyish pout on his face that nearly sent her into a fit of laughter. But she caught herself when she saw him shirtless and indeed wet from working on the plumbing and ….dripping all over her clean floor. At that she playfully shoved him again and ordered in her most serious voice she could find, "Out you! You'll have my floor soaked and then I shall have another mess to clean up!" she jokingly commanded, pushing his tall frame toward the opened back door.

"I come begging your help and all you can do is scold me," he moaned dramatically. He allowed her to push him all the way out and then turned suddenly and grabbed her around the middle again.

"Stop!" she giggled, as he walked backwards toward the end of the porch where the shower was. "What am I to do with you, eh?

You beg more then your baby brother. How could I possibly help you with the plumbing anyway?" Srenna gave Matthew just enough resistance to tease but she knew too that he probably did indeed need her help. Once they reached the end of the porch Matthew reluctantly let go of her and turned towards the entrance of the shower.

"Actually, you can. I need you to hold the wrench while I tighten the seal the other way. I can't do both at the same time," he explained with a huge grin on his face. There was still some water dripping from the fixture that he was trying dutifully to fix. Srenna had only to look at his blue eyes again and the incorrigible pleading in them and she would have stood on her head for him.

"All right. But if I get soaked...I'm..." she started. But Matthew hushed that sentence with a quick kiss and the handing over of the wrench he wanted her to hold. He walked into the shower where the leak was still dripping and motioned her to follow.

"Now here's what I need you to do," he instructed, taking the wrench and placing it on the part of the pipe he wanted her to keep in place. "While you're holding it still this way I can turn this one and tighten it. Every time I tried, this one turned and ...well...I really need you to try." He smiled down at her and waited for her to take hold of the wrench.

"I'll have to hold it with both hands Matthew and even then I don't know if I'm strong enough to keep it from moving," she argued gently.

"Just try...please...only for a moment...that's all it will take me," he promised.

Srenna reached up above her head and grabbed the tool in both hands gripping it as firmly as she could. When Matthew was sure she had a firm hold on it he began to turn the other wrench in his hand and felt the seal begin to turn as it should. But it suddenly stuck and no amount of turning it would budge the stubborn coupling. The harder he tried the more it seemed to stick. Then Srenna could feel the pipe joint she was holding begin to move...the wrong way.

"Matthew...is it supposed to move this way/" she asked gently, gritting her teeth and holding on with all her might. Her arms were beginning to ache from holding them over her head for so long and squeezing the tool.

"Just a little more Sren...hold on just a little more and tighter if you can," he begged.

"Matthew I can't much longer. My arms are screaming...I..." Suddenly the wrench in her hands slipped and fell to the floor with a deadening clang. Almost simultaneously the seal she had been straining to hold slipped enough that the one Matthew was trying to tighten came loose all together. Water spewed everywhere...mostly in Matthew's face. Srenna however was able to make a mad dash from the shower and down on the grass, escaping most of the deluge that he got. She couldn't help herself as she watched with hand over mouth and laughed at him taking a soaking with the wrench in hand.

Matthew walked from the shower and dropped the tool in his dripping hand. He gazed down at his wife of only two days and thought of a thousand ways he would like to get even with her for laughing at him but only one idea leapt at him as she stood holding her sides from giggling so hard. With no hesitation at all he was off the porch and after her, determined he would take her back in for her own thorough soaking. But she was quick. She knew his intentions the moment he looked at her and she had already sprinted for the nearest tree in the yard. That was however not nearly fast enough by the time Matthew caught up with her. Before she could reach any safe harbor, had there been any, he had her in his arms, over his shoulder and was headed for the porch. But Srenna wasn't about to go without a fight. She started tickling Matthew's sides, to which he turned suddenly as though he were going to put her down. Instead he swatted her playfully on her backside sending both of them into even more fits of laughter...that was until both of them heard the angry question that came from the back door.

"Matthew Lucas Patton! What in the name of God is going on here?"

Srenna was the first to see the austere headmistress standing on the porch, hands on hips, glaring as though she had just witnessed the most horrible act in progress. But in an instance Matthew whipped his body around so quickly that it sent Srenna's head nearly snapping.

"Put me down...Matthew...put me down, you," she whispered loudly, trying to wiggle free of his grip.

And drop her he did... with a thud!

Srenna caught herself against Matthew's arms. The expression on his face was somewhere between that of total embarrassment and total disbelief that his grandmother had just witnessed their frolic across the yard. Srenna smiled encouragingly at him, pulling at his arm and whispering, "She'll be right Matthew, eh?"

Matthew stared down at the young woman who had been holding them all together for the last twelve weeks and suddenly realized how fast everything had happened. But one look into her dark eyes sent a flood of warmth and strength through him. She was right. They would be right...all of them.

"Well...are you going to tell me what in the blazes is going on here? Where is Mrs. Wrightman? And who in the world is this brazen young woman?" Madelaine Brewster was angry, there was no doubt about that as she came off the porch and walked toward Matthew and Srenna. They were both frozen in their spots, but finally Srenna found her tongue and stepped past Matthew with her hand extended.

"Grandmother Brewster, we wondered when you'd be here. You must be very..." But Srenna was cut off sharply.

"I don't believe I addressed you at all, young lady," she snapped indignantly, never even looking at Srenna. "Well...Matthew!"

Srenna turned and looked at her new husband's face. For a moment she was sure she was seeing a young boy who felt whipped and beaten...and the expression sent a chill down her spine. But she spoke Matthew's name over Madelaine's attempt to ask again and then slid her arm through his, squeezing it reassuringly and praying fervently. That was all it took.

Srenna felt a noticeable change in Matthew's demeanor. He suddenly stood up to his full six foot and stared straight into his grandmother's eyes. "This brazen young woman...is my wife," he started softly, gazing at Srenna and finally smiling. "Grandmother I would like you to meet Srenna...Srenna Adelaide Patton." Before his grandmother could recover from the gasp that escaped her lips Matthew went on. "As for Mrs. Wrightman...she's gone bush. We don't know where she is or your money that you sent with her. She made it for... four days. Isn't that what I told you Srenna?" he asked the young woman at his side. Srenna could feel something else rising up in Matthew's demeanor and his tone. It wasn't good.

"Yes I believe that's what you..." she started answering him. Before she was able to finish he had pulled away from Srenna and was walking towards his grandmother. He stopped short of a few feet away from the older woman and simply stared, almost defiantly, waiting for her next reaction.

"What did you do to her? She just happened to be one of the best governesses in all of London," Madelaine Brewster spit out. "I paid very good money to send that woman here to keep all of you in line until I could retrieve the girls." She was angrier now and Srenna could feel Matthew's temper getting hotter by the minute.

"Keep us in line? Retrieve the girls? Is that what you call it, eh? You're form of care and concern for all of us after mum's..." But he found himself cut off...by Srenna.

"Matthew! Wait! Can't we all go inside and I'll make some tea and we can sit and..." But Srenna never got any further.

"Where are the girls? I have the papers I need to take temporary custody of them and I want them ready now." Miriam's mother was so adamant that Srenna felt herself beginning to believe that the woman might just be able to carry out her threats.

Matthew wasn't having any of it.

"We've been to a lawyer as well! There's to be a court hearing...soon...and the judge will decide if they stay here with Srenna and me as their legal guardians or go with you. Until then they go nowhere, but here." He folded his arms across his bare chest and glared at the woman, defying her to continue the fight. She was determined to get the last word in as she began to walk around the house towards the car she had driven to the sheep station.

"I have no time for this little battle with you Matthew. Have the girls ready in the morning. I'm going to see the law enforcement in this God forsaken town and at the very least I will be back to get them in the morning. We leave in two days for England." That last statement brought all three of them around the side of the house and to the front gate. Madelaine Brewster never even stopped to look back at her grandson as she opened the door to the automobile and slid her angry body in.

Matthew was ready to let another rebuttal fly when he felt a slight arm slip through his and a steady hand on his back. For the first time in several minutes he felt the fight in him...the anger...and yes...even fear begin to roll off of him. He watched as the car sped up the lane and through the gates it had passed under. When it disappeared over the top of the hill he finally glanced down at the one steadying him. There were tears in Srenna's eyes even as much as she was trying to encourage Matthew and he realized how his anger with his grandmother must have felt to her. He pulled Srenna into his arms and kissed the top of her head.

"I'm sorry...I shouldn't have let her get to me like that, eh?" he apologized. But she was crying...quietly so ...but none the less crying. "Srenna...we'll figure this out...no worries right?" he breathed into her ear. He kissed her cheek again and pulled her face up gently away from his chest. He was about to encourage her more when they both heard the woeful cries of a disturbed infant. Benji had no doubt heard the grandmother he had never even met as she yelled out her last orders on her way past the baby's window. Srenna immediately tore herself out of Matthew's arms and headed for the front door.

He stood for a few moments and shook his head tiredly. He felt a great urge right now to simply get on Samson and go bush himself for a while just to pray. He might have too if not for the fact that at that exact moment Mary came over the top of the hill and through the gate, returning from their shopping expedition. He walked slowly towards the car and the excited little girls who came bearing shopping bags galore. The joy on their faces made him want to scoop them up and hold them close and then run with them as far away from their grandmother as he could. But a clear, loud voice was ringing in his ears. It was the same voice he'd heard on the mountain top when he was agonizing over his lie to Srenna, the same voice that spoke comfort and direction to him so many times in his young life every time he'd cried out, the same one that told him undeniably that He would provide for this motherless, fatherless little family. And He had.

Matthew caught up Emma first and started laughing when the vivacious five-year-old exclaimed "You're wet?" He stepped in time with Lilly as she began to pull out first one thing and then another to show her big brother their accomplishments. He nodded his head in rote response but was really trying to read the expression on his oldest sister's face as she silently tried to read his. It was almost an unspoken conversation with her; the kind two people have that know each other so well. "Was that grandmother?" her eyes asked. His response in silence was to nod slightly, put his arm around Mary and hug her all the way into the house. Tonight the prayer needed to rise up from this house and not from the hills. "A family that prays together..." he thought to himself. The rest of that saying was burning on his heart, screaming in his spirit. He could hear the promise he'd made to his mother on her death bed, that screaming the loudest.

He would do anything to keep them together if it meant praying all night, all of them. He felt sure that the children wouldn't miss a beat where this was concerned.

And they wouldn't…they didn't.

Chapter 38: If Only

Once again the Patton family congregated in the master bedroom for the night due in large to the girls being so upset when they found out that Grandmother Brewster had arrived. Matthew tried to keep it as low key as he and Srenna could but anyone could see that they were concerned as well. A phone call was made to Jimmie and Irmani and of course Irmani's first suggestion was to return to her ancient ancestor's way of handling things and simply boil and eat the woman. However she ended that thought with, "Sorry God" and "the old goat would probably give us indigestion anyway, eh?" She apologized for her crude remarks, but then announced that "no one is taking any of Miriam's babies off this island!"

Much prayer did go up over night. Even after the children dozed off, Srenna, Matthew and Mary discussed in hushed tones what they might do if Madelaine Brewster insisted on testing the system before a hearing. Matthew knew all the community officials both in Castle Point and in Tinui. Many of the older men had either served with his father or known him well and Matthew was certain that he could count on them to help him within the confines of the law. He did however call Philip Cramer and inform the lawyer that Grandmother had landed and was extremely agitated. He included the information that she came bearing papers of some sort. Mr. Cramer assured Matthew that "papers" written up by the courts in England had no jurisdiction in New Zealand. The playing field, so to speak, was level for both parties. That brought a small measure of comfort to Srenna and the children when he relayed the news.

That night while all their whispers and prayers were being uttered, Srenna felt some deep unction stirring in her. She never said anything to anyone as it formed in her mind and began to take shape as an idea. Matthew was so weary from all the past days of events and so were the children. The weariness was actually a blessing in disguise as first one child and then another drifted off in relatively blissful peace. But even after Matthew finally succumbed to slumber and the room became still, Srenna couldn't push away her thoughts about the grandmother she had just met that afternoon.

As you would guess, it brought up painful thoughts of another grandmother she never knew. Her memories began to flood over her again of family she would never know, people she would never have in her life. She was extremely grateful that her own grandmother had come to some form of peace with herself at the end of her life and in that had brought an abundant blessing into Srenna's, of which she was now able to pass on to her young, new family. But Srenna could not get rid of the feeling of loss…as well. No amount of inheritance would ever replace what she wished she'd had; the opportunity to spend time with her own grandparents as she grew up.

This one thought began to cultivate a plan in her mind. By the time she finally gave in to exhausted sleep she was sure of what she would do in the morning. Being who she was and how determined she had been her whole life when it came to something she knew should happen…well, that is as they say…that!

Matthew was as always the first to stir in the morning but it wasn't long before everyone else was awake, whinging and complaining about how tired they still were. Srenna ordered the girls back upstairs with Mary to sleep for a little while longer, fed Benji and laid him down again and then saw Stephan off early to help Matthew take the sheep to the low fields. Neither of the boys wanted to be very far away on the offside chance that Grandmother would indeed return and try again. It was only after they had both disappeared into the pastures just beyond the house that Srenna dressed quickly and slipped into Mary's room to speak to her.

"Mary…" she whispered lightly over the girl's head.

"What's wrong Srenna? Is she here? Did she come back?" Mary asked as she rubbed her worried eyes and started to rise up off the bed.

"No…no…She's sweet, Mary. I just wanted to let you know I'm going to run an errand real quick and then I'll be back…before lunch. Can you hold down the fort until I get back?" Srenna questioned the baffled girl.

"You know I can…but what on earth do you need to do…right now, you?" Mary asked with a great amount of concern in her voice. "What if she comes back?"

"Mary…I promise you she won't be here this morning while I'm gone. Trust me." Srenna stood from the side of the bed and prepared to leave the room.

"You're going to talk to her…aren't you?" Mary already knew Srenna well enough to know that when she got an idea in her head there was no stopping Srenna Adelaide… "Patton," came out of Mary's mouth with a grin.

"What?" Srenna asked with a frown on her face.

"You're a Patton for sure. You've a mind to accomplish something…better no one get in your way, eh?" Mary sat up on her elbows with an eyebrow raised in jest.

"I'm just going to try and reason with her, that's all," Srenna explained, "If you're brother insists on knowing where I am, and I know he will, tell him. But tell him this too." She heaved a big sigh and smiled at the young girl who was her sister now every bit as much as if she had been all of Srenna's life. Then with a completely serious expression she finished her thought. "We may never have the chance for mending like this again and this time I'm not going to sit around and do nothing about it." She smiled one more time at Mary and slipped from the room as quietly as she had slipped in.

Srenna went back downstairs and grabbed up her handbag off her bed. She also remembered to grab up one more item off the bedside stand and held on to it with a definite goal in mind. She was out of the house and into the car before a full two minutes had passed. She glanced briefly in the direction of the fields where Matthew and Stephan were and felt such a strong pang of love for first her "husband", even if the word still seemed so new, and then for Stephan, whom she had come to relate to so very much over the last few months as the boy still processed his grief. She loved all of them so much. She couldn't imagine any of them being gone from her life…at this moment…for any reason. This drove her determination into a rush of action as she turned the car onto the road above the house and headed for Masterton. She didn't even know where Madelaine was staying but she knew someone that would.

It took her only thirty minutes to pull into the train station and only one more to reach the ticket master's booth.

"G'day, sir. My name is Srenna Patton. I live up by Castle Point," Srenna began, addressing the elderly gentleman behind the window. "My grandmother arrived either yesterday or the day before on the train and would have wanted a place to stay in town. You couldn't miss her. Older woman, very British, immaculately dressed..."

"Oh sure...that one...Yeahr. She was a proper sort, that one...strict like, called herself ...um...Headmistress something or other. Would 'ave been scared of that one in school, eh?" The kindly man grinned. "No offense Miss."

"No offense taken sir," Srenna chuckled, "And you have no idea. But I really need to see her. Would you by chance have given her any ideas where to stay...a hotel...or hostel maybe?" Srenna pleaded with her eyes.

"Well bein' it's your nana... I guess I could tell ya. I sent her over to Dunham's Hotel. She looked like she could afford a nice place, that one," the man offered.

"Sir, thank you so very much. You have no idea how wonderful this is. I want to surprise her." Srenna smiled gratefully at the man and turned back towards the car. Within minutes she had found the stately hotel, one of Masterton's English styled accommodations. Inside and at the desk she wondered for a moment how she would even get to the woman, but once there she simply spilled her story out to the concierge behind the front desk and then pleadingly asked him to send a message to Grandmother Brewster's room. The man could hardly refuse the big dark eyes begging him for help and quickly sent a valet upstairs to inform the austere British woman that she had a visitor.

Srenna went over to a fountain in the lobby and stood facing the elevator. Her heart was beating so fast and furious that she thought for sure she might turn and run at the last minute. Her lips were moving in a silent fervent prayer that when the moment came, and she hoped with all hope that it would, that God would give her the exact words to speak. She was almost ready to give up that hope when first ten minutes passed and then another ten.

"God...there's been enough pain in this family. I'm begging you for healing...please...pour out your healing. I know that's what you want or you wouldn't have put us all through so much to be together. There's a reason for us to be together; all of us." Srenna felt tears brimming in her eyes and threatening to spill over before this conversation even had a chance to happen. But her prayer plowed on as she pleaded with the Father that had held her and consoled her and directed her for a long time now. "If Madelaine Brewster can be a part of this little orphaned family will you move this mountain so it can happen...Please Father?"

Srenna had inadvertently turned her back from the elevator when she thought she was about to cry. Her last request had just rolled off her lips when she heard a stern voice behind her.

"What on earth are you doing here young lady?" snapped Madelaine, bringing Srenna around quickly and at full attention. She wondered if the children's grandmother was always angry or if this display of emotions was only because she was being challenged.

"Grandmother Brewster...uhm...I mean Mrs. Brewster...I wanted to see if you would have tea with me...or let me take you to brunch...please," Srenna stammered. She tried to keep a smile on her face...while she held her breath.

"If you've come here to plead with me Miss...you've wasted your time. I have things to do this morning and the sooner we get this unsavory business taken care of the sooner you can get on with your ridiculous marriage with Matthew," Madelaine continued to spew.

Srenna let out the breath she was holding and took a deep one in its place. She dropped her head for a moment and without even thinking about her actions as she shook her head, she stated, "I wish so very much that I'd had the opportunity to know my grandmother when I was younger. She died about six months ago." Srenna said nothing else but her eyes came up from the floor and caught Madelaine's gaze. She thought for sure the angry woman would snap something vile back at her but she found the British headmistress staring straight at her...speechless. The woman's face had gone ashen and her eyes hinted of her own tears threatening to give way. But with a last attempt to be bitter and brutal Madelaine Brewster pulled her frame up stiff and staunch and tried desperately to unleash a rebuttal.

"Whatever happened between your grandmother and you, young lady, it has nothing to do with me and my daughter's affairs.

You can't possibly think that there is any comparison to what I have suffered at the loss of my child." Madelaine could not hide the tremor in her voice or the pain she was feeling at that precise moment as her grieving memories began to flood her senses.

Srenna smiled mercifully at the older woman and answered with all the determination she knew. "Oh… but I do," Srenna said softly, her own tears welling up and drowning her dark eyes. But she never lost her gracious smile. "My family was gone…in only a few precious minutes when I was only twelve." One tear escaped, slipping slowing down her cheek. But before any more could follow Srenna brushed her eyes with her hand and stood up as tall as her slender frame could afford.

"Please…won't you just give me fifteen minutes of your time; only fifteen. Just hear me out and then I promise I'll leave and you and I will be done and you can go on with whatever it is you think you must do."

The stubborn young woman must have raised Madelaine Brewster's curiosity and/or the headmistress was just becoming embarrassed with the audience they seemed to be drawing in the hotel lobby. "Stop your begging," she reprimanded Srenna sternly. "It's neither lady-like or dignified, especially in public." Srenna thought for sure the conversation was over but to her great surprise the children's grandmother took her arm rather forcefully and began to lead her towards the hotel dining room. Once at the doorway Madelaine Brewster let go of her young visitor's arm and requested a table of the host. They were quickly escorted to a quiet corner of the room and Srenna immediately pulled out a chair for the headmistress to be seated.

Srenna lowered herself slowly into the opposite chair and waited for a moment. She was nearly ready to begin her fifteen minute dissertation when a waiter came to take their order. She held her tongue until Madelaine could request tea and scones. Once done, she watched the woman's face for any sign that dignified pleading could begin.

"Well…your wasting your fifteen minutes, child," Madelaine snapped, "and mine."

Srenna took yet another deep breath and prayed a quick prayer and then opened her mouth.

"I was raised in a private school in Sydney after my parents died. I lived there until I started training as a governess when I was sixteen. I was very fortunate to be hired by a wonderful family in Sydney and stayed with them until I came here three months ago after three governesses just up and left the children. Right before I came to New Zealand to take the position with your grandchildren I received word that my own grandmother had passed…only a year after my grandfather had been gone. I never had the chance to know her because they were both estranged from my mother before I was born." Srenna hesitated for a second or two, catching her breath…again uttering a silent prayer before going on.

"I regret never having known my grandmother and I believe deep down inside she felt the same way. The letter that she left me apologized for never having come for me. It was because of my grandfather's bitterness when my mother married my father that I was robbed of ever having them in my life. None the less before she died she willed all she had to me…a considerable amount."

At this statement Srenna looked away from the woman sitting across from her and unabashedly began to cry quietly, as she had been doing much in the last week or so. She neither heard a rebuke or a consoling word coming from the other side of the table…but Srenna was too afraid to even look at the children's grandmother. At the moment she did not want to know how she was reacting to her story.

"She left me all her riches and yet…the one thing I wanted more then anything was …just…family," Srenna wept softly…well aware that the waiter that had brought their tea and scones had set the provisions down quickly and humbly backed away. But she still could not look at Grandmother Brewster.

"I fell in love with your grandchildren…Miriam's children…the very first day I met them. I knew before the day ended that I would never be able to leave them…that I was meant to be there…in whatever capacity. And do you know why?" Srenna asked, not really wanting an answer and not really getting one. She never saw the silent shake of Madelaine's tearful face.
"The minute I walked into the house I felt your daughter's presence…I saw it everywhere I looked. It was in every one of those children. And every day that passed I saw her strength…her graciousness…her kindness in them. She and John poured so much goodness into them…so much determination…especially Matthew and Mary."

Srenna finally turned back and gazed at the elderly woman who was now staring away as if fixed on a spot on the wall, but Srenna knew she was still holding Madelaine Brewster's attention. Before any interruption could come from the woman's lips Srenna plunged on. "They were so strong when I met them. Matthew was holding everyone together with what help Mary could offer at sixteen years of age. He works hard every day…harder then most men. He has so much respect from the men in the community. They've watched him grow up without his father and still stand like a man even when he was just a boy. And Mary…she learned so much from her mother. Even though I've never met Miriam I look at Mary every day and I know I'm looking at your daughter…smart…beautiful…compassionate. She wants to go to the University in Auckland next year." Srenna uttered that news with a smile and obvious pride in her voice as though she were speaking of her own child. "It's truly amazing how those children make it day to day. Sure, they've had help from neighbors and Reverend and Patricia Davidson. But their real strength comes from all John and Miriam taught them…how to love one another…serve one another…protect one another."

At this point the headmistress could no longer hold her tongue. Srenna could hear the deep breath that came from the woman and knew she had run out of time.

"All these details will not solve the issue of who needs to finish raising the children," Madelaine began, her voice a bit quieter but still sharp. Srenna feared she had made little or no impression with all she had shared. "You and Matthew are far too young to be bringing up all these children. With me taking the girls back and enrolling them in the school they will have all the refining a young woman needs in life. It will leave the both of you only the responsibility of one teenage boy to raise and the baby. I'm doing you a favor by taking some of this off your hands. Matthew will thank me later…so will the girls." The children's grandmother was looking full into Srenna's face assuming that this would settle the argument. Madelaine was use to getting her way. She was however not prepared in the least for Srenna's reaction.

"Mrs. Brewster!" she began, trembling just a bit and feeling as if pure unadulterated anger was about to explode from every pore in her body. She pulled herself upright and stared back into the woman's face and held her gaze with all the unction Srenna Adelaide James Patton knew…ever.

"The children…the girls …or for that matter especially Matthew and I will never thank you for splitting up John and Miriam's family for the sake of your unforgiveness." While Madelaine was gasping, Srenna plowed on…now that she had truly lost her temper. "They will hate you every day of their lives…resent you…count the days until they can leave you and ….your grudge. And then you'll have nothing…no one. When what you could have…" Srenna stopped for a moment and caught a sob in her throat, trying desperately to compose herself and ashamed that the woman had provoked her after all.

"Have what…young lady?" The woman had set back in her chair waiting for Srenna to give her a sound reason why she should drop her intentions.

"You could have your family back." Srenna fought hard to calm her quivering lips but she was nearly spent by her attempt to appeal to this stubborn woman. She wanted to keep on fighting but suddenly the fight was gone out of her.

"Family…I lost the only child I will ever have. I will never get her back," Madelaine cried.

"Neither will I…but God gave me something to fill that enormous hole in me where my family use to be and I can not…I will not stand by and see them ripped away from me this time," Srenna was done. She stood and prepared to leave while Madelaine stayed seated. She quietly composed herself and then forced a smile at the woman. "It doesn't have to be this way, "she pled one more time.

Srenna reached into her bag and pulled out the item she had been guarding since she left the house. It was one of Matthew's journals. She laid the small book down and looked at Madelaine.

"You need to read some of this…maybe all of it. It's your grandson's heart in this book. It will tell you better then I ever could what kind of man he truly is," and then without another word Srenna shook her head and walked away. She was to say the least a bit surprised that no retort or retaliation was flung at her as she left.

Srenna went straight to the car and began the drive back to the sheep station. For several moments she cried as though her heart was once again broken. She had barely gone ten miles and she finally had to pull over. She laid her head against the steering wheel and sobbed, crying out to God with what was left of her emotions...her thoughts...and then finally...her will.

"Why did you bring me here, you?" she cried out to her Father. "All this to let them be snatched away...it's not right...it's not. It can't be. She's so...so hateful...so vindictive...I can't let her...I won't let her...even if I have to spend the last penny I have...I will...I will...I..."

Srenna tried to get the last "will" out of her mouth, but it never made it. She sobbed a few last sobs and then hung onto the wheel spent and empty. But just a soon as she felt she could feel nothing more that same incredible presence that had engulfed her on the mountain top came flooding into the car. It was the same one that had tapped her on the shoulder in the alley when she feared leaving Sydney...the same omnipresent cloud of comfort that had blanketed her when she was plucked from the frothy waves of the Sydney harbor...the same tender, loving, gentle Shepherd that had kept her all these years was sitting in the car with her at that very moment. And just as she had felt on the mountain she feared even opening her eyes or looking up for fear she would simply be consumed by his awesome presence. She felt immediate remorse for her stubborn will, her angry words with the children's grandmother.

"Oh Father. I'm so sorry. I should have never..." Srenna suddenly had an image of Madelaine Brewster sitting alone. And then she saw herself sitting at a table full of happy laughing faces and Matthew smiling at her from the other end. Then again she saw Madelaine beside a
warm fireplace but no one to share it with. She felt as though her heart would burst as God showed her first one and then another scene of Miriam's mother suffering in solitude over the years. It sent a flood of fresh tears down her face but this time her prayers were quite different.

"Father...she's so hurt. Like Stephan...so grieved. She'll never have the moments back with her child. Please Father, set her free so she can love again. So she can be loved again. We would love her...I know we could. I know that's what John and Miriam would have wanted. Give us a chance to do that for her...for us...please." Srenna looked up from the steering wheel and waited. She heard no response, for which she was just a slight bit disappointed. But just at that moment she needed Matthew. She was exhausted from the confrontation with his grandmother...exhausted from her encounter with God and in dire need of her new husband just holding her and reassuring her. With what was left of her strength she started the car again and finished the drive home.

He was waiting for her at the gate. One look at her tear stained face and Matthew could no more be angry with Srenna for going to see his grandmother then he could have been with Emma or Benji. He simply caught her in his arms and consoled her. They walked away from the house for a while until Srenna could relay all that had been said, all she had encountered in the car coming back and all that she felt at that exact moment. He gave her plenty of time to explain all that had happened. No response came from him when she was spent. He simply just kept holding her, so Srenna turned the conversation to the most important thought in her head…and her heart.

"Matthew…all this time we've been praying for ourselves…we forgot how she might feel…how grieved and lonely she must be," Srenna suggested. She leaned against his arm as they came up on the barn and for a moment neither one spoke. Then Srenna heard a deep sigh escape from Matthew's chest at nearly the same time she heard an automobile coming down into the lane.
It made her whip her head up in the direction of the sound and to her dismay it was the vehicle Madelaine had driven to the station the day before.

"You'd better start testing your theory now Srenna…the one where we should feel pity for her," Matthew remarked sarcastically and tiredly. "She isn't wasting any time, eh?"

"She didn't bring anyone with her," was all Srenna could think of saying in response. They both realized that that might be a significant point to say the least.

Matthew grabbed Srenna's hand and they made their way back towards the house in time to meet the car at the gate. They waited in front of the walk and watched as Madelaine stepped out of the car. She stood still for a moment looking all around her as though for the first time ever she was actually seeing the surrounding landscape. Then she turned her head and directly addressed her grandson in what was the surprise of both their lives.

"Well…I suppose you and I have much we need to discuss…Matthew…" she began in a much more subdued tone then the one last heard. "But first…."

Matthew arbitrarily cut her off. "There doesn't need to be any discussion because they are not…"

"Hold on young man." Grandmother Brewster took a few steps toward the young couple clinging to each other for moral and physical support and went on. "No one is leaving, at least not until they are old enough to make that decision on there own. But we will discuss that later. Right now… I believe you and I would do well to …maybe talk…alone." Madelaine Brewster looked straight at Srenna and gave her the faintest of smiles…but Srenna saw it and something in her heart began to leap. It was hope. "Just maybe," she thought to herself.

"Matthew," Srenna whispered gently up to his face. She gripped his hand firmly hoping he could feel the encouragement she was trying to send him.

All Matthew had to do was look into Srenna's eyes…her pleading eyes…feel her hand squeezing his and know that whatever prayers had gone up in the car along side the road for his grandmother had indeed been heard and quickly. He heaved a deep sigh again and knew the next steps of healing in this family were up to him. He smiled into the face of the young woman who would be standing with him for a lifetime and was extremely grateful for the one who had more determination then ten woman put together. He kissed her cheek and then turned to look at his grandmother.

"Srenna…would you excuse us for a little while? Grandmother and I need to go for a walk," he grinned, letting go of her hand and turning towards the older woman. Matthew took a step towards his grandmother and motioned to her to follow him. She stepped in line with him and before any response had come from Srenna the two were walking away towards the sheep pens and the fields. But Srenna didn't need to respond. She fairly flew into the house to let everyone know what was going on and to start praying. As badly as everyone wanted to run to the windows and try to assess the conversation going on between grandson and grandmother, no one did. But they made up for it by preparing the best meal they could in the bright hope that Grandmother Brewster would be staying for lunch.

Chapter 39: In Loving Memory

"Emma Narah Patton! Where are your shoes and socks, you?" Srenna exclaimed, half frustrated, half laughing at the energetic five-year-old. The little girl had been skipping up and down the hallway leading to the Judge's chambers with little or no thought of what was about to happen. She also went unnoticeably barefoot as was the general condition of the child at home and at church. Today was no exception where she was concerned. Her carefree child-like approach to these unusual surroundings was to enjoy the cool of the tiled floor under her tiny feet and get as much play in before they all had to sit down and do business. She wasn't even really sure what business had to be done, even though Matthew and Srenna had explained to all of them what would be taking place in family court on this day and at this time.

Emma looked up at Srenna to determine if her governess/new sister-in-law was angry, but as usual there was a slight smile on Srenna's face. Before Emma had a chance to answer she was scooped up by her biggest brother, who had snuck up behind her to assist Srenna.

"You must wear shoes today "Little Bug" or the Judge will think we're raising uncivilized urchins, eh?" Matthew laughed at his littlest sister. He squeezed her just about as hard as she could tolerate and this brought giggles and squirms.

"I swear, you're both incorrigible," Srenna giggled along with them. But she was frantically scanning up and down the hallway to see the much needed shoes and socks.

"I have them," answered Stephan who had been watching his sister for a while and then had gotten preoccupied. He sounded somewhat annoyed but wasn't really. There was a slight grin on his face as well as he handed both over to Srenna and poked his baby sister in the side just because he could. "They were under the bench." Of course Emma had to stick her tongue out at him, at which, of course, he in turn imitated.

"All right everyone. I think we'd better settle down before we get called in, eh?" Matthew offered as Srenna desperately tried to shoe Emma. He was still grinning though, this time at his beautiful young wife of only two weeks. He couldn't help but still feel overwhelmed by all that had transpired in such a short amount of time. Fortunately, most of the events had been good, far better then he could have ever imagined less then five months ago. He distinctly remembered his despair in Reverend Davidson's office that day when they devised a plan to get him help. Now he looked around this hallway to see joyful, albeit nervous, smiles and sounds of happiness instead of the sheer grief that had been surrounding them for a very long time.

Matthew looked at each of the persons in the hall waiting anxiously for the hearing to begin. Standing against one wall was Jimmie and Irmani, holding little Benji and trying to keep the nearly one-year-old occupied for a little while longer. Sitting beside them on a bench was Mary and Lilly discussing the return to school only a few days before. The biggest surprise of all was the older woman who sat across from the girls with the Reverend and his wife Patricia. Grandmother Brewster had stayed over for this day, making arrangements to return to her school late so she could accompany the children on this pivotal day.

Matthew watched his grandmother deep in discussion with the couple, knowing full well that a few weeks ago this could have been another scene of tragedy. Instead, today it was the fulfillment of his dying mother's last wish. The memory of her words in the hospital that early morning when she drew her last breaths threaten to bring tears to Matthew's eyes...until he felt a little hand on his face and a little larger one on his arm. Emma was looking at her favorite brother as though even in her young little life she had a deep awareness of when Matthew was sad. But instead of frowning…she was grinning.

"No worries, eh?" she laughed in her best imitation of her brother when he was consoling the rest of them.

"Right, "Little Bug". No worries," he chuckled as he smothered her cheek with kisses.

"Hey! I want some of that, you," Srenna whinged playfully, pulling on her husband's arm until he bent to kiss her too.

"Now stop…the both of you…there's plenty of me to go around," he jested with them.

"There'd better be, because you're about to sign your life away to this brood," Srenna laughed, looking around the room at each one of the children. She couldn't help but think about another time when she sat in a court hallway waiting to see what her fate would be. Images of herself at thirteen, wedged between Daniel and Ruth Carmel made her misty eyed for a moment, remembering how scared and unsure she was about her future after the death of her family. It had crossed her mind numerous times over the last two weeks how the children might be feeling as they prepared to go through this important day. She made sure each of them, Matthew included, were able to talk about how they felt. She and Matthew had spent tremendous time assuring the children that it would all be good. They of course had to ultimately trust God on that one.

Philip Cramer had worked incredibly hard to expedite the court hearing with the family services Judge in Masterton. A home study was done, as well as interviews with countless people, including school officials, teachers, the Reverend and his wife, and of course Jimmie and Irmani. Even Grandmother had been consulted.

Srenna caught the eye of Miriam's mother as the woman watched her grandson with his baby sister. She smiled at the woman who only two and a half weeks before had been their greatest threat and now was one of their strongest allies. There was much more healing to be received, especially where Madelaine Brewster and Matthew were concerned, but so many walls had come down that fateful day when she and Matthew walked and talked for nearly four hours.

They had walked well into the foothills and found a quiet place to discuss and at sometimes even argue about the events that had transpired in their family. It was the most difficult thing either one had ever done. In the end it brought the beginning of a workable plan for the well being and welfare of the children. She and Matthew agreed finally that to disrupt the children's environment would only cause more grief, something they both were extremely tired of. Matthew convinced her that they would indeed welcome her visits at any time and that the children needed to get to know her... and she them. It also brought the much needed forgiveness for grandmother and grandson. For Madelaine it opened the floodgates of closure, something that would change the woman's entire personality over time. It was decided that she would return when her school was on holiday break and actually be here for Christmas.

When they finally returned to the house, tired and hungry, Madelaine had her first opportunity to observe the tight-knit family that her daughter had birthed and raised until the day she died. She watched with amazement at how each child contributed to the supper meal and the poise in which her grandson and his new wife steered the children through the evening. In the end she made arrangements to stay longer and moved into Matthew's old room so she could spend time with the children.

It wasn't to say that there weren't moments when everyone felt awkward, but all in all the children were like most children are...ready to receive anyone that will give them a chance. And Madelaine Brewster was ready to try. Several times over the two weeks she and Srenna spent time alone, mending their moments in the hotel dining room and getting to know one another. The coveted journal was returned quietly and no mention of it to Matthew was every made. It was a variable though in the softening of Madelaine's heart towards her oldest grandson. A little at a time she attempted to inquire of each of her grandchildren and their persons. Srenna and Matthew watched as she even attempted to resolve her issues with "that Irmani woman" when she realized the intricate role Jimmie and Irmani Rainga had played in her daughter's life.

Now today it seemed almost an impossibility that they had come to this after all they had been through. It astounded Matthew that at the near age of twenty he was about to legally become the guardian of a family full of siblings. But that thought spun him around to look full into the sweet face of his loving, determined and sometimes downright stubborn wife. She caught his gaze as she turned from sweeping the hallway one more time, her usual mothering thing to do where the children were concerned. There was no doubt in Matthew's mind just looking at her encouraging smile and knowing first hand her heart that he could do this amazing thing with her standing beside him.

Srenna had proven her dedication to he and the children so much over the last four months…it made him feel as if she had always been there somewhere in his life. Maybe she had…somewhere in that corner of his conscience, wondering who it would be that would share life's responsibilities, it's joy and sadness, challenges and hurtles. He knew beyond any shadow of a doubt she was standing with him now about to take on the same incredible brood of children he called family.

Those thoughts were suddenly all interrupted as Philip Cramer came to the doorway leading into the Judge's chambers. Everyone fairly flew to their feet as the kind faced man signaled to them that it was time for their hearing. Matthew put Emma down, much to her dismay, but not for a moment did he let go of the little girl's hand in his. With his free hand he led Srenna and Emma towards the door where everyone else stood waiting. Srenna instinctively held out her arms for Benji who was very ready for his "Mim" to take him. All were to go in as each one would have a significant role in this decision today.

"Everyone ready for this, eh?" Matthew asked his young brood and closest friends. He even made the effort to smile at grandmother before taking a deep breath and indicating to the lawyer that they were indeed ready. After every head shook a determined yes, one little voice rang out as usual with her steady child voice. "We ready!" Matthew squeezed his little sister's hand and took one more breath.

They all filed through the doors and Philip Cramer escorted them to the two rows in front of the Judges bench. The social worker who had come to the house and visited with them a week ago was there sitting at a table across from the seats. She had been a nice enough woman but had peppered them all with what seemed like a thousand questions. But in the end she had praised Matthew and Srenna and those who had supported them for the hard work they had done to keep this family together.

The nervous group had no more sat down when the Bailiff announced the Judge's entry and everyone stood as one is supposed to. For a few moments the Honorable Judge Malcolm Havens reviewed the file in front of him. He then looked up from his papers and asked if everyone present was ready for the proceedings. They were, of course, ready and anxious to get the hearing over.

"I would like Matthew and Srenna Patton to approach the bench please, Mr. Cramer," the Judge requested with an air of authority. Srenna reluctantly passed Benji to Mary and hand in hand they walked to the front of his bench with Philip Cramer close behind them. Srenna could feel the warm pressure of Matthew gripping her hand. She could only wonder what incredible thoughts were going through his mind at this moment. She knew she had better not let go of him whether it be her to falter or him. But they held each other up and stood facing Judge Havens with the greatest of hope.

"I have had the opportunity to review the contents of the study done on behalf of your family, Matthew," the Judge started. He was still scanning a paper when he finally looked up and straight into Matthew's blue eyes. He stared hard at the couple standing before him and as he did he saw what he was looking for. As his gaze locked with Matthew's the Judge watched the young man pull him self up and stand straight and tall. It was not a proud or haughty look he saw...but a determined one. There was no less expression or stature in the lovely young woman next to him.

Judge Havens sat back against his chair and smiled at the young couple. "Have either one of you any idea what you are taking on?" he questioned bluntly. This question made the both of them look at each other and grin.

It was Matthew who began the answer first. "With all due respect, your Honor..." Matthew glanced again at Srenna and then they both turned back to the Judge and soundly finished the answer together. "Yes!"

"Well I can see you are both equally determined to see this through, albeit in time you will no doubt fully appreciate the brevity of raising this bunch." The Judge looked around the room at the group of people sitting with the children and continued. "In most cases I would be a bit skeptical about allowing this sort of thing, due in large to the number of siblings, their age span, and your age of course and other factors. But, to say the least, placement of a family this large is a tedious undertaking and one in my opinion does nothing but cause more problems down the road for all involved."

Judge Havens stopped for a moment and once again scanned the room. He then made another request. "I would like James and

Irmani Rainga and Reverend and Patricia Davidson to approach the bench as well please."

At this request both couples, who had set themselves down directly behind the children, stood to join Matthew and Srenna at the bench, one couple on one side and the other on the other side. The judge smiled again at the obvious public display of love and concern for the young couple. He first addressed the Reverend.

"It has been duly noted Reverend Davidson that you and Mrs. Davidson have offered to act as guardians in the event that this family is in need of support in future times. Is that correct, sir?" he questioned. Both Hamilton and Patricia gave him a sound yes and smiled at both Matthew and Srenna.

"And likewise and no less, you James and Irmani Rainga have also petitioned the court for the same responsibility." The judge peered over his glasses at the other couple beside the young man and woman.

Jimmie Rainga, who seldom said anything in public, while his demonstrative wife said all, beat her at the draw and firmly answered the Judge, "We would do anything for these kids your Honor and that includes takin' the lot of them in under our roof if need be." Irmani looked at her husband of nearly twenty seven years and grinned.

"He speaks for us both…your Honor!" she agreed firmly.

"I'll accept that as a yes then," the man chuckled. Judge Havens looked out over the row of young faces staring anxiously at him and knew by the strained expressions that he'd better finish this proceeding. Even little Benji was staring at the man as though knowing something was about to shape the rest of his little life.

"Well I guess we'd better get the "lot of you" up here then so we can finalize this guardianship, eh?" He then began shuffling some papers and waited for the reaction he knew was forth coming.

This announcement not only sent up whoops and hollers of joy but sent a flood of children running into the arms of those that loved them the most. But even as they all were embracing each other with the greatest of elation, Srenna sensed to turn and look at the one person still seated in her chair behind the lawyer. Grandmother Brewster sat watching the sight, not really sure what she should do, but Srenna solved that in flash.

"Wait, your Honor. We have one more person that needs to be up here for all of this…right Matthew?" she inquired of her husband, catching the warm smile on his face and the welcomed prodding of his helpmate.

"She's so right." Matthew turned to his grandmother and for the first time since he had taken Srenna's hand he let go. Before another word could be spoken he had walked to the aisle where his grandmother sat waiting. He extended his hand to the woman and grinned his unmistakable boyish grin. "We can't start this without you," he offered.

Madelaine Brewster looked up at her grandson and felt a thousand reasons why she should not be worthy to take that hand as the memories of her past infractions with this family threatened to flood in. But Matthew would not have it. He pushed his hand a little further towards her and smiled again, "It's alright Grandmother; no worries, eh?"

Madelaine reached for her grandson's hand and allowed him to escort her up to the Judges bench where he pulled her into the circle of children and turned to face the man.

"Now we're ready," he announced, sweeping one more look at everyone, his gaze landing last on his "Little Bug" who of course had to resound, "We ready!"

Several cars made the winding trip back up the roads leading to Castlepoint. The entourage of people who left the court room beyond the point of ecstatic happiness were now on their way to a celebration at the Davidson's home at the church on the coast. It had been decided earlier that some form of festivities had to be planned to herald the hopeful decision made by the Judge to award custody of all the children to Matthew and Srenna. In the end and after much document signing the young couple found themselves to be the proud guardians of Mary, Stephan, Lilly, Emma and Benjamin Patton. Papers had also been signed by both the Rainga's and the Davidson's to share the responsibilities of guardianship at any time during the years the children were still minors if need be. Even Grandmother was admonished by Judge Havens to stay involved in the children's well-being, to which she assured him she would as long as God gave her breath.

Now all of them were rattling and sharing their feelings about the events of the morning. Stephan and Lilly were doing most of the talking in the family car to which Emma nobly attempted to get in her two cents worth. Benji was tucked safely in Srenna's arms fast asleep after his momentous morning. He had been as good as any baby could be, but it was finally his cries of weariness for the whole event and his deep seeded need to eat that sent them all finally headed for the cars. Matthew and Srenna couldn't help but keep looking at each other and smiling, a deep satisfaction for the Judge's decision.

Behind them came Grandmother and Mary, who had asked if she might accompany Madelaine on the trip back. Matthew was glad to see Mary's attempt to engage with the older woman; Srenna was even more elated as she watched the two walk to the car chatting as only she wished she'd been able to do sometime in her life. It was a melancholy feeling, but Srenna was genuinely glad that grandmother and granddaughter were trying.

In front of Matthew and Srenna were the Rainga and the Davidson cars. Patricia and Irmani had once again put their efforts together to prepare a luscious picnic meal, which at Matthew's insistence would be the way all of them should celebrate. He had waited for Srenna's disapproval on this idea but was relieved when she whole-heartedly agreed that they should all embark upon the beautiful setting of the parsonage and … maybe even the beach. Bathing suits had been snuck into Grandmother's car by Mary just on the offside chance of their use later.

It took very little time to make the trip to the sunny New Zealand coastline of Castle Point and the church. Each car pulled into the lane in front of the parsonage and as Matthew exited the car and sprinted around to open the door for Srenna he caught his brother's eye and the slight grin on his face. For the first time in a long time the two had a secret that was nearly causing both of them to explode with anticipation. For a short while they had been too preoccupied with this morning's agenda, but now, that past, they were both excited with what was about to unfold. As Matthew took Benji from Srenna he stole a glance at Lilly and unmistakably saw the grin on her face as well.

Everyone exited from their cars. The entire group formed in front of the path that led either to the parsonage or to the little cemetery above the beach. Immediately Patricia suggested to Irmani that they go on ahead and finish preparing the lunch. She also motioned to the men to follow, as well as Grandmother, leaving only the Patton family still waiting at the path.

"I really should go with them and help, eh?" Srenna began, her usual need to be involved in things at hand. She started to follow before Matthew had even responded, but he stopped her short.

"Not this time, Mrs. Patton," he ordered gently and a bit playfully. He grabbed her arm with his free hand while nestling a sleepy baby against his shoulder.

"Why ever not, you?" she asked, frowning at Matthew's tone and then realizing that none of the children had even attempted to follow. One look at all their faces and Srenna knew they were up to something. "All right…all of you…what is going on?" she demanded. She glanced at Mary who could never keep anything from her and saw the determination on the girl's face to play along. But Emma…dear little Emma could not.

"We have a secret!" she exclaimed, thoroughly pleased with herself that she had been entrusted to keep one for the very first time in her life.

"Em! You're not suppose to say!" Stephan growled at his little sister, to which he immediately received another intense sticking out of the tongue.

"All right! Enough…all of you," Matthew scolded them both. This conversation brought Benji's head popping up from his nap and looking around at all of them until he saw his "Mim".

"Not this time, little man. We have a surprise for Mim, eh?" Matthew announced as he grinned at each of his siblings and rested his eyes on his beautiful wife.

"A surprise? What surprise, you?" Srenna quizzed everyone.

"Blindfold please," came Stephan's instructions, to which Lilly produced a scarf she had tucked away in her pocket this morning and had guarded with all her might.

"Blindfold? What in the world?" Srenna gasped. But she wasn't allowed any more questions or speculation as Stephan came up behind her and began to place the scarf around her face.

"Matthew, what…?" she tried to ask.

But Matthew came up to her and kissed her cheek softly and whispered in her ear. "We wanted to get you something for everything, so just play along, eh?" he ordered again. He slipped his hand through her arm and laced his fingers through hers and then began to lead her carefully down the path towards the bluff above the sea. Within moments Srenna could tell they had gone in the direction of the little cemetery and the path leading down to the wavy surf below. But instead of continuing the trip down the path as she thought they might, they stopped in the grassy bluff overlooking the beach. She could feel the warm breeze of the ocean below against her face and smell the salt air as she breathed. Even still the sensation of both sent the hair on her body to stand upright.

Matthew felt her body lean into him for a bit of support as they led her over some rough ground and he was quick to whisper in her ear. "All right?" he asked with a small amount of concern for her reaction to their location. They had not been back since that day she had fallen apart and shared her tragedy with him on this bluff. He knew he was taking a risk bringing her to this spot…but what was about to happen could happen nowhere else but here.

"Yes…I'm fine," she offered encouragingly, not wanting to spoil anything this glorious day.

"Good," Matthew remarked, kissing her face and motioning to Stephan to get ready to unmask her. "Because we all wanted to get you something…something we hope you'll like. Something we all thought you should have …after all this time." He finished the sentence with a nod of his head for Stephan to remove the blindfold from Srenna's eyes

After blinking a few times to adjust to the bright afternoon sun, Srenna found herself inside the picturesque little cemetery. In front of her just offside were the unmistakable grave stones of John and Miriam. She could not for the life of her wonder why the children would want to come here on this day with the death of their mother so fresh in their minds. But as she gazed at all of them she saw an incredible look of satisfaction on their young faces that they had done something so special in spite of their own recovery.

Finally little Emma could stand it no longer. She stepped in front of Srenna and pointed with her tiny hand and bursting with enthusiasm exclaimed rather impatiently, "See what we got?"

Srenna smiled at the dear child lovingly but it was when she glanced past the child that she drew in a deep breath. There behind the little girl next to John and Miriam's markers was a beautiful white stone standing about three feet tall. It was surrounded by vivid blooming flowers that had been recently planted around the stone. Srenna stood in amazement as she began to realize what it was she was looking at. As though moving in a dream she stepped past Emma and walked up to the grave stone. The words carved in it finally made her understand what was happening. The first three words brought the beginning of tears to her eyes. "In loving memory…" was all she could see as she blinked and sent a cascade of tears down her cheek. But it was the remainder of the inscription that brought a sob up from deep inside her.

"In loving memory of Harrison and Sarah James
and their sons, Douglas and David.
This to honor them by a most loving daughter and sister."

Srenna felt strong arms go around her from everywhere, even little ones around her middle as all six of the Patton children embraced her and held her up. Even little Benji seemed to know his Mim needed his love at that moment. But it was Matthew who, with his arm around her neck and his face against her cheek breathed these words into her ear, "We thought you needed a memorial, Srenna. We're we wrong?" he asked carefully, with a hint of concern in his voice.

"No…no…you were not," she cried softly as the girls began to cry with her. "Oh no…this is the most…beautiful thing any one could ever do. It's…it's so…I never had…you know…" Srenna simply could not get the right words out of her mouth, the words she wanted to find to truly let the children know how she felt.

"We know…" cried Mary, holding her new sister tightly. "We wanted you to have this here with Mum and Dad…because we're all family now…all of us and…" But Mary could not go on either.

Even Stephan was sniffling unabashedly, but it was him in the end that put into words what he thought Srenna might be feeling right at that moment. "We know they're not really here Srenna, they're with God, but we can come here, anytime and just remember what was good about them and how much they loved being near the shore." Srenna could only guess how his encounter with God on the mountain had enlightened the boy to his own pain of losing his parents. His words made her immediately remember all the precious moments she and her father had spent in and around the sea. She would never want to forget that ever again after today.

"I think it's time we leave Srenna alone for a little while and let her have some private time, eh?" Matthew gently suggested to his brothers and sisters. "Would that be all right?"

Everyone nodded, whether in agreement or not and started to move towards the gate. Matthew lingered next to Srenna after depositing Benji into Mary's arms.

"We'll be waiting for you down on the beach, Mrs. Patton," he smiled slightly, as he kissed her face and squeezed her around her waist. "I love you," he whispered softly. He reluctantly let go and moved to join the children who had only made it beyond the gate and waited tearfully for their brother. As he began to herd his flock of children towards the path leading down to the waves he glanced back at Srenna who could not take her eyes off of the monument. He was praying what ever had not been completed the day of the storm when Srenna had tried to come back here …would indeed be finished for her now.

She stood for what felt like an hour and simply stared at the marker, reading and rereading the inscription and the loving names it bore. It had been so long since she had actually seen her family's names or for that matter spoken them. She wondered if this time she would be able to really say goodbye. She knew she had to try. With feeble voice still trembling and with more tears she began what she had never spoken before.

"Daddy…I miss you so much. There's so much I wish I could share with you…all my adventures…my discoveries. You were right. There are so many in life. I can't even imagine what will happen over the next few years, so much has already." With that statement Srenna suddenly lifted her head and scanned the beach below her. From where she was standing she could see her new family on the warm sand below. They were milling around as though waiting for something to begin.

"Just look at them…all of them, Daddy. Their mine now…all of them…can you believe that?" she smiled, with tears still flowing freely down her face. "And Matthew…I love him so much. He's such a good man, Daddy, just like you; so strong and kind. And he loves God so much."

Srenna turned back to the marker and continued. "And Mum. I know now how much Dad must have loved you. He wanted to take care of you and the boys. I know you had to be proud of him for all his hard work because I know how proud I am of Matthew. And Douglas and David. I'm so sorry I didn't have more time to be a better sister …but I promise…" a sob caught in Srenna's voice, but she plowed on any way. "I will be."

At that promise Srenna turned back to the group waiting for her below. She was startled though by Madelaine's presence standing just off the side of the little white fence surrounding the cemetery.

"I'm so sorry dear. I did not mean to interrupt or frighten you," Grandmother apologized. She stayed where she was until Srenna had brushed away some of her tears.

"No…it's quite all right really. I probably should be joining everyone down there," Srenna assured the woman as she gazed at Matthew in the distance. She started to walk towards the gate when she noticed Madelaine's eyes fixed on the grave markers past her. It was then that Srenna realized that this woman also had never been present for a funeral or memorial for her daughter. Her heart ached for the woman. But Srenna being the sensitive person she was knew what needed to happen and it was precisely what the children had just lovingly forced her to do.

She walked up to Madelaine and much to the woman's surprise the young Aussie woman embraced her with all the strength she could muster. Srenna felt one lone sob wrack the woman's body and then true to her form Madelaine Brewster attempted to steel herself. But Srenna knew what she was trying to do and as she pulled away from Miriam's mother she smiled lovingly at her and simply stated, "It's your turn."

Srenna hugged her one more time and just as she began to leave she remembered something in her pocket. She had had the presence of mind to stick it in before they had taken off this morning. This something had been in her bag the day she and Matthew had been married, and more times then not it had been close by if she thought she might need it. The lovely lacey handkerchief bearing the initials S.J. she had kept all these years was pulled out and handed to Madelaine along with one more smile of encouragement. Then without looking back she hurried down the path leading to the waters below and the family she wanted to be with more then anything right now. As she came up on the sand she couldn't help but begin to laugh, a pure joy beginning to bubble up from deep inside her to replace the momentary bittersweet feeling she had just been experiencing.

Matthew turned just in time to see her approaching them and watched carefully for the signs of how Srenna was feeling at that moment. To his relief the broad smile and the pace in which she was coming towards them gave him all the hope he needed. The rest of the children saw the smile on his face as Srenna came closer. Before they could all turn she had reached them and they watched as she playfully pulled off her shoes and headed for the water, pulling her skirt up above her knees.

"Well, you?" she shouted at all of them as she ran into the first lap of the waves. "Are you just going to stand there and watch me get wet all by myself?"

The joyful answer from them all… of course…was no.

SHEPHERD'S GAZE

Lord when the darkened clouds obscure my sun
And all my world has seemed to come undone
I've only but to keep my eyes on you
I'm in my Shepherd's gaze

And when the angry waves crash from the sea
And threaten to surround and frighten me
I've only but to lift my arms to you
I'm in my Shepherd's gaze
I can feel you watching

Now I know that to really grow
I must trust in you
Now I see to be truly free
I must let go
Now I see what's really meant to be

And when the mountains quake beneath my feet
And life has brought a heart its final beat
I've only but to rest my heart in you
I'm in my Shepherd's gaze

And when my path is treacherous and unknown
And I begin to feel I'm all alone
You never missed a single step I took
I'm in my Shepherd's gaze
Always in your gaze
In my Shepherd's gaze

www.ingramcontent.com/pod-product-compliance
Lightning Source LLC
Chambersburg PA
CBHW070744120726
47910CB00001B/157